NOT ONE
AMONG THEM
WHOLE

A Novel of Gettysburg

EDISON McDANIELS

Northampton House Press

First Northampton House LLC edition, 2013. ISBN 978-148250516-0

10 9 8 7 6 5 4 3 2 1

All that is loathsome, drooping, and decayed is here.

—Charles Dickens, *American Notes*

NOT ONE AMONG THEM WHOLE

Book I

The In-Between Time

ONE

T he end of the before time, and of Cuuda's childhood, came fast and without warning in the summer of 1857, on a day that dawned cloudless with the sun flooding a vivid blue sky.

When that day ended, in a soaking rain, everything had changed.

Forever.

***

"No! No, you cain't put me in there. Please Pa, don't!"

Cuuda's protests sounded weak and mealy even to himself. He was seven or nine years old—keeping his age was no priority and to say he was about seven or nine was good enough—and in he went, forced into the ground at his father's own hand, kicking and bucking all the way, up to the last moment. That moment was, far as Cuuda could tell, the last in all the world and he suddenly stopped his carrying on and stared into his pa's face. The huge man had hold of him, his great hands wrapped around Cuuda's wrists, and the boy thought *Don't let go Pa, don't ever let go.* "Don't do this! Why you doin' this?"

His pa's face seemed to break open. His head tilted—as if a great weight pushed it so—and his lips quivered and pulled back, baring gapped and yellowed teeth in a regretful grin. One eye squinted, closed completely, then opened before squinting again. Cuuda would think forevermore that his father had wanted to say something in that instant. But he didn't, and what passed between them was unsaid. Both their faces welled with tears and neither could take his eyes off the other.

Bucking again.

"Ya keep shut up now boy!" The words came out hard, like saying them was akin to cutting your own arm off. Not something you'd ever want to do, except maybe the world had gone to shit and right here, in this time and place, cutting your own arm off was about the only thing that made any sense. Tears welled anew in his father's eyes and that's what Cuuda would always remember, how the last time he saw his pa alive he'd been crying. The only time he ever saw him such.

He opened his mouth. "But Pa—"

He never saw the hand coming and probably his father had meant that. His hand was big and strong from working years in the field, could palm a melon and squeeze it one-handed till it popped like a ripe berry. His pa jerked his head first one way and then the other, and if he took his eyes off him, Cuuda never saw it. Listening was what he was doing, crooking his head to gain a better ear. The big man paused yet a moment longer. His eyes were a witch's brew of warmth and love and everything that was safe and Cuuda thought he could go his whole life entire without ever looking elsewhere. His pa's breathing was loud and labored and heavy. His own eyes watered and his nose ran with snot. He sniffled and caught the rank odor of an animal caught in a trap, maybe a wolf. He and his pa had caught a wolf once...

His pa's hand struck him upside his head and Cuuda's childhood ended.

***

He awoke to the moldy earth smell of wet dirt clogging his nose. He could barely move his legs and even in the dark, the close confines of the box hugged him in a claustrophobic shroud. His arms were across his chest and only a few inches' space separated them from the board above. He raised his head and struck that board and fell back dazed and in his mind heard his pa shouting at him all over again: *Ya keep shut up now boy!*

He almost wet himself. Then heard his father's words over and over again, each more insistent than the last: *Ya keep shut up now boy! Ya keep shut up now boy!*

His breath hitched in the close dark and he struggled against the box. He took to chewing his lower lip and somehow that made it better, forced him to slow down.

He thought, *In the hole then.*

He heard voices, or thought he heard voices. Like in a dream, the kind that comes in the middle of the black night unbidden. The kind that make a little boy piss himself cause he's shaking so bad and there's nobody around to comfort him. He'd known a few nights like that.

"Where's that nigger boy o' yours?" A phantom voice. Real?

Then his mother's sweet, golden song. That was real. She sang: "Will the circle be unbroken? / By and by, Lord, by and by / There's better home a-waiting / In the sky, Lord—"

The sharp—very real—smack of skin against skin. Now Cuuda did piss himself. He began to squirm in his confines, to cry, to pummel the boards of the box. Then more of his father's words came.

Don't ya cry boy. Ya cry, dey finds you.

He became still again, bit his lip and sucked in a breath and tasted dirt. A cruddy, earthy flavor that lingered after he spat. He took in another and felt his chest heaving, felt his parents going away, going to the *sure dead*, the place old Prosper had told him folks went when they died. A nice place he hoped.

Don't ya cry boy. Ya cry, dey finds you.

"Who they, pa?" Soft words, but they sounded loud in the box.

Toubob.

Monsters.

In his mind, he walked the *sure dead* with Prosper. Neither of them could read, but that didn't seem to matter. They found the stones of his parents. Erasmus and Sara Monk. They bore no dates because slaves didn't get dates on their stones. Their deaths were as anonymous as their lives.

Toubob. Monsters. Or White folks. Same word for both.

***

They beat Cuuda's father senseless.

He heard his father wailing, heard the scrapings as they dragged him to the tree, then hung him first when his mother refused to give away her son's hiding place. Then her sweet singing again, strong and bold as ever. She could have been projecting to the heavens, but he knew she was sending her love to him. She sang and they waited for her. They waited for her.

"Amazing grace! how sweet the sound / That saved a wretch like me! / I once was lost, but now am found / Was blind, but now I see. "

"That's just about the best nigger singing I ever did hear. Real sweet lady. Damn shame you won't tell us where that boy be."

"You leave my boy 'lone. He ain't hurt no one."

"Say goodbye, woman."

Under the earth, Cuuda said goodbye.

A long time later—no idea how long in the silent dark—he kicked his way out of the box and rose out of the grave his father had fashioned for him. He was back a piece in the woods at the side of the road. The sun had gone away and the earth had cooled. When he came out on the road it was pouring rain and at first he didn't see them. He heard the heavy ropes complaining as they swung in the weather though. Then the lightning came and he saw them suspended in the tree like flying shades.

He wasn't big enough to cut them down and sat under the tree for the better part of two days trying not to look up except to scare the crows away. On the third day hunger and the natural tainting of their bodies encouraged him to move on.

***

"Boy!" someone shouted, "Boy! Y'all hold up there. Come here now boy!"

Cuuda stopped rummaging in the garbage, pulling a half-eaten orange out from its depths. He turned toward the hollering voice, recognizing the speech. He'd long ago learned toubob came in two classes: those who treated negroes like property or wayward children, and those who regarded them as on a par with skunks. The former were a nuisance, but tolerable; the latter were like mad dogs—unpredictable, with a tendency for a nasty bite.

Which is you? He took a few reluctant steps toward the man, saw he was tall, stringy, twenty or twenty-five, with glasses that flashed so you couldn't see the eyes behind them. Cuuda looked him over warily, the way one might do a snake. Avoiding his gaze. Shoeless, he squished cold mud between his toes. The same cold climbed his spine. "Yassuh?"

"What's your name, boy?"

"Jim, suh."

"Don't sass me, boy."

"No suh. Never suh." *Don't move no closer.*

"So what your name, boy?"

Hesitation. In toubob's world, according to Prosper and verified by his own experience, one name was good as another. That he was asking again was uncomfortable. "Most folks, they jus' calls me Jim, on account of m' pappy, big Jim." He smiled, a stupid grin that made him look simple.

"I could beat it out of ya, boy."

Cuuda stood bulging his leg muscles, preparing to run. But where? He'd been running two months, every place as awful as the last. Back in the before time, he'd heard Prosper say how the world was a place with thorns, how a man could get himself dead without trying. The seer had been wise to the ways of the world.

"Jim, eh?" The white man stared at him with his head cocked. His forearms were done up with crazy wrappings. No, Cuuda thought, not wrappings. Bandages. Cuuda palmed his half orange—his, he'd found it, wasn't about to share it with nobody—and rubbed it against his shirt like he was polishing it. He held it out. "Yassuh. Jim, suh. Orange, suh?"

"Do I look like I wants a orange, nigger?"

That ain't no question you wanna answer. The voice in his head was Prosper's—old and creaky like the old man, but strong too. The strange thing was this man talked like a poor white, but too, he was talking like a man talking like a poor white . . . like he wasn't, really, like he was something else. His clothes sort of said that, too. Cuuda listened out for the old seer's voice and kept his mouth shut and made little squishes in the mud with his toes. He was hungry in the worst way a boy can be, deep down where the taste for food is a poison that'll get you killed. He wanted—needed—to sink his teeth into the orange. The weight of it in his hand was a tease and his mouth watered. He saw now that the wrappings, the bandages if that's what they were, had come partially undone on one arm. Cuuda was close enough—too close, he felt—to see something ugly under those bandages. A burn maybe, below the elbow.

"You simple, boy? That your problem?"

Yeah, simple. "Yassuh. Orange, suh?"

The man smiled. "You just a dumbshit baby nigger darkie, that's all."

Okay, if'n that suits ya. Cuuda redoubled his smile and stuck his tongue out like he was trying to catch flies with it. "Yassah," he said. He bit the orange and its juices ran down his chin, over the skin of his neck. It would have tasted good in any other place, but here he barely tasted it. He just wanted to get it down, to have something filling the hollow under his ribs for whatever was coming.

"Well I could use me a dumbshit baby nigger darkie. Maybe you come with me. Then you eat good." Toubob stepped toward him, put a bandaged arm out. Both his forearms had been wrapped, but the wraps were dirty and old. The one side that had come undone, unraveled further. The skin under it was either dirty or charred going on black. Cuuda stepped back a pace. He barely breathed, as if chewing was the important thing and breathing came second.

"Leave him be." A tall, thin man in a green bowler hat stepped from the shadows.

"What's it to you, mister? I'm maybe looking for a nigger boy. Got me some work what needs doin'." Toubob turned to Cuuda and sucked air through his teeth. Cuuda's glimpse at him was quick but he still couldn't make eyes out behind the flat glasses. "How's about it, boy? Where your master?"

Cuuda swallowed, hesitated. His eyes went to the man in the green hat.

"He ain't for sale."

Toubob eyed them both. "What?" The word came out of the corner of his mouth, as if escaping.

"You heard me. Ain't for sale. He's mine and I ain't interested in selling." Green hat turned to Cuuda and gestured behind him. "Get on back to that wagon, boy. Be quick about it. Ain't got all night."

Cuuda wolfed what was left of the orange and looked past Green hat. In the flickering light of a street lamp stood a painted wagon, a mural on its side. Letters too, though he couldn't read them. The paint was worn, the wagon old and tired. A miscellany of pots and pans and ropes hung from it.

"Yassuh. I's sorry, suh," he said, and stepped toward the wagon.

"Goddammit, that ain't your boy."

"Prove it."

"Ah shit, what the hell. I'll find me another." He said it loud enough for Cuuda to hear. "Ain't like they don't breed like sewer rats." Toubob snickered and it echoed down the alley.

Cuuda approached the wagon, biting his lip and looking back at the pair. He leaned against the side, trying to decide if he should run or not. The green hat man was coming toward him and he had just about decided yes when a little door opened above his head and a small creature with a face reminiscent of a man—only not—appeared. It had bright eyes and slender arms and tiny, perfect fingers. It climbed out and up and hung by its tail from a crossbar that seemed made for the purpose. A moment later it jumped onto Cuuda's shoulder and the boy gasped.

"Archimedes, mind your manners."

And that was how Cuuda met the man in the green

bowler hat and how the in-between time ended and the now time began.

Book II

The Dust of a Thousand Men

TWO

Liza Coffin faced into the breeze and closed her eyes, feeling the gentle wind blow over and around her. There was still a hint of cool in the air, the day new and promising and not yet the furnace it would become, and the sky was high and clear and beautiful, and without a hint of trouble anywhere. She filled her lungs with the good air, which smelled of spring honeysuckle and pear blossoms.

It was dawn of a Wednesday, the first day of July 1863. In the days and weeks to come she would not infrequently close her eyes, breathe deep, and try with all her might to remember this last morning before the world went to hell.

She turned her head to the ground, where lay her baby boy Sam in his basket. She waved a hand at him, said, "Howdy doody, Sammie," in her baby voice, the one she used for him alone. A high pitched, sugary sweet speak. He smiled up at her, sort of. He was a generally plain faced baby, just three months old, and she hadn't yet decided whether or not he'd learned to smile. He pulled up one side of his mouth anyway, and it might just as well have been a smile she decided. The novelty of having another soul around—let alone her own child—had not yet worn thin. She'd spent so much of her life alone, parents gone and no other family, that to have this little bundle seemed a daily miracle.

"You're lovely, like your pa. And you have his nose."

She knelt and rubbed his hair, laughing at how it stood up with electricity, then reached into the pile of laundry beside him. She began to hang things over the clothesline— diapers, a few blouses, a flower-patterned dress she was particularly fond of, pieces of her underthings. She talked incessantly all the while, with Sam in his basket a captive audience. "Your pa, he'll be home soon." She said this every day, or something very much like it. She had no particular knowledge of his return, rather just a deep longing. "I don't mean today of course, but soon. I ain't exactly sure on account of him being in the army. Soldiers ain't got a whole lot of time these days on account of the war. But he'll be home. You'll see."

Sam made a quizzical little face, like he wanted to ask a question but couldn't think of the right words, and Liza went on, both with her laundry and her talking. "You're such a quiet thing," she said in her baby voice, then back to her own. "I do love your pa, you know. When he comes home, I guess when this killing war is over, we gonna be a family. You'll see Sammie. You, me, and your pa. I'll introduce you."

She smiled at that last. Thought, I hardly know him myself. She was just seventeen, he was twenty or so, couldn't remember for sure. Older than she, but not much. She didn't even know his birthday. They'd known each other six months, but that had been a year ago. Hadn't seen each other since. But it had been an intense six months and sometimes in the night, when her longing for him crossed into a physical need, she would lie with her pillow and believe she could feel the shape of him against her. They were in love—young love—the kind meant to last a lifetime and then some.

Liza, Mrs. Ezra Coffin she liked to say because it

reminded her she was part of a family now, finished with the laundry. She picked up Sam, kissed him, and he glomped on to her tit. "You hungry? Go on, take yer fill. After breakfast we got to get that old cow over to the barn. Might be we can get some milk outta her yet. Something to trade."

Twenty yards behind her cabin, buried in the scrub and thorn berry bushes with an entrance all but invisible, was an old root cellar. After milking the old cow, it was a good day and she gave up the better part of two gallons, Liza carried the milk bottles under one arm and Sam under the other.

She was on her third trip between the cellar and the barn when the first soldiers came. She dropped the milk.

There were two of them, dressed in a dirty, slipshod sort of way, wearing what she took to be Confederate uniforms. One was shoeless, and the other's toes showed through the holes in his boots. They were friendly, and too familiar, she thought. They asked did she have anything to eat.

"Nothing," she said, hugging Sam close.

The one with the holey footwear spat. "That thar baby don't look too hungry," he said, in a lazy drawl.

"We got a little milk's all." She didn't like their eyes, how they roamed over her. "In the barn."

"Where there's milk, there's a cow."

"She's old, don't produce much," Liza said.

"She ain't too old for eating," the shoeless one said.

Liza said, "That ain't right."

"Well, that's war. Just about the least right thing I ever seen in this life," the shoed man said.

The pair left trailing the old cow behind them. She stood watching them go, Sam in her arms, stripped to his diaper as the day was starting to heat up. From across the wheat fields, the irregular sound of repeated gunfire startled her.

"They'll be back," she whispered to her baby, "them or

others."

***

They marched in the dust of a thousand men—a hot, dry dust spewing the kind of heat that paws at a man and drains the vigor out of him. These men were the common part of a larger machine, indeed the gears that made that machine work. Privates, corporals, sergeants, junior lieutenants, seasoned captains, majors, and colonels. Soldiers to a man, they had an undeniable familiarity with the march. The army to which they were both an insignificant part and the most consequential element had been ever on the move for two years now. This road, and hundreds more like it bridging the miles between ten thousand different places scattered wide across the nation, was their home. Marching was their stock and trade as much as, if not more than, fighting. For every hour in combat, they endured hundreds on the road. They wore shoes down faster than the cobblers could make them. They slept on the side of the road, ate on the side of road, relieved themselves at the side of the road. They rarely went where the roads did not, and when circumstances forced them to do that, they built a road. And so even with raw throats and feet made leathery by too many miles, they pressed on. As if their bones knew the way of their own accord; as if they'd been born to a world of miserable stepping. Such was a soldier's life.

As a certain private in this army watched, a hawk flew high overhead. It soared gracefully on some unseen air current, growing small in the distant sky until this certain private could no longer pick it out from the other specks of dust. After it was gone, he remarked, "If I was a bird I'd get on outta here too." This man was a member of 'E' Company, a part of the 115th Pennsylvania. An infantry regiment in the Grand Army of the Potomac, what had once been called the showpiece of the Union Army. But on this, the last day of June in the year of our Lord eighteen and sixty-three, such a time as that seemed far removed. The rebels had nearly bled the Army of the Potomac to death at Chancellorsville, seven weeks past. Six months before that, this certain private and other members of the 115th Pennsylvania, held in reserve, had watched with a gut-boiling awe as their fellows assaulted the heights above the Rappahannock River no less than fourteen times. No blood looked quite so red as that silhouetted against new fallen snow. A massacre in the cold December wind. Such was Fredericksburg.

A sheen of grubby sweat coated this private's skin and he crooked his neck this way and that. All the while, he followed the man in front of him, who in turn followed the man in front of him, who followed ... The land seemed to blight in their wake, to quake under their feet. He choked on the russet dust and spat dirt. Unwashed, he smelled of last week's march, the burnt ashes of last night's campfire. As he walked he chewed a half cooked piece of fatback, ignoring the taste of grease. The straps of his pack dug into his shoulders but he no longer tried adjusting them. It was a slight discomfort, like a small pebble underfoot. A trifling thing. The better part of a year at war had taught him to ignore trifling things.

This certain private's name was Ezra Coffin and he had no idea where they were going, only from whence they'd come—a place best forgotten. At Chancellorsville, he'd come across a man he knew slightly from before the fight, a Corporal Dalhausie. Dalhausie was from Poughkeepsie and had a wife and two daughters. On his arm was a big heart-shaped tattoo with 'Liza' in the middle. The private's wife was also named Liza and so he'd admired the tattoo as the two bivouacked. The next day, they'd been standing together when a bullet tore through Dalhausie's elbow, completely separating it at the joint; the glistening, polished bone stuck out like the white hot glow of embers in the ashes of a dying fire. Two hours later, the private had recognized that tattoo—half of it anyway—on a heap of flesh beside a big oak. The ground was soaked with blood for ten feet around the tree and when he walked across it his boots slid on the burdened grass. He stared at the arm, at the broken heart and the inked letters on the skin, *za*. He thought of his own Liza, of the baby boy he'd never seen, and he conjured that Dalhausie himself and not the arm had been amputated.

Private Ezra Coffin fixed his eyes on the back of the man in front of him. His legs ached and he had to piss. He spat and took another chew of the fatback and wished for a breeze. Even the tiniest. The trees, still heavy with leaves in late June, did not sway. It occurred to him there was no such thing as perfect weather for marching. Always too hot, or too cold, or too wet, or too dry. Too much of this, or too much of that. And so, over a sun-parched, dusty road on the last day of June, in the year of our Lord eighteen and sixty-three, Private Ezra Coffin marched along as he had a hundred times before.

He couldn't know his marching days were just about over.

***

Another army was on the move on a road remarkably similar to the thoroughfare used by the 115th Pennsylvania. Though not in the immediate vicinity of each other, the roads were close enough that the vanishing speck seen by one army was an enlarging bird in flight from the vantage point of the second. More precisely, as seen through the field glasses of Major Tom Jersey, the bird was a red-tailed hawk. The major whistled as he saw the soaring wings come into distant focus. He hadn't seen a raptor in Northern Virginia in almost a year. Such a bird could mean only one thing: food.

Jersey had been born in Kitty Hawk Village, a fishing town on the Outer Banks of North Carolina. A banker before the war, he was a balding man of slight build who wore wire-frame spectacles and spoke with a Carolina drawl. A quiet family man in his mid-thirties, the worst day of his life had come not as a soldier, but as a father. Little Tom, his ten year-old son, had gone fishing one afternoon in the summer of '60. He'd never been seen again. A few months later, a black boy walking the back roads near Albemarle Sound, not two miles from the major's home in Manteo, had spied a wicker basket in the roadside mud. Inside he found a bit of tackle, the remains of several fish long since rotted, and a smear of muck which might have been fish guts. It was black and crusty though, the exact hue of old blood. On the underside of the creel's lid, scrawled in faded, barely legible letters, was the single word 'tom.' A search of the creel's hiding place turned up only one other object: a boy's left shoe.

It had been a year since Major Jersey had seen the Outer Banks. As second in command of the 18th North Carolina, an infantry regiment in the Army of Northern Virginia, he'd had little time for home visits. Now that regiment, three hundred strong, was strung out and raising a billowing cloud of dust in their wake. They'd crossed the Potomac a week before, were in the North. Enemy territory. They had orders to quickstep it; the battle was joined and men were dying. Or soon would be.

Replacements were needed.

The hawk came closer. This North was a bountiful place, with lush, green fields and crops aplenty. Jersey stepped out of the column and stopped. He took a swig from his canteen, swearing at the drops that trickled down his beard. On a day so hot, water was too precious to waste. He knew much about waste. The land they'd left across the river, a place most of the soldiers called home and became melancholy about, was a wasted land indeed. Picked over by the two armies, whole valleys had been scorched to ash—first by fleeing Rebels, then invading Federals, then retreating Federals going back the way they'd come in the first place. In the ruins of Northern Virginia, even the chickens were starving.

He urged the men forward, holding the canteen high in the air with his arm extended as he did so. "Git on now," he said, "and mind you drink. It's a hot one and we ain't got a man to lose. Drink up, you sonsabitches." He ran his gaze up and down the column. "You – Collins, ain't it? Step up there, son. No stragglers today."

"I got shurt legs, sir. Caint hardly keep up," the young soldier said. He showed a wide, crooked-teeth smile and those around him burst into laughter. The rebuked fellow moved up smartly just the same.

"Well," the major hollered after him, "I guess you just gonna have to two-step-it then." He turned to another, a corporal whose right sleeve hung empty. "Good to see you back, Miller. I thought you was a goner sure."

"Ain't no Yankee lead whatever could kill me, sir. This," the stout corporal pointed to his vacant sleeve, "this here's no more'n a flesh wound."

And so it went. They were in Southern Pennsylvania now, taking the war to the enemy, giving them a taste of what they'd felt for far too long. The major looked out across the countryside. Rolling green hills as far as he could see, the land broken only by the occasional copse of oak. He thought of his son, as he often did on long marches, and tried to imagine him running through the tall grass. He wondered what the boy, gone these three long years, would have looked like today. As was always the case, however, the boy he saw in his mind's eye was the same ten-year-old he'd been the morning of his disappearance. And as the hawk soared above him, Jersey had a vision of that boy chasing butterflies in the hills before him, his step uneven.

He was missing a shoe.

***

Surgeon Josiah Boyd leaned toward the corner, pressed his tongue against his lips, and spat. Reflex mostly, something he did without thinking whenever the need presented, which was often. The gob splattered against the wall, joining the smear already there. Assistant Surgeon Tobias Ellis gave little thought to the smear of tobacco, keeping his mind on the task at hand. Like Boyd's, his hands and forearms were streaked with the blood of scores of men. They looked raw, almost skinned.

"Artery clamp." Boyd stretched a palm out.

Tiny, the surgeon's helper, was a heavyset kid in his early twenties, though he looked younger. He'd spent the better part of two years—the worst part of a lifetime—with the field hospital. He rummaged in the dirty water of the basin even as he held a chloroformed mask over the patient's face. His fingers made quick work in the cool, blood pink water, finding the instrument by feel. He slammed the clamp into Boyd's hand with a sharp smack and Boyd squeezed the clamp around the femoral artery as Ellis lifted the great vessel out of its bed, the thrum of the pulse fighting back from within. The clamp clicked as it locked, and the artery beyond the obstruction went limp. "Ligature," Boyd said with a practiced calm.

Major Josiah Boyd was thirty-eight. His hair had thinned up top and he hadn't shaved in days. He was of lanky build and sallow complexion, possessed of a long drawn-out face almost ghoulish in its particulars, with prominent cheekbones high under his eyes. His lower jaw had been twice broken (once by a horse, once by a man) and poorly set. It jutted obtrusively and his teeth came together at an angle off the expected, so the whole of his face was skewed. His hands were large and his fingers long and spindly like the legs of a great spider. They were economical in their wanderings across the surgical field, however, with no waste of motion.

The soldier on the table lay on his back. He was insensible to the workings both around and upon him, heavy under the influence of a chloroform-soaked towel. Boyd and Ellis worked quickly, their movements somewhat frantic at times. They had about them a look of resigned experience, showing both intolerable exhaustion and inordinate energy at the same time. They'd been working feverishly at one task or another since first light a dozen hours before. Their efforts had made not a dent in the queue awaiting their services. At times, they worked so fast and the wounded spent so little time before them, it seemed they were cutting the same man over and over again.

Tiny passed the silk ligature and Ellis encircled the artery twice with it, just above the clamp. His fingers blurred as he tied the thread and occluded the artery. He repeated the exercise on the thinner-walled vein beside it. Tiny retrieved a pair of scissors from the basin and slapped them into Ellis's hand before he could ask for them. The assistant surgeon divided the vessels—artery and vein— below the ligatures and removed the clamp.

They'd cut away the soldier's trousers and filleted his thigh to the bone midway between hip and knee ten minutes before. Now, with the last of the muscle and flesh parted and only the bare thigh bone joining the lower leg to the upper, the amputation was complete in all but fact. Only the saw cut remained.

"Capital saw," Ellis said, and out of his side vision he caught Boyd turning to spit again. This time he had time to consider the action, something he'd seen Boyd do a thousand times in a dozen hovels like this one. In the instant before the handle of the bone saw struck his palm, Ellis wondered at the incongruities of his direct senior. He had 'good hands'. *Goddammit that ain't true,* Ellis thought, *he's more than that, a genuine honest-to-God born surgeon.*

Ellis had seen a lot of men work the tables in almost two years as an assistant surgeon and Boyd was, hands down, the best cutter out there. But it was also true the man had odd ways. Like his wont to chew during surgery, which perhaps wasn't all that bad, except it meant he was always spitting. And his fits of sudden abstraction in the middle of an operation. He'd suddenly walk away from the table, turn his back or go behind a wall, then reappear before too long as if nothing had happened. Except something had, Ellis would always think. At such times Boyd looked different. Certainly not better, and not worse (or probably not worse, he'd had occasion to think a few times—and how curious was that?). Just different. It showed most in his hands, which looked somehow, he tried to think of the correct word, revitalized? Was that it? Upon returning to the table, those hands, which had seemed worn and tired, would now be spirited and quick to perform. But it was Boyd's eyes that bothered. Once the surgeon reappeared, Ellis always found those eyes...*unsettling.* As if Boyd's eyes had developed an unpleasant 'lag,' a sort of disparity with his hands. *As if the one had given to the other,* Ellis suddenly thought. He swallowed hard, tried to put that absurd notion out of his head. A fevered product of his own exhausted mind. After all, once a battle was joined and the bloodletting began, there was never enough rest.

Tiny put the saw in Ellis's palm and he came back to the

moment. He curled his fingers around it—they seemed to have conformed to it over the endless months of the war—and went to task on the soldier's femur. Boyd held the meat of the leg out of the way as Ellis laid the business edge against the lower end of the bare thighbone and began to run it back and forth. The blade's teeth bit at the glistening bone with a gritty feel and flecks of ivory dust and crimson blood peppered the air. The sawing took more force than Ellis supposed it should and he made a mental note to have Tiny replace the blade before the next patient. When he'd about sawn through the whole of the femur, the remnant snapped with the pop of a dry twig and the leg fell away. Tiny stuffed a wad of lint against the bleeding stump as Boyd removed the now useless limb.

"Bone file."

Tiny anticipated the request and passed it without hesitation. Ellis grasped the narrow, five-inch flat metal file and worked the roughened side against the sharp edges of the bony stump. When he was satisfied with its appearance and feel, no sharp edges to work through the skin later, he nodded at Boyd, who took a quick feel as well. "That'll do," the senior man said. Ellis handed the file back to Tiny and Boyd took up an amputation knife—its long, sharp edge might easily slice a ham—and carved away a bit of remaining muscle and flesh on the back of the thigh, until he was satisfied with the flap to lay over the stub of bone.

They continued to work largely in silence, with no idle chit-chat. Ellis removed the lint from the end of the sawn bone. Satisfied the wound was not oozing too much blood, the surgeons flapped the skin up and approximated the edges with several silk stitches placed an inch apart. Ellis dressed the incision with a plaster cap and Tiny fanned the man to purge the chloroform from his system. A quick whiff of liquor of ammonia served to bring him back to consciousness, where upon he began to groan. Judging the man was safely over the effects of the chloroform, Boyd dribbled a few drops of laudanum, a sweet concoction of opium and alcohol, on the soldier's tongue to dull him to the agony to come. Ellis had seen its effect on men time and again. Some the laudanum slept, others it simply relaxed. Ellis himself had taken it once or twice to kill a headache. Its effect had felt akin to salvation—removing him from the horrors of the field hospital and the tussle of war, albeit transiently. *Good stuff,* he thought, *and dangerous. Too much of that could turn a man out.*

A pair of stretcher bearers stepped forward and lifted the patient with only a bare afterthought of gentleness, grabbing him under butt and armpits. The private's grunts as they carried him outside to be deposited alongside the other unfortunates were lost in the chaos of the battlefield hospital. Boyd stood off to one side of the room, several men interposed between him and Ellis. Ellis watched as the surgeon put his hands out, looking at the trembling, blood soaked palms as if they might suddenly fall off. Another of Boyd's odd behaviors. There followed a curious moment in which Boyd looked about, spotted Ellis, and slipped awkwardly out the back of the building.

Another soldier, younger, was placed on the table. As Tiny pressed a cloth over the lad's nose and mouth, Ellis probed the wound in his calf with a stiff finger, feeling for splinters of bone and the ball that had done the damage. The soldier winced, not quite under yet. As Ellis pulled his finger from the boy's innards, Boyd appeared at the side of the assistant surgeon and chuckled in an odd, not at all funny way. "The truth of the flesh," he said, or something very much like it. Ellis couldn't be sure. It was a small thing, but as Boyd called for a scalpel, it disturbed Ellis nonetheless and he had no idea why.

THREE

Major Tom Jersey watched the dog through his field glasses, temporarily distracted from the heat. It wasn't clear which side the animal belonged to, a mutt of no particular distinction, an ordinary thing caught in an extraordinary time. It moved in the borderland between the two armies, racing among the dark forms of the day-old dead, stopping now and again to sniff at remains or lift its hind leg. Somewhere along the way, the animal had lost part of an ear and every time its head came up, the gap was silhouetted and stood out peculiarly. He watched the dog move to within fifty yards of his line, then bound off across the field as the men taunted it.

He removed his cap and wiped his sleeve across his brow. "Damn heat," he muttered, thinking of his wool uniform, of the heat wringing him dry. His jacket, a dirty yellow-gray, stuck to the small of his back. No wind meant the smell of twelve thousand men on the edge of battle was penetrating and musk-like, as of a barnyard at branding time.

Jersey stood with his regiment in a screen of trees, line abreast, arrayed for battle with the enemy a mile distant beyond a treeless grassy divide. Before them flowed a shimmering field of wheat, broken only by a rail fence three-quarters of the way across—and by the ugly bodies of those who'd fallen the day before. *Yesterday*. His company had numbered one hundred and eighty-two then, had assaulted the Federals a half dozen times, had nearly broken them. But nearly didn't count, except maybe to the thirty soldiers who'd been lost. Half had been killed—their bodies still lay out there, on the scorched earth between the armies—and the other half were missing or with the surgeons.

Among the dead had been his colonel, and Oppley's last words still rang in Jersey's head. He'd raised his saber toward the enemy, shouted something like "That way men, the enemy is that—" and then had fallen dead, a dribble of blood staining his blouse over his heart. Jersey had known Colonel Charles Oppley since their days together at the bank before the war. Oppley had been a good man, full of integrity and bound to duty. An honorable man. Neither he nor Jersey had thought of themselves as true gentlemen, but if that had once mattered, it seemed foolish now. They'd done their duty to North Carolina and Oppley had paid the ultimate price. His had been a merciful soldier's death, Jersey understood, to be killed quick in the heat of battle at the front of his men. He supposed that's what he'd tell Cora Oppley.

An officer came bounding up on horseback, drawn saber held before him. The major thought he looked the archetype of a mounted warrior, too good for actual battle. "Major, you must take that hill there." He thrust his saber out to indicate the ground to which he referred. "It's the enemy's extreme left flank and the commanding general believes they are vulnerable there." The horse danced skittishly as the rumble of a distant shell shook the ground. "Can you do that, Major? Can your men take that ground?"

"I, eh, yes sir," he said. "We can, yes, we can take that hill, General. Yes sir, my men will take that hill, sir. This will be a proud day for the 18th North Carolina. Sir."

"Very well, Major. The 18th will lead the charge on this end of the field." The general nodded, said, "Godspeed, sir."

"Sir, my regards to the commanding general."

"Of course." The brigadier wheeled his horse and galloped off down the line.

Jersey surveyed the ground before his troops. To the south was the edge of the wheat field, with numerous boulders the size of houses, and woods beyond. Off in the distance in front, the field narrowed to half a mile and a rail fence bordered a dirt road running parallel to the trees. The ground beyond the road angled steeply upward; a thickly wooded hillside. The Federals were dug in on that hillside, among the trees and rocks. They'd argued over the ground between for a day and a half now. They'd taken it, lost it, taken it again, and lost it again. The hill was good ground for defense, deadly ground for an assault. The remnants of his company were proof of that. As he surveyed the ground through his field glasses, Jersey imagined he could pick out Colonel Oppley's body just in front of the fence.

He put the glasses down and wondered why he'd been so positive his men could take the hill. Hadn't Oppley been just as positive yesterday? What was it about war that made a man stupid, made him less—and more—than he was? The sulfur stink of gunpowder? The close feel of sweat parading your back? Of fear twisting your gut? Was it the anticipation of glory? Or just the simple sense of duty?

Jersey looked up and down the line, squinting as his eyes fought to adjust first to bright sun, then to shade, then sun again. He was on the extreme right flank of the army. Thousands of men crowded the trees in a long line to his left. It seemed to be alive, to have a pulse and a breath all its own. A slight corporal some distance away pulled an item from a breast pocket. It must have been close to his affections as he first kissed it, then flipped it open and stared at it. A picture case of gutta percha . . . perhaps it held an ambrotype of the soldier's girl back home. Jersey suddenly had a notion he was intruding. He himself had had such a case. Within it had been the likenesses of his beloved Elspeth and their three daughters. The damn case was now at the bottom of the Potomac River, lost the week before. But the images it held were still fresh in his mind.

A large tree burst not far up the line, close enough that he felt its report on his face and was stippled with the blood of those closer. The blast jerked him into the present and he saw a dozen men splintered in its wake. Others stepped forward to replace them, as though the shell had wounded not men but the line, and the line had healed itself. But they no longer existed . . . he wiped the proof from his face with a kerchief. He turned away, to face forward, toward the enemy. That was where his attention properly belonged.

A pasty-complexioned private sniveled beside him, mumbling something very fast, his face wet with tears. A veteran stood on the other side of the sniveler, tall and with a full beard and a dusty blouse. He said, "You'll be okay, Benny," and he rubbed the other's shoulder. "We'll all be okay if'n we jus' please to do our duty today."

Tom pondered the words, took their measure, and decided the advice was sound. Someone else was praying, and the Lord's Prayer became loud for a moment as others joined in. Jersey felt he should say some words, something inspirational. He was at a loss for what, though; could think of nothing beyond that which they were already saying to each other.

The moment passed and the command came. At three o'clock, he and the other soldiers stepped out of the trees and began to move toward the Federals. The rumble of five hundred score pair of feet pounded the earth; the hard, deep clamor of good men exerting themselves to the utmost. No silence, no stillness—only the lethal din of Federal artillery, only the sound of men ready to give their full measure. He was pushed along as the army became a sea of gray flooding the ripe wheat, the tide moving slowly, inexorably forward and upward. His men marched bravely. The sun caught the glint of polished poles and company colors flapping in the smoke. They moved with muskets shouldered, at the route step, side by side, five and six and eight deep in places. A grand spectacle. The surge of blood swelled his veins. He was hot again, and his blouse seemed too small. He stank of sweat but didn't care.

"Onward now! Over thar! Men, show 'em what we think o' Yankees in North Carolina!"

As he labored forward, he noted terrible gaps blasted in the line and learned what men are made of. Great chunks of flesh and bone mixed with bits of earth as the Union batteries turned the wheat field into a place for dying. Canisters of grape thickened the air with metal shot, like a swarming mass of black bugs. Arms, legs and fingers flung skyward yielded a peculiar mortal rain.

Jersey was painted red by the mist of diffused blood.

He was halfway across the field—running hard but he might as well be running into a stiff wind—when a trooper next to him went down. The major stopped beside him, along with a second trooper. They made themselves low in the grass. The wounded man was bleeding heavily. A minié ball had shattered his knee. The major tied a tourniquet above the wound, the two troopers talking incessantly as he did so.

"Do it hurt?"

"Not much, burns a little."

"I got to get you back."

"Can't walk, no way."

"Lookahere, just lean on me."

"I just wait here."

"This ain't no place for waitin'. And what I gonna tell ma?"

"Help me up then, I kin hobble along."

Jersey glanced at both troopers for the first time, and did a double take. The two had the same face; identical in every way except the blood streaming down one's leg. He said nothing; helped them to their feet. One slung his musket over his shoulder, then hooked an arm around his wounded brother's torso. He looked Jersey in the eyes. "I promised..." and the rest was lost in the blizzard of battle. They stumbled in the direction they'd come and Jersey knelt to regroup, breathing deeply in the closeness of the burnt air. He watched the two go a few paces, then began to move forward again. He looked back a moment later, saw they'd gone fifteen or twenty yards, but something wasn't right. The scene was off kilter and at first he thought it was how the smoke obscured them, then understood. A shell had taken one brother's head off, though his body still stood with its twin as if yet living.

A lone horse, saddle empty, hide fouled by gore, bounded between him and the brothers. In that instant, the twins disappeared as if the horse had erased them. Jersey's gaze followed the animal as a hole opened in its neck, the blood spurted. It fell to the ground in a clumsy mass of flesh.

Jersey took off at a run, leaping others as he went. No longer a man, he'd soared into the soldier's Valhalla—where glory abounds and death is sanctified; where blood is a badge and bone a medal. He put a hand up to signal, felt little pain as a fragment chiseled a finger off. He ran past three pairs of legs lying in the grass—nothing more, just legs. He kept moving.

The air tasted of dirt and cinder. A canister of grape hit the air beside him and subtracted another man, as if the air itself had opened and swallowed him whole. Another soldier, one leg blown off, dragged himself yet toward the enemy, leaving a wide trail of red. Jersey viewed this last as if from a distance; it didn't seem real. None of it seemed real.

An explosion flung him to the earth beside a winded infantryman. The man sat the ground trying hard to catch his breath, clutching desperately at his chest. Jersey talked to him but received only a blank stare. He eyed him for a wound, saw no tell-tale red. The infantryman's breath shallowed, then stopped. A flag bearer slumped at their feet, shot through the head. Jersey picked up the flag as its bearer fell. He turned, shouting with his last ounce of voice.

"Over there, men! The enemy is that way! That way, men, the enemy is that way!" It occurred to him these were the same words Colonel Oppley had shouted twenty-four hours before. He held his saber aloft in one hand and the flag of the 18th North Carolina fluttered over his head as he gripped the pole hard in the other. He advanced, and it had the desired effect. His men ran forward, yelling, trying to fit themselves to shallow folds of terrain as they came on. He found Oppley's body, recognized it only because of the rank insignia—the face was unpleasant and ugly. He thought of the waste—the terrible waste—and his determination was renewed. He took another dozen steps and dropped beside the split rail fence. Bodies were piled high here, cut down by close and grueling fire as they'd risen to climb it. As he watched more were cut in half trying to clamber it, dismembered in ways terrible to see.

Jersey looked back at the colonel's body, saw the colonel's saber lying broken in the soiled grass. The words of the brigadier came to him: *Major, you must take that hill there. It's the enemy's extreme left flank and the commanding general believes they are vulnerable there.* The words branded his mind. *Can you do that, Major? Can your men take that ground?* Jersey recalled too the sniveling private, and the tall, bearded veteran: *We'll all be okay If'n we jus' please to do our duty today.* The words echoed in his skull. They drowned out the clamorous rush of battle; focused his mind like rays of sun through a magnifying glass. *Yes sir, my men will take that hill, sir. This will be a proud day for the 18th North Carolina. Sir.*

Jersey stood and clambered over the fence, using those who'd come before for traction. He accomplished it smartly, in one fluid motion, both flag and saber held high. He crossed the road quickly and gained the shade and safety of the trees. He caught his breath and watched others come the way he had, then passed the flag to a soldier with no words going between them. The hill loomed before him larger than even the field had, and he wondered that he still breathed. Looking back the way he'd come, he glimpsed the army still crossing the wheat field; vast, jostling blurs of men. Smoke obscured the detail, and it was as if the earth had frayed, as if the surface had been abraded and what lay below was hell itself.

Jersey motioned to his boys: move into the trees and up the hillside. They charged forward, screaming and shouting exhausted pleas. They knelt and fired their muskets, moved forward, knelt again, reloaded, fired again. They made it fifty yards through the trees before being turned back the first time, twice that far the second. They charged six times up that hill, certain the next lunge would break the Federals. The seventh charge broke their spirit, however, as the Federals came running down the slope with bayonets shining.

A fierce hand to hand ensued. Men choked, stabbed, kicked, punched, clubbed, shot, and otherwise burdened each other. Some of the Southerners ran out of the trees and scooted over the rail fence, retreating into the wheat field beyond. Jersey fell after a sharp blow to the back of his neck and lay momentarily paralyzed. He was up again before long, though, saw the day was lost, and retreated with his men. His soldierly edge was gone. Exhaustion crowded its place. He fought off two Yankees as he climbed the fence, dropping his saber in the process, and began to run back across the field, where he was tackled by a third. Holding his side, Jersey regained his feet and reached for his sidearm. Before he could pull his pistol, though, a terrible jolting struck his hip and knocked him to the ground like gravity defined.

As the world dissolved around him, Major Tom Jersey found himself staring into the face of the gap-eared dog. At intervals, the mutt's skewed body jerked. It grinned pathetically at him, tongue dangling at an odd angle, eyes shot with blood misaimed crazily. A trickle of blood dripped from an ear. The thing kept circling a paw, uselessly, as if unable to right itself. That seemed to Tom a measure of the day's losses. With the last of his strength, he drew his revolver from its holster and, lying there beside it in the crushed wheat, shot the dog.

***

Private Ezra Coffin was just four days past his twentieth birthday, but he feared he'd drawn his last breath in this world. In the hour just passed, he'd seen a half dozen comrades, the best friends he had, killed in one rebel charge after another. On the extreme left of the Federal line, the beleaguered 118th Pennsylvania had turned back the Confederates five times, though at a high price. The 118th had numbered three hundred tired and weary souls ninety minutes before. A third of that number now lay wrecked and bloodied, doing little more than soiling the ground. And, while those still able whooped and called to the rebels down the hill—taunting them to come meet their betters once again—Ezra stood behind a large oak and tried to calm the pounding in his chest. He tore open yet another powder cartridge with his teeth. Its bitter taste mingled with the metal of blood as he bit his tongue in the process. He cursed and with a shaky hand—he'd never gotten used to the thrill of battle—poured the black grit down the muzzle of his Springfield. He dumped a lead minié ball into the barrel and drove the lethal mix into the weapon with a brass ramrod. All the while, rivulets of sweat carved streams through the soot on his face.

Behind the dirt, that face was a rounded mass with simple features; in ordinary times, not the face of a killer. His eyes, a soothing hazel green, were large and their whites stood out boldly against the burnt powder encircling them. His nose was blunt and crooked and his yellowed teeth were still crudded with bits of the salted pork he'd chewed on the march hours before. His pale lips were hidden behind more black soot and his dirty hair scragged this way and that. A few blond whiskers curled from his round chin. Overall, the face of a boy, of any son, on either side of the line.

Ezra made himself small against the bole, musket tight between his fingers, and looked to the tree beside his. A soldier sat, neck extended, head back as if dead weight. His face was dirty, his eyes wide, dazed. His mouth was a dark O mocking the hole in his forehead. Beneath the blank sleeve of a private, dead hands still gripped the musket, clutching so hard his fingers were ghostly white, the blood long since drained. Ezra looked upon this with no emotion. Emotion created hesitation, and hesitation would kill him. This much he had learned. So he tried not to think how much the boy looked like him. Actually, the dead soldier didn't favor him at all, or so he decided.

Ezra gripped his canteen, shook it. No splash within. The dead private stared up still, the canteen against his belt apparent for the first time. Ezra tasted the salty powder on his lips anew, grit dry as dirt. His throat was raw and scratchy. Water seemed as necessary at that moment as breathing, and each breath renewed this idea. His eyes stung and he closed them tightly. He ran a hand over the whole of his grimy face, the woods closing in on him.

The air was heavy with sulfur and stank powerfully. Smoldering clumps of dead leaves lay all about. The boom of cannon was far off. Close in, the laborious breathing of the soldiers caught his ear, and the cries of the wounded—unavoidable, pitiful, nearly unbearable—assaulted his senses. Ezra thought them prayers to a merciless God, saw the woods become one large church. Everyone was a believer now. Chaos. Misery abundant.

He timed the booms of the cannon to his heartbeat, every ten or so. His breathing slowed. His fear waned. He gripped his musket and saw his fingertips blanch, like those of the dead soldier beside the tree. Where were the rebels? He hated waiting. The worst part of battle. Anything could be imagined in the waiting.

Ezra felt his parched throat again and shook his empty canteen. He tossed the useless thing aside, and reexamined the dead private's canteen, still at arm's length. His throat was stinging now. Too much waiting. Too much thinking. Too much noise. Too much of everything—except water.

He swallowed and the little spit he had hung in his throat like a thick web.

He scanned the hillside before him. Bosky on his arrival, trees the size of men's thighs had been gnawed in half by the close fighting. The bushes were stripped of leaves. Soldiers crouched under any cover they could find, like kids in a game of seek. A fellow had his member out, pissing in the dirt. Beside him another bled from the neck like a butchered hog. Unfamiliar, and he was thankful for the fact. Discarded haversacks, abandoned cartridge boxes, blankets, empty shells, kepis, leather straps, gloves, jackets, a single boot with a fancy silver spur (the light caught it just so and it sparkled like a jewel). All these things and more littered the place. He saw a soldier with a harmonica peeking out his breast pocket.

I know him. Ezra waved and Tim Jewel waved back. Ezra patted his breast, put his fingers to his lips as if playing. Jewel pulled the instrument out and held it up to see. He put it to his mouth, played a few notes. They flittered away, unheard in the scourge of battle. Jewel pocketed the harmonica.

A mosquito buzzed Ezra's face, and he slapped at it. The only real winners today were the bugs. He began to chuckle at how it must be high carnival for them. *The meek shall inherit the earth after all.* He threw his head back, and grinned wide. He felt himself slipping, felt his grip on the scene around him coming undone. He'd seen men come undone before. Men who were a damn sight stronger than he, too. Officers even. He'd heard about a lieutenant at Bull Run, in the first year of the war, who in the midst of the fighting had inexplicably—and calmly—turned his sidearm on himself and put a hole in his own head. One of Coffin's sergeants had been there and had witnessed the whole thing, had spoken of it around the campfire. "Now the durndest thing I ever did see," the sergeant would say in his down home way, and then he'd launch into the tale all over again.

Ezra folded his lower lip over his teeth and bit down. Hard. He righted his head, the grin now gone, and darted his sight back and forth across the trees in front of him. He sniffled and his nose drooled black snot in the sooty air. His shirt and pants were uncomfortably close in the humidity. He couldn't stand the aching in his throat any longer. A thousand fire ants roosted there. He eyed the dead soldier's canteen, still only an arm's-length away. He leaned from behind the tree and grasped it in his right hand.

With a single clear ping, a ball broke the flesh of his hand and passed through the tin skin of the canteen. Ezra snatched his hand close as the canteen fell, spilling water over the ground. He made himself tight against the tree once more. *Goddurn water. Goddurn rebels.*

"They's comin', men!"

He made his neck long and peered around the bole. Movement down the slope. The trees themselves trembled. Men in gray were moving with purpose up the hill. They might own the forest. Too many. A terrible yell, hard to believe men could make such a noise. The air once again filled with lead and popping. Bits of rock and splinters rained like a storm. He thought his position no longer tenable; saw nothing else any better.

Ezra sighted on the first thing that moved, pulled the trigger. The musket bucked his shoulder and a puff of gray smoke obscured his vision. Bits of burnt powder stung his face. A ball whizzed past his ear, close enough to prickle skin. He turned his back to the tree once more and tore open another cartridge. He rammed a ball home, capped, cocked, turned, and fired again nearly a minute after his first shot. The gray men were closer now, though still behind a fair screen of trees seventy or eighty yards down-slope. He reloaded. Only three cartridges left in his box. Standing erect, he bit down on his lower lip again and stepped out from the safety of the tree. He took a bead on one of the gray men. His opposite moved in the obscurity of the smoke, hugging the earth. Ezra waited the smoke out, aimed for the man's chest but struck him in the head and watched him fall. Another stepped over his fallen comrade, not bothering even to look down but finding his footing nonetheless. He seemed to eyeball Ezra as he did so, but an instant later he dropped as well. The oncoming rebels took another step or two forward. Then, as they'd done five times already, the wave of gray halted and reversed itself, the men backing carefully but hastily down the hill. Ezra watched them withdraw, reloading as they did so.

His right hand throbbed, the pain only now becoming apparent. Sharp and burning. He slid to the ground and looked uneasily at the hand. He had no idea what to expect. A hole in the center of his palm was large enough to pass his thumb through. Only a little blood. His hand still fisted, but he had some difficulty opening it again. He'd always imagined nausea at such a moment, but had none. A tolerable wound. He fumbled with his haversack and pulled out a faded red kerchief. He wrapped the cloth, a gift from his wife—oh, how he wished he were home by Liza's side just now—around his damaged hand.

"Ammo, I need me some ammo!" he shouted.

"Me too!"

"Over here as well!"

He glanced about. The place belonged to the dead. The 118th was shredded, more men down than up. Tim Jewel with his tall frame was still up though—a small mercy. The ground was littered with the only waste of battle that really mattered.

Dead men clogged the space between the trunks like fish in a net.

Ezra swallowed, his thirst no less parched. He ignored it and counted his cartridges. Two shots left. He glanced at Tim. Jewel smiled back. Ezra couldn't bring himself to return it, waved his bandaged hand instead. "Lookahere fella, we're giving 'em hell!" Jewel hollered, or something like it. Ezra's ears rang, were no longer reliable. He nodded with more certainty than he felt and sniffled again.

The word came along the line to fix bayonets. It occurred to him that the day, already far along on the road to damnation, was about to tilt further in that direction. Jewel fixed his sticker with barely a hesitation. Ezra noted the quick compliance of others as well. But he no longer cared. He wanted out, then and there. Wanted out any way it came. Amid the smoking and bleeding ruins of the 118th

Pennsylvania, death was as good a way as any other. He looked about again. A good place for dying. He fixed his bayonet and waited for whatever would come.

He didn't have to wait long. For a seventh time, the rebel attackers howled up the slope. The first cry an hour before had made Ezra weak with anticipation. This time it sufficed only to warn him.

"Let 'em get close boys!"

"Make Pennsylvania proud!"

Ezra stood and stepped from behind the tree. He aimed on the third rebel he saw, supposing others had already eyeballed the first two, and not wanting to waste the shot. He waited for the order to fire, concentrated all his energies on the effort, stilled his breathing. He and the rifle were one.

"Stead-y... Stead-y... fire!"

Ezra pulled the trigger, and the man dropped. Another filled his place as he reloaded. *Live or die, ain't no longer my decision.* He felt lighter than air, as if some burden had been lifted—as if every burden had been lifted—from him. He took four steps forward, knelt in the bloody soil, aimed at another boy across the way, squeezed. The ball missed, rattled away high in the trees.

The enemy came in force, a mass moving with deadly purpose. He wondered where they'd all come from. They moved with frantic effort, pulling bodies aside, stepping on some, stepping over others. The musket fire was as thick as it had been all day. More men went down.

Crying. Screaming. Confusion.

"Charge! Men, chaaaaaarge!"

Ezra raced down the slope, bayonet thrust in front. He, all of them, whooped as they ran. They took the Confederates by surprise. The two lines became an intermingled killing zone, a no man's land of blue and gray bleeding red onto the scorched ground of the woods. The entire mass surged downhill as the gray line turned and ran, the Federals in pursuit. As he ran, he stopped once to reload, though in the confusion he lost the ball and charged the weapon uselessly. He half ran, half stumbled, and the trees thinned before he realized they'd done so. He crossed a road and climbed a fence, all the while continuing to move at the double step, other blue-clad soldiers running with him. Many of the routed rebels stopped and threw their hands up. One such did so a few yards in front of Ezra and he stopped and raised his musket.

"You my prisoner, Johnny Reb," Ezra said, his weight shifting foot to foot, his nose running again. He tried not to sniffle as he looked the man in the eye.

A second gray-clad soldier, musket raised, stepped from behind the first. The two men, the gray in the screen of his comrade and the blue with nothing before him save his raised rifle, stood close enough to exchange pleasantries, yet said nothing. Ezra, not awed, pulled his trigger.

The hammer fell and the rifle bucked too-soft against his shoulder with the blast of an empty powder-load. The two rebels fell back, stunned and off-balance, perhaps surprised to be still alive. They hesitated at their good fortune, but somewhere off in the cover of the trees, another rebel did not. He fired and a large chunk of meat peeled from Ezra's left thigh. His boot began to fill with blood.

Ezra both heard and felt a loud snap. A corkscrew of pain spiraled from his hip to his knee. He sank to the ground, put an arm up against the blue sky. His heart pounded double and this time there was nausea, instant and unavoidable. He feared he'd pissed himself with the warmth in his boot. He had an incredible sense of falling, that he could fall forever...

With him on his knees, the lucky rebels before him swung their muskets as clubs. One caught Ezra's raised arm and he knew another moment of pain. He groped for his own weapon, but the butt of a musket slammed into his forehead. The last thing Ezra Coffin saw before the bright day receded into darkness was the stain of red pooling the grass beneath him.

He thought, *I didn't know it would be like this.*

***

Captain Tobias Ellis knew the man would die from the moment he first laid eyes upon him. He was propped against a post, the last remains of a picket fence. He slumped with arms at his side, palms up in the dirt. His foraging cap sat askew his head in such a way so as to show off his eyes, which owned a distant, melancholy look, as if he was already somewhere else. The soldier was chest-shot and each time he sucked a breath, air and blood both bubbled through the wound with a sickly glick-glick sound. Ellis judged by the man's blue lips and fingers that his time in this world was about up. He'd been wrong before, though, so he placed a bare hand on the bubbling wound, felt the yet strong throbbing of the heart within—mighty, like a great engine racing out of control—and the slickness of warm blood before it congeals lifeless.

The man acknowledged him with a bare flicker of a glance. Assistant Surgeon Ellis was in his mid-twenties, a little less than six feet tall, of stick-thin build with wire frame glasses perched upon a similarly thin nose. He had bushy burnsides of youthful black hair, no beard or mustache. He was bookish, disciplined, no stranger to work, no stranger to death. He'd experienced two years of war. It seemed to him alternately a giant sloth brooding over its next move, or a great clawed creature that chewed men to pieces. In the former instance, tens of men died day in and day out from typhoid, diarrhea, dysentery, pneumonia, smallpox, camp fever, and a host of other maladies that attacked the human body like rot on meat. The daily toll was small, but the accumulation was steady, the sum incomprehensible.

The latter instances were stuttering moments of unmitigated chaos that stretched into eternity for far too many men.

Like this one. Ellis opened his hospital pack and took out a vial marked 'morphine'. He sprinkled a liberal amount of the powder on the hole and stuffed the wound with a lint dressing by way of arresting the leak. He looked the man in the eyes, said "Easy, easy. It'll be done soon, it'll all be over soon." The man's head fell back then, knocking his cap to the ground and giving the illusion his neck had suddenly lengthened. His adam's apple bobbed beneath the stubbled skin of his jaw as if he was swallowing a large stone over and over again. Ellis took the man's head in his hands and righted it. The soldier's breathing, which had been slow, deep, and regimented, became short, shallow, and rapid. Tiny beads of sweat gathered on his face and neck, magnifying the dirt there. His lips pursed, relaxed, pursed again.

The wounded man mouthed something. Ellis strained to hear, but could make out nothing more than the sound of something wet caught in his throat. A growing smear of purple bled across the blue fabric over his right nipple; the leak hadn't been arrested after all. His body began to shake violently, and Ellis imagined a miserable, terrible cold engulfing it. He understood the man was beyond any help he could give. He had neither time nor desire to watch him die and so took only a moment to lay him flat upon the earth. "Don't fret," he said. "The war's over. You'll be going home soon. It'll be nice. You'll see, it'll be nice." Then he moved on.

Ellis had set up shop in a slight depression near a front which kept shifting back and forth across the field. The only cover the meager surroundings afforded were the remains of a Federal artillery wagon and the horse that had pulled it. The wagon rested atilt on the ground, one wheel a splintered memory while the other, large wooden spokes fanning out from the center, held its end of the axle out of the dirt. An open artillery box sat upon that axle, its job now to shield the living. The horse lay dead on its side, still hitched, belly bloated grotesquely in the summer heat. Tiny burps of escaping gas ripened the air with each bullet that struck it.

Having taken a medical education and volunteered his services to the United States Army, the not yet thirty-year-old assistant surgeon had the task of making the first decisions that might mean a man's life or death. Ellis and an aide, a hospital steward named Archer, worked at a frenzied pace to stop bleeding and splint broken bones—both as quickly as possible. They splinted bones, dressed wounds, and tied tourniquets. They weren't priests, but more than once they'd heard a man's confession. All this with shells whizzing overhead and exploding close enough to shower them with dirt. Each carried a pack of bandages, needles, silk thread for ligatures, ether for the occasional small operation they had to perform, aromatic spirits of ammonia to boost a failing man's temper. A bottle of whiskey wasn't regulation, but Ellis knew from long experience the raw rye he carried was the best medicine there available.

A shell-burst knocked him off his feet. He regained himself and saw a man face down in the aftermath of it. He closed the distance in three steps, the air heavy with lead all the way, and dropped hard in the churned dirt. He felt for a pulse, then rolled the man onto his back. Most of one side of the fellow's face was missing and his breathing seemed the last ratcheting of a broken gear. Ellis coughed in the sulfur-laden air and turned away, looking for another distraction. He found one a long twenty yards away, propped over on his side in a shallow gully of mud and grass.

He crawled most of the way, found a gaping hole where the soldier's abdomen had been. Loops of bright pink bowel bulged through the opening, writhing about like a ball of snakes, and Ellis immediately classed this one too as a cadaver, though he yet breathed. He hated that he didn't have the time or expertise to help them all. This was just another he couldn't save.

He was turning to crawl back to the dead horse when the gutted man reached out and grabbed his arm. Ellis tensed at the touch and shot him a sideways glance. He regretted it at once, for the soldier's face shone with a fierce intensity. Life still touched him.

"I can't help you. The wound is mortal," Ellis said. Direct, but the dying deserved the truth.

The hand fell to the grass and he thought for a moment that was it, the end of it. But then the man slowly reached to grasp something beneath him. A paper of some sort. Blood smeared. It became clear the soldier wanted him to have it. He accepted it, a scribbled note. No time to glance further at it, not then. He repeated the mistake of looking into the man's face. "You can't leave me here," he whispered. 'Yes, yes I can,' Ellis wanted to say. But didn't. He looked across to the dead horse, saw the wounded piling up through the smoke. Others were waiting, men he could save. "Okay." He stuffed the note in his shirt and saw Archer moving from man to man across the way. "Archer! I need you!"

They made quick work of dragging the wounded man back to the wagon and laid him in the lee of the bloated horse. While Archer poured a jigger of whiskey down his throat, the assistant surgeon sprinkled the man's exposed guts with morphine powder and pushed them back in as best he could. Terrible work, and when Ellis was done it was over. With thumb and pointer finger he drew the lids over dead eyes. He sat back a moment and the scribbled note came to mind. He pulled it out, read a part of it, and stared too long at the signature on the bottom: 'Tucker A.' He had not even asked the man his name. He started to read Tucker's letter a second time but a gust of dirt blown up by a burst shell startled him back to action. For a short while after that, he worked with the note balled up in his fist, then stuffed the wad in a pocket.

He moved on to attend an unconscious man. Pushing aside the spiritless man's blond hair, he discovered a nasty hole in his scalp. He probed the wound with a finger and found a hole in the underlying skull as well, with fragments of in-driven bone rough against his digit. As he worked, the soldier abruptly stopped breathing. Ellis buried his finger to the knuckle and swept it circumferentially around the hole, then pulled it out. Bits of clot, bone, and gray matter bubbled after his finger. The unconscious man shuddered and opened his eyes and Ellis hoped he'd done some good.

A sudden shell-burst flung him to the dirt. Those who could crouched low. Others hugged the bloated horse. A moment later Ellis ducked and covered his head as a volley of musket fire ruptured the belly of the dead animal and spattered him with rotted entrails.

Deafened, he blinked up into the smoky late afternoon, at the smoke rolling across the green hills of southern Pennsylvania. Moving across and between those hills like a gray-white veil.

Dusk of July second, 1863, and across those fields and hills lives were being either ended or changed in ways both inconceivable and irrevocable. In a shadowland where the only real commodity was suffering and the only true coin was death, men lived or died with apparent randomness, and there seemed no sense anywhere.

FOUR

T he man in the green bowler hat stood in the street brushing the dust from the sleeves and lapels of his suit coat, first one side, then the other. He'd put the coat on only fifteen minutes earlier, just before entering the town proper, but the churned dust had settled on the coat, turning its dark undertaker black to a somewhat lighter dirty charcoal that wouldn't do against his white shirt. The shirt too had been recently laundered, and now he crooked his neck side to side and adjusted his string tie with all the familiarity of an act done a thousand times before. He coughed into a kerchief (an act he was also too familiar with), looked at it, folded it, and pocketed it.

He searched the lane prior to crossing the street, taking pains to avoid the muddier places, then stepped across a gangplank and up onto the wooden sidewalk, where he continued his stroll past a few storefronts. He could tell the character of these small towns by their main street. He saw nothing in the mud, dirt, and dilapidated buildings to differentiate this pissant little town from a hundred other similar mudholes he'd passed through since the beginning of the war. It had a worn look, like a wagon that had been used hard over the years and was out of square. You could change the wheels, but the axles were so warped the effort would hardly be worth it. Change out the axles, and you'd discover the frame was rotted. *Might as well burn the goddamn thing. Jesus K. Reist.*

The burb did have a bank though. The First State Bank of Monroeville. Monroeville. Moronic name. And why was it every goddamn little one-horse town he passed through had a bank with either 'first' or 'state' in the title, when the bank was in fact neither of these things? He had an idea it made people feel big, or at least bigger. No matter. They could call their bank *The First State Pisspot* for all he cared.

He'd just talk to these good folks, he tried hard not to think of them as suckers or even as pissants though in fact that's exactly what they were when you came right down to it. He would just talk to these good folks, make them the usual offer they couldn't resist—though most would, he knew from experience. Well, that was their loss. They'd regret it when the war came back this way and the bodies started piling up like flies in an outhouse, but that wasn't his problem. *No sir. Jesus K. Reist.*

He finally stopped in front of a pair of smoked glass doors with Jake's Saloon writ in fancy gold script across the upper half. The glass in the right hand door was fractured and a crack wormed down between the o's in Saloon. He touched it and the door opened several inches. He pushed it open still further and stepped through.

It was midday, not quite noon, and the local watering hole was quiet. The inside was dark, or at least the bright street made it seem so, and his eyes took a moment adjusting. He was drawn to the lazy sound of a broom—shuh, shuh, shuh—sweeping back and forth across the floor. Its owner was a boy in dirty coveralls and bare feet, ten or twelve. The room, which was not large, was crowded with perhaps a dozen empty tables and their chairs, most of which had been set on the tables. An upright piano occupied one wall, looking lonely and out of place. The man in the bowler wondered if it had ever been played. Probably not, or at least not in a long while. *What a shithole. Jesus K. Reist.*

The barkeep, a softlooking dude who ran to chubby, stood to one side behind the bar, the top of his shirt undone and his sleeves rolled to the elbows. He had only four fingers on his left hand, a fact which the man in the green bowler identified immediately and thought *proof of life.* He had an unconscious habit of checking for such idiosyncrasies, though in this case it was easy: the remaining four fingers were curled ulnarwise. The hand was useless. A blind man would have seen as much.

A dozen or so bottles of various liquors sat the shelf, labels turned outward for easy reference. The four-fingered keeper had been tinkling glasses or bottles or both when he'd entered, but now the tinkling had stopped and the barkeep just stood leaning on the bar. "Help you, mister?"

"Name's Jones. Jupiter Jones. Purveyor extraordinaire, sir. At your service." Jones doffed his hat. "Perhaps, sir, you'd favor me with a shot of your finest."

The barkeep made a face like he was trying to suck a piece of food stuck between his teeth, then nodded and pulled down one of the bottles behind him. He stepped down the bar until he was directly in front of Jones and poured. As Jones reached, he put his good hand over the shot glass. He held the other in front of his chest. A grimace flashed across his face, then nothing. "Color of your money."

"Absolutely sir, absolutely." Jones produced a yankee greenback and the man moved his hand away. "Leave the bottle, if you please," he added, tossing out another greenback.

The barkeep shrugged and walked away. Jones drank the shot and poured the rest of the bottle's contents into his glass. He fingered the glass like a man in heavy contemplation, his fingers scrawny and wasted.

"What's with that hand?"

"My hand ain't none a your business," the barkeep said.

"Looked like it might be some painful, that's all. I guess I could help that."

"Like I said, ain't your business."

"That your wagon, mister?" the boy asked of a sudden. He'd stopped his sweeping and was peering out a window.

"Yep." The mural on the side of the wagon read *JUPITER JONES TRAVELING MEDICINE SHOW*. The letters were big, bright gold surrounded by red and blue stars of varying sizes against a black background. The paint was worn, the wagon an old one. Tin cups, lengths of rope, an old pair of spurs, two pots for brewing coffee, a fire grill, a miscellany of other pots and pans, and other accoutrements hung from it. It had all jostled about with a musical quality like a traveling minstrel show as the fancy cart lumbered down the road.

"Sure is inneresting. What you got in there?"

"The wonders of the world, my boy." *And the secrets too. Oh yes, the very secrets of life itself.*

"Huh?"

Jupiter Jones was tall, cadavericly thin, and looked as if the stuff of life had mostly ebbed out of him and living was a burden. He was drawn, with shiny, sickly yellow skin that glistened like polished brass under the hot, midday sun. Up top, a thin crop of hair covered an otherwise bleak landscape, which by long habit he covered with a green bowler's hat. His face looked as if hollowed from the inside, and a man could get lost in the dark sunken holes that were his eyes. His cheekbones, high and thin, were dotted with the faded scars of the smallpox that had killed his mother before he was five. His chest too was bony and narrow and he wheezed near constantly, interrupted at occasional intervals by an anemic, washed-out cough, which more often than not brought up a wad of his insides.

"The world, boy." Jones doubted the lad had ever been out of this pissant town, had certainly never been out of Northern Virginia even though Pennsylvania was just across the river. "Jesus K. Reist," he said sotto voce. *What an inbred lot.*

He turned and glanced out the window. As expected, his wagon was drawing a crowd. "Come here, boy."

The boy looked at the barkeep and the barkeep nodded. Still holding the broom, he crossed the room and stood in front of Jones.

"What's your name?"

"Billy."

Billy had a moronic smile and needed a bath, but neither one of these things disqualified him. "You look like an enterprising lad," Jones said.

"You want something of the boy, just say it plain, mister," the barkeep said.

Jones had always moved among people with the awkward ease of one who'd never learned the social graces. He was queer, not given to friendship easily or intimacy ever. He was, in fact, Dr. Jupiter Jones, for he possessed a medical degree for which he had studied the better part of six months some thirty years before. Notwithstanding this, the actual practice of medicine had never been of interest to him. He didn't like sick people, never had.

Jones coughed into a kerchief again, a wad of something black and green. He pocketed it and produced several candy canes. "Give these to your friends and tell them to bring their parents over to the wagon at two this afternoon." He added a shiny new coin. "This is for you. There's another, and one for a friend too if'n you set up a stage I have beside my wagon."

The boy's eyes widened at the sight of the coin. "Yes sir, mister!"

***

A little over an hour later, Jupiter Jones stepped out of the saloon and observed the crowd gathering at his wagon. There might be fifty people, he surmised, and the majority adults. He smiled despite how he felt, an action he'd grown accustomed to long ago; there wasn't much he took pleasure in anymore, though he could still get up for a good crowd.

He took a half deep breath—the air filling his chest stiffly—and ambled forward, saying nothing at first. He let their curiosity grow, let anticipation build in their petty murmurs and pointing. He might have waited even longer, but a grunt gripped him just then and he made as if clearing his throat to cover it. He lifted his hat clear of his baldness, and said, "Welcome! Welcome one and all. Jones is the name, Dr. Jupiter Jones. I have a degree in medicine but I'm humbled is all, humbled to be here among friends." His voice was old, scratchy.

The crowd turned at his sudden appearance. He waved his hat in the manner of the great showman he'd once been and moved through them with a robustness he'd husbanded strength for all day. They were interested if not awed and parted to allow him to pass. Reaching the stage, he ascended the steps and turned to look out over the assembled folks.

"Jupiter Jones's the name and healing's the game," he began, suppressing another cough. "Neighbors, I've traveled the land far and wide to bring you the miracles you will see here today." He spoke in an easy singsong, gaze wandering, crossed one moment and walleyed the next. Those below had difficulty telling where the good doctor was looking at any given moment. 'You could fry the fish and watch the cat at the same time,' the tactless mother of a girl he'd courted many years before had remarked at their one and only meeting. His eyes, crossed since birth, seemed to look everywhere. "Who be ill here, I ask? Who among you will be the first to come forward and witness the awe..." He paused. *Let it build.* "...of Jupiter's Oil?"

"I will," a young woman said, raising her hand before the others and stepping boldly out in front of the crowd.

Putting the hat back on his head, he said, "Wonderful, wonderful. Your name, lovely lady?"

"My name's Mary."

"Mary is it? A Christian name." He smiled, first at her, then at the crowd. "So lovely to see you today Miss. Are you afflicted?"

"I am," she said, and the suffering in her voice was unmistakable.

"Can you show us?"

The day was warm, too warm for the long cotton sleeves covering her forearms. She began to roll up one, hesitated, then continued. She was sobbing.

"Do not be afraid, Miss."

"I'm not. It's just, well, I've had these sores so long." She glanced up at him with a knowing smile.

"Sores?" Jupiter said. He turned to the crowd. "She has sores," he repeated, as if making an announcement of great portent. "Great and terrible sores!"

She gave her sleeve a final tug and revealed the full extent of her affliction to the onlookers. There was a collective gasp—the susurrant stour of fifty throats inhaling as one—and those closest to the woman, no more than a girl really, stepped back.

She was afflicted, all right, that was plain. Like something out of a charnel house. Blue-black pustules, oozing a greenish crud, covered the forearm. For those closest to her, there was a smell as well, akin to the black odor of a rodent three days dead. The entire forearm had a dusky, diseased look, and anyone in the know would have asked how such a person was still breathing.

An elderly woman fainted. Somebody uttered the word "smallpox" and the crowd stepped back further. Jupiter quashed this, however; he wanted their attention, but not their terror. Fear would be useful as well of course, but not if they dispersed. Perhaps he'd overdone it; too much of the green crud maybe, or the odor. Not so long dead next time. "All is well, good people, very much all right. You see for yourselves the girl does not look ill. She has the devilpox, not the smallpox. A common mistake of those without a medical degree."

Nobody in the assembly had ever heard of the devilpox (how could they, it didn't exist), but that hardly mattered. Another rush of air, this time a collective exhale. The people of Monroeville took a step back toward Jupiter's stage. Those closest held their noses.

"Can you help me?" Mary sobbed.

"Of course. I have the treatment—THE CURE," he corrected in a stilted, loud voice that would have made any showman green with envy.

Now came her tears, like a burst dam. *Jesus K. Reist,* Jupiter thought, you had to love this girl's skill with a mob. He pulled a kerchief from inside his jacket and dabbed at the sweat collecting on his forehead. "Well, my dear Mary, calm yourself; for this is your lucky day. I got me a remedy straight from the jungles of Africa." Jupiter cast his good eye about the crowd, feigning a look of amazement; his face had gone from tubercular to jovial in an instant. His wayward eye tumbled up and back and only the white was visible then. *Like lambs to the slaughter, you stupid sonsabitches. Jesus K. Reist. It's all in the showmanship. Convince them, Jupiter, you can do it.*

"Mombasa. On the equatorial coast of Kenya, the great and wild continent of Africa." He pronounced it Ah-free-

Ka and it came out sounding shoddy but nobody knew any different. "An ancient city, filled with awe and mystery. It was there I first heared of Jupiter's Oil." His voice wavered slightly as he spoke, his own sickness never far off. "I learnt how the oil was used to heal the broken people of the world's oldest civilizations. – Come on up here, Mary."

He took her hand—would never allow this crowd to see his own scrawny hands, they were safely hidden in white gloves—and helped her negotiate the steps up to the stage, the way any gentleman would. In truth, she needed no help and their hands barely touched. She sat upon a chair and laid one hand to her forehead, as if about to faint. She laid the afflicted forearm on a small side table. Jupiter buried a cough in his kerchief (a quick and subtle glance showed a mostly greenish wad this time) and tapped his cane twice.

A small door in the side of the wagon opened at stage level. A monkey—no bigger than a small dog—rushed out. It looked to and fro, radiating a bright intelligence. The crowd gasped. The woman upon the chair acted out a moment of surprise. The monkey had slender arms and tiny, perfect hands and fingers. Its long tail bobbed gracefully behind it. Dressed in a black suit that mimicked the showman's right down to the string tie, it stood beside the girl, offering a dark blue bottle in its paws.

"I see how you've met my friend, Archimedes," Jupiter said, one eye looking knowingly at the girl, the other turned to the crowd in a wide-eyed stare that might or might not have seen them. "An industrious and curious sort, friends. Got him in Africa too, from the knowing niggers that ran the place, if you can believe that." *Believe it,* he thought, *those sonsabitches knew what they were talking about when it came to life. And death too. Especially death.* "Archimedes, if you wouldn't mind?"

The monkey smiled and bared a broad swath of bright white teeth. He nodded energetically and the crowd roared with laughter. "Allow me to note, friends, that Archimedes uses the oil to clean his teeth." With that, the monkey held up the bottle and made a big deal of showing the label around. That label recalled in great detail the side of Jupiter's wagon, except that the bright gold letters spelled out JUPITER'S OIL. The animal untwisted the cap and poured a bit of the contents into a cup held by the showman. Jupiter passed the cup to Mary, making a show of even this small maneuver. She sipped of the mixture after a moment's hesitation for dramatic effect. She trembled violently for a second or two, during which she looked to be having a fit.

The crowd pushed back a step or two, and in the same instant Jupiter swiped his hand across her forearm with a practiced gesture. The pustules came away in his palm, leaving only a red and inflamed-appearing arm. He coughed, this time on purpose, and the pustules went into his kerchief alongside the wads of his own insides. The whole thing was done smartly, with the accomplished stealth of a master showman.

"Praise be the Loooooord," Mary cried suddenly, and rose. She raised her arm for all to see.

The spectacle was catching. The crowd murmured and several folks pointed. Somebody said, "oh my Gawd." Not a one among them recognized the girl, but that didn't seem to matter. They were entertained, and to be entertained was to be interested. Jupiter knew this as surely as he knew his own name. Keep them entertained and they would be happy. Keep them happy and they would stay, and the longer they stayed, the more likely they would buy. His mind worked the problem every moment he stood on the stage. "Jesus K. Reist," he said, in a tiny voice with lips that barely moved.

The crowd guffawed as Archimedes took a seat on the chair vacated by the woman. Jupiter asked: "Is there one who is lame? I beg you to come forward, make yourself known. Do not pass up this once in a lifetime opportunity. Who among you wants to walk again?"

An old man leaning on a crutch put a hand up. He waved it, but Jupiter ignored him in favor of a small black boy on the outskirts of the crowd. Jupiter pointed to him and the boy hobbled forward with great difficulty.

"Plez massa, Ah's borned dis heah way, one leg shirter 'an duh udder. Plez."

"Come here, lad. I ain't one to make no difference by the color of a man's skin. In fact, Jupiter's Oil was first tested on negroes in Africa." He swung around to the crowd, away from the boy. "Cain't be too careful, ya know."

The crowd snickered.

The boy, Jupiter didn't ask his name, schlepped his way forward. He made his way through to the stage, hobbling with obvious discomfort, his gimp leg not bending. His hips were crooked, one leg shorter than the other so that when he walked, his pelvis ambled up and down. It was a trick his father had taught him by way of disguise while crossing from the South to the North a few years before. That father was dead now, lynched. The boy had learned his lessons well, though.

He climbed to the stage with obvious discomfort. Once upon it, Archimedes took him by the hand and led him to the chair.

"Boy, I ever seen you before?" Jupiter eyed him carefully, as if he didn't know how he would respond.

"No suh, don't recalls we ever did meet afore."

"Of course not. You say you ain't been able to walk right since being birthed?"

"Long time, suh."

"Archimedes here is going to pour you a drink of Jupiter's Oil." Jupiter held a bottle of the stuff high in the air for all to see while the monkey held a cup for the boy in one hand and poured with the other.

"It smell funny," the boy said.

"Well of course it does!" Jupiter said, wiping a bit of phlegm off his lips before the crowd could notice. "That's the medicine in it. You ever heared of a medicine what didn't smell funny?"

"S'pose not," the boy said. The crowd murmured agreement with him.

"Of course you ain't. Now drink if you've a mind to, it's all the same to me. But hurry up with it, we ain't got all day."

The crowd watched as he took a long gulp of the medicine. He played it up, pinching his nose and making gagging sounds as he drank. When he had at last finished, he gave the cup to Archimedes and looked at Jupiter.

"Walk, boy."

He was hesitant.

"Go on now. Don't waste these fine folk's time." He waved his arms out over the crowd in an expansive fashion. *"Walk."*

He stood on his good leg and took a step, hobbling only slightly and looking out at the crowd as if for sympathy.

"Again, boy." Then, with more compassion, "Go on, you're fine now. I know this and you do too." He said this last rather simply and matter-of-factly, not even looking at the child.

The boy stepped forward and there was no hobble, no tilt of the pelvis. He took another step, then two, then jumped down from the stage and danced a jig before it, casting his crutch toward the crowd so they couldn't help but see it and have to move, have to respond to his display of new-found independence. "Ah's been touched by Gawd! Glory be tuh Jesus an' Jupiter Jones!"

The crowd applauded. But then a voice was lifted.

"Hey, mister," somebody said, "I ain't never see'd that darkie 'round here. How we know yuh ain't just bring him wit yuh?"

"Mister, you meaning to question my integrity?"

"I guess I does."

"I assure you Mister—eh, sir—that the good name of Jupiter Jones does not participate in such skullduggery."

"I know the boy." A white kid, slightly older than the previously crippled child, stepped forward. "I seen 'im around, knowed his folks too."

"That's all well and good, boy, but I don't recalls I see'd you either," the man said.

"Nor does I know you, Mister, so we're even. But I know Mr. Brimmer there, was in his store just yesterdey. Ain't that right Mr. Brimmer?" The kid, who'd been standing in profile at the edge of the crowd, turned and faced the group.

Mr. Brimmer, proprietor of the local goods shop, gasped as he looked at the kid. His eyes had betrayed a moment of doubt when the kid first spoke up, but now that he looked at that face full frontal, doubt changed to recognition on the spot. You couldn't not remember such a distorted visage. Jupiter knew what the proprietor was thinking: *What the hell happened to you, boy? What in God's name ravaged that face?* He'd seen the kid all right. He'd been in his shop on several occasions and Brimmer said as much now. "Mark, ain't it?"

"Yessir."

"Mark was in my store yesterday, knocked over a jar of candy as I recall."

The kid he knew as Mark tried to smile at that. As he did so, the scars that had so twisted one side of his youthful face into a hideous melted caricature of its former self prevented the edge of his mouth from curling up. Brimmer and the others looked at that still, distorted half a face.

Some must have thought they were burn scars. Others might have guessed he'd been mauled by an animal. Brimmer, perhaps haunted by his slight familiarity with the boy, trembled slightly. "I'll take a dozen bottles of that there tonic," he said quickly, turning to Jupiter.

Of course you will. Anything to obliterate the image of that boy scarring your mind's eye. Jesus K. Reist but I do love a good bit of make-up and wax. "You are obviously a man what knows quality sir, one who knows the value of a good product when you see it. You ain't gonna be disappointed, no sir, not with Jupiter's Oil." Jupiter's eyes struggled to converge upon the storekeeper.

Brimmer looked both eager and uncomfortable at the same time.

"And I knows him as well," the smith said. "I shoed his donkey just last night. Doctor Jones—"

"Not doctor. Never doctor. Call me Jupiter, sir."

The smith nodded, said, "Jupiter, you think that stuff'll help my—"

"How you mean you can help my hand?" a man hollered out from the back of the crowd.

"I'm sorry. I didn't catch your name, sir."

The hollering man stepped forward and Jupiter saw it was the portly barkeep. "Name's Magruder. John Magruder. You said back in the bar you had something what could help my hand."

"Does it pain you, Mr. Magruder?"

"It does."

"How so? Tell these good neighbors how it hurts."

John Magruder looked like a man who didn't like being the center of attention, but once having made the mistake of stepping into it, he owned up to how his fingers always ached. "Since the day that old threshing machine took my one finger and crushed the others. I wasn't but fifteen years old. Ain't slept a good night since I guess."

Jupiter addressed the crowd: "Hear that, folks? He ain't slept a good night since!" Now back to Magruder: "Would you like to sleep, Mr. Magruder? Would you like to have a day's peace from that there ache? A week? A month?"

"Yes. Yes!"

"Then step forward, sir. Join me up on this here stage." *Jesus K. Reist but the power of suggestion is awesome.*

Magruder did as commanded. He'd been convinced, had become a believer without one ounce of proof. And once on that stage, Jupiter made a big deal of showing Magruder's hand to the crowd, of making sure they had plenty of opportunity to see the barkeep grimace as he squeezed that hand in both his gloves. Finally Jupiter tapped his cane twice and Archimedes came forward with a bottle of Jupiter's Oil. "And now sir, hold your crippled limb out that I may restore it to you."

Magruder held his hand out, wincing. Jupiter unscrewed the cap and held the bottle high, giving the crowd another gape at the colorful label. "Are you ready, sir?"

Magruder didn't answer, just stared.

Jupiter poured a helping of the Oil over the hand. "Go ahead, sir, rub it in, please."

Magruder rubbed and his wince disappeared. Then he blinked. "I ain't believing it."

"What's that, sir?"

"It's gone. The pain is...gone."

"Course it is," Jupiter said matter-of-factly. He turned to face their audience. "Ladies and gentlemen...I give you Mr. John Magruder and Jupiter's Oil. You know him, he is one of you. He is a believer."

"Hell yes, Mr. Jupiter. I been trying...been hoping for years...Thank you." Magruder had real, honest-to-god tears on his cheeks. "How long will a bottle last?"

"Long enough." He wanted to say 'as long as you live' but that didn't seem a wise promise.

"Long enough?"

Jupiter smiled. It was the best answer he could give. Certainly he could say more, but why? Why stir up a hornet's nest? Besides, it was the truth. John Magruder would discover that the bottle lasted long enough. *Exactly long enough.*

Over the next quarter of an hour, Jupiter Jones sold three dozen more bottles to the residents of Monroeville. *Not such a poor town after all.* The name was moronic, and the people were still suckers to be sure (John Magruder not the least among them), but those who had bought would discover in due time they had made a unique, if not exactly sound, investment. The label read Jupiter's Oil, but in fact it wasn't Jupiter's at all. A lot of what he'd said and done that afternoon had been bullshit, but not the *Oil.* No sir. That snake oil really had come from Africa, from the equatorial coast of West Africa, to be more precise. And whatever the hell was in it, it damn sure wasn't the usual cheap mixture of spirits, sugar, and water. Jupiter was certain of that much.

Jesus K. Reist.

FIVE

The evening of the second day of battle. The sky ran blood red against the setting sun and beneath it, beside a river two miles east of the field where Ezra Coffin had been shot down and clubbed earlier that day, an old wooden building towered like a monument. A two story structure with a vestry above and pews below, the old Lutheran Church dominated the surrounding land, and the stretch of Rock Creek flowing past it.

Within its holy walls, the US Army had set up a temporary field hospital. Here, in the chancel beneath tall, empty windows once filled with colorful stained glass, the surgeons plied their trade over a pair of heavy wooden doors. Pulled from their hinges in the front hall, the doors had been laid flat over several pews and were now unrecognizable as anything save the operating tables they were. So when Surgeon Boyd stretched himself erect and stalked from the nave to the vestibule, he looked out into the somber light of dusk without the obstructing doors. A three foot high stone wall enclosed a large side yard off the front steps. A thin, smoky veil had drifted across from the battlefield and hung above the churchyard, like a pall of visible suffering.

Hundreds of men crowded the yard, and not a one among them was whole. They covered the ground thick as maggots on a week-old carcass, the dirt itself hardly anywhere visible. No one could move without all feeling it and thus rising together in a hellish contortion of agony. Everywhere men moaned, shouting for water and praying for God to end their suffering. They screamed and groaned in an unending litany, calling for mothers and wives and fathers and sisters. The predominant color was blue, though nauseations of red intruded throughout. Men lay half naked, piled on top of one another. Bloodied heads rested on shoulders and laps, broken feet upon arms. Tired hands held in torn guts and torsos twisted every which way. Dirty shirts dressed the bleeding bodies and not enough material existed in all the world to sop up the spilled blood. A boy clad in gray, perhaps the only rebel among them, lay quietly in one corner, raised arm rigid with a finger extended, as if pointing to the heavens. His face was a singular portrait of contentment among the misery. Broken bones, dirty white and soiled with the passing of hours since injury, were everywhere. All manner of devices splinted the damaged and battered limbs: muskets, branches, bayonets, lengths of wood or iron from barns and carts. One individual had bone splinted with bone: the dried femur of a horse was lashed to his busted shin. A blind man, his eyes subtracted by the minié ball that had enfiladed him, moaned over and over "I'm kilt, I'm kilt! Oh Gawd, I'm kilt!" Others lay limp, in shock. These last were mostly quiet, their color unnaturally pale.

It was agonizingly humid in the still air of the yard. The stink of blood mixed with human waste produced a potent and offensive odor not unlike that of a hog farm in the high heat of a South Carolina summer. Swarms of fat, green blowflies harassed the soldiers to the point of insanity, biting at their wounds. Their steady buzz was a noise out of hell itself, a distress to the ears.

Townsfolk, who themselves had little more than the clothes on their backs, moved among this human flotsam, who seemed now to resemble humanity only in the vaguest outlines of their being. Here and there women wept, as if to do so was helpful, and others brought water or dumped slop pots. No modesty here; if a man had to go, he went. A score of hospital stewards moved about as well, recording names and hometowns for records and death registries. Nurses—all male—offered laudanum, morphine, and whiskey against the pain, as well as a reassurance someone would soon help them. But there was too much work to be done in this churchyard and 'soon' was a day or more away. For too many, time would be their only salvation.

***

Tobias Ellis, who'd just ridden in from the battlefield in a horse-drawn ambulance, stood at the base of the steps as Boyd stood atop them. "Merciful God in heaven," Boyd said, turning to go back inside. Apparently he'd seen enough, perhaps heard too much.

"No God had anything to do with this. It's devil's work." Major Solomon Hardy shifted his segar from one side of his mouth to the other, then added, "And the sonofabitch wears gray." Hardy was Boyd's senior, the surgeon at the other operating table inside. He was the officer in charge of the makeshift hospital, the one the others answered to. He'd come up behind Boyd, looking out on the churchyard as well. Their eyes met briefly, and Hardy took the chewed nubbin of his ever present segar from his teeth. He ignored Ellis standing in the yard below, looked up at the sky a long moment, and his face changed from contempt to something that might have been disappointment. He squinted as he shook his head, but if he said anything more, Ellis didn't catch it. Replacing the segar, the senior physician chewed it until he was apparently satisfied he had the taste of it, then stalked back inside.

Ellis saw Boyd's eyes were red, almost crimson. The skin around them was red too, as if scalded. Later, Ellis would recall they'd both seen their share of hell on this earth—their share and more to be sure—but that the scene of devastation outside that church seemed to have loosened something in Boyd. The surgeon stood at the top of the steps, making no effort to move. He began to shake, and had he not been leaning against the jamb, Ellis believed he would have fallen. Boyd looked at Ellis, but Ellis felt he was looking past him, not at him. Ellis turned, following Boyd's line of sight as best he could. He appeared to be staring at the chanting man. "I'm kilt, I'm kilt! Oh Gawd, I'm kilt!" became loud for a moment, then receded once again into the background clamor. When he turned back, Boyd was gone.

Ellis climbed the steps and passed through the doorway, looking toward the altar, which was now an operating room. A large cross hung from the ceiling. On first entering the church the day before, Boyd had mumbled something about finding little comfort in the symbol. "Only a piece of wood after all," he'd said to Ellis. Ellis, who'd had as much cause as any man to abandon every belief he'd ever entertained in an omnipotent God, had said a silent prayer.

Now, as he gazed across the wide nave at a mass of injured every bit as disconcerting as those outside, he had another thought. "God in heaven," he said, thinking maybe Hardy was right, thinking God might be in heaven but he damn sure was nowhere to be found about this place. He panned the room for Boyd, who likewise was not to be found, then turned and saw Hardy probing a belly wound. The patient was a fat man who reminded Ellis of a dead cow as he lay face up. His blouse was open full down his wide front and it hung sloppily on either side of his exposed bowels. Threaded gold eagles informed the epaulets on his shoulders. A colonel.

Hardy looped a finger around a piece of dusky pink gut, but it kept rolling away from him. Finally securing a hold on it, he ran his hand back and forth along the intestine by way of inspecting it. A long two minutes passed before he looked up. "Goddammit, Boyd, these boys ain't gonna sew themselves up." The worn stump of segar bobbed with each word. A wisp of smoke curled up toward the cross.

Ellis saw that Boyd was here now, had appeared as if from nowhere. The surgeon stood beside his empty table, his look blank and unfocused once again, as it had been the day before for just a moment. Ellis tried to take a step toward him, but the place was a maze of prostrate bodies and getting around them was no quick task. Boyd's lips were moving, but he couldn't make out the words.

"Boyd, you hearing me?" The senior surgeon clearly had no patience for Boyd's antics.

"He's gonna die," Boyd said.

"Damn well may. But it's a sure thing if we don't try." Hardy sniffed the air close to the table. "Don't smell a hole."

"He ain't dead."

"What's that you say? What the hell you talking about?"

"The man in the yard, he ain't dead," Boyd said.

"What man? They all going to be dead you don't get your ass to operating." The segar bobbed again as Hardy grinned, apparently satisfied with what he'd found. It settled back between his lips as he stitched the colonel's belly.

Boyd didn't move, and his lack of action made Ellis uncomfortable. "The truth of the flesh." Boyd said.

Ellis did a double take. The phrase was familiar, the same one Boyd had uttered the day before.

"Dammit, Boyd." Hardy picked up a bone saw—the first thing his hand found—and flung it at Boyd. The heavy handle struck a glancing blow to his shoulder.

This seemed to bring him out of his stupor. "You need me?"

"Hell yes. Get the lead out. Best look after them." Hardy jerked his head toward the pews, toward the terrible humanity congregated there.

Boyd drifted over as a stretcher bearer tossed the saw back in Hardy's basin. Wearing a butcher's apron that looked as if crusted with the entrails of a dozen animals, he stooped over the first pew and eyed the soldier who lay sprawled on the bench. One foot had fallen over the edge and its leg dragged uneasily at its owner. He seemed about to tumble to the floor. Wide eyes gazed at the ceiling. His hand clasped the side of his neck and a large amount of blood had pooled beneath him, creeping along the bench like spilled molasses.

The hand fell away as the surgeon touched it. At the same instant, Ellis touched Boyd on the shoulder. The surgeon tensed as if he'd been branded with a hot poker. "You okay, major?"

"Sure, sure. I'm all right. Stink must be getting to me."

Ellis could agree with that. "Yeah, this place is a little fetid, I guess."

"Fetid, hot, humid. Like working in hell." Boyd looked down at the open, dead eyes of the soldier on the pew. "Like operating beside the devil himself."

"Major—"

"Take care of the boy, Captain. Then get some food. I got it here. I'm fine."

***

Tobias Ellis exited the church in a bone weary state, rubbing his forearms, which had a tendency to pain him at such moments. It was dark, so the forms sprawled across the ground in front of and around the church were just that, forms. They had little definition beyond that of a writhing mass, but his ears filled in what he couldn't see. Men howled in shock, pain loosening their tongues until they cried like babies for their mothers. The screams made Ellis think back on all he'd seen that day and the one before. Their collective noise, even their breathing, drowned out the other sounds of the night; the rustling trees and chirping crickets seemed impossibly distant. He leaned against the stone wall of the churchyard, looking for Archer. The hospital steward was already somewhere out among the injured. Ellis passed an ambulance, nodding to the driver. He slung his hospital pack over a shoulder and passed a pair of negro stretcher bearers coming forward to remove the newly wounded from the wagon. He needed a latrine and something to eat, in that order.

He found Archer sitting at a campfire. A tall man, big-boned and rough about the edges, he was younger than Ellis, from the woods of Minnesota; a backwoodsman with the muscles to prove it. By the orange light of the fire, Ellis saw the top of Archer's blouse was unbuttoned and that he'd pushed his foraging cap back so that the black visor pointed up somewhat. He was eating a roasted potato he'd bought from a sutler. He'd gotten some honey too, and spread a generous amount of it on a piece of hardtack by way of making it palatable.

"Mind if I sit?" Ellis asked.

"No sir," Archer said, appearing hardly to notice the assistant surgeon.

Ellis opened his haversack and withdrew a few strips of jerky and hardtack. He asked Archer if he'd share his honey, but the man didn't answer. He asked a second time and Archer nodded vaguely, as if he'd have said yes to the devil taking his soul. "What's got you, Corporal?"

Archer finally looked at him. "Captain, I don't like what

this here war's doing to me."

"None of us do. You just got to put it out of your head, not think on it. That's all."

"Sometimes that's hard to do, yes sir, hard to do." Archer chewed and looked off into the dark, away from the church. In the slow, steady way of a man just barely in control, he told of a soldier he'd found lying at the base of a tree an hour or so before. He'd come upon the man, an artillery sergeant, as he searched out a latrine. "My God," his face contorted, "the way he looked at me—eyes so full of suffering I couldn't pass him by, no sir." In retrospect, however, he wished he had. He'd lifted the man's dressing, which had been only lightly soiled and so he hadn't steeled himself against what might be under it. The sergeant's lower jaw was gone, only a gaping hole the size of Texas beneath his upper teeth. "Each time he breathed in, something at the back of his throat wiggled the way the crop of a bird does when feeding." Archer stopped there, his face a painful mix of humility and anticipation. It was clear there was more, that it needed getting out.

"You couldn't see how he'd ever eat again," Ellis said matter-of-factly.

"Yes sir, that was a part of it." But obviously not all, or even most. Archer looked as if he would cry any moment. He'd put his plate down in the dirt and was just talking now, talking as if it was just him and the wolves out there. He told how he'd replaced the bandage and said a few words, something like how a surgeon would be along shortly and that the sergeant should lie still. A flat out lie. He'd moved off fast after that. And then came this revelation: "I'm ashamed to say that all the time I was knelt there, all I could think was: I have no time for the dead. I was all the while watching the poor man's chest move up and down, but I was thinking of me, not him."

"He was dead already far as you were concerned."

Archer looked at Ellis for the first time since beginning his tale. "Yes sir, I guess that's just about the truth of it."

"It doesn't mean anything, Corporal."

"No sir?"

"Not a thing. And you ought to know by now there'll be something else to take its place tomorrow. And that something won't mean anything either."

Archer had looked about to weep, had wanted to, Ellis was sure. But he hadn't, and it occurred to Ellis that was one of the many costs of the war. Archer might be cried out, or at least Ellis hoped he was anyway. Crying was like being eaten out from the inside; too much of it, and a man was apt to fold in on himself, like a chicken egg drained hollow and dried to a fragile shell. A little too much pressure one way or the other, and that shell would crack and crumble to the wind.

"Listen now," Ellis said, "we got a job to do, eh? We get stuck in the details, like too much of who lives and who dies, well, it just won't work. It all evens in the end anyway." He paused, itched at the scars on his arms just above his wrists, and repeated "one way or another, it all evens in the end." Archer just looked at him and Ellis sighed and went on. "We don't decide who lives and dies. There's not a man here we could save if the Lord saw fit to take him. And not one of us lives any longer than the Lord wills. We're just servants of His bidding. Don't ever forget that, Archer."

The corporal's face warmed a bit and the two eased into less weighty matters. Archer poured a cup of hot coffee for himself, not bothering to ask Ellis if he wanted some. Ellis didn't favor the drink and they'd been together long enough to know each other's likes and dislikes.

Both were tired and their need for sleep acute, but the wounded got no such respite, so neither would they. As they finished their dinner, Ellis chanced to reach into his pocket and found the letter from 'Tucker A.' He hadn't exactly forgotten it, but in all the work that day, he'd set it off in a corner of his mind with other things he'd come back to later.

"You recall that soldier whose bowels were out, the one on the field by the horse?" He asked his assistant.

"The one you called me over to and we dragged him back to the wagon?"

"That's the one. Name was Tucker. Tucker A. actually."

"Wasn't doing much talking by the time I got to him."

"Nor for me. But he wrote something." Ellis removed the note and unfolded it, passed it to Archer.

The corporal glanced in a cursory fashion at the crumpled pages. His attention caught, he read.

> Camp at Coaltown, VA
> June 24th
> Dearest Mary-
> It is about 10 o'clock in the evening just now, though I cannot be certain as my watch has once again quit me. Oh well, it is a trifling. I feel now I should have taken your mother up on her kind offer all those months ago. At the time, to take your father's timepiece seemed a callous thing, though her offer was a sincere one I am sure. But, alas, she has needed it more than I this past year. I am certain it has given her great comfort as the only one of his possessions returned after Gaines's Mill. Can't hardly imagine it has been a year since he fell. Time creeps out here, but it passes nonetheless. I guess you must know something about the passage of time, too.
> There has been little fighting these past

weeks. I guess General Lee pretty well whipped old Joe Hooker and the rest of us at Chancellorsville. I have heard that Scotty Irvin was killed there. Also Morgan Masterson. You must express our sympathies to Anita and Jane, which I am sure you will do in the kindest way. Jimmy Michaels is in a hospital up in Washington. He is shot up pretty bad and may take some time getting on again, if the butchers don't do him in. I wish I could go up there and watch out for him.

Jeff Powderhorn (you remember him? I brought him up to the house once some time back. He has the blind sister. His girl, Melinda, lives over in Tarrytown) broke his leg last week marching. He stepped in a pothole. More than a year the two of us have been together, through at least a dozen skirmishes and fights, without a scratch on either of us, and he goes to the butchers with a broke leg from marching. His bone was out of the skin and they said there wasn't nothing but to amputate, which they did day before yesterday. Poor Jeff. He loved that leg that's for sure. I go over his way just every morning and he's pretty down in the face. They took his leg off just below the knee. He looks to be healing okay, though I'm no doctor.

The children are well, I trust? Not a day passes I don't think of Agnes and Henry and wish to give them, and you, a hug. If you can, keep Henry from playing at war. Nothing good can come of that it seems to me.

Camp at Coaltown, VA
June 27th
Dearest Mary-
It is afternoon here, a hot day. I have once again come from the hospital. The stump where they took Jeff's leg is draining something the nurses call 'laudable pus.' They say it is normal but he didn't look so well today. I gave him a little brandy mixed with coffee to perk his spirits. Didn't tell the nurses. That got him to smiling, at least for a short while, as I didn't warn him of the brandy either. Put a warm smile to his face and it was good to see him such. He does nothing but lay in that bed, staring at his leg. I don't know what he thinks about but he hardly says any words at all.

Pretty boring here just now. Used to spend some time at checkers, not much now though. I met a former shoemaker from Ohio, a man named Geary, and he helped me mend my boots. I suppose they are still going to leak in the wet mud, but at least my feet will be snug otherwise. I had a hole in each sole I could put my thumb through and my shoes kept filling with dirt. You might send me some new socks. Two pairs. Decent socks are pretty hard to come by, almost as bad as shoes.

Listen to me. Jeff lost his leg and I'm talking about mending my shoes and not having a decent pair of socks. This here war makes selfish people of us.

Send the socks just the same.

Some of the men here are fairly deficient in matters of soldiering. I watched just yesterday as a general scolded a lieutenant. The poor fellow was sitting barefoot under a tree and eating what I suppose must have been an apple. The general stopped before him, well within earshot of me, and the lieutenant did not so much as look up. When the general finally said "Lieutenant, what's your name?" the junior man stood and saluted, apple and all! He then proceeded to give a rather poor accounting of himself and the general asked him what sort of man he was. He answered that he had been a farmer before this war and hoped to return to that work before too much longer, pointing out as well that he had been promoted to his rank from sergeant and had never asked for it. The general replied that the man had better get back to farming because he wasn't much of a officer.

The next day I saw this lieutenant again, but he was wearing the stripes of a sergeant.

I've decided to have a picture made when I return home for leave at the end of summer. We'll all sit for it, you, me, Agnes, and Henry. Maybe your mother too, if you like. Perhaps you can make something for the children to wear. You have time. I can't get leave before the end of July and maybe not for another month after that.

On the road in PA, June 29th
Dearest Mary-

We broke camp early this morning. I asked for and received permission to visit Jeff at the hospital before moving out. Didn't have much time. He seemed a mess. They have been feeding him opium and that stuff makes a man less himself I guess. His leg was very swollen and smelled too bad. A surgeon visited while I was there, said they will have to take more of his leg off. My God! Can they really rid a man of such ills by chopping him apart a little at a time? It seems unholy. You well know I'm not a religious man, but I prayed this morning. You have always taken comfort in such things though, and I ask you to pray too. Pray for my friend Jeff Powderhorn.

We marched the whole day today. Made ten miles if we made one I guess. My shoes held out alright, good as my feet anyhow. Nobody knows where we are going, just somewhere north. No hurry. We stopped to lunch by a creek and I and some others took a swim. Not long mind you, but you'd be amazed what five minutes in the water can do for the spirit. I'd just about give my boots for a hot bath. And a little soap.

PA, June 30th
After midnight
Dearest Mary-
Jeff's dead. He died of marching. Poor Melinda.

Kiss Agnes and Henry. Wake them now and kiss them for me. Hold them and tell them I love them. Tell them I will always love them.

I wish I could lay with you. Now. Right now. I want to grow old with you.

***

The letter almost, but not quite, ended there. The easy handwriting gave way to an increasingly crowded script. And whereas parts of the note were lightly blemished in crimson, here the paper was stained and crumpled with the author's bloody handprints, as if he had gripped the paper over and over again in his last desperate moments.

***

The battlefield. July 1. Mary I never saw a leaf fall before. How they float down, flittering and turning every which way and such. They are all around me here. Oh how the sun goldens them on their journey. A beautiful thing. Just beautiful. Mesmerizing even. Could watch all day but there is no time. So it's come to this. I'm lying in a field, the green grass and good earth beneath me, the sky blue and the sun above me. I never knew before today just how bright and lovely is that sun. But I am done. July 1, 1863 I am killed. Do not fret my dearest wife. The pain is little. My heart is heavy with the loss you and the children will feel in reading this, but I have done all I can do and now you are to be a widow. Conduct yourself with dignity, teach the children well, and tell them of me every now and again.

Mostly, let them chase leaves.

I think I would have made a good father.

You have been the most wife a man could have.

Tucker

***

"I hate this damn war," Archer said after he finished reading.

"I'd say that's a fair sentiment," Ellis replied, taking the letter back and folding it once more. "Yes sir, I'd say that exactly."

SIX

O n the battlefield, Ezra Coffin passed a fitful night with consciousness waxing and waning. Knocked silly by the blow of a rebel soldier, he kept seeing Tim Jewel waving at him, kept seeing that fair-skinned, thin kid from Fever Creek—way up in the northern woods of Minnesota that was—sitting at his bedside. Kept hearing the rhythmic chords of Jewel's harmonica. The coarse notes were soothing, reassuring. The tunes alternated between *John Brown's Body* and Ezra's own favorite, *When Johnny Comes Marching Home*. This last was a soothing, melancholy air that had him sitting on the porch and looking out at the fireflies in the cool, still air of a fall evening. When he was young, he used to eat his ma's apple pie and delight in the tangy flavor of the green apples she favored, in between catching the insects and watching them light the tiny bottles he put them in. But his ma was gone now, God rest her gentle soul, and it was Liza he caught fireflies with anymore. The shrill but melodious notes of Jewel's harmonica poured through Ezra's mind like melted butter over fresh baked bread. Then the music stopped.

A year earlier he'd been in hospital in an old warehouse near Washington, alongside the Potomac River. The stench of sickness was everywhere, the foul odors of men too long abed. The warmth of fevered men lay nearby; the heat of his own was a fire that boiled the strength out of him. The twisted form of the soldier in the bed next to him was vivid. Cowdry had been his name and Ezra hadn't thought of him in months—indeed had made an active job of forgetting him. The tetanus that had taken him was the stuff of nightmares, a creeping stiffness that edged into grotesque rigidity. His muscles had betrayed each other, pulled him six different ways at once. He'd died with his spine arched like a taut bowstring, head extended back to touch impossibly between his shoulders. Even in Ezra's fevered state—or perhaps because of it—he'd heard Cowdry's joints popping apart. If a less Godly sound in all of nature existed, he couldn't imagine it.

Ezra had still been a mere country boy. He'd had no experience then with the fetid swamp of army quarters, no protection against the ills that plague such places. Camp fever had nearly killed him. He'd spent ten fevered days near death. At the end, he'd discovered himself luckier than most, for he'd survived with some measure of his verve intact. Tim Jewel had rarely left his bedside—had rarely stopped blowing his harmonica—during the whole of his time in that sick bed. In the months since, Tim had been his constant companion and, in the hours of boredom that framed their days, had taught him the rudiments of the harmonica.

In the here and now, the certain knowledge Jewel was dead came to him unbidden. Ezra's mind reeled around in the darkness, like a ship's anchor seeking bottom. He tossed frantically, not quite awake but unwilling to sink into complete sleep. A distant shriek—a ghastly, pathetically human sound—twisted the night into something unfamiliar. Another followed, this one long and tortured like that of a wolf caught in a trap.

Putrid air wafted by him. Ezra shivered—the night wasn't cold—but when he opened his own mouth to scream nothing came save the gritty taste of wet dirt. His head pounded. He felt death encircling him. "Not like this. Oh God, not like this." He passed out again and for a long while lay still as a casketed body.

When he opened his eyes again, his first thought was that he was blind. He saw nothing except an inky darkness—and the ill-defined shapes of the monsters lurking in his own mind, a nocturnal inner house of horrors. In that long, panicked moment, he began to cry, and the salt tears dissolved the clotted blood that had crusted his eyes. Through the dirt and grit he began to recover a filmy, distorted view, like that behind a dusty window looking out on a storm.

He sniffed and the sour smell of death was still there. The sense of impending doom had left, however. He closed his eyes and the grit scratched his eyeballs, a sharp, prickly hurt that tortured him every time they moved. He got an education on the subject of gritted eyeballs. If he stared straight ahead and didn't move them when they were closed, the pain was much dissipated. They felt best in the few seconds just after opening, but he had to blink before long and blinking was the worst, like scraping his eyeballs with a knife. And once opened, it was impossible not to move them side to side anyway. All things considered, best not to open them at all.

Images of the wooded hillside raced by. Bits and pieces of the day peppered his thoughts and he was none the better for it. He tried to move his leg, was racked with pain for his efforts, the thigh throbbing in concert with the thumping in his chest, which was impossibly close. He felt nothing below his knee, neither his booted foot nor his cramped toes against the hard leather. Another moment of panic, of fear he was a one-legged, blind cripple. He groped around with his other foot until he found his missing leg. It came alive and agony like a razor peeled along his flesh from thigh to ankle. That pain was some comfort, though. He still had two feet, whatever else.

He tried his arms. Slowly and carefully, like a man handling acid. They weighed in stiff and heavy. His left hand lay oddly twisted behind his back. His right lay across his chest and he picked it up with little trouble, though it felt unnaturally large. It too pained him, though not so much as his leg. He made an effort to close the fingers and found he couldn't. The skin seemed too small, or the bones too big. Opening his eyes brought a new wave of misery, but he made out the smeared outline of his swollen hand, the faded red of something wrapped around it. He struggled to focus, paid the cost with another surge of nausea. What he could see of the hand was blue and mottled. He worked his fingers and they felt foreign, detached. He vaguely recalled reaching for a canteen. When had that been? Yesterday? The day before? Or even this morning?

His left hand was another matter altogether. With some effort, he rolled his body—more agony—and pulled the hand from beneath him. The wrist was busted, that was obvious, though the hand beyond might not be so bad as its opposite. When he moved it, a familiar dance of pins and needles shot through the whole arm. More odd than painful, the sensation passed before long. After this, he discovered he could close the hand, though there was no strength.

"Liza?" He'd dozed again and it took a moment before he recalled he wasn't home in bed beside her. He had never wanted to be home with her so much as he did now. "I love you."

"Anyone? Anyone here?" The words sounded raspy, the voice figmented. He wasn't clear why, not sure if his voice or his hearing had failed. He called again. A bit louder, but still a long way from his own sound. Was he deaf too? Could a deaf man hear himself talk? He listened and heard what sounded like running water. A creek or stream nearby?

As if never interrupted, his thirst came back and it was as if it had never left. Of all the pains he'd woken to, thirst was the worst. Its ugliness consumed every pore of his body. It out-throbbed his ruptured thigh, the sting of his shot-through hand, the ache of his broken wrist, even the scrapings of his gritted eyeballs. Nothing compared to the insistent, dry scratching of his throat and later, as the sun began to climb toward a new day, he discovered exactly how thirsty a man could get. With the stream bubbling somewhere in the distance—a sound at once both a welcome and a hellish tease—Ezra's torment rose above the level of pain.

Before long, he knew what it was to suffer.

***

The third morning of fighting found Assistant Surgeon Tobias Ellis advancing across a wheat field. He and the several others with him, Archer included, kept their heads down and eyes straight ahead, tried to blot out the noise around them, and moved with all possible purpose toward a small house they could just make out from the scrub and bush in the distance. The place was on the edge of a woods and an hour before Ellis had been informed of the great need present there, of the wounded hunkered within its walls. He'd been told it was accessible too, and maybe it had been at the time, but with the coming of dawn the fighting had closed in and it was all but under siege now.

By the time he made it to the house, they'd taken a dozen casualties. A half dozen more had fallen on the field behind them, and left for dead or some unforeseeable period when the face of War could look back over its shoulder for them. At the house, he found more wounded inside. The worst was a boy of fifteen or so. He'd been shot through the neck and was pale from choking on his own blood. He breathed as if weighed down. Ellis understood immediately that suffocation was his problem, and an advanced case by the look of things. The boy's features were a dusky blue and his eyes rolled back in his head listlessly, as if all manner of control had already left him and passed to the Maker of all men.

Ellis examined the wound, probed it with a stubby finger. A hole in the windpipe. He managed to clear a bit of meaty debris such that a few breaths of air entered the lad. His countenance brightened and his eyes took on a more earthly appeal. The boy's throat clicked and his lips moved as if to form words, but he couldn't speak. Removing his finger, Ellis saw that the folds of skin and torn muscle surrounding the wound collapsed the pipe and occluded the boy's air passage. At first it occurred to him that he needed a stick of some sort to prop the wound open, but quickly understood such a thing would never work. A hollow cylinder was what he needed, something the boy could suck air through. He turned to Archer, ever present. "Search this place. Find me a quill, something hollow, a tube of some sort, any sort. And be quick about it or this boy, well, he'll be gone." He spoke fast, rapid fire.

Archer moved off and was gone too long. Ellis repeatedly propped the boy's throat open with his finger. A poor solution though, a temporary fix that allowed in only enough air to keep him from dying outright. His color faded in and out with each breath, more out than in. When Archer finally returned, he'd found nothing except an old wine bottle with a twist of wire around its neck. He handed it to the assistant surgeon, who turned it over in his hand several times. "Too big, and no way to break it true. But maybe." An idea, something he'd seen demonstrated once in school, came to him. "Put your finger here," he said, removing his own and plunging Archer's finger into the muck of the kid's neck wound. "Hold it thus, see he breathes."

Ellis broke the bottle against the wall, shattering the glass and spraying the wine. A fruity aroma filled the air. He poked past the glass and retrieved the wire, then worked hastily to untwist it. When he had the full length of it fairly straightened, it measured the length of his arm from elbow to mid-palm. He picked a thin stick off the floor and began to wrap the wire around it. He was careful to make tight circles, each loop closely applied to its fellow. When he removed the stick what remained was a leaky but serviceable wire spring two inches long.

"Remove your finger."

As Archer did so, Ellis inserted the makeshift tube into the hole in the boy's windpipe. The outer end stood proud above the skin of his neck, a half inch or more. As the boy began to breathe better, the color rolled back into him, and his features pinked up.

"Well I'll be hog tied," Archer said. "Never seen such a contraption as that, doc. I always knew you were some kind of genius."

"Just seen too many men die, that's all." He thought then about Tucker. A fleeting thought, now not being the time for such remembrances.

"You stay with him, see this thing doesn't come out."

"You bet, doc. I can do that."

SEVEN

Cuuda stood beside the old man, Mr. Jupiter, and together they gazed at the nude soldier. He was down an arm and was a wasted, sorry looking fellow besides. In the mid-morning light the body was still and the boy knew it would be cold and stiff even before he touched it. He looked up at the old man. As always at these times, Jones had a look of deep concentration about him, as if praying, and Cuuda was reminded of Prosper and the before time.

The pair had left Northern Virginia a few weeks before—the immediate and overwhelming need for their services in the aftermath of Chancellorsville had waned— and after a few days in DC had moved out once again. As was his routine between battles, Jupiter had steered his tiny but efficient enterprise into yet another small town. The town lacked a bank, and so his first stop had been the office of the town doctor. There had indeed been a death, he was informed upon asking.

Would the doctor be so kind as to introduce him to the family?

"Of course, my pleasure," the old sawbones had said. "The soldier's beyond any help what I can give 'im. Only thing is, the single introduction what need be done is to his mother. She's all what's left of them. A strong but peculiar lady, that one."

Once again dressed in his undertaker black suit, white shirt, and string tie, Jupiter met the 'peculiar lady' in her home. Cuuda, left outside with the mules, did what he had always done. With Archimedes on his shoulder, he moved around to the side of the house and crouched under a window, watching the scene unfold.

Jupiter removed his green bowler and tried to shake hands with the lady, a stiff looking woman dressed in the black veil of mourning. It looked well worn on her and Cuuda had the impression she'd always worn black. She ignored the undertaker's proffered hand and remarked something to the effect her son had sinned in the taking of another's life, war or no. Her exact words didn't come through the pane, but their sense did. She said he now had all eternity to atone for his wrongdoing and hoped the fire pits of hell wouldn't be too hot for him. Cuuda winced. She said these words with one hand hard upon the family Bible and the other clasped to her face with a lace kerchief in its fist. That face, Cuuda saw, was like a weathered piece of leather—etched with lines only a great misery could account for.

"Do you know how long I've been in mourning, Dr. Jones?"

He nodded no.

"Since the first day of this damned war." She turned and looked out the window. Cuuda had to drop quick to avoid being seen. He gathered Archimedes in his embrace and the monkey kissed him. She stood a long time before the glass, long enough that Cuuda got used to Archimedes' rooty smell. His knees pressed the mud and when he was finally able to rise, the knobs left small, parallel impressions in the flowerbed.

"Madam?"

Cuuda heard a stifled cough and he and the monkey peered over the sill.

The lady turned and her head bobbed like she'd noticed Jupiter for the first time. Cuuda saw the old man's eyes were crossed, as they had wont to do at odd times. He looked thin too. Too thin, the boy thought.

She moved back to the window, apparently by way of dismissing the undertaker. Cuuda ducked again, but she looked right at the monkey and apparently didn't see him. Cuuda looked again and saw she was looking at Jupiter even as she came to the window. Her words were clear when next she spoke. "I've read few of the soldiers get a proper burial."

"Yes madam, I'm afraid that's true. You see—"

"My husband, God rest his soul. I fear he got no proper burial."

"Your husband was a soldier, madam?"

"Yes." She did not elaborate, but by her tone a painful memory was close. Maybe Cuuda should have felt something for her, but such a trick he'd never learned.

"You need a bath, Archimedes," he whispered. The monkey slowly drew back his teeth, holding his gaze like a poker player.

"I can prepare your son very proper, madam. No odor a t'all." Even Cuuda heard the eagerness in Jupiter's voice, the huckster in the old man. It came out when he hankered for something. Cuuda had seen hankering turn the old man every which way a man could be turned.

The lady looked at him as one might look upon any creature that scavenged a living off the dead. The undertaker met her stare without shrinking back.

"I had three other sons."

"That so, madam. Ain't that something—"

"Had."

So the burial'll be for all of them. Cuuda almost did feel sorry for her.

"They too are gone."

"Yes, madam." Jupiter kept his distance, as always. Cuuda had never seen the old man touch anyone in sympathy. Except for Archimedes, he seldom touched the living, period. He'd never touched Cuuda. Wasn't his way. "The cost—"

"I don't want to know of such details, Dr. Jones. Just give me my boy so I can look upon him once more..." She wept, concealing her tears behind the lace hanky before suddenly staring Jupiter hard in the face. "Do that, sir, and I shall pay your price." She turned, and Cuuda saw she was fleeing the room. But she stopped short of the door, not looking back. "And goddamn you for making money off the dead."

***

So it was the two of them were bent over the young man. Archimedes, wearing his little green jerkin, was at his post on Cuuda's shoulder. The dead man's body testified to the ravages of disease and was—not unlike Jupiter's—thin and worn in the trunk; deep, sunken eyeballs hidden in the hollow of their sockets; a belly caved inward as by starvation. The left arm was missing below the shoulder and the stump had healed but poorly. Jupiter nodded and Cuuda followed. Archimedes nodded his tiny head in turn. They all read pain on that stump. Jupiter had taught him how every corpse told a story. Reading the leavings of the dead was his special lot in life, his true calling.

They were set up with the storied wagon along the banks of a small stream. It was morning, the sun not yet too hot and the remains not yet so spoiled as to be intolerable. By their good fortune the soldier had died only the night before. The corpse was set under an awning off one side of the wagon, upon two planks pushed close together. The planks in turn were laid upon two half-hogsheads standing on end. The work was waist high and convenient to Jones. Cuuda stood on a small step he'd built especially for the purpose. Archimedes moved between the pair, sometimes occupying a shoulder, sometimes clinging to their front or back. The monkey didn't seem to like The Concoction though, and once he smelled it he tended to escape to a perch in the awning.

The Concoction, Jupiter's self-made embalming fluid, was a strong solution of arsenic and chloride of zinc mixed with alcohol and some modest amount of water. Caustic stuff that ate at the skin of the living despite its propensity to preserve the same in the dead. Jupiter never took precautions against this; by the time he finished, his hands were always bronzed and pitted by the acid-like fluid. He remarked how they tingled the way a summer June bug buzzes when caught in a closed fist. This was one of his favorite feelings in all the world. It made him feel closer to his subjects. He had told Cuuda these things time and again.

"Look here boy."

Cuuda was small, but strong. He'd been a runt when Jones had discovered him six years before, but he'd grown muscles in the intervening time. Lifting the dead, who were always heavier than in life, was no small affair. Cuuda's assistance had become more and more essential as Jupiter's body failed him. They'd had help from time to time, but who would stay with a man the likes of Jupiter Jones given a chance to do otherwise? Jones was a man who knew—preferred—the dead. So far as Cuuda could tell, he gave not one whit for the living. Cuuda supposed he himself would have left if he'd had anywhere else to go. To his surprise, he'd discovered he had a talent for this job, this peculiar art, of reanimating the dead. He was useful with a hammer and saw as well and fashioned the pine boxes the work called for. He sewed a tolerable canvas bag too.

He missed Mary. She'd been fun, had never judged him by the color of his skin so far as he could tell. She hadn't minded the showmanship, but messing with the dead hadn't sat well with her. She and Mark had run off when Jones had switched from hocking his oil to collecting and preserving the dead. That's the story the old man was telling anyway. You never quite knew what the real story was with Mr. Jupiter. Cuuda had learned that much over the years. That much and more. Much more. "Good riddins to 'em," Jones had said after they left, "we don't need the ungrateful sonsofbitches. Jesus K. Reist."

And so now it was just the two of them.

***

"Look here, boy," Jupiter repeated.

Cuuda, who'd been measuring the dead man for his box, looked up. Archimedes dropped from his shoulder and climbed into the awning. "Yassah?"

"Pay a mind now." Jupiter took up a small knife. The blade was no more than two inches long and he ran it back and forth several times over an emery board, the way a barber might a razor before a shave. He then addressed the nakedness before him by name, begging his pardon for the intrusions to come. He debated out loud whether to cut the thigh or the neck. For a moment he was having an argument with himself, as if moving between sanity and insanity:

Jupiter: "Cut down on the thigh?"

Jones: "Naw, the neck. The vessel's some easier to find."

Jupiter: "The vessel's bigger in the thigh. It'll go quicker getting the concoction in."

Jones: "Lookie how fat that leg is. You'll be half the morning finding the artery."

Jupiter: "So."

Jones: "So it'll take too long and you'll get more concoction to the face going through the neck anyway. He'll look better when and where it counts."

Jupiter: "It counts ever'where. Just cause you can't see it don't mean you can do a shoddy job."

Jones: "Nobody cares what his innerds look like when he's laid out."

Jupiter: "I do."

Jones: "But you must know you're the exception."

Jupiter: "Ok, the neck then. I do want him to look good."

Jones: "Jesus K. Reist."

Cuuda took in the measure of the body lying on the boards. It really was that of a boy, doubtfully out of his teens. The single hand that remained had clean fingernails and a palm short on calluses. The fingers were spindly and lacked the brown-yellow mark of tobacco use. All of these things were so obvious he hardly needed to think on them.

"Proof of life," Jupiter said.

"How's that?" Cuuda asked, looking for what he'd missed.

"He's right handed," Jupiter said, showing his habit to speak of the dead as if they still lived.

"How you know?" Cuuda tried to see what the old man saw.

"That callus there. That's his trigger finger."

Cuuda looked, saw it.

"He don't smoke neither," Jupiter said. "Chews though. He chews tobacco."

Cuuda's mouth turned up at the one side and he grunted by way of questioning. The monkey hung above them, looking interested but keeping his distance.

"Boy, you got to look on a body—on a patient—the way you would a horse. One you was thinking of buying. Don't worry about the incidentals, the common things. You know it's got four legs, a tail. But what about its hooves? Where's the wear? Do it got cracked teeth? It's the mistakes you gotta see, boy. The imperfections what make each of us..." he paused, trying to find the right word, "human." Jupiter had a hand in the soldier's mouth now, pulling and tugging on the lips the way one might examine that horse. His manner was gentle. "There," he said, pointing at something hidden in the pouch between the inner side of the soldier's cheek and his teeth.

Cuuda peered into the depths. "Don't see nuttin."

Jupiter produced a locofoco from his pocket and struck it against the table. It flared and he held it between two fingers, close to the black hole of the dead mouth. The monkey screeched something in his little voice. "Quiet, Archimedes," Jupiter said and stretched out the cheek with his free hand. "Look now, boy."

Cuuda leaned closer and recoiled at the smell, though it was no worse than the putrid, dead raccoons and possums he sometimes collected for Jupiter's medicine shows. "The way to a crowd's wallet," the old man like to say, "is through their noses." He held his breath and at last made out a brown stain discoloring the soldier's gum line and cheek, like rust on an axle. "I see."

The undertaker dropped the match before it singed his fingers. Apparently satisfied he'd made his point, he reached up and stroked the monkey's back. Archimedes jumped down onto his shoulder. "One more thing, boy. Where's his heart?"

Cuuda ran his fingers over the dead man's chest. The skin was splotchy blue. "Here, he said, laying his small fist over the left side of the ribs between breastbone and nipple.

"Very good, excellent, boy. Now where would you needle him?"

He and the old man had been over this a hundred times.

It had never been necessary, but Jupiter insisted he know how it was done anyway. "Sooner or later, it'll come in useful," he'd say.

He felt the tip of the breastbone, then for the hollow just below it. "Just there," he said, pointing.

"And the aim?"

"Upward, up under the ribs. A little to the left. About..." Cuuda hesitated.

"About three inches, boy. Jesus K. Reist." The undertaker coughed a black crud into his hand. Jupiter looked at it and wiped his hand on the underside of one of the planks. "Jesus K. Reist, boy, you gonna kill me someday you don't remember that."

"Three inches, Mr. Jupiter. I remember. I was just joshing is all."

Archimedes seemed to understand this and screeched.

Jupiter tossed the monkey to Cuuda and bent to his work on the dead man. He made a one-inch incision in the front of the soldier's neck, along the border of the meaty muscle that stretched from behind the ear to the breastbone. No gush of blood, all was as still inside as out. His finger slid between the bands of muscle and found the pulseless carotid artery an inch deep to the skin. He made a slit in the stilled vessel and inserted the needle tip of an old pewter syringe. The length of this device looked something like a long, hollow knitting needle. The other end was attached to a metal hand pump about ten inches long with a plunger handle of polished white ivory. Jupiter pointed and Archimedes climbed back into the awning. Cuuda began to work the pump, slowly at first and then with greater confidence. The concoction flowed through the syringe and needle—Cuuda had to stop now and again to refill it—and into the dead soldier's system; after a while, the body hardened under the embalming fluid's influence.

As Cuuda continued to work the pump, he watched the

undertaker apply Jupiter's Oil to the soldier's face and other exposed skin with a small artist's brush. The apparent spoiling, so obvious a moment before, disappeared as if a magical wand had been waved over the body. Not much later, the odor died away as well. That was impossible—the morning cool had burned off and even now Cuuda felt the humidity in the air—but it was a fact nonetheless. What lay on those two planks didn't exactly smell like roses (more like roses in the midst of a manure field), but the odor was more than tolerable and they both pulled off the masks they'd been wearing.

The undertaker motioned and Archimedes scampered over to a locker in the side of the wagon. The monkey opened it and withdrew a roll of bandage and carried it over to Jupiter. "This will be uncomfortable, but only for a moment," he said, and gently picked up the stumped arm and wrapped it in several layers of lint, then bandage. The old man worked hard at his many tasks, all the while talking to the dead man in the present tense, as if to a patient and not a cadaver. Jupiter's eyes crossed now and then as he concentrated and the monkey continued to gather the things he called for. All of this was a tedious process taking several hours; Jupiter being meticulous in his work. But as it went, Cuuda saw the dead man's features liven up in ways wondrous to behold (he didn't like the way the dead man watched him through those now perfectly lifelike eyes—no clouding of those orbs, no siree) and when it was done, he understood that what the soldier had been in life, he was nearly so in death.

"Looks like if'n his chest could just move up and down, he'd up and walk away," Cuuda said.

Jupiter admired his work a moment, perhaps even feeling pleased. Before a minute had passed though, a frown creased his forehead. The lines of the old man's face strained, relaxed, strained again. It was like watching

Jupiter's mind working. The undertaker grunted under his breath. Archimedes, from his perch on the old man's shoulder, jumped down and touched the dead soldier's cheek. "Of course. Damn near forgot," Jupiter said. He went to his wagon, rummaged, then came back to the body. He stuck a wad of tobacco into the pouch between teeth and cheek. The cheek bulged, appearing pregnant with his chew.

"That's got 'em tingling," Jupiter said as he opened and closed his fists. "Yes sir, I'd say that's a job tolerably done." Archimedes screeched again.

The funeral was in the late afternoon that same day, an open casket spectacle befitting the burial of five members of one family. The soldier was well preserved and cooperative to the last with no smell at all. At the end, Jupiter collected twenty-one dollars from the mother— fifteen for the embalming and five for the pine box. The final dollar was given at the peculiar lady's bequest; she was a mother after all and hadn't seen her son so peaceful and full of life since before the war she said. "I never approved of his chewing the tobacco, but that's who he was and that's who we buried today. I thank you, Dr. Jones. And those eyes, exactly as I remember them, except...except I felt he was watching me throughout the whole of the service today."

Cuuda didn't attend the funeral, of course; heard about it only later. Neither he nor Archimedes were welcome at such goings-on. They spent the late afternoon tearing down the setup, putting away the wares.

Word had come. The Army of the Potomac was on the move, which meant they should be too. All they had to do was follow the army. Either or any of many armies might have sufficed, but in the two years of the war to that point, the last day of June 1863, following the Army of the Potomac had proven the most lucrative. The incompetence of the Union generals guaranteed a bonanza every time the two sides clashed. It got so that on the eve of an expected battle, Jupiter would spend extra time sharpening his trocars and boiling up extra concoction. Never a happy man, on such nights Cuuda thought him perhaps a bit less morose and sullen. "Jesus K. Reist," he was apt to say, "we gonna have us a goodhap tomorrow."

EIGHT

E zra Coffin fingered his haversack. He had not eaten in almost a full day and was hungry despite the pain of his wounds. He contemplated the haversack, unable to turn it upside down draped as it was over his shoulder. So he proceeded—all but blind, his eyeballs still gritted—to remove the contents one item at a time, his broken wrist hurting all the while. A knife and fork, a deck of playing cards, a tin cup and the plate that went with it, a pouch smelling of coffee grounds, a smoking pipe, a second pouch half full with tobacco, a few lucifers, and a pencil and notebook. He found a bundle, these would be Liza's letters, and tried to open an eye. The ball watered though, and the pain was the wrong side of a hot ember burning it. He gave up the effort and stuffed the letters in his shirt best he could. Going further, he discovered the remnants of a few biscuits, two strips of jerky, and another kerchief. Unwrapping the kerchief he found a shriveled apple. He bit into it and it grated against his dry throat like so many shards of glass. He couldn't get it down.

He pushed the jerky and biscuit back into the haversack. He dozed and the sun baked him. He dreamed of the swim hole where he'd romped with Liza not too many years past. And of Tim Jewel and his harmonica. Gradually, as he moved in and out of such thoughts, it occurred to him the canteens of the fellows around him might have some water.

It pained him to move, but the agony of thirst was worse, so he rolled onto his back, propped himself on his elbows, and pushed off with his lone good leg. In this fashion, more blind than not, he moved across the ground. Slow going, but he didn't have to go far. The place was strewn with bodies.

He came first to a soldier dressed in blue. The man was up on his side, back to him. Try as he might, Ezra had not the strength nor the dexterity to turn the man over. His vision was still miserable—he had none at all in one eye— but the feeling had mostly returned to his left hand beyond the busted wrist. He groped around as best he could, reaching over the back and side of the soldier. What he felt was a crusted, wormy thing, warm from the sun. His fingers broke through the crust, and the inside was wet and mushy like the innards of the pigs he'd used to slaughter back home, with the same shit smell too. He jerked his hand back and rolled off, his body spasming with hurt.

He regained a sense of himself before long and pushed around the body. He couldn't help looking as he did so and saw that in the heat the poor devil had swelled. His face was unrecognizable and his smell the worst part of a latrine ditch. Ezra was about to turn away when metal glinted in the sun. At first he thought it a blouse button, but that wasn't right. He took a second blurry look, reached out. As he touched it, he understood what it was. And what it meant.

Tim Jewel was dead.

It was a moment Ezra could have lived without, but his bullet-holed hand twisted around that harmonica despite himself. After all of a night and half a morning lying against the ground of that place, Tim certainly didn't care. *When Johnny Comes Marching Home* flashed through his mind, then twisted into the haunting and lively *Dixie* as Ezra was drawn to the instrument. He knew this harmonica like a friend. It represented something good, and he would take any good he could deal himself in this hellish place.

He retched the little he had in his belly, followed by dry heaves which plagued him for some time thereafter. He clung to the harmonica as to a trophy earned in battle. He stuck it in his breast pocket, tried not to think of its owner, and crawled on, his thirst now worse than ever. That thirst was a madness, the engine propelling him forward.

Only a few feet further on, he came upon a haversack and an abandoned canteen. There were a few more crumbs of biscuit and another piece of jerky in the bag, but he ignored these for the canteen. He gave it a shake, not much because he didn't have the strength, but enough to hear a splash. He unscrewed the cap and gulped half the contents before he stopped himself. Too late, though. The water was like poison to his parched stomach and he immediately chucked it back up.

He lay there, the taste of his own spew a tease on his tongue that he could only gum around his mouth. *Easy now,* he thought, *easy now.* He calmed himself and took small sips of the warm water, taking an hour to down the remainder. His thirst was dented, but only just. He checked the haversack a final time, found a physic for headaches, and downed it as well. It didn't help so far as he could tell.

There was a spate of open ground here, ten feet or a little more in any direction except backwards. He couldn't go backward, though, too many memories, no water, and his leg wouldn't move that way anyhow. A snake slithered through the grass in front of him and he understood that was what he had been reduced to. He crawled and his progress was agonizing. He stopped halfway across the open glade to rest. He peed as he lay there, realizing he'd just let go more than he'd drunk in a day or more. In one end, out the other. He took the harmonica from his pocket, the memories rushing through him as if the thing was some sort of touchstone. He put it to his lips, but they were too cracked and he had not wind enough to do more than blow a weak note. He clutched the harmonica in his good hand, that's how he thought of the one with the busted wrist, and began to mumble in a scratchy voice.

"When..." he began slowly, "Johnny comes marching home again..." He pulled himself along the ground. He'd seen a dog run over by a wagon wheel once and he imagined he looked very much as that dog had pulling itself across the road.

"Hurrah...Hurrah...We'll give 'im a hearty...welcome then..." His voice was dry, no more than a whisper, but the words focused him and so he kept them up.

"Hurrah...Hurrah...The men will cheer...the boys will shout..." The sun rose higher in the sky and its heat seemed made for him alone. His eyes tremored in the hot sweat. He concentrated on the words, ignored all else.

"The ladies...they will...all...turn out..." He chuckled, didn't know why, so thirsty he would have licked dirt to get the small moisture there. He thought of the dog with its back broken.

That dog had died.

"And we'll...all feel gay...when...Johnny comes...marching...home." He pushed forward.

The world seemed to be dead all around him. He reached his goal, a rebel lying on his back. He didn't immediately see a wound. He saw something else though, something hard to place. The body wasn't discolored like the others, and its smell was different, even familiar. Sweat and stale piss. Ezra reached for the canteen beside the man's shoulder.

The rebel stirred, opened his eyes, and in one motion brought a pistol to the thin part of Ezra's temple. "That'd be a poor choice, stranger," he said. His voice was weak and uneven, but it made its point.

Ezra let the canteen lie where it lay and slumped back. He saw the man was a Confederate officer. A major. "Go ahead, sir. I'm mostly done anyway. You'd be shooting a dead man."

"All current evidence to the contrary," the man said, letting the arm holding the pistol go slack.

***

Major Tom Jersey looked at the blue clad soldier slumped before him, propping up on his elbows to get a better look. A dirt covered boy with a round face and swollen lips. His eyes were clotted with dirt and blood. A large gash marred his forehead. He couldn't immediately decide if the soldier's eyes had been gouged out or if the blood had come from the forehead wound. The edges of the wound were a purplish-yellow color and a large blowfly squatted in the depression of the macerated flesh. He allowed to himself how he'd seen worse.

The boy's torn and dirty blouse was streaked with blood and other incidentals Jersey didn't make the effort to categorize. He noted something in his hand—a mouth organ?—thought little of it, had no care of such details. The soldier's right hand was tied with a red kerchief, was badly swollen and discolored, a sickening shade of blue he couldn't recall having seen before, except maybe in the mottled skin of the amputation pile. "Can you use that hand?" Jersey asked him, more or less idly.

"Think it's busted," Ezra said, and held up his left hand.

Jersey had been referring to the other, but didn't presume to correct him. "What about your legs?"

"I'm thigh shot. Can't feel nothing below my knee."

"Lemme see it."

Ezra shook his head. "Too dang much effort. You wanna see it, do the moving yourself."

Jersey slumped back. "Well, we a pair. We so busted up we don't make a whole man 'tween us." He started to laugh at that, but it deteriorated into a barking cough and blood appeared at his lips.

"You gut shot?"

"My right hip. Leg's useless." More coughing, more blood. "Feels like I'm busted up inside too. Could be I got a broken rib or three."

"Name's Ezra Coffin, private, 115th Pennsylvania, Wadsworth's Division, Reynolds' Corps."

"Tom Jersey, Major, 18th North Carolina, CSA."

"Major Jersey, sir, I'd be much obliged if'n you'd share whatever's in that canteen you got. My throat's feeling like a plucked turkey, sir."

"Why would I do that?"

"Well sir, I guess you don't have to. But I'd sure be obliged, and I guess maybe my Liza would be too. Liza's my wife and she's a lovely sweet thing. Sure would hate to disappoint her. You married, sir?"

Jersey thought on that, and an image of his son came to him, the same image he'd seen all night. The boy had been sitting on the grass beside him. He thought too of his wife and daughters back home. How beholding Elspeth would be to any who saved his life. How very much he wanted to see her and his girls again. "Okay," he said, "Guess the war's 'bout over for us anyhow."

Ezra fumbled with the canteen a few moments, the clumsy workings of his injured hands apparent. The major took it from him and put the canteen to his lips. He let Ezra take a long swig.

"I feared I was alone out here," Ezra said when he lowered the canteen.

Jersey said, "So did I."

NINE

Jupiter Jones had spent the better part of his adult life as a showman and purveyor of the extraordinaire. An opportunist. The war had brought something akin to a windfall. He had realized early on that a great many men would be going off to fight in this thing, and more to the point, a great many would not be coming back. Death was his calling, his stock and trade.

He was rather more than an itinerant undertaker, however. Anyone could build a box and plant the dead, but Jupiter had perfected a concoction of chemicals by which a body might be preserved, for days on end and, as he put it, "without the unpleasant odor and unsightliness normally accompanying such business". Once preserved, the dead could be shipped to points all over the country. As he imagined it, death was an industry waiting to be born. He dreamt it in his sleep and lived it every moment of his waking life. Death was his business.

It was his canvas, too.

Three o'clock in the afternoon and the blue sky was obscured by the formless, nocolor smoke of war. The still, humid air was a lifeless miasma of decay. The undertaker and his assistant tied scarves perfumed with the oil of rose petals across their lower faces. By midmorning, Jupiter had stripped to his undershirt and Cuuda wore nothing but a pair of worn trousers. They had casketed or embalmed a dozen cadavers by noon. They couldn't work fast enough to meet demand.

Simple casketing took twenty minutes, give or take, those in the worst condition a half hour or more. Embalming took longer, half a day if he did it right, but he had no such time here. The heat and the circumstances demanded speed. He might have used the Oil, that would have made a difference with the smell anyway, but he had an idea there wasn't enough of it in all the world. And so many of the bodies came to him in such poor condition. He doubted even the Oil would work when the decomp was so advanced they had to take care not to pull off an arm or leg inadvertently.

Sometimes he worked three bodies simultaneously. Officers were worth more than the enlisted and Jupiter was always on the qui vive for them, but he had discovered long ago that a family who wouldn't pay $2 for a doctor would pay $10 for an undertaker. Simply the way of things, what the market would bear. *Jesus K. Reist you gotta love the free market*, he often thought.

He didn't embalm unless the soldier had prepaid, he had a commitment from the family (which meant he had the money in his pocket), or a particular body caught his attention. Occasionally such would happen. He'd see the potential in the lifeless form before him, like a sculptor eyeing a block of stone. He'd go to work then, carving that stone, drawn by the temptation of it like a moth to flame. A beautiful thing to watch a man in his element and undertaking was no exception. On such a case, the Oil proved invaluable.

It wasn't just the Oil though. Jupiter was a master at his craft, a perfectionist of the highest order. When he said he was gonna 'do a body,' he damn well did it right.

Opportunities to reconstitute the broken and tortured clays that came his way were nonetheless few. Mostly, the heat and the elements had spoiled them beyond repair. The least he did was seal them, inserting a wad of clay in the ass and a plug of lint in the penis. A dead man turns liquid from the inside out and plugging these openings... well, it was just common sense. As best he could he closed the death wound. If embalming was feasible, this was the next step. Finally, he worked a bit with the Oil on their faces, getting the eyes to fill out, the cheeks to bulge, keeping their jaws from dropping. He'd step back and read them quick, always looking for that one telling detail that was proof of life, that one item that would give their loved ones a final moment of comfort in their grief. Then he and Cuuda would casket them and tack this notice to the lid of the box:

> *To The Undertaker or Friends Who Open This Coffin:*
> *After laying back the lid of the coffin, remove entirely the pads from the sides of the face, as they are intended merely to steady the head in traveling. If there be any discharge of liquid from the eyes, nose, or mouth, which often occurs from the constant shaking of the cars, wipe it off gently with a soft piece of cotton cloth, slightly moistened.*
> *This body was received by us for embalmment in a _____ condition and the natural condition is _____ preserved. Embalming was/was not possible.*
> *After removing the coffin lid, leave it off for some time and let the body have the air.*
> *Dr. Jupiter Jones, Embalmer & Keeper of the Dead*

Let the body have the air. Jupiter liked that. He knew

exposing them like that made damn little difference when these poor fellas were gonna be planted anyway. But the families had paid good coin for his artistry and they should at least take some time admiring the result, so, yes, let the body have the air.

It couldn't hurt none.

And he did so love the idea of showing off his work.

***

All of that very long third day of July, Ezra Coffin and Tom Jersey struggled in the heat. They had no shade and the sun baked them. Ezra felt his skin frying at the worst of it. *I'm a done tom turkey,* he kept saying in his mind.

Ezra moved off a few yards and found a Union private slumped over a Confederate soldier. The two were chest to chest, locked in an embrace at the moment of their passings by the look of it. A blood puddle sealed them together. A canteen hung from the belt of the private and Ezra cut it away, spending a tortured hour in the effort. The dry burn of Monongahela whiskey rewarded his efforts when he finally put it to his lips. The day was a little more tolerable after that.

He crawled back to the major but kept the whiskey to himself. The officer, who was less mobile in his condition, had managed to garner two canteens himself. Looking around, he judged it was about all that field was going to offer. As an hour became two, and two hours four, time slowed until each moment became an ordeal in itself. Ezra became conscious of the ground underneath him, of his weight upon it and its weight upon him. Each blade of grass discomforted him as if designed to do so. A pebble under his ass became a nuisance, an irritation, finally an exasperation. When he removed it, another took its place. Sweat streaked his face as the heat boiled the juices out of him. He lay on his back, foraging cap over his face. He counted the boom of cannon in the distance – were they still fighting? – listened to the major's breathing, wondered if the rebel was listening to his. Anything to occupy his mind. He gummed his lips, sipped the whiskey again. Just a drop. Make it last, he told himself.

The hottest part of the day came and time slowed still further. The sun hung in the sky as if painted there, a smeared golden dot on a blue canvas. Even the sounds of the place seemed against him. The ripple of the stream (it had taunted him from his first tortured moments on that field) became a hammer knocking against his ears. The bubbling never varied. At intervals he could even smell the water, or thought he could. Such moments occupied his mind in the worst way.

He went up on an elbow and pulled Tim Jewel's harmonica from his pocket. He ran his fingers, numb and tingly, over the raised lettering on the brass plate. H O H N E R. The name was Dutch or German. Tim had told him but he'd forgotten. No matter. He blew a few notes in the hot stillness of the mid-afternoon.

"Where you from, Yank?" Jersey asked between notes.

"Pennsylvania."

"Pennsylvania, eh? Whereabouts?"

"Cashtown." He slipped the harmonica back into his pocket.

"How's that?"

"Cashtown. Born and raised."

"Well ain't that a hoot and a holler." Jersey chuckled.

"You people are invading my home. Don't see nothing funny about that."

"Nor do I. But you got it wrong, soldier."

"How you figure?"

"This war's been on Virginia soil the best part of two years now. It's you who been doing the invading."

"I don't got no argument with anybody down Virginia way. Or anywhere else for that matter."

"But you got no hesitation against shooting us either."

Ezra, whose eyes still focused only poorly, turned toward the rebel, who appeared to be up on his side now. They were close enough to touch, but it wasn't that kind of moment. "I expect you know as much about that as I do, Major. I'll tell you this much. Just now, that decision don't seem so good. You got any more water?"

"Some, but I think I'll hang on to it for the time being."

"Not for a Yankee, eh? Is that how it is?"

"Way I see it, it's every man for himself. Doesn't matter you being a Yankee."

Ezra relaxed back against the grass. "You know something, Major?"

"What's that, son?"

"I don't much like you. Sir."

The major chuckled and Ezra heard the click of the officer's revolver as he cocked it. His eyes remained closed. If the major was going to shoot him, he wasn't going to give the man the satisfaction of acknowledging the fact. He refused to beg for his life.

The sound of the shot was louder than he'd anticipated. He flinched, which surprised him.

"Sonbitch." The major set the weapon in the grass beside him. "Thought I saw some movement in those trees yonder. Guess not though."

"Anyone coming?"

"Nope, didn't work." The major slumped over on his back.

"How long you suppose we'll have to lay out here?"

"Depends."

"On what?"

"On how long it takes someone to find us."

That was all the talk for a long while, until the silence

seemed as pressing as the heat.

"You got folks, Ezra?"

"I got me some loved ones, yes sir. A wife, a son."

"Well, go on. Let's hear about them."

"What you want to know?"

"Whatever, it don't matter too much. Not interested in the telling. Just want to hear a voice is all."

"Even a Yankee voice?"

"Right now, I'd listen to Abe himself."

Ezra began to talk and the sun moved across a fair piece of sky as he spoke. "I ain't never seen my boy. Three months old. Samuel. Samuel Coffin. Sound good, don't it?" He didn't wait for an answer. "I'm still getting used to it. Liza, that's my wife, she chose the name 'cause it was my father's. I didn't know he was going to be borned when he was. Should have been there. She had a hard time, I hear.

"Liza and me, we were married a year ago this past June. I was home on two weeks furlough. She was just about the prettiest girl who ever was done up in white lace, I guess. Of course, I might perhaps be a tad biased on that, and I ain't seen too many brides, mind you, but she sure was sweet looking. And sweet on me besides. That's the best part of it. How she was and is so sweet on me. Liza's my gal.

"I didn't know we were marching this way till we were here. It was already too late when I found out and I couldn't get a pass. I wish I could have seen them. I keep imagining what Sam looks like. I close my eyes and see him lying in his mother's arms. Liza's a great mother, I just know that. She says her ma was a great ma. I never met her on account of her dying when Liza was just five. I guess she got snake bit or something. Her pa died too. Drowned in a storm back in '58 or '59—whenever that big nor'easter come through a few years back. Liza just sort of took care of herself after that. She's resourceful you know. She's been working the land all her life but you wouldn't know it to hold her hand. Soft as fresh baked bread. Her smile, too. I'd walk through a hornet's nest to see that smile."

Ezra fumbled his sack coat open and pulled out the small tintype from the pocket closest to his heart. The pale image of a young woman standing beside a willow stared out at him, though his eyesight was too poor and he filled in the details by memory. "Want to see?" He passed it over without waiting.

Jersey didn't look at it. Instead he ran his fingers over the image as if he were a blind man gleaning its shape.

"I got me a son. Name of Sam Coffin. Now that's something. Even if I die out here, that's something. Ain't it, sir?"

Tom Jersey didn't answer immediately. Instead, he told of how he'd been a banker before the war. He spoke of his daughters and of his wife, Elspeth. He hadn't wanted to leave them, hated war in general and this one in particular, but whatever other sentiments he'd had back then, honor and duty had demanded certain things of him. He wondered out loud how much of this war was secondary to honor and duty, spitting the words with a contempt borne of too many letters written to the loved ones of dead soldiers under his charge. He never mentioned his own boy.

He told of Colonel Charles Oppley, who lay dead even now somewhere on their field. He told about how the two had known each other for years in better times. "The finest man I ever knew, and when he volunteered, there was no question I could do otherwise." He didn't add he now thought that decision the worst of his life. He was no coward, and he took pains to make this clear to Ezra by reciting a resume of the battles he'd participated in: Second Manassas and Sharpsburg, as well as every skirmish in between; wounded at Fredericksburg; picket duty during the recent battle at Chancellorsville. He supposed he'd seen too much fighting, guessing it had to catch up with him sooner or later.

"It's like chasing a hog wallowing in a mud pen. That hog's going to keep sliding out of your grip, least till it gets tired. Then that hog's going to get pinned in a corner and there'll be pork for supper. I guess in the end that's all we are. Hogs wallowing in a mud pin, all of us trying to avoid getting pinned." He took out a canteen and unscrewed the cap. "I really only want two things: to get home to my family and be with my children. A girl needs her father, and I've got three of them."

"That's only one thing," Ezra said.

"So it is. You still want a drink?" The image of his boy stared at him as he passed the canteen.

TEN

By the evening of July third, the guns were silent. The whole of the land seemed to bleed though, and the wounded came to the hospitals in droves, as if the battle had planted a crop and the wounded were its bountiful harvest. By ones and twos they came, sometimes by the half dozen and more. Some walked and found their own way, friends brought in others. Still more came by ambulance. However they came, they were a miserable lot.

Assistant Surgeon Tobias Ellis did his best to sort through them. He examined a butternut boy who said through the twisted lisp of a harelip that he was sixteen, from Georgia. He was shot through the pelvis and it took no time to know nothing could be done. He gave the youth water and a little laudanum, but it was small comfort. He moved on to others, but the memory of that harelipped boy stayed with him. When he asked about him a long time later he was told the boy had passed before morning and that they'd buried him a hundred and fifty feet behind the old mill, under a cherry tree that someone imagined would shade him in the hot days of summer. Nothing marked the spot because nobody knew who he was.

That's how it was. The evening was a string of miserable minutes strung together in tiny clusters. Three minutes for a man shot through the shoulder; Ellis put first a finger in the entry wound and then another in the exit and when his fingers touched, decided he was only lightly injured and didn't need a surgeon. Three minutes to set a broken wrist and splint it with a strip of cowhide and a piece of wood from a sycamore. Two minutes to tourniquet a leg, then extract a piece of wire deep in the meat of it. A minute to peek under a pink, saturated bandage several inches below a slender belly button; he saw thin, red water leaking from a hole and smelled urine, knew the ball had breached the bladder. It would either heal or it wouldn't, but nothing to do about it so he set the soul aside, a case not to be operated upon. He turned a man's head looking for the source of a trickle of blood and had ten terrible minutes trying to stop torrential bleeding from under his clavicle; frantic moments during which he could get neither a finger nor a clamp around the pulsating source. All bleeding stops eventually though, and this case did not violate the rule. He took two minutes to settle his own breathing, then four minutes sewing a torn scalp, and half a minute saying a prayer over a fat, cigar-shaped dead man. After a while, he had the impression he wasn't seeing men, but parts—an exploded chest, a blood-swollen thigh, a busted jaw with its teeth spat to the wind or swallowed.

It was more than a man could take but a lot less than there was to be seen.

***

In the black dark of an already too long night, Ellis worked by the soft glow of a dying candle on his last patient. A loquacious young fellow named Haskell, his wounds were slight but his tale an intriguing one.

He had a girl in town, the young man said, a pretty young thing named Susanna. They'd writ letters back and forth for months, though never met. She was the sister of a late member of his company and it was with the news of her brother's death that he had first written to her. The brother himself had introduced Susanna's letters to him as he lay dying on the field. He'd found him, Chuck was the brother's name, groping at his breast after taking a ball in a skirmish the previous October. With his last words Chuck had asked the soldier to read out loud the letter in the pocket of his breast. What Haskell had found in the man's pocket were two weathered pages, which he still had now and showed as proof of his tale.

Ellis stopped pulling birdshot out of the man's backside and perused the worn pages, tilting them back and forth so as to gain the advantage of the candle in the dim room.

>2nd March 1862
>Dear Chuck,
>I take a few minutes to write you this beautiful Sabbath morning and tell you the comings and goings here. Your letter of the fourth inst. reached me day before yesterday and I have told the Rev. Davies what you said about the sermons there. Mrs. Sadie says that she has not heard from her boy Joey for 4 months now and she is very worried that something is wrong. You remember Joey? He was at the town picnic just before you went off last summer. Mrs. Sadie is a young woman but she looks old now. We have become good friends as people should have someone to be with at times like these.
>Father is down much lately with the rheumatism. I think he works too hard. There are simply too many things to attend to around here without you. But we make do. Mother is well. All send their regards.
>There is one here who says he saw you about two months ago. His name is Ackerman, a

somewhat crude man who says you will remember him because you shared some tobacco and coffee with him after he was shot in the leg. He says you spilt hot coffee on him and started to show me the scar, though I did not wish to see his naked belly. I am not sure he is talking truth but he described you pretty good, even your funny broken tooth. Do you recall this man?

Now something a little fun. The other day I was sitting in the yard by that shed where you fell off the roof. I was thinking deeply of you and I had the curious urge to go into that shed, though I knew not why. When I did so, I found on the floor this drawing, which I remember we made together when we were children. Of course, I immediately thought this a glad omen and determined to keep it near my heart then thought better to deliver half to you so you can do the same. This glad memory of better times will see you safe in the days to come. I am sure of this.

Write soon as it is dreadful here in your absence. I need some word of you to cheer me. If you see Joey tell him to write Mrs. Sadie.

Yours in God and All things.

Your loving sister, Susanna

Haskell told how he'd read the letter out loud, and how Chuck had died somewhere in the middle of its telling. At that, Haskell had turned his attentions to the second page, which was but half a sheet ripped down the middle.

Ellis looked at the torn sheet, more worn than the first page. A child's drawing of a house, or rather, half a house, for it was torn down the middle. The marks and squiggles suggested a chimney with smoke curling out. An animal of some sort, it could have been a dog or maybe even a horse, stood in the yard. Ellis laughed.

Haskell had fallen in love with this woman at once. He'd written to her, giving her first the sad news of her brother's death, then asking if she'd allow him to continue writing her. He'd thought, he said, it might be better to put such in two separate letters, but what if she got his request first? Such circumstances aside, she'd agreed to the arrangement and they'd been "a-courting ever since, by golly." Through it all, neither had ever seen the likeness of the other. Now, as luck would have it, Haskell's unit was posted to an area near the girl's home on the second day of battle. Gaining his sergeant's permission, he'd slipped away under the cover of the July night to see his sweetheart for the first time. All of the romantic interludes he'd ever heard tell of were on his mind. She, of course, was not expecting him. Over the months, however, he had learned a great deal about her, including the layout of her home. This stood him in good stead that night. Haskell told how he had secured her attention by the old ruse of a pebble at her window and proved his personage by showing his half of the drawing. Elated, the pair escaped to the cover of the shed—the same one as in the letter—and had only been speaking a few minutes when Susanna's father showed up. He'd not even had a chance to spark her—to steal a kiss! Misconstruing the circumstances—dad apparently thought Haskell had come to call on his daughter in the manner of a man seeking a lady of the evening—Susanna's father ran him off, firing a load of birdshot up his ass in the process.

As Ellis resumed pulling bits of shot out of Haskell's backside, he suggested that if the boy intended to go back, he'd do well to apply to her father for permission first. Such a simple suggestion, Haskell wondered why he hadn't thought of it in the first place.

"'Cause love is blind and boys are stupid. God made it such. Ain't a man among us what ain't been shot in the ass at least once by love."

The discussion jogged Ellis's mind with regard to another letter, that of the late Tucker A. The evening was far advanced however, and he was exhausted. He crossed the camp as he fumbled for the letter. As he went, it seemed that not a man could breathe without making a heavy pant or rasping noise. He heard mumblings of need here and there, but never stopped until he got to his own tent, which was next to that of Hardy and Boyd. A light glowed in their tent and he went over, letter still in hand. Boyd was nowhere about, probably operating, but Hardy sat on his footlocker, eating beans from a tin. In his dirty undershirt and blood-splattered apron, he slouched like a man whose spine had gone tubercular. The space was just large enough to stand in the middle, and as Ellis came in Hardy looked up but didn't speak. Two cots stood along opposite walls with a three foot aisle between them. Each had a footlocker. A small writing desk occupied a corner and on it sat a coal-oil lantern, the source of the glow.

"Major," Captain Ellis tipped his head by way of greeting. He'd hoped to see Boyd. Hardy he thought a queer sort, not easily given to conversation.

Surgeon Hardy ran a piece of hardtack through the beans and took a bite of the mix, then sipped from a cup. "I hate cold coffee."

Ellis turned to leave.

"Have a seat, captain." Hardy pointed to Boyd's footlocker. "I hate cold coffee, but it's one of those things a man gets used to in the army. He never likes it, but he gets used to it. Don't you think?"

"I don't drink coffee." Ellis turned the folded letter over in his hands.

"Now that's peculiar." He took another sip. "Can't say I know too many men in this here army what don't drink coffee."

"Just never developed a taste for it's all."

Hardy spooned himself a mouthful of beans. "Can't see how that'd be a handicap. Hell, half the time it don't taste like coffee no how."

Hardy took another spoon of beans. Ellis tried to find something to say, but the moment lay awkward between them until Hardy finally said, "I've had the devil's own day here." Ellis made to ask about it, but Hardy moved and the moment was lost. He put the tin down and reached for the stub of segar balanced on the edge of the writing table. He struck a lucifer on the sole of his boot, and his face disappeared for an instant in the bright sulfur flash. He sucked back on the segar, shook out the match, and puffed. A coarse-smelling smoke filled the tent. "I been in this man's army a long time. From the beginning of this goddamn war just about. Today was about as unpleasant a day as I ever did see. As I ever want to see."

"Yes sir." Ellis knew something about that himself.

"Want to know something? I used to like watching the sunset every evening. I'm from Penobscot, Maryland. Don't suppose you ever been there?"

Ellis shook his head. He was from the Pennsylvania coal country and prior to the war had never left his own state. He and his brother had been happy there.

"Well, it was a real fine place to grow up. It's on the eastern side of the Chesapeake and there was this place not a mile from my house where you could climb this big spruce and sit in its branches and watch the water turn golden every evening as the sun rested down on it. I guess I made the hike up that hill and climbed that tree at least a thousand times. Never was disappointed, not with a view like that. When I was nine my mother passed, and I watched the sun hit that water and it was like an angel kissing me."

Ellis had known Hardy for over a year and never known

this about him.

"Well, I won't never be able to watch the sunset again. The one thing in this whole damn world I loved doing, and I won't never be able to do it again." He took the segar out of his mouth and carefully pinched the lit ash off, then stuffed the segar in his pocket. Ellis couldn't recall him ever having done that before. "You see the sunset tonight?"

"No, I don't guess I did." Ellis supposed he had seen it actually, but it hadn't left an impression.

"Well I did." Hardy seemed to falter then, just the barest hint. He seemed far away the next moment, somewhere else completely. He might have been talking to the wind. "The sky was blood red, like the whole world was bleeding. And below it, all these parted men. Men missing arms and legs, or lacking a jawbone, or with only half a chest or one eye. And it occurred to me that I had removed just those very parts over the course of the day and how I could maybe use those parts to put these men back together. I saw all of this in an instant mind you; one moment I had no thought of it, the next it was a fully developed notion. Only...only I got it wrong. See, I put the wrong parts with the wrong men—they aren't interchangeable, no matter how much you think they might be. And after that, none of the men worked, they were all broken, every last one."

By the time he finished, Hardy was near to crying. Ellis, who still held Tucker's letter in one hand, took a long step across the tent and placed a hand on his shoulder.

At Ellis' touch, the surgeon stiffened. "I'm sorry, it's just this...I'm a damn fool."

"I understand. I've cried plenty myself."

"Excuse me, Captain. I've patients to attend to." With those words, Hardy stood and walked out into the night.

"Of course, Major," Ellis said as he watched his senior go by him. Only much later did it occur to him that Hardy had turned away from the church and its unholy operating room.

***

Ezra slapped at the bugs, an oft repeated but useless gesture. It served only to waste the little strength he had. The insects, which had eaten at them all that livelong day, redoubled their efforts in the coolness at dusk. The blowflies swelled with their blood meals and when he did manage to smack one, they popped the way a cockroach does when stepped on.

"I seen me a angel once," Ezra said.

"That so?"

"A real honest to God angel."

"I don't doubt it."

"Was the night before my ma passed. I guess I was maybe eight. Ma was sick a long time and I didn't get to see her but once near the end. My pa took me in and there she was, sitting upright. She looked small in that bed. I guess now she was some pale, but just then I didn't notice that so much. What I noticed was how thin her hair was, how it hardly covered her head. She always had such pretty hair, but not that day. I noticed too how she smiled at me. A good smile, like she weren't sick at all. I guess that smile must have taken most all her strength. I held her hand and she smiled and that was the last I ever did see of my ma. Later, when I was lying alone under my blankets, I saw the angel. She wasn't what I'd call beautiful. She had wings though, just like they say. My room was dark but I could see her no problem at all, like the sun had come up special for me. It's her hair I remember most. Thick like my ma's hair used to be. Long too. My ma's hair hung most the way down her back and that's how the angel's hair was. Thick and long. Most all the way down her back."

"She say anything to you?"

"Didn't talk if that's what you mean. But I knew just the same that everything was going to be okay. That my ma was going to heaven and I had to be brave."

Jersey stared at the moon, which had risen high and was near full. "I saw something in a picture book once. A sketch of a long tunnel. At one end stood a man, just a shape really. He was outlined against the light of..." the major coughed and a bit of phlegm hung in his throat for a moment, "...against the light of celestial paradise, according to the note under the picture. At the other end were two angels, their wings spread wide. It said they were custodians that accompany souls toward beatitude."

"What's beatitude?"

"Sort of like heaven, I guess."

"That about figures it then."

"Figures what, Ezra?"

"Ain't enough angels to go around. That's why we're still here. Waiting on our angels."

"I guess that's one possibility. But I'm not ready to look for no angel. You suit yourself."

"Major Jersey?"

"Yeah."

"I messed myself, sir. Sorry."

"Don't be. Done the same. Held it most all the morning, couldn't hold it no more."

"Don't seem fair, does it?"

"What's that?"

"That all these men get to die so well and easy and we should suffer so."

"Suffering has its uses, Private."

"I'd be obliged if you'd name me a few then, sir."

"Well, if you never suffered, how would you know when you weren't suffering?"

"I'd know."

"Maybe so, but I guess the good Lord sees fit to remind

us of our plight on this here earth every now and again."

"I don't know about you, sir, but I'm feeling plenty reminded right now."

The late night brought the black sound of hogs feeding on the ungathered dead. Ezra dreamed he was one of those hogs. That laid out before him was an unimaginable feast. The dead suddenly were not the dead, but large and abundant sides of beef to devour at will. He dreamed he snorted in glee as he tore into those sides, that he rutted in the guts and bellies of those delicious carcasses until he satisfied his hunger. And when he awoke in the wee morning, he was horrified to discover that in the fever of his dream he had chewed at the leg of the dead man beside him.

NOT ONE AMONG THEM WHOLE

ELEVEN

Jupiter Jones worked the mortar and pestle, his scrawny hands rolling the stone and crushing the pellets into first a chalk and then a paste as he added a bit of stomach juice. The juice—usually he took it from a muskrat or squirrel Cuuda had trapped, although he wasn't above using juice from whatever stomach was available—was an activator. It was the acid he was after. It softened something in the pellets, he had no idea what. In fact, he had no idea at all what was even in the pellets.

He'd acquired them a dozen years before, while a ship's surgeon. *SS Brittany* had been forced to lay over in Africa, on the equatorial coast of West Africa to be precise, after taking on water in a storm. She had nearly sunk, and it had taken her sailors the best part of four months to refit her. Four months because the heat, the ungodly and some would say unnatural heat, had nearly killed the lot of them. Two had died the first day, dropped dead in the high noon sun within minutes of each other. The Captain went mad—some said it was hot enough to boil a man's brains in his skull—until he could do no more than babble incoherently. The Captain did so for weeks, until one morning it was discovered he'd simply wandered off in the night. They all suffered in one way or another after that.

The coastline was inhabited by a primitive, barefoot, dark-skinned people, naked above the waist with what

Jones believed to be banana leaves below when they cared to wear anything at all. They mostly ignored the whites— they'd perhaps seen their like before and no telling what those encounters might have wrought—but they made no effort to hide either. Jones moved among them, mostly out of boredom, less out of curiosity.

Whatever the reason, he discovered a truth in those months: the local people seemed an unusually healthy lot— and unusually old. He saw it mostly in their faces and hands, grizzled, taut features which showed the bones underneath in all their anatomic detail. Looking at those faces, with their eyes like black pools of churned dust, he had the crazy notion some had to be a hundred years old. Thing was, they didn't act a hundred. Their spines weren't bent, they didn't limp, and they shambled around at what might be termed a gentle—certainly not doddering—pace. In that hellish heat, the fact anyone lived past thirty was a minor miracle. But those darkies didn't seem to get sick *ever*. Jones supposed they maybe stayed to themselves if they felt the need to up chuck, but he didn't really believe that. Not after the boy fell out of the tree, anyway. Seeing that had made him a believer. You could take that to the bank, Jesus K. Reist.

It was a banyo tree, or anyway that's what the darkies called it. Jones had never seen their like before, and none of his shipmates had either. They'd discussed the subject around supper one night (after three months of baking like human potatoes in that oven-like strange land, the men had given up talking about home) and it was generally agreed that wherever those shiny black trees had come from, it hadn't been a place any more hospitable than that Godforsaken coastline. The goddamn trees were everywhere, like maggots on a hog three days dead. And full of curious little black bugs (everything that thrived in that place seemed to be black, as if it was a world of burnt offerings), as well as thorns that had a tendency to produce a nasty little scratch. Finally, there was the smell. Arriving on that shore, all of their eyes had had gone to watering and noses to a fullness of thin snot. It was days before they realized it was on account of those stinking banyo trees. The men took to wearing scarves, but that didn't help much. Might as well spend your days living in an outhouse.

But the darkies made good use of those banyos. The tree produced a fruit something like a banana, only the taste wasn't palatable, not to the whites anyway. Jones had tasted a lot of things in his time afloat, most recently monkey skulls boiled with their natural filling still in place, a delicacy he'd been at least able to keep down once it passed his gullet (getting it past his gullet had been another thing entirely). That banyo fruit had smelled like the tree itself, which was to say pungent, but tasted like something else altogether. Jones supposed the closest he could get was to say bitter rotten eggs. That wasn't quite it, the bitterness was in a class all by itself, but it was close enough. He'd tasted it only twice, once on the way down and again on its way back out. He hadn't cared to try it again. Not then anyway.

Apparently the shiny black wood was useful, both for building and for burning. The leaves too—Jupiter had mistaken them for banana leaves early on. But it was the fruit and those curious black bugs the darkies craved—needed?—most. Craved enough to send young boys into the tree tops to collect them. The boys were remarkably agile at this. Jones only ever saw one fall. He wasn't yet a teenager; the older boys and men wore a kind of sleeve on their manhood and this boy had nothing.

He fell from twenty or twenty-five feet, high enough to have been killed. Jones had seen him hit, had seen his leg crumple underneath him, folding like a cheap parasol. In his position as ship's surgeon, he'd approached the youngster and those gathered around to offer his assistance. The boy was obviously badly injured, maybe fatally so.

What happened next haunted Jones for a long time.

The other darkies gathered round the boy, all but cocooning him and shutting out Jones and his offer of aid. Perhaps they didn't understand, he had thought, and raised his voice by way of emphasis, gesturing to his own leg. He was still ignored and his view was obscured, but he managed to catch bits and pieces of the mayhem that followed. The crowd was loud, shouting in that repugnant tongue of theirs. A woman wearing one of those banana leaves on her lower half arrived in a matter of minutes, Jones recognized her as one of the ancient ones, and they parted for her. She carried a bag of some sort and knelt beside the injured boy. Jones thought the child had either passed or must be having trouble breathing because he had grown unaccountably quiet.

The woman poured a handful of something that looked like rabbit pellets into her hand and spat on them a half dozen times. She worked the pellets the way Jones had seen artisans work clay, molding them back and forth until she had a small clump, which she of a sudden placed in her mouth and began to chew. Before too long she began to spit again, this time on the boy. She and the others—they were chanting something now, *glubok, glubok, glubok*, or maybe the word was *kubok*—rubbed the spit over the boy head to foot. He hadn't been bleeding, not that Jones had seen anyway, but he looked to be now because the spit had been the color of blood.

This ritual (Jones could understand it no other way—he was witnessing an ancient and primitive ritual of some sort, a death chant maybe, or the twentieth generation of a witchdoctor at work conveying the soul to the next land) continued for five or maybe ten minutes. He had no watch, and he had learned enough to know how time dragged out there, so he couldn't be sure. All the while the chanting continued and the boy lay still. Jones had just about concluded the child was dead when the old lady, still chanting, reached into her bag and withdrew something that looked—Jesus K. Reist—like a large knitting needle. Only it wasn't. She attached a bulb or bag of some sort to one end, and then, incredibly, she pushed the other end—the pointy end—between the ribs and into the boy's chest.

The chanting continued, louder now, some sort of meditation, or maybe a hypnotic. "Glubok, glubok, glubok..." Jones had taken his own pulse then, had felt himself about to pass out. He found he was breathing too fast and had to concentrate to slow down. *Don't miss this,* he told himself, *you won't see its likes again.* She pushed the point inward, two or three inches Jones thought, and squeezed the bulb. The boy's body jumped then, and he screamed. A throaty, full voiced scream Jones recognized as having heard from time to time coming from the surrounding jungle. He would hear that same scream several more times before his tenure in that hell ended, and each time he would understand the old lady was at it again. He had an idea she was some sort of voodoo woman. Or doctor. Or both.

Jesus K. Reist, he'd thought, *what is going on here?*

***

The boy survived. Jones knew this because he saw him.

It was only a few days later. The boy was back in the trees. The idea he was seeing a ghost crossed his mind before all else. What he'd seen, the ritual he had witnessed, had loosened something in his mind. It couldn't be. It wasn't the same boy.

Except that it was. And it hadn't been a week. That leg had looked like a corkscrew. His neck might have been broken too. Yet here he was, twenty feet up in another one of those banyo trees. Not even a goddamn week.

He had to know the answer or he was going to go bat shit. He was going to go the way of the Captain. He'd spend a few weeks babbling incoherently about darkies falling out of trees and then being spat on by old women, and one day he'd just up and walk off into the hot West Africa sun.

He thought at first it might be their black skin, but that idea never sat comfortable. It might have provided a modicum of protection against the heat, but against a fall? Twenty fucking feet? Not a goddamn chance in all the universe. Besides, he'd seen the boy's leg. And he had lived around negroes half his life and had never observed any special advantage in health among them, at least not in the States.

It had to be the pellets then. The pellets and whatever was in them.

Jupiter, who was even then a showman, had gone to the old woman. He tried to convince her to give over her secrets, but the black bitch didn't speak his language. She babbled in that harsh, repugnant tongue of hers. As if he was supposed to learn their ways.

In the end, he'd stolen the pellets.

***

All these years later, he still had no idea what was in them. He had, however, developed a way of compounding them into a useful and lucrative tonic, which he called Jupiter's Oil. The compounding required breaking the pellets to a powder before activating them with stomach acid (he guessed that's what the woman had been doing by chewing them). He then mixed the resulting paste with some sort of alcohol filler: wine, sometimes brandy, even whiskey once or twice. He'd have preferred water alone, but that mixture always came out with an unpalatable bitter coppery taste—vaguely reminiscent of the fruit of the banyo tree—and with both the look and consistency of blood.

Jupiter went into a minor coughing fit, bringing up several thimblefuls of lung. He looked at what came up, saw what he took to be flecks of blood. "Jesus K. Reist," he muttered. His coughing waxed and waned with the seasons. It usually increased in the winter, decreased in the summer. Either way, he always looked at the wad that came up, at the color and for the presence of blood.

Jupiter Jones was not a healthy man. Once upon a time, he'd been a consumptive. Tuberculosis. But he'd long since dealt with that. Actually, Jupiter's Oil had dealt with that. But he had discovered, too late, there was a price.

He cursed those damn African niggers. If they'd just given him the pellets in the first place—if he had not had to steal them—well then he might have been able to get directions for their use out of them too.

Put another way, he lacked a prescription. Which meant he experimented. He tried different things.

Of course he'd miscalculated. Or the darkies had somehow allowed him to steal tainted pellets. He had to laugh at that notion. If the best they could do was spit on each other, they couldn't have much going on between the ears—the equatorial coast of West Africa was dark. Ha ha.

Mostly though, he believed the pellets simply had a certain, shall we say, unfortunate side-effect.

Madness.

The pellets would cure whatever ailed, all right. He had seen them work again and again. They even worked on the dead. One swipe of the pellets in the form of Jupiter's Oil not only reversed decomposition, it actually produced some weird kind of reaction in the tissues that halfway livened the dead. It didn't exactly reanimate them, but with a skilled undertaker to back them up the effect could be uncanny. A certain 'strong and peculiar lady' (who had recently buried her son and felt through the entire service that the dead boy had been watching her) could attest to exactly how eerie that might be.

But in the living, the result over time was almost always the same: madness.

Use the Oil once or twice and you might be all right. More than that, however, and a person was apt to start talking to the walls or insisting Uncle Billy had come back from the dead to supper with him.

Jupiter had discovered the madness could be controlled, though only by the hardiest, and only by continued additional use of Jupiter's Oil. Without its ongoing use, well, a person might as well consider himself to have a golden ticket to the funny farm. He'd seen that a time or two as well.

He coughed again, saw the blood in the sputum. He'd already poured a shot glass of the Oil, his nightly dose. He picked up the glass and downed the contents, feeling the brandy burn in his throat but not caring. He poured another half-shot of brandy straight and downed that too as a chaser.

He spat and Archimedes appeared beside him. His loyal and dependable friend. He motioned and the tiny primate ran up his arm and perched on his shoulder.

He gave the monkey a small shot of Jupiter's Oil and watched him imbibe the cure-all. Not the first time, but if the Oil had any effect beyond whitening his teeth, it never showed. Well, almost never; there was the obvious. Before long, Archimedes had a tough time holding his place on Jupiter's shoulder. His head lolled as he scampered around the little fire. His eyes crossed and Jupiter grabbed him up and stroked his back and laughed into his ear.

As the night wore on, he felt a curious and telling vibration underfoot. *Army on the move,* he thought, *no, less than an army; repositioning a corps maybe. Or collecting their dead.*

Jesus K. Reist but a man could get to love this war business,

Several hundred yards away, the first of scores of wagons began to pass in the trees along the road. They were two and four wheeled horse-drawn ambulances carrying the wounded in from the field. They moved at a creaky pace as uncomfortable as it was slow. As he watched from back in the trees, one after another pushed across his view. The yells of teamsters at work were suddenly all around him: curses, shouts, moans, more curses. Like a tired and spent incantation. He couldn't make out any of it with certainty.

With Archimedes passed out under the wagon and a whip cracking the back of some used-up horse out on the adjacent road, Dr. Jupiter Jones shut his crossed eyes and tried to sleep.

***

Tom Jersey slept only fitfully. He roused once or twice when the hogs rutted too close or the urge to piss overcame him. He voided then, and the stink of urine joined the other smells on that field. The night was cool, the air close, the odors unforgiving. To breathe was to choke. The air in the early hours of the fourth very nearly choked the life out of him.

Sometime in the early hours, with his mind either overwrought or under fueled, he thought he was back home in North Carolina. It went something like this:

He lies atop Elspeth in the night. He takes her in their bed, the lumpy feather mattress conforming around them, knowing their shape after so many years beneath the pair. In the morning, he breakfasts with Elspeth, Little Tom, and his three daughters, then walks the few blocks to the bank, where he works until early evening. On his return home, the house is not the gay place it had been just hours before. There is a brooding atmosphere, a gray, dismal mood he can't discern. Rounding the corner and seeing the white clapboard home, he feels a heaviness. A hand at his throat.

He runs.

The next instant he's in the house, moving down the long central hallway. It has lengthened grotesquely and he takes forever to reach the parlor at the opposite end. Along the way, he meets folks he knows. They don't belong in his home. Miss Rogers for instance. The ancient spinster taught him in school twenty years past; he hadn't even known she was still alive. She stands before him looking as old as dirt, her face a mask of taut skin stretched over a too bony frame. She lifts an arm and extends a skeletal finger toward the parlor. He moves on, the hand at his throat now covering his mouth, making breathing hard. He tries to run again—the hall just lengthens further.

Uncle Harry, the old negro stable hand, an ever present fixture of Tom's childhood, looks every bit of seventy years old. Tom guesses he must have survived his bout with pleurisy after all, though lying fevered abed three years ago it hadn't looked likely. As Tom passes him, Uncle Harry's eyes meet his and the two lock upon each other. Their heads turn and their necks crane as if yoked like oxen. Uncle Harry has the drawn face of one who has been mourning for a very long time, and Tom has the distinct and uncomfortable feeling Uncle Harry knows something.

The hand at Tom's mouth is smothering him. The closer he gets to the end of the hall, the worse it is. He can feel the fingers of the hand digging at the skin of his cheek. His heart thuds, his breaths are forced and fought for. His forehead creases till it hurts. His lungs burn. The figure of a child looms in the middle of the hall. Tom rushes to it, thinking it one of his girls, or maybe his son. It's a boy.

"What is it? What's happened?"

The boy turns toward Tom and points toward the parlor. In that long instant Tom recognizes Jimmy Classen—and sees everything he has ever held dear melt as if it is a thousand degrees in that place. His breath fails him altogether. Jimmy Classen was his best friend for years, right up until the summer of their tenth year, the summer Jimmy fell from a third floor balcony and broke his neck.

Jimmy Classen is dead.

Tom no longer wants to get to the end of the hall, no longer wants to go into that parlor. He no longer wants to be home. He turns and runs the opposite way, fleeing past Uncle Harry and the spinster schoolmarm, but when he reaches the end of the hall and steps through the doorway, he finds himself standing in his parlor.

The candle flame flickers and the furniture seems to distort with it in the too generous room. A box of polished wood, rosewood, sits in the middle of the room, dominating the dim scene by its half size. Tom's footsteps echo as he moves toward the stunted casket. Three figures stand in the shadows. Three girls dressed all in black, crying softly. His girls.

"Where's your mother, children?"

They seem not to hear him, not to see him. He runs a hand along the polished rosewood. He doesn't want to run his hand over it, but he does just the same. His own reflection stares back at him in the polish. He's no longer wearing a suit. Now he's dressed in a pair of worn coveralls, one strap broken and dangling in front of him. Oddly, his bare chest glares hairless out of the rosewood. And then he sees his face, which is at least thirty years too young, too boyish.

"Where's Little Tom—"

Jersey cried out, the sleep washing from his eyes like warmth fleeing a dead man, a curiously apt description of him at just that moment. Suddenly awake, he stared at the black sky, at the polished black sky with its fine veins of redwood. His stomach fell away and his bowels emptied. He could do no better than lie there and search for the boy. He found him despite the dark. He'd moved a few yards in the night, but he was still there, still kneeling beside him with the creel draped across one shoulder and the strap of his coveralls dangling uselessly on one side. Still close. Still smiling. Still silent. Still watching him. Or watching over him.

It wasn't like that. Wasn't like that at all, Jersey thought. No funeral, nothing to put in the ground. No headstone to lean on in the hard moments. Nothing but an abandoned rod and two-bits worth of fishing twine tossed in the mud. And that damn creel with its rotted fish remains. *That's how it was. My boy rotted like those damn fish.*

He curled into something close to fetal, the pain like a bomb going off in his head, over and over again. *—Oh God, make it stop. Make the hurting stop. Take me now and make the hurting stop.*

***

Solomon Hardy and Josiah Boyd worked through the dark night by candlelight, little encouraged by the cross above their heads. Whether in a barn or a church, men still bled the same irritating and unfortunate red. And like some twisted Midas touch, everywhere the two doctors touched seemed to turn that unfortunate sanguinary color; it coated everything.

At some point during the previous day someone had secured several large sheets to the overhead cross, obscuring the operating theater from the waiting wounded. This was a merciful act, and though it did nothing to shield the wretched cries of those concealed behind it, at least it offered some form of absolution to those present in that house of worship. A large window behind the altar, the glass long removed, provided a breath of fresh air all the long night.

By two-thirty in the morning, Surgeon Boyd was exhausted. The work was disagreeable enough to make him wish he'd taken his education in the clergy rather than surgery. He'd been up for three days, stopping only for the occasional cornmeal and beans. Hardy, working at his usual feverish pace, had been on his feet almost continuously as well. As Boyd's latest patient was lifted from before him, the surgeon tilted the board and the blood ran in thick streams over the edge and onto the floor. He rubbed his forehead and spat between his feet, the brown tobacco juice having long since stained the spot an ugly brown. Boyd preferred that to its alternative.

As he waited for his next patient, Boyd leaned against the wall, hands in his pockets. He closed his eyes and contemplated quitting. And not just for the night. He was tired to the very marrow of his bones. Tremulous and flushed by a sense that no matter how long or how hard he worked, there'd always be one more patient waiting for his knife. Ten more, a hundred more. He had the curious notion this war was a cruel hoax designed to drive him insane. He withdrew his hands and put them out before him. He watched his fingers skitter restlessly in the air, dancing the keys of an imaginary piano. His stomach twisted and the room spun around him. He leaned hard into the wall, opening his eyes and looking up at the cross suspended above his head. He removed a small brown bottle from his pocket.

Boyd's first lesson with laudanum had come two years

before, not long after First Bull Run. Following a minor skirmish, he'd encountered a single Secesh propped under a birch tree. This was in the early months of the war, before he'd yet seen the horrors to come. Lying there with his foraging cap on his head the boy had looked almost natural; Boyd had at first thought he was just sleeping. His posture struck the surgeon as odd though and removing that cap, Boyd had discovered a hole in the youth's forehead big enough to set a plum in. And as he had knelt there contemplating the soldier and his severe wound, the soldier had opened an eye.

"I's Thomas Ellerby," the boy had said. "My folks has...a plot for me up...up on Sumter Ridge, South Carolina."

Apparently, Thomas understood he was dying and wanted to get this information out straight away. The surgeon had still believed in the compassion of a higher God then (only later would he determine that compassion— and God—had no place in the affairs of man), and had tried to make the boy comfortable. He dressed his wounds.

Then he waited for Thomas to die.

"How old are you, Thomas?"

"I woulda...been twenty next...next month, sir," the boy said.

"I'm sorry, I've got a boy just twenty myself," Boyd had lied. The silence of the next few minutes was broken only by the gasp of the boy's breathing. A wet and frothy rasp, as if a soaked rag was caught in his throat. It had sounded melodious and grisly both and in the years since, Boyd had come to recognize it as the sound of a man's lifeblood draining from him.

Not much later, Thomas had made one other request. "Sir, I'd be much obliged you'd...tell my folks...that I...that I died well and for my country."

"I can do that, Thomas."

"Thank you...sir." And when Thomas had finished those final words, he drew a last wet breath, tensed, and died. His body went slack then, like the way a person sighs when relieved. That was something Boyd always remembered, how Thomas relaxed after he died. He saw that tiny moment over and over again in his dreams for months. That, and the boy's first words: *I's Thomas Ellerby. My folks has...a plot for me up...up on Sumter Ridge. South Carolina.*

Boyd never wanted to know the name of one of his patients again. As he had stared down on Thomas's corpse, Boyd's hand brushed the front of his own trousers and discovered a bottle of laudanum he'd placed there the day before. He'd intended to return it to the medicine box, of course, but he'd forgotten. A small oversight and these things happen in war, in the heat of battle. He pulled that brown bottle out and stared at it for a long moment. He kept going back and forth between it and Thomas's wounded face, between the bottle and that plum-sized hole above Thomas's eye. He had wondered how a man thus injured could speak, wondered if he might not have imagined the whole thing. This had got him nowhere, though, or at least nowhere good, for if he had imagined the conversation with the soldier then he was crazy. And if he had not, then it seemed to him the world must be insane. He hadn't been sure which of these ideas he preferred and he felt caught between, as if trapped by the dead gaze of the rebel youth. That gaze, and the dilemma it supposed, was too painful to contemplate on his own, and so he'd gulped the bitter contents of the bottle as a sort of nepenthe. The sweet and delicious euphoria that followed broke the stranglehold of the dead youth's gaze, though it didn't offer up a solution to his dilemma. Not then, not since.

Standing now in the ruins of an old church in the middle of the Pennsylvania countryside, Boyd had to admit that

Thomas Ellerby had died well. In fact, separated from that moment by almost two years and an education by the devil himself, he had to admit the boy had passed just about as well as anybody he'd seen since.

He cursed and spat again, this time sending most of his chew to the floor. He uncapped the bottle and turned it up. The opiate mixture spilled down his throat, and a queer warmth permeated his person even before he finished.

When he turned back to his table, his anxiety had dissipated and his fingers no longer skittered in the air.

***

The early hours of July fourth were long ones for Assistant Surgeon Ellis as well. Tobias spent much of it working the ambulances, which again and again went out into the dark fields, following the plaintive cries of the injured. He rode along not because he had to, but because he was not one to send others after danger while he stayed behind awaiting the outcome.

So it was that he and Archer found themselves back on the field of carnage. The place stank of gunpowder and much worse. In the terrible darkness, they went from man to man, ignoring the dead and reviving those still short of the grave. Ellis doled out whiskey like a generous barkeep, but mostly the doctoring had to wait until they got the men off the field.

Making the best use of their time waiting on the next ambulance, Ellis and Archer split up. Ellis came upon a trooper burnt red by the sun. A nasty gash exposed his ribs and the spongy tissue beneath, which moved with his breathing. The same gash extended across his arm, which was mostly off and hanging by no more than a piece of flesh just below his shoulder. He was barely alive, begging water when Ellis found him.

Ellis filled the soldier's mouth with whiskey, which served to bring him around abruptly. He asked again for water, and Ellis poured the last of his canteen into him. It seemed not enough though—a man could die of thirst sure as a rebel bullet—and Ellis left him where he lay and retraced his steps to a small spring he'd found earlier in the evening. Approaching it through the trees though, he heard talking. He froze in his steps, quickly ascertaining the direction and tone of the words. A Confederate trio, filling their canteens by the same spring. He swallowed hard, held his breath, wondered where Archer was. Still not breathing, he slowly backed out, taking great care in his footing. The words of the rebels grew faint, then died out.

He took a breath and it seemed his first in a very long while.

***

Cuuda hated the nighttime. Never able to sleep under the wagon, to coffin-like he said, he wanted a wide open space where he could lie down and see the stars. The old seer Prosper had often told him of "hebben-goin' spirits," the traveling spirits that left the "sure dead" at night. Although Cuuda hated the dark, he spent the nights searching for his parents.

Cuuda stood in the dark on the edge of the field watching the healer go from man to man. He assumed he was a healer. Who else would be out there?

The corpsman bent over a soldier. A rifle protruded from the man's chest and on the instant Cuuda realized the soldier had been spitted on a bayonet.

"Please," the spitted man's voice carried across the quiet field.

"Name's Archer. Ain't no surgeon but I'll do what I can," the corpsman said.

Cuuda stood transfixed. A long silence ensued as he watched the healer alternately grip and release the spitted rifle. He saw the man pull a flask of some sort from his bag and take a sip, then pour some down the wounded man's throat. He heard a "thank you" maybe, couldn't be sure.

The healer gripped the stock of the protruding musket. His medical bag fell off his shoulder as he did so and he stopped so as to let it tumble to the ground before resuming. He gripped the musket again, hesitating, perhaps building his nerve. Cuuda watched. He had no idea to help, no thought to run. Just a thing to see.

He jumped as Archer pulled the musket and the spitted man screamed. He clutched at his heart. Archer put his foot to the man's chest and yanked again. The bayonet slid out and the healer stood in the moonlight holding the weapon.

At exactly that moment, a trio of rebel soldiers appeared out of the darkness opposite Cuuda. As they looked on, a brother Confederate on the ground bubbling blood, a Yankee standing over him with bayoneted musket in hand—its blade still dripping—they simultaneously brought their muskets to bear.

"Scoundrel," one said. He spat and wiped a long drool on his shirt sleeve. He eyed the Federal the way one eyes a mangy dog lose in a chicken coop, as if he was something that had to be destroyed.

"Youse'll burn in hell, Yank," another said.

Archer dropped the musket, put his hands out before him and shouted. "No! No, wait—it's—it's not what you—"

The night shattered with the loud report of musket fire.

Cuuda fell behind a tree, looking up. The sky seemed immense. But not a single star was visible.

***

The noise was close—too close for Ellis' comfort. With his heart climbing his throat, he came around a tree in time to see three rebels fleeing across the countryside. They disappeared into the night even as he bent to his friend.

Archer's open eyes were distant. The steward had fallen on his back, hand across his chest. Three fingers and half his palm were missing. He was bleeding from a hole through his breastbone. The wound was mortal.

"I, I, tried to, help..." Pink froth appeared on Archer's lips as he coughed out the few words.

"Shhhhh."

"He was, I tried..."

He took Archer's head in his lap, groping for his medical bag at the same time. He stuffed a fist-sized wad of lint into the wound. It turned red and did nothing to stop the bleeding. "Goddammit! Goddammit!"

Archer paled. He died, looking like a spirit on the moonlit field.

Ellis heard the ambulances rattling closer in the following silence, the only other sound that of the wounded rebel breathing stertorously beside him. He rocked the dead Archer in his arms for a long time, listening to the hard, throaty sound of the other choking on his own blood.

When that choking finally ceased, Ellis stood. He looked down on Archer, dead in the high grass. Then he kicked the confederate in the head, pissed on him, and left.

Book III

The End Of The World

TWELVE

Dawn of a new day and the soft light revealed a meandering stream barely a stone's throw from where the wounded Tom Jersey and Ezra Coffin struggled to survive. A tributary of the larger Rock Creek, and if it had a name, it was unimportant. The creek wound across the base of a ravine, a rocky crevice of irregular stones and granite boulders. These boulders were massive, some the size of houses, with cracks and fissures and jagged edges interspersed between expanses of rough granite. Nothing thrived here except the crawlers and bugs that must have been here at the beginning, a thousand thousand millennia past. Dry skin lizards with claw feet scurried between the rocks; snakes slithered for a perch in the warming sun. Flies buzzed in abundance and feasted on the peculiar sticky ooze which crept down the face of several boulders and dripped slowly into the water. A tiny, hard shelled black beetle scurried through the ooze and over the rocks before coming to a swath of butternut gray— a sickly, jaundiced color. The beetle scampered onto the material and was soon lost in the hive of activity found there: a festering, wormy mass that recalled the spoiled remains of last week's butchered cow.

Only this was no cow and the jaundiced material not a hide, but a trouser leg. The same fly food ooze spreading over the rocks soiled the trousers. The cuffs were a frayed remnant, the knees patched haphazardly with whatever the owner had had at hand. Within the trousers the pair of legs had not moved in two days—except once, in the black dark of the night just passed, when the pull of gravity had finally caused one socked foot to slide several inches to the water. The guppies and minnows had nipped at the shoeless foot in the hours since. One hand also rested in this same creek water, and it drifted silently up and down with the vagaries of the current. The other hand rested at an angle painful to look at, the wrist flexed fully on itself with the back of the palm pressed hard against the granite. If not before, the message of death was telegraphed unequivocally here—this hand had turned a putrid blue-black, a degree of spoiling accelerated by the heat of the sun baked into the rock upon which the hand rested, which acted something like a hot griddle. A canteen lay under the small of the back and the knees and hips were flexed. The soldier seemed to defy gravity sitting there, dangling precariously on the edge of a boulder above the nameless creek.

The head with its dirty, brown hair tilted way back on a long neck, canted crazily to one side with eyes blissfully shut. The mouth was open though, almost as if in surprise or perhaps mid-shout. Crusted blood drooled from one side and a tongue swollen to three times its normal obscured most of the ugly, yellow stained teeth. The torso had begun to bloat as well, straining the sweat-stained undershirt beneath the open blouse, which was the same shade of butternut gray as the pants. Vermin of the kind that thrive on the dead moved everywhere over the muted remains, crawling in the ooze and stink of it.

Dawn on the fourth of July, and on this battlefield life seemed no more than a twisted caricature.

As if any further reminder of man's inhumanity were necessary, a young boy approached this sorry scene. The straps of two muskets crisscrossed his shoulders and he moved with the phlegmatic ease of one who has seen much. He bent over the body without hesitation, holding his breath against the stench. The shoes were already gone, so he pulled at the blouse. Nothing of interest save the canteen. He unlooped the strap with some little difficulty. All of this without a word. He kicked at the dead thing as if it had not been a man and the bloated body finally slid off the rock and fouled the creek.

The boy sipped from the canteen, then spat the warm water to the wind. He bent to refill the canteen in the cool waters of the creek, the body bobbing beside him. He stood, took another sip, then looped the canteen strap over his head and moved on.

***

Tom Jersey awakened in the shadows at dawn. A figure loomed over him and at first he thought: *I'm dead. Dead and going to hell. It's the devil come to get me.* But when the devil didn't speak and instead bent beside him, a bite of pain climbed his leg and chewed his mind open. He knew then he was still on earth, hell or not.

"Mister...what...what you doing?" Jersey's voice was raspy and weak the way an old man's voice can sometimes teeter between being there and not. He'd aged twenty years over night.

The devil figure stopped pulling at Jersey's leg, and the major howled in pain as his foot fell to the dirt. The agony reverberated through him in ever decreasing waves of nausea but he understood that the world, which he had thought had no more use of him, had found him. Salvation was at hand.

"Please."

"This one here, he alive!"

Another figure appeared, taller, the sun bright beside

him. He stepped to the side and the sun moved behind him, at his back. Jersey blinked, saw now the haggard rags of a man, the dirt-smeared clothes of a young boy. The man had a bushy head, woolly face, and wild eyes. Damn near mad, those eyes were. A half dozen muskets, and several pairs of boots, hung over his shoulders. He carried a bundle of clothes under one arm.

"Well, what we got here, boy?" His front teeth were chipped and he spat as he spoke.

"He talked at me, Pa."

"That so, boy? He don't look like he could do no talking to me." He kicked Jersey squarely in the head.

"MOTHER OF HEAAAAAVEN!" Jersey screamed. His head whipped to the side then rolled back, constrained as it was by its attachment to his neck. His heart pounded between his ears, the lights seemed to go off, on, then off again. He blinked, tried to make sense of the world around him, lights on again, saw a boy of eight or nine. Dirty face. A slew of muskets and canteens hung off him. Blood on his hands.

"I guess you was right, boy. The dead do talk."

"Maybe he ain't so dead, Pa?"

"I expect you right 'bout that much. Goddamn. Go figure. You make grams proud, boy."

The inane chatter echoed in Jersey's head, which ached as if squeezed between the gnarled hands of a vise. A wetness trickled behind his ear where the skin had been laid bare to the bone by the toe of the boot. "Mister," his tongue was heavy and he struggled with the words, "I'm Major Tom Jersey."

"I bet you is."

"My friend and I. Help us." He lifted an arm toward Ezra, who didn't stir, lay dead as far as he could tell. Ezra's feet were bare below his leggings. His boots were missing, pockets turned inside out. "Ezra? Ezra?"

"He dead." A grim smile gripped his face, wicked in its apparent satisfaction in delivering this news.

Jersey fingered the pistol at his side. Not salvation, but looters. Scavengers of the dead. The thought sickened him and weighed heavy on his trigger finger, where there was no longer any weakness.

"Now ain't that something. I's touched," the man said. He bent over Jersey, saw the dark spot at Jersey's hip and rooted around in the bloody material over the wound, as if maybe he knew of such things. "Get that musket there, boy," he pointed to a body a few feet to one side of the major.

Jersey tensed with the man's touch. He'd been near two days on this field but hadn't rested a minute of it and didn't want to get this wrong. *Now ain't that something.* The man's voice was crooked, like a bent railway tie that would throw whatever came its way. *I bet you is.* Not salvation, but damnation.

The boy, who seemed impossibly weighed down by his pilfered burden, stepped over Jersey's head, and knelt at the remains of another rebel. He reached for the musket, tried to pick it up by the bayonet.

The woolly man was now patting Jersey down with one hand. He had a smoke in the other. Jersey eyed the glint of metal in the man's patting hand. Ezra's harmonica. Seeing it was more than Jersey could stand. His arm began to stir and the pistol rose slowly out of the dirt. *Bend closer,* Jersey prayed, *closer, closer.*

The next two seconds passed in an instant. The kid reached for the musket and pulled. It discharged—the trigger caught on the dead man's finger—and the boy was lifted up and backwards by two feet. The canteens around his neck clinked with loud, hollow sound of wind chimes. The better part of his skull was carried still further, no better than food for the crawlers now. A look of confusion crossed the man's face as the kid slumped to the ground, heart so still his blown-apart head hardly leaked blood. In the final fraction of the instant, Jersey put his pistol to the man's temple and squeezed the trigger. The powder blast ignited his hair, then his hat; he was dead, though, so there were no frantic flailing movements of his arms to put the flames out. He fell to the earth beside Jersey, where blood and gray stuff bubbled out of the hole as his skull cooked.

***

For Surgeon Josiah Boyd, hell was fifty-six sleepless hours, most every one scalpel in hand, standing under a cross in a nameless church atop a dusty hill after a pointless battle. For too many good men, this was where the world ended.

The camp of wounded filled with men of both sides and the surgeons used them, Johnny Reb and Billy Yank, alike, making no distinction as to the color of a man's uniform—the life-blood being all the same. The men waited their turn with an eerie patience, as if their fate had already been decided and it was the duty of those present in that time and place to carry it out. The pile of severed flesh grew at a hideous pace. The wounded moved on and off the tables with nary a word, except for the occasional groan that couldn't be suppressed. Indeed, at such times each participant in the drama knew his place and the universal language of blood and pain spoke for all.

On this sleepless morning, Josiah Boyd toiled beyond exhaustion. He hadn't had so much as a latrine break in hours. The muck on the altar floor was two parts blood, one part shit from exploded bowels, one part tobacco juice. The mothy taste of the tobacco he chewed obscured the worst of the stench and allowed him to keep going. Except for the ever-present hum of flies (they were everywhere, a constant distress), it was mostly quiet now. No sounds of battle broke the dawn stillness, only an occasional random shot. Outside, those who had survived the night waited their turn. They were a quieter lot now. Natural selection had exacted its toll.

Boyd gazed at the stilled face of the dead man on his table. An overdose of chloroform, he supposed. He stared as if the dead man might have a message for him, saw only pain and the anguish of a life poorly ended. A mistake. Not the way things were supposed to go. But then, none of this was the way things were supposed to go. Outside, the night sky had cracked to open another day, but it had not made one damn bit of difference in here.

"Need to sleep. So tired." He wasn't sure if he'd actually said the words or just thought them. He dozed off looking at the dead man, or at least thought he did. He lost track of the world for a moment. Like looking at scenes of a play: the curtain came down, attention lapsed, and when it came back up everything was different. Everyone had changed places. *Goddamn.*

"Major? We got another. Sir?" Tiny said.

Boyd willed himself to stay awake, tried to follow what was happening in his piece of the world.

"Major, there's another, eh, only one more just now. Urgent I think."

A goddamn lie. There were another thousand urgent cases out there, and beyond those another thousand, and beyond... He had the sense all of this was hardscrabble surgery, that he was trying to eke a healing out of the diseased and dying human corpus. In the dim light, he saw the church for what it was: a festering sore on the ass of humanity.

"Hardy?" Boyd said.

The hospital steward pointed. Hardy stood at his own

table, had his own problems to contend with.

He wanted to tell them all to go to hell. He needed an hour's sleep—a week's sleep wouldn't have been enough. "Well," he began, but couldn't bring himself to say the words. In the end, he waved an arm and his consent was implied.

They brought the soldier in. A corporal with a nasty upper thigh wound. The leg was a mottled, blue wreck, but Boyd found a pulse in the foot. A good sign, though useless if the bone was broken. Need to probe it. Boyd worked off instinct now. He stared into the corporal's face. A hint of dusky gray, eyes absent and faraway. For a moment, Boyd imagined he was looking into his own face. He was the one dying. He discovered he couldn't die fast enough. He kneaded the skin above his eyes like a man working clay and shook the intrusion off. Before too long the soldier would be beyond help. This too he understood without actually thinking it. It was what he did. His job was to save lives, to make men whole again. Too often, the two were mutually exclusive. Thank God for the little brown bottle in his pocket.

Tiny prepared to administer the chloroform. He started to place a rag over the man's mouth and nose, but the patient's hand came up and grabbed his. The wounded man's eyes, suddenly very wide and alive, darted back and forth between the medical men. As if he'd pulled back from the edge, had been resurrected.

A tired-looking captain with a slinged arm stepped around the sheet suspended from the cross overhead. He clasped a hand over that of the corporal's, which in turn lay upon the assistant's hand. "What y'all intend to do?"

"What is this?" Boyd said.

"Let go my hand," Tiny said.

"Don't want to sleep," the wounded man said in a voice stronger than expected.

"You ain't goin' to take this corporal's leg."

"Captain, you don't know what you're talking about," Tiny said.

"Ain't nobody going to butcher me," the wounded man said.

"I know enough to know you butchers ain't taking this man's leg off."

"Listen to me, you sonbitch," Boyd said. "I been operating damn near three days with not an hour's rest. Don't know if it's night or day, don't know if we're winning or losing. Don't much care, truth be known. Which all means I could give a rat's ass about who the dang you are. You best get out of my hospital, Mister."

"Name's Chase, Captain, 21st Pennsylvania."

"You're not hearing me—" Boyd said.

"This man, his name is Wooster. He's got a wife, Anna, and three sons, Nathan, Connor, and little David. They run a farm in upstate New York where they grow—"

"Goddammit, Captain, I don't want to know his name. I ain't debating this with you. Every man here's got a life story what would make us crazy if we stopped to listen. Family or no, that leg needs coming off, it's coming off. His name, who he was, who he might become—it don't figure and I don't need to know."

"He needs that leg." Chase placed a hand on the wounded corporal's shoulder.

"Yeah, well, they all do," Tiny said.

"But he wants his leg."

"Please," the wounded man said.

Boyd looked at the corporal. "I'm guessing you want to live too." Turning to the captain, he said, "You get out of here now, let me probe this man's wound and do what needs doing."

"I'm not going anywhere, doc."

"Suit yourself." Boyd turned to Tiny. "Drop the

chloroform."

"No, no chloroform," Wooster said.

"Corporal?" Boyd asked, sure he'd heard the man correctly but questioning him just the same.

"He said no chloroform."

"I heard what the hell he said, Captain," Boyd said. "I just don't think he knows what he's saying."

"He can handle it."

"You can handle it. Him, it'll hurt like hellfire," Tiny said.

Corporal Wooster reached up and put a hand on Boyd's arm. "You goes ahead, doc. I can handle it if'n you can."

Boyd, who had had a strong education in reading the faces of men, looked at the wounded man's dirt-smeared expression and knew he meant to do this thing awake.

"I been lying here better part of a day, doc. I knows exactly what's coming my way. You cut if you needs to, but—" A spasm of some sort racked the man.

"But you don't take his leg," the captain said. "He'd rather just die."

Tiny shrugged his shoulders. Boyd turned away from the wounded man's face, not wanting to see the expressions to come. He pushed a finger into the bloody hole in the thigh, stirred it around, wasn't particularly gentle. He understood speed was more important than gentleness. The captain swallowed and his adam's apple grew large at the front of his neck. His eyes grew big, as if this was necessary for him to catch all that was occurring.

"Knife," Boyd said.

The captain drew a Colt from within the sling on his arm. He stood beside the patient, across the table from Boyd, and brought the weapon to bear on the surgeon. A foot in front of Boyd's face. "If it even looks like you're taking his leg off, I'll blow your brains all over that cross up there." He gestured upward with the barrel.

Boyd's eyes followed the gesture, his head rock steady and unmoving. He stared at the revolver, had never looked down the likes of its black barrel before. It loomed like a cannon before him and he wondered what it would feel like to die, wondered if his tired-to-the-bone fatigue would follow into the next life. He looked past the muzzle to the captain's eyes, saw the fire burning there, felt the burden of his education again. He meant business. He might damn well use the gun if pushed. Boyd spat a dirty gruel on the floor. His finger was still in the wound and he gritted his teeth, said again, "Knife."

The wounded man stirred. His leg tensed, the muscles in spasm against Boyd's fingers. His breathing was barely audible.

Boyd twisted his fingers in the man's wound, said, "Breathe dammit. I need to hear you breathe, you sonbitch."

The wounded man gulped big and began to cough.

Tiny slapped the knife into Boyd's palm.

The captain cocked his revolver, a loud click. "Goddammit, I told you. You ain't taking this man's leg off."

"I ain't here to cut off legs, man. That bullet needs getting out. But it's all the same to me if I go to bed and leave you here to work this out, seeing as you know so damn much about it."

The captain gave a single nod.

Boyd sliced the corporal's trousers. The smell of solid waste assaulted him and he chewed briskly at the wad of tobacco in his cheek. He probed again the wound, two fingers to get the measure of it. The corporal was jumpy now, anxious like a man going to his execution.

The surgeon turned from the table, spat, took a deep breath, and turned back. With his fingers still buried in the corporal's flesh, he made a two-inch cut in line with the bullet hole. He cut quick and deep, nearly to the bone, and fresh blood welled dark and venous. His fingers poked around in the muscle and fat making a wet, sloppy sound— like a boy groping for pollywogs in the mud. The corporal cried out, bucked, tried to get off the table. Tiny laid his considerable weight on top of him and all he succeeded in doing was flailing his arms with no purpose.

The revolver aimed at Boyd's face wavered like weight on the end of a wilting branch. "Go on," the captain said, though he was taking on the limp look of a fish too long out of water.

Boyd had the lead ball between his index and middle finger. He worked the thing out, moving it first along the bone, then worming it between the muscle and his fingers. When it finally came out, it felt heavier than the ounce it weighed. Boyd dropped it on the corporal's chest. "Here, a souvenir."

Passed out, the corporal didn't hear him.

The captain lowered his revolver. Boyd sewed the skin loosely so the pus would have a way out. As he looped the needle through the corporal's thigh, the captain slipped to the floor as if suddenly boneless. He fell over, face down in the muck.

"Maybe the sonbitch'll drown there." Boyd finished sewing and came around the table. He stepped over the unconscious captain and walked out into the dawn.

When he got to his tent, his hands were shaking so badly he could hardly get the laudanum to his mouth.

***

Ezra's shoes had been stolen sometime in the night. Beyond his thirst, beyond the aching numbness of a leg he could no longer feel, beyond the agony of raw broken bones scraping each other, beyond even the ever present hum of what must have been a thousand thousand insects, the missing shoe on his good leg was what first grabbed his attention when he awoke shortly after sunrise. He wondered who might do such a thing. After near two days on that field, this thought all but finished him. He began to cry. It seemed he'd spent his entire life lying there.

"Help me, Liza, help me."

"Ezra? Oh God. Ezra, that you?"

"Major, sir, I'm going to die out here."

"Well, you ain't dead yet and glory be for that."

"How can you be so calm, sir?"

"No choice. The way I figure it, we can either lay here and die, or we can lay here and live. I want to live."

"I can't feel my leg no more. I stink too."

"The whole field stinks, you ask me. And as for your leg, you're better off not feeling it. Think of it as one of God's blessings."

"God's blessings?"

"Yeah. I can feel my hip and it sure as hell ain't no blessing. Aches like the devil himself is inside."

"I'm sorry about that."

"Don't be sorry, ain't your fault I got myself shot. Just don't go giving up on me," Jersey said.

"I won't."

"Better not."

"You thirsty, Major?"

"I am if you got something to drink."

"It ain't much, just a couple drops I guess. But you have it, sir. Go on."

Jersey took the proffered canteen and turned it up to his lips. When he'd emptied it, he opened his mouth wide like a man who'd drank his fill. "You been holding out on me, Private."

"No sir. I believe the sun's getting to you. Got so you can't tell water from whiskey. Damn shame." They both chuckled, and the major removed something from his pocket. At first, Ezra thought it was a coin.

"I found this just this morning. Forgot I even had it. Bought it for two bits off a sutler some time back." Ezra's hands were too swollen to grasp it, so he set it in the grass where Ezra could see it.

"What is it?"

"I think they call it a pocket angel. It occurred to me this might be the angel you been looking for. Had it all along."

The sun rose higher in the eastern sky. After awhile, dark clouds moved in from the west and by mid-morning it looked like rain would be on them before long. Jersey told Ezra about the scavenger boy and his father, whose ruin of a head lay beside them still. He didn't tell him about the other boy there with them, about Little Tom.

"Sonofabitch," Ezra said. "What kind of strange you have to be to do something like that? Hope they rot in hell."

"The man at least," Jersey agreed. "Sure could use some food."

Ezra groped at the haversacks lying near him, but all were empty, not so much as a crumb of hoecake.

Every time Jersey moved, a sharp pain shot from his hip through the whole of his person. He tried not to cry out, but this was mostly futile and after a while a series of groans announced his every move. He began to babble. "Little Tom, what you got in that creel, boy? Give me one of them fishes. Whyn't you go down to that stream and fetch up some water?"

"What's that you say, Major? Who's Little Tom?"

The major was crying. Ezra pulled himself to a sitting position and felt the man's forehead the way his mother used to feel his. It burned. He wasn't surprised the major was not quite right-minded. He reached over and lifted the material off the officer's hip wound. "Oh Jesus." Ezra's vision had cleared some overnight. He almost wished it hadn't. "Maggots."

"I know. I feel 'em squirming. Damn things are eating my insides out." The words came with little emotion.

"Oh Jesus," Ezra said again, imagining it took everything he had to maintain his sanity just then. He was wrong.

"Told you it was a blessing you can't feel your leg."

Ezra hadn't really looked at his leg before that moment, either because of his blurry vision or his leg's position. He did so now. His subsequent screams did nothing to quell the mass of white worms crawling in and out of his flesh. Ezra felt his mind slip with his hollering, then understood it was made of good stuff if it could tolerate the likes of this. "Oh God. Liza. Oh God."

"We need help, Little Tom," Jersey said as Ezra came undone. If Little Tom was out there, he didn't answer.

***

The only place worse than a field hospital on the day of battle is a field hospital on the day after battle.

On the grounds surrounding the church where Hardy and Boyd worked at their palliative measures, a growth of trees shaded men in the midst of a modest cemetery. There had been no time to arrange and lay out a proper field hospital, of course—the battle had been enjoined before the first surgeons arrived—and the result was a mish-mash of tortured humanity. Scores of men lay about the churchyard and cemetery both; every hour saw their number increase. They lay grouped under trees or among the carved wooden markers and crumbling stones that were the last remains of bygone souls. Some sheltered in the lee of hastily improvised works. Most had nothing more than a blanket between them and the ground. They were in various states of dress, but none had more than the tattered clothes they'd been wearing in battle and many had considerably less.

Even for those used to the odors of an army encamped—common knowledge informed you could smell an army before you could see it—it was a bad business. The pestilent froth of a thousand festering wounds made the air redolent of corruption. Not a place for weak stomachs or frail constitutions.

Within the church itself, the pews remained occupied by those worshippers still waiting their turn at the tables, some glued to the wood by the crud of their wounds. Comfort was sparse here. A lone minister moved from man to man—those not yet corpses but still amenable to salvation—and offered blessings, absolution, last rites, prayers, whatever the comfort of a few words could offer. He couldn't hide his tears as he went about the work.

In the mid-morning, Ellis walked the grounds with several nurses, men all. They had a numb, beaten look, so far beyond fatigue that fatigue itself was a memory. Tobias examined some patients and neglected others in a more or less random fashion. He listened to men breathe through the wooden cylinder of a rigid tube, counted the beating heart against his own pulse, and laid a hand upon the forehead by way of feeling for fever, which he expected to come in every case followed before long by the laudable pus. This pus was a putrid mix of the body's humors, the sick man's way of ridding himself of those essences that would otherwise do harm; a green-white, foul-smelling seepage which took three or four days to show itself, then weeks or months to dry up. Sometimes it might not dry up for years. This timetable could not be hurried. It belonged not to man, but the Creator.

He lifted dressings and probed wounds for this laudable pus. In some cases he pushed a naked finger into the swollen flesh to get at the putrid matter; the same finger in each case. He never changed a soiled dressing for a clean one, though more than once he took the bandages from a dead soldier and placed them over the wound of one yet living. In all of this, he washed his hands only once per dozen or fifteen men; he had two hundred wounded in his charge.

Here was a man, a private of infantry, thirty-five years of age, a farmer before the war. Name was S.H. Howard. The scant notes recorded he had been wounded on the morning of the first, admitted that night, and finally operated on the afternoon of the second. His constitution had been feeble at admission, practically exsanguinated from a gunshot wound which had entered his face just above the angle of the jaw on the right, passed clean through his neck, and made its exit only after fracturing the left arm as well. Ellis had amputated his arm on the battlefield to control hemorrhage. His pulse was ninety and he was very hot. Lifting the dressing, Ellis noted the first signs of erysipelas in the stump, which was black and weeping and blistered. He applied powdered quinine and gave supplements of iron.

An enfeebled corporal of artillery, twenty-six, name of Murphy. The exposed end of his stumped femur already jutting through the gaping incision at the flap; a troublesome bedsore also eroding the skin of his ischium. Diarrhea as well. "Mark him for a return to theater," Ellis said. "I'll revise his stump. See that he's not getting purgatives."

Yet another, this one not operated. Charles Babcock, thirty-one, a druggist before the war. Constitution good. Gunshot wound, the ball entering near the middle of the posterior border of the scapula, two inches or so from the spine, passing upwards and exiting anteriorly, fracturing the clavicle at its middle third. Patient was and has remained conscious, able to give a history of severe hemoptysis and dyspnea. Little constitutional disturbance.

Some fever. Ellis noted the wound in the front was suppurating freely, the posterior wound not so much. "Transfer to hospital in DC," he directed.

A boy of eighteen, a student before the hostilities, had apparently died alone in the night of secondary hemorrhage after a relatively simple gunshot wound to the right forearm. According to what he'd told before being operated, he was from Marietta, Georgia, but had sided with the North. He had two brothers and an uncle fighting for the South.

And so on.

When he finished, Assistant Surgeon Ellis stepped aside for a few moments to himself. He was tired and his arms were bothering him. Or rather more truthfully, the scars on his arms were itching again. At times those damn scars itched incessantly. Usually, and blissfully, he just worked through it. Blissfully because if he wasn't gainfully occupied he would get to thinking about how he'd gotten them. He'd think about his father then, about how it would have been better to have had no father at all. Sometimes, this would be when he was working the operating tables or making one of his gut wrenching runs across a battlefield strewn with the injured he dearly cared for. At such times he might in the moment look at his scars and see healing. At such times, he was at his best and nobody could have outperformed him. At other times, when he was idle and the fire in his gut had stoked down—while at the same time the hate in his soul had stoked up—he'd look at those scars and see pain. He was impossible to tolerate at such moments, loathing himself, hating his father, and needing...what? Companionship? Intimacy? A scapegoat? Or maybe all of the above?

Best, he knew from experience, not to think of his scars at all.

He wasn't much for tobacco, but he preferred the stink

of it to the reek of the ward, and it sometimes helped him clear his head. In his pocket he had ten bills and a letter from Archer. He had gone through Archer's belongings. The steward had stashed the money in his bedroll with a note the money was meant to send his body home in the event of his death.

Just now the money was useless. Archer's body was still out there.

Standing in the humid air, Ellis rolled himself a cigarette. The tobacco stuck to his fingers, which more clumsy than usual, and his fingers stained the paper red. He fumbled for the letter in his pocket, came out with Tucker's letter instead. He struck a lucifer against a headstone, lit his cigarette, and read Tucker's final thoughts again. He took another drag and his mouth filled with the copper taste of blood not his own.

THIRTEEN

A light rain began falling as Ellis found the old undertaker stooped over a makeshift table, a cadaver laid out before him. He was working some sort of a hand pump and the body jiggled under its effect now and then. He wore a green bowler hat, pushed back on his head, revealing a receding hairline.

The monkey, Ellis recalled his name was something like Archimedes, hung from the awning overhead.

The assistant surgeon watched the undertaker squeeze the dead man's cheeks, as if giving him a massage. Jupiter didn't seem to notice he was there. He continued to work on the cadaver, smiling and talking as he did so. "That oughta do you, Mr. King. You like that? Yes sir, I believe your folks'll be right pleased with how that extra little bit fills out your jowls. You should be proud. Hope I'm not presuming too much by saying so."

"Mr. King?" Ellis said.

"The poor deceased lad. My patient, if you will."

"Why do you address the dead as if they still live?"

"Ever been dead, Captain Ellis?"

"Not yet."

"Then what possible criticism could you give on how these dear departed souls are supposed to be addressed?"

"Same ole Jones."

"I certainly hope so."

They both laughed.

"How are you, Jupiter?"

"I'm tolerable."

"I doubt it. You been working too hard. I hear there may be ten thousand dead."

Jupiter said, "Could be. I ain't one to count 'em though."

"The hell you say. You the countingest man I know."

Jupiter motioned to the monkey and Archimedes dropped onto his shoulder. He made his way out from under the awning, into the drizzle. Across the muddy lane, a campfire occupied the middle of a small clearing and Jupiter took a seat on a chair beside it. Tobias followed and sat down on pine box across from him. The coffin creaked under his weight. The wind skittered the trees around them.

"I address them, because I respect them," Jupiter said. "I buried my pappy when I was ten. Me, by myself. He died beside me in the night and I dressed him in his trousers and shirt and buried him before noon."

Ellis paused as he tried to figure where this was going.

"Later, I dug him back up."

"You dug up your father's body?"

"I buried him didn't I? We was alone, figured I needed the money left in his trouser pockets more than he did."

"That' a tad ghoulish, Jupiter."

"He'd been in the ground two days by then, so I guess looking back he had some corruption, but that's not how I remember it. When I think back on it, the most remarkable thing is how quiet he was."

"He was dead."

"I know, but that's not what I mean. You see, and I don't expect you're going to understand this, but the dead, they got a certain way about them. It's not exactly talking, and yet that's exactly what it amounts to. They tell a story." He stroked the monkey's tail and the two men stared across the fire at each other. The rain was coming harder now. "They talk to me, Captain. As God is my witness, the dead talk to me."

Ellis watched the fire's reflection dance off the wet on the old man's face. "That sounds some crazy. You know?"

"I guess that's an old man's prerogative. Sounding crazy."

"Dead people don't talk, Jupiter."

"You're young. I been undertaking a long time. This here war's two years old, but I seen a lifetime of death. They talk if you listen. Got something to say too, more often than not." He coughed several times and took a moment to study the kerchief's contents, then sat back and tipped his bowler hat over his eyes. "Go on. Let me enjoy this here good rain now."

"You still taking your own medicine?"

"That what you came here for?"

"You don't take something, you're gonna be joining these here..." he hesitated, tried to find the right words, "...friends of yours, right soon."

"See that's just the thing, Captain."

"What's that?" Ellis said.

"Nobody gets outta life alive. Look around you. Proven fact." Jones put his hand up, said, "Bring me a cup of that coffee, boy."

Ellis was confused for an instant until a negro boy appeared as if out of nowhere. He was in his early teens, stick thin but muscled like an ox. He wasn't wearing a shirt and his black skin shone in the rain, just as the old man's face had. Tiny orange diamonds danced over his chest in the firelight. "Didn't hear you come up," Ellis said, eyeballing him hard.

"That's 'cause you weren't listening," Jupiter said from under his bowler. "How you expect to hear the dead you can't even hear the living?" He made to get up and rose to his feet. "Damn shame you ain't gonna let me enjoy this here rain. Good rain's hard to find, especially nowadays."

"The boy didn't make a sound," Ellis said.

"That so?" Jupiter turned to the boy, who handed a cup to the old man. "You make any sound, Cuuda?"

"Nope."

"Then how'd I know you was there?"

"Cause you just know things like that Mr. Jupiter. You funny like that." Cuuda pursed his lips and bid Archimedes over to him. The monkey jumped from the undertaker's shoulder to Cuuda's.

"How long you been with me, Cuuda?"

"Six years near about, I guess."

"You see, Captain, the boy's been with me longer than any soul ever has, except my monkey Archimedes. And my pappy of course. Cuuda's a righteous fella and I've seen plenty of men thrice his age who weren't half his character. He's strong as a bull, honest to a fault, quiet the way the wind is on a fall evening—you know it's there but it don't intrude—and I can't recall ever hearing him curse the Lord in vain."

"And you're telling me this why?"

"Cause he, too, has the gift. He listens. You'd be obliged to pay attention to him. There's something in that boy. He's a keeper."

"Maybe it's my problem, but I don't always follow you, Jupiter," Ellis said. He was looking at Cuuda though. "I know you, boy?"

"I don't guess we ever met, suh," Cuuda said.

"You'll understand when the time comes," Jupiter said.

Ellis stood in the rain, nodded at Jupiter. "I have no idea what you're talking about, old man."

Jupiter stared at him. "You come out here for a reason, Captain?"

They talked a bit longer and the rain never let up the

whole time. Talked about Archer, about retrieving his body, about sending him on to his folks.

Jupiter would do it all for ten bills, which was, coincidentally, exactly what Archer had left for the job.

***

Ezra Coffin and Tom Jersey had lain forty-eight hours undiscovered in the grass of a field not three miles as the crow flies from a Union hospital. This last they couldn't know of course, and it would have provided small comfort if they had. As the sun fell beneath the horizon, hunger began to add to the miseries they'd seen and felt. A light rain pelted them.

Except for a few bits of biscuit, one or two strips each of jerky, and a couple of stale hoecakes, they had had nothing of any substance since before their wounding. Battle exacts a heavy toll from a man, not the least of which is his last meal, and thus their stomachs were about as empty as empty can be. Damaged as they were, with the fever burning through their bones, they'd begun to consume themselves the way a burning house consumes itself in the flames.

The two lay side by side, Ezra flat on the ground and Jersey propped intermittently on an elbow. Neither had strength to move about any longer. They'd raided all the knapsacks within crawling distance. They were quiet now, listening to the out of kilter rhythms of nature.

Jersey looked at his boy. Little Tom sat in the grass at his feet, staring silently at his father. His hands rested like a still life atop the creel. "Blessed are the meek, for they shall inherit the earth," Jersey said.

"Blessed are those who hunger," Ezra said.

"Who hunger and thirst for righteousness, for they shall be filled."

"Blessed are the merciful, for they shall obtain mercy."

"Blessed are the merciful, for they shall obtain mercy," Jersey repeated.

"Blessed are the pure in heart, for they shall see God," they said as one, and followed it with "Blessed are the peacemakers, for they shall be called sons of God."

Little Tom nodded his head and never took his eyes from his father.

Jersey tried to take Ezra's hand, but neither was good for gripping. The left one was the better of the two. It held Tim Jewel's harmonica most of the time.

"I think maybe I'd like to say the Lord's Prayer, Major."

Jersey stared a long moment at his feet, looking at Little Tom, then said "I got no plans to die out here. I don't think the good Lord would bring us this far and abandon us now, do you?"

"No sir, I suppose not."

"Whyn't you play something Ezra, something with kick to it."

Ezra gripped Tim Jewel's harmonica and brought it to his lips, now moistened by the rain and so some less painful. "Something with kick," he repeated, then played *Dixie*. The major joined in with the words.

"I guess that had kick enough," Jersey said when the playing was done.

"Yes sir, Major. Thought you'd like it."

"Thank you."

They rested awhile, not saying much but much passing between them nonetheless. Jersey finally spoke up. "I had a son once. He was a good kid, every father's dream of what a son should be. Laughed a lot and had a smile you'd'a walked a mile in the rain just to see."

"Sounds nice," Ezra said.

"Had a winning way about him. We used to go fishing together in the evenings, but sometimes he'd go alone during the day. He was eight years old when he didn't come home one afternoon. Just eight years."

Ezra blew a couple of random notes on the harmonica. "God in heaven."

"We never found him. I found his rod where he must of been fishing, but nothing else. Searched for days, months even. Elspeth..." he coughed—a sad, pathetic thing to see, not from the throat but from the heart—"...she thinks he's still alive, but I know better. He'd never leave that rod."

"No sir, I bet not."

"I see him sometimes, plain as the day. He's carrying that creel I gave him too. Just appears, never says much, just looks at me. Like he's—like he's watching over me or something."

"Amen."

"That make sense? That make me crazy?"

"I can't imagine. Sam's only a few months old, and I ain't even seen him, but I guess I'm a father. I got me a boy, I think every day. I imagine him in his ma's arms, imagine him standing in the yard, imagine him atop a horse. I think maybe from the minute they're born, our lives revolve around them whether we know it or not. Maybe that's what you're feeling, or seeing—the caring."

"He's here now, you know."

"Your boy?"

Jersey pointed with a shaky hand and Ezra's head turned, his face grimacing against the pain of moving his eyeballs. He saw only the skein of rain.

"Ezra, you got to live, you hear me? Got to live for that boy if nothing else. A son needs his father. I know. I had me one once."

FOURTEEN

Drs. Josiah Boyd, Solomon Hardy, and Tobias Ellis had to contend with both the rain and a thousand men who had rather to die than live just then. The church-turned-hospital had become a place where the work of the doctors went on side by side with that of the undertakers; where four men died every hour day and night and the rain and blood ran as red mud across the ground.

Tents were scarce. The wounded faced the elements, making little enclaves for themselves where they could. Some watched after the senseless, lifting their heads onto earthen mounds to keep them from drowning. In the occasional flashes of lightning, these scattered groups looked as much like the ungathered dead as they did the tortured living. The able-bodied moved among the stricken in small but increasing numbers, holding a hand here or a head there, dispensing medicaments when they could. The favorites were whisky and apple brandy and they doled these out liberally. The men shivered less with liquor warming their insides. A few women from town, who a week before hadn't any greater care than whether their baked goods rose in time for supper, now washed the distressed. They sang lullabies, wrote letters, and spooned a lardy gruel of beans and fatback into their charges.

Assistant Surgeon Ellis moved in and about the churchyard. The men were quieter than he had any right to expect them to be, a silence painful in its solemnity. The broken bodies and sad frames of farm boys, carpenters, blacksmiths, shopkeepers, wheelwrights, coopers, tellers, ministers—the list was endless—ran on forever.

Fifty yards or so behind the church, he came upon a boy with yellow piping on his jacket, a cavalryman. He might have been eighteen, but his size and the peach fuzz on his cheeks suggested younger. He lay under a tree and someone had taken the time to place a pillow under his head. He looked almost comfortable, except that he'd been shot through the skull. He was generally unconscious, except that his left foot kept moving. That heel had dug a hole deep enough to bury his whole leg and even now did its work. Back and forth it went, back and forth. Ellis put a hand on the foot, but this made no difference. He felt the pulse at the ankle, rapid and weak, skin hot and dry, features a dull, listless gray. Looking at the helpless soldier fairly tortured him, though it was not as difficult as it would have been four days ago. Archer was dead and you could get used to anything.

Tucker came to mind, the letter still in his pocket. *What's it like to know you're dying? Worse,* Ellis thought, *what would it be like to not know you're dead?* Here was a man, his heel obviously laboring without the knowledge and authority of his God-given mind, as gone as any soldier in the dead house and only a breath shy of the undertaker's table. Yet, that breath was enough. Without any future, the boy hung onto life like he had a right to. Here life lingered but didn't thrive.

It seemed the definition of war.

***

Surgeon Solomon Hardy dropped the scalpel and it clinked as it struck the plank floor. He'd operated with barely a break for three and a half days and his hands were cramping badly. His boots had never fit well and a blister on the instep made standing a chore. A sharp pain pierced from the small of his back down both legs with every move. Not a pain that incapacitates, rather that special kind that exhausts a man in his efforts to ignore it. He hurt to breathe. His eyelids felt pinned open one moment, glued shut the next. Worst of all, he'd been pissing razors for a day and more. The wounded in the yard still numbered in the hundreds though, and Hardy stood at his operating table refusing to leave.

His back ached and he stooped to rest it. A pain—it ran like a hot poker from back to foot—hauled him up short. He stooped beside his table looking like a man twice his age with half his health. He was finished operating—for the moment and maybe always. He left a soldier lying face up on the table. The man was insensate and cared not an iota for this or anything else. An orderly helped Hardy descend the altar and make his way through the throng between him and the door. He was a bent man in a bent place and thinking was beyond him. He had only one place he could go. Not so much a place as *the* place, arguably the one spot where he truly belonged—even beyond his presence at the operating table.

In the middle of the night a day earlier, Hardy had taken his only real time away from the tables. A brief melancholy respite he'd spent eating alone in his tent until interrupted by Ellis. He had a reputation as a man of few words, but had somehow needed the company at just that moment and his words that night had been as heartfelt as any he'd spoken in the army. He'd lost control and come back around to his senses, all in the space of a few weeping moments in front of the junior surgeon. He'd excused himself then. Not ready to return to the tables, though; he'd stolen a few moments more. He went out among the soldiers in the yard, over the low stone wall to the fringes where the light of the lanterns just barely touched the dark. There were wounded there too, men who had lain much of the day without any attention from the doctors. A few hollered his way, but he ignored them. For whatever reason, he focused on a lone soldier lying against an old picket fence on the far side of a wide dirt trail. The man lay alone, despite the fact the trail was freshly rutted; the wagons had come this way recently and often. There, in that quiet place, with only an occasional cough or groan to remind him of the disordered world, Dr. Hardy cried with his head in his hands, kneading his face. He'd seen a thousand men bleed out and it was as if he was drowning in all their blood.

The lone soldier again. The man all but beckoned him. Even in the dim light, Hardy saw the yellow stripes on his trousers and knew he was thus a cavalryman. He edged closer, no idea why. Maybe it was the way that heel dug at the ground, an odd sort of activity, at once mundane and unholy. He moved closer yet. He'd not bothered to remove his surgeon's apron, and so when he knelt the apron buckled upon itself and was the first thing to touch the youth.

"My God." Hardy looked into the cavalryman's face and saw...

The private's eyes, which had to that moment been rolled up and back so that only the whites showed, came around to a more earthly appeal and seemed to register recognition. He held a hand out, took a deep breath, and uttered something frothy and unintelligible.

"Don't talk, Spencer."

Hardy took his son's hand. He laid him carefully out on the dirt beside the picket fence, enough so as to examine him. He had been shot through the right side of his head, front to back. The ball had entered above his right eye and exited just above and behind his right ear. Gray matter bubbled out at regular intervals with his pulse. "A mortal wound," Hardy whispered.

The surgeon inhaled as if he had to take in enough air to last him the rest of eternity. He was looking at the final hours, if not the final minutes, of his son's life—his only child, all the kin he had in this world. "They've killed you." He took his son's head in his arms and wiped away the blood on his forehead. He kissed the bare skin. "Maggie, they've killed our boy."

He carried his boy around to the back of the church, fifty yards or so, to a spot near a branch of Rock Creek. He wanted him in the open, where the combination of fresh air and fine humors might do him some rest. He laid out a little straw and dressed his son's wounds. The boy all but stopped moving, except for that foot which kept digging its heel at the dirt. As if all the parts of him had died save that heel. Hardy wept as he watched that heel work. It was the best he could do, the best anyone could do. His son was already dead for all practical purposes and every moment he stayed with him might mean the passing of a life he could save. He asked a negro litter bearer, a rakish man he'd worked with for some time and trusted as much as you could trust any negro, to watch after the boy until he could return. The black nodded and Hardy took Spencer in his arms. He arranged his tunic just so, fussing with it for several long moments. He said him a solemn goodbye then, promised to meet him in a better world, and caressed his son's cheek with a warm finger. It left a washed-out smear of pink. He apologized for leaving, but the workload was great and the time was short. The negro handed him a clean piece of linen and he put it under his son's head. He said a prayer for forgiveness then, imploring Maggie to look after their boy in heaven as he had not been able to do in life.

That had all been a day and more ago. A lifetime. In the

intervening hours, the rakish negro had been killed and Hardy had destroyed his own health standing at his operating table. He had made it his mission to save as many of the boys as he could.

Now he had only to watch his own son die.

***

In the silence after dark, Ezra's stomach growled like a bear just up from hibernating all winter. A long, low, embarrassing rumble. A reminder of better times.

"You should've seen the way my mother used to cook up wild turkeys," he said, perhaps lost in an image of the glistening bird turning on the spit, its sumptuous juices falling on the coals below, those coals singeing with each drop. His tongue jutted in and out with a frenzied motion.

Tom Jersey watched Ezra's tongue move in and out, an eerie sight that recalled for him a baby bird waiting on its mother. All afternoon he'd been staring at his son, trying to work his way around a thought that first came to him when Ezra had pulled back his trouser leg that morning and begun to scream. Even now he could feel the maggots boring into his hip, just below the emptiness in his stomach. *What if?* he wondered, *what if...*

Too much for Jersey to contemplate, too awful to consider. Yet, lying beside Ezra, the last light showing that tongue moving in and out like the lash of a mad man, maybe things weren't so bad after all. They had plenty of food, if he could just bring himself to stomach it.

Jersey closed his eyes and reached into the loose crud that was his right hip; the soup of creatures was warm to his touch. Trying not to think of what he was doing, he picked out a handful of critters and brought it to his mouth without looking. He gagged, but not as much as he'd thought he would, and swallowed without chewing. A few of the things stayed in his mouth though—that was the worst of it—so he was forced to chew them. He'd imagined they'd crunch between his teeth, but they were mushy, somewhere between overcooked grits and too-ripe melon. The taste was like undercooked beef or the near raw chicken he'd had to eat on the march: a dull, nonsensical taste that wasn't offensive by itself, but with it came a tinge of something metallic—an awful coppery flavor he understood too readily was his own blood.

Still, it was not so bad as he'd imagined all day, and he repeated the effort several times. It might keep him alive.

It might keep Ezra alive as well. Jersey shook him and the Northerner came out of whatever place his mind had retreated to. He explained what he'd done.

Ezra was horrified.

"Either you live off them or they live off you," Jersey told him.

"I can't do it. No way."

"You've no choice, man. Eat 'em, Private. That's an order."

Ezra wondered for a moment if a Confederate officer had any authority to command him, then stared hard at the wiggling mass of worms in the major's hand. He turned to the major's face and every thought he had suddenly vanished. It could only be one way. This one way. He opened his mouth and Jersey dropped the critters in. "Swallow fast, don't chew unless you have to."

Ezra gagged more than Jersey did, and was near to bringing the whole mess back up. He didn't, though, and in holding them down he realized a reserve of something he'd never known he had.

"Again, Private."

This time Ezra closed his eyes as he opened his mouth, not wanting to see that look on the major's face. By the time he swallowed the second handful of maggots, he'd left the horror of it behind.

It would be another hour before the two had eaten their fill.

***

Once, when he was fifteen, a cricket had crawled into Josiah Boyd's ear while he was asleep. Awakening, he'd felt a peculiar heaviness in the ear, as if he'd been swimming and it was full of water. Only he hadn't and it wasn't. He slapped his fingers against it, gently at first, but couldn't dislodge whatever it was. This had served to rouse the bug though, and the result was hell indeed. Either the cricket liked the warmth of the canal or it was too stupid to find its way out. Either way, the pain had been horrendous. The thing scratched at Boyd's eardrum like the razor edge of a knife drawn back and forth against his brain. And the chirping was out of a nightmare. Its high strain had echoed on forever. He would have cut his ear off to stop that noise.

The same feeling that had engulfed him that night came back now. It began the way it had then, as a small thing. He ignored it and spat on the floor, but as he worked on the soldier before him, the need grew. It came to occupy his mind slowly, like blood leaking from a poorly tourniquetted wound. A man could bleed to death from such a wound.

He felt a sty in one eye and blinked. Then blinked again. Before long, the blinking became a spasm and Boyd struggled to open the eye. It seemed to have its own agenda, and he was losing to it. The pain in his head mounted and the patient before him dissolved as his other eye filled with tears. He wiped at it with a red hand. He wondered if those around him could see the desperation in his actions. His gut twisted. He considered a quick amputation. He'd cut off the soldier's arm in two minutes and be done.

He looked up. The room was cloaked in dim shadows beyond the ring of light around his table. His eyes ached from straining all night under the flickering lanterns. One eye closed, he looked like a man escaping the sun. His need for laudanum was acute and it scratched his mind every bit as hard as the cricket had scratched his ear. And as he'd hated the cricket, so too he hated the laudanum.

He spat again and turned back to his patient. The man slept under the chloroform. He stuck a finger into the innards of the forearm, searching blindly and quickly for the ball. He felt the fleshy muscle and the strings of ligament, but no projectile. No shards of bone, no evidence of a fracture. He couldn't justify an amputation under such a circumstance—*Chisolm's Manual of Military Surgery* called for him to cut the man's forearm open and search out the ball under direct visual inspection—the best hope for the man's recovery.

The worst thing for Boyd's peace just then, however. It might take ten minutes or more, minutes his own needs wouldn't allow just then. He had to have a swig and, increasingly, he had to have it then and there.

The idea was a cricket in his head that wouldn't die.

He called for the saw, which was the wrong order of things and he knew it. He knew full well he was going to cut the man's arm off too. He didn't want to, but he had no choice.

The cricket was in control.

The saw slipped his grip; his palm was sweaty like a greased axle. The saw hit the floor with a vibrating twang that might as well have been Boyd's mind shattering. He looked at Tiny, and caught a strange look about his assistant. He was saying something, speaking gibberish. Somewhere in the back of his mind, in a place the cricket hadn't yet gotten to, Boyd struggled to understand what was happening. As his gut twisted a second time and his hands began to tremor, a wad of chew built in his mouth. His saliva became a thick gruel and he needed to spit. He tried to call for a scalpel, but it came out hollering for a saw again. He was losing the battle. He had lost control.

—*Amputate. Cut the man's arm off.*

—*No. Unnecessary.*

Boyd leaned to spit, but in that single instant it hit him. The full weight of the cricket collided with all he was and he knew if he spat, he'd lose everything. So he swallowed instead.

Boyd vomited across the patient on the table, then his legs gave out and the floor rushed to meet him. Tiny was there with him an instant later, as were several others. They helped him to his feet, the world swaying all around him as they did so. He heard someone ask if he was feverish? Sick? He couldn't speak. Tiny pulled him to the window, where the air was less dense with the smell of rot. The hospital steward called for Hardy, but the other surgeon's hands had cramped not long before and he couldn't be found.

Boyd was conscious but lightheaded. He vomited again, managed to enunciate a single word. "Laudanum." Tiny was gone a long minute or two, hours they seemed to Boyd, and returned with one of the bottles. Boyd fumbled with it a few seconds, like a man dying for lack of its contents. He tilted it to his lips.

The cricket died away as Boyd collapsed in the shadows of the operating tables.

***

Inside, the church was dry but the misery was no less for it. The wounded covered every speck of floor space, squeezed in tight against the elements until one more might have burst the walls. The only area with any room was the altar, set up for surgery. In three hard days of operating, Hardy, Boyd, and their assistants had parted enough men from their limbs to string a line of withered flesh from Washington, DC to Richmond, Virginia. Still plenty of woe, that much was sure, but most of those they could immediately help had already passed their tables. Those left were mostly the dying, those they'd set aside earlier who'd somehow managed to hang on despite themselves. For these, they had few answers.

Ellis stood in the doorway of the church, the cavalryman in his arms. The interior was dark and oppressive, with flickering sable shadows moving everywhere across the walls. The darkness drained the color out of the place and the people moved about as if in a world of figments; no detail anywhere. Even so, one could not look upon any object for long without coming to know it substantially and unfortunately. It was warm and swelteringly close within the walls and not a man entered who didn't at once prefer the wet weather to the purulent fever within.

A limp-armed sergeant led the way with a stub of lit candle as Ellis crossed the nave, stepping carefully but producing unpleasantness just the same. They approached the altar and found Boyd passed out in the corner. His hospital steward sat on one of the tables. Tiny was chewing something, it might have been a piece of chicken but Ellis couldn't have sworn to it. The steward stood as the group approached, but only slowly moved out of the way as Ellis laid the injured man before him. "What we got here?"

It had taken an hour to trudge the muddy churchyard. The soldier's leg had kept kicking all the while, like a busted engine that wouldn't give up. It flopped on the table even now, as if animated by the strings of a mad puppeteer. Ellis pointed, though he wasn't accountable to the steward. "He's been shot in the head."

"That so." Tiny was not quick to look, took another bite of the chicken leg, or whatever it was, and chewed slowly. He regarded Ellis as if his presence couldn't mean anything good. "Can't help him."

"What're you talking about? Wake the major up," Ellis said.

Tiny tossed the chicken leg through the window. "Can't do that." A last mouthful of bird made the words almost unintelligible.

"Corporal, wake the damn major. I'm sure Dr. Boyd's capable of making his own decisions in this matter."

"Beg pardon, sir. Dr. Boyd, he's, eh," Tiny leaned close, the way one will in imparting a secret, "he's not himself, Captain."

"Corporal, you best say what needs saying."

"The doctor's exhausted is all, sir. Been operating three full days with no rest. He can't go on. I won't allow you to disturb him. Sir."

"Corporal—"

"They call me Tiny, sir."

"I know what they call you. I seen you and Boyd together. He speaks highly of you. And the last thing I want to do is upset a good man and you're a good man, Tiny. But this ain't a thing for you to decide. I got a man injured bad here, needs a surgeon."

"Truth is, he ain't in no condition to operate. He collapsed a couple of hours ago, Captain. Weren't too pretty neither. Got all shaky, started talking gibberish—"

"Shit." Ellis looked carefully about the room, trying to make out detail in the faces. "Where's Dr. Hardy?"

"Couldn't go on either, sir. Hands cramped. I think he went to his tent."

"This is madness," Ellis said to no one in particular. He looked at the man on the table. His eyes had opened and a torpid look haunted them. His left leg rocked back and forth, digging at the air. It made a faint thumping against the table every time the foot came down.

A commotion in the nave and someone came forward. As the shadowed light of the altar illuminated the figure, he felt relief. Hardy. Thank God.

But it wasn't a Hardy he'd ever seen. The surgeon looked like a man who'd lost his best friend, who'd lost everything. His face was dark even in the light and he stooped as he walked. And he was hot too. Ellis could feel the fever coming off him. There was something else as well, but he didn't quite get what.

Hardy stroked his son's face, and Spencer grimaced. "Goddamn you Ellis, what'd you do?"

"How's that, Major?"

"What you intend to do with this boy?" Hardy didn't look at Ellis.

"Major Hardy, look for yourself. He's been shot in the head."

"I goddamn well know he's been shot in the head. But why's he on the table? He should be—" Hardy stopped short of saying whatever was on his mind. "The wound's mortal."

"No sir, I don't think so."

"You what?" Hardy asked, finally turning to him. "I don't give a bucket of bull piss what you think."

"Sir, I looked. The injury's one-sided. That is, it don't cross the midline. I heard a talk recently about saving soldiers in such a case." The something else occurred to Ellis then: he couldn't ever remember seeing Hardy without a segar before.

"Bullshit. Don't you think I'd have operated on my son already if the boy had a chance? If just one chance in hell?"

"Your son?"

"That's what I said. His name's Spencer."

Tiny choked.

"I'm sorry, I didn't know," Ellis paused, reconsidering what he knew. "You didn't know, sir. That's all, didn't know. But I've heard about operating to relieve swelling and remove the clot."

"Pssssssshaw." Hardy dismissed the notion.

"He's right, you know." Boyd, stirred from his stupor by the argument, stuffed a wad of chew in his cheek. "I saw it done once. Can't say it amounted to much though."

"You saying there's a chance of saving my boy?"

"I'm saying I've seen a gunshot to the head operated is all. Nothing more," Boyd said.

"This is crap," said Hardy, "you can't help him. Nobody can." He rose and rubbed a weary hand across his eyes. "I should've had the guts to take him to the woods myself, but I couldn't do it."

Boyd shuddered at the at the mention of the woods. "Yeah, that might've been the place for him, but no one here's faulting you, Sol. I guess I'd have done the same." He examined the injured man's head, noted the blue-black discoloration of a large bruise on the temple, the hole in his forehead, another behind his ear. He probed it gently with his index. Spencer stirred slightly. "Course, time sometimes decides these things. He's survived this long..."

"There's no fracture, if that's what you're feeling for. I already checked," Ellis leaned over Boyd as he worked.

Boyd continued nonetheless. "No," he said, "I suppose not." He pulled Spencer's eyelids back. The pupils were almost equal. Their gaze was skewed, one up, the other down, but not much.

Hardy shook his head. "My boy needs a priest, not a surgeon."

"Quite possibly, Sol," said Boyd.

"Dr. Hardy," Ellis said, "I never did much like you."

Boyd made a furtive smile at the statement, turning the corners of his mouth up a bit. Those very words had been on his own lips a few times. To Ellis he said, "He's right, you know. The man's stuporous, shows evidence of concussion of the brain. There's not really much we can do for him."

"Dr. Boyd," Ellis said, "I've always known you to be fair and honest, a bit quirky they say, but a good surgeon, maybe the best I've seen. I know you care more than just about anyone else here what happens to a man placed on your table. I've seen it in your eyes more than once. I know it eats at you, the way these men die and we can't do nothing about it. But this ain't like that. This is one you don't need on your conscience. You can do this, sir. You're good enough to save him. I know you are." He turned to Hardy. "This is your son, for Christ's sake. What you going to say to your wife?"

"My wife is none of your damn business, Captain."

"I'm begging you, sir, give the boy a chance."

Boyd spoke up. "You didn't let me finish, Tobias. I didn't say nothing could be done, I said there wasn't much."

"What's the difference?" Tiny asked.

"The difference?" Boyd knew he was going to hate himself for what he was about to say, but he'd hate himself more if he did nothing. The image of Thomas Ellerby popped big into his mind, though he'd had no chance at saving that boy. He stared at Ellis. "Drilling a hole in his head, I suppose. Yeah, that'd be the difference, a hole about the size of a two-bit piece. A hole in his skull." He didn't wait for a response. He was done with talking. He descended the altar and began to work his way out of the church. "Where you going, major?" Ellis hollered after him.

Boyd twitched again. His stomach squeezed a little, high in his belly. *God I hate this place.* He stopped and turned very deliberately back towards the men on the altar, said:

"With your permission, Captain, I need to move my bowels."

"But sir—" Ellis said.

Boyd clutched at the bottle in his hand, and if it had been anything but the thick glass it was, his stranglehold would have broken it. As it was, the contents had a stranglehold on him. He glanced at Hardy, who clearly wasn't in any condition to operate himself. "I'll be back, Solomon, and then we'll see to your boy. You have my word." His word was about the last thing Boyd could promise anymore.

***

In spite of his meal of worms, Ezra's strength was waning. He used the near last of it to pull a few corpses around them as a shelter against the weather, which was blowing and raining hard now. He failed to take note of the dead faces, a mistake he would pay for later. He and Jersey lay huddled in the nook of cadavers, a patent mackintosh pulled over their heads. The steady drum of rain against the material was a dirge they could have done without.

Ezra was soaked through and shivered uncontrollably at irregular intervals. In between, he caught the spill of rain in his mouth as it came through a hole. "Do you think we'll go to hell?" Ezra's ever weakening voice wavered with the question.

The major didn't immediately answer the question, wishing for the first time out there that he had a flint and steel or a lucifer to strike in the dark. He wanted to see Ezra's face just then, didn't feel comfortable with the question and thought if they could just see each other things might be different. "Why you ask such a thing?"

"Cause we're gonna die here."

"Don't give up on me, mister. Remember Liza,

NOT ONE AMONG THEM WHOLE

remember your boy."

"I can't do this no more. My leg feels like a stick of wood, my arms burn every time I move. I'm lying in my own stink and filth. And that damn rain, why won't it just stop?" He began to sob.

Jersey pulled Ezra closer. He was himself constantly nauseated now and his head swam in the darkness, as if he was foundering amidst a storm on the high seas. As he groped for means to sustain himself, he realized Little Tom was beside him, kneeling Indian style as had been his habit. Jersey looked hard at the boy, at the blue flannel shirt he was wearing under the coveralls. Long-sleeved because that's what he had been wearing that day—had it been three years already? He closed his eyes and counted the months since February, 1860. Three and a half years and still the worst kind of hurt imaginable. He had the idea that the worst part of the years since his son's disappearance was the silence, the incredible silence. If he could have just once heard his son's voice again—the way he rolled his r's or the small squeak in his laugh—everything would have been okay. And of course it would have been, because that would have meant Little Tom was still alive, still a growing boy with vital flesh and real needs. He was none of those things now, just an apparition conjured by his father at difficult moments. Jersey knew this, but this conjuring was all he had of his boy and so he kept on conjuring. It wasn't under his conscious control anyway. Not so far as he could tell.

He opened his eyes again and there the boy was. A grin from ear to ear. The boy was up close, as close as he had ever been, and he saw something he hadn't noticed before. Though pitch black under the mackintosh, Little Tom's neck stood out as if lit by the sun. Pressed into the skin of his small neck, now suddenly as plain as a red flag waving big on a bright, breezy day, were splotches of contused blue. Bruises they were, and an idea crashed through Jersey like a raging bull. The idea had eluded him for three and a half years—since the first moment he'd learned of his son's disappearance on that cold February afternoon—and suddenly everything he was or had ever been vanished. One moment he had shape and weight, and in the next instant gravity disappeared and he came apart like a bag of rags flung skyward. Another instant and his bones were suddenly made of lead, held down by the weight of just one word. Jersey put a hand to the boy's throat, saw his thumb covered half the indentations there. Not a perfect fit, but good enough. Then he saw how easily his hand—any hand—could slide around Little Tom's neck and he thought: *murder*.

Jersey felt Ezra's warmth against him. His eyes grew wide and his mouth gaped. He might have been about to say something, but before Jersey said anything he went rigid. His back arched hard. He began to shake, his arms and legs writhing back and forth in wide, vigorous sweeps that pulled the mackintosh aside and allowed the rain to pour in. His breath caught in his throat and nothing save guttural clicks escaped. The stain of urine at his crotch renewed itself and his eyes rolled up and back until he appeared pupilless.

***

Ezra was horrified. He shook his head back and forth in quick, panicked gestures, muttering "no, no," over and over. Anyone watching might have thought he too was having a seizure. He hugged Jersey close with all his might, as if he could impart some measure of his own remaining strength in doing so. Jersey's skin was cold and wet and dark blood dribbled out of his mouth after he bit his lower lip. "Oh God, not like this!" Ezra said, and the rain pelted

NOT ONE AMONG THEM WHOLE

him in the face, beating them both incessantly.

The fit seemed to go on unmercifully. When it finally stopped, Jersey relaxed in his arms and Ezra knew he was hugging a dead man. He couldn't bring himself to let the major go though, and so lay there holding him against his breast, using his elbows and forearms rather than his injured hands and wrists. A cramp finally made him let go, and when he did Jersey rolled back to rest against another corpse.

With Ezra's eyes long adjusted to the opaque darkness, the outline of Jersey's face was a faint wraith. The stilled curves of his lips had come to rest in a pout, as if to show their disappointment with him. And those eyes. Once or twice those eyes teased Ezra as they appeared to flicker—a mockery of life and nothing more he realized after the third time.

His mind broke and for a long time he sat without making a sound, the stillness around him pouring in like the rain. When at last he opened his mouth to scream, his tongue was dead in his throat and the resulting gasp was hardly worth the effort. He decided at that moment there was nothing left but to die himself, but try as he might he couldn't bring it about. He stared at the several corpses around him and found now he envied them. They stared back through ugly, soulless eyes, and he thought it a cruel thing to put a man through, showing him the object of his desire and not letting him have it. His fever was up again, and in it, he coveted death and felt cheated, wronged. As his brain baked, he slipped periodically into odd snippets of conversation with the late fellows.

"Come on now," he said, "Give it over to me and I'll be forever in your debt."

But it's the darndest thing, it ain't something we can just give over, one of the fellows was heard to say.

Another time, Ezra asked what death was like.

Oh, it's the peach, one of them answered, all jittery and excited-like. *Warm as your momma's belly and no joshing besides.*

And all the drink you want, that's true sure enough, another chimed in as Ezra ran his tongue over his lips, longing for the warm taste of whiskey.

"Is it warm being dead?"

Warm? Like a Joo-lie summer day in Ohio. That be warm enough for you?

"Oh God," he said. "I got to have me some of that."

Well, it's right here. The dead men smiled in unison, taunting him with their miserable teeth. *Right here for the taking.*

"How?"

You just stop breathing, that's how. Just stop breathing. It worked for us. You done see that.

"Yes, yes, I see," Ezra said, and he was excited. He sat up and tried to hold his breath.

Well, that ain't never gonna get you nowheres.

"What're you talking about?"

It ain't breath holding, it's no breathing at all.

"Well I can't do that!" Ezra had a mind to punch the fellow, but he lost his balance reaching for him. He fell over and found himself in the very lap of the dead man. "Christ. Get a grip." He somehow managed to pull himself back to a sitting position. "You dead sonsofbitches is starting to get on my nerves."

Hey, we didn't ask for this. Maybe we ain't so thrilled with the company either.

"Yeah, well, the least you could do for a guy is share. Didn't your mommas ever teach you about sharing?" He began to laugh hysterically. "Share share share share share."

What the hell's wrong with you? Stop your whining.

"Goddammit. That's easy for all of you to say, sitting

over there all comfy and dead."

You'd be the first person dead if I could oblige you.

"Dead dead dead dead dead," Ezra said, the laughter still going strong.

Dead dead dead dead dead.

He stopped rollicking back and forth and the expression on his face changed quickly and completely, as if he'd donned a mask in an instant. "Don't mock me! I may still be the wrong side of living, but I ain't crazy."

We ain't the ones what's talking to the dead.

"Hell," he said, "With any luck I'll be dead by nightfall."

You don't want that.

Ezra did a double take. The familiar voice took a moment to place. "Major Jersey? Sir, that you?"

"Ezra. Ezra wake up."

Ezra opened his eyes and the dead men around him were suddenly just that, dead men. Jersey lay beside him, but his position had changed somewhat. And he was shaking Ezra with one hand. Ezra's throat bobbed like he was swallowing an egg and his hand went to the harmonica in his breast pocket. He'd have given his last two bits to play it just then, but he had neither the two bits nor the breath. "Mine eyes have seen the glory," he said aloud.

"Little Tom," Jersey said in the next instant.

"How's that?" Ezra asked.

"My boy. I never told you his name. It's Little Tom."

"Major, don't die."

"I just wanted you to know my son's name is all."

FIFTEEN

D r. Boyd left the church and walked out into the darkness. He had an image in his mind of Spencer Hardy and a hundred other boys abandoned nearby. Perhaps in a bosky woods, perhaps an open field left fallow. He wasn't exactly sure what the place looked like. But he was sure it existed just as the ground he walked on existed, as the broken, exhausted men inside the church existed. Such a place always did. It held those poor souls he and the other surgeons had rejected, those too far gone to be operated, but not quite gone enough for burying. Boyd, like his colleagues, divided his patients into three groups. The walking wounded he patched and sent back to the lines; the more seriously wounded he operated on; the hopeless—the living dead—he sent to the woods.

Boyd's chest hurt. Exhaustion had long since escaped him. His second and even a third wind were days behind him. Ancient history. He tremored, played out like a cheap fiddle with three busted strings and the fourth frayed threadbare. He found an abandoned ambulance, crawled inside, and drank the last of his laudanum. The opium and alcohol left him giddy, and he felt as if the walls of the ambulance were expanding outward. The world around him began to spin. He closed his eyes, lost all orientation, and opened them again just short of vomiting. He reached out to either side of the stretcher to steady himself. The effect wasn't entirely unpleasant, certainly preferable to the hideous wails of those he'd cut this day and all the days before this one. His chest, which had been tight and painful all night, loosened somewhat. He finally closed his eyes and found a fitful rest.

At some point in the middle of the night, the exact time was lost since he had no timepiece, he found himself awake in the terrible darkness. He hated the night, always had, and wondered now what had awakened him. His chest still ached. He might as well be breathing molasses through a quill.

I'm kilt, I'm kilt, oh Gawd have mercy I'm kilt!

The words, coming as they did out of the dark, bellowed as if the woods themselves had spoken. The hollering was followed by a low moan and Boyd knew at once he'd seen the last of his sleep. "Damn," he said, and pulled himself to a sitting position. It took a moment to realize he was in his tent, and he wondered how he'd gotten there from the ambulance. His left arm ached and rubbing it only made it worse. He redoubled his efforts at breathing. The shakes were coming on and he cursed a string of profanities as he groped for his boots.

He was bent over with one boot on when he felt someone standing beside him. He saw the shoeless feet first, then ran his gaze up the intruder's body. All the while he found himself blinking and scrunching his eyes, as if trying to bring the shadow into focus. He couldn't quite do it, though, and a moment later the presence was gone. Boyd had neither seen nor heard him enter or leave. His presence remained an enigma.

I'm kilt, I'm kilt, oh Gawd have mercy I'm kilt!

The word Gawd, with its prolonged crescendo-decrescendo tone, gave the whole thing the sound of an incantation. The world toppled about Boyd, but he steadied himself and took a few tentative steps before finding his measure. Outside, a thin mist had descended on the makeshift hospital, making the grounds murky and unclear. Its tendrils crept lazily over the earth, enveloping the corpses and near corpses alike in a wispy veil of teased cotton. Boyd was disoriented by the cacophony coming alive around him. The haggard rants of the not quite departed and the wet breathing of those too long invalided and in the midst of their death rattle was as distinct as the hooting of barn owls, the chirping of frogs, and the whining of crickets in the swamp back home.

I'm kilt, I'm kilt, oh Gawd have mercy I'm kilt!

They were the worst words he'd ever heard. They echoed in the mist and so each utterance seemed to do double, or even triple duty. The surgeon found himself wishing to finish the job the man was so certain had already been done. In the thickening fog, he was uncertain as to which direction the lunatic voice came from. He turned first one way and then another, finally deciding upon a tack calculated to bring him upon the mad rants as quickly as possible.

He stepped out already tired. The mist gently parted and then rushed back on itself to fill the void as he moved. He'd never seen a fog move so fluidly, and he was reminded of water devouring all in its wake. Or blood pooling on the floor beneath his operating table. As quickly as it occurred to him, he put this last out of his head and groped his way forward.

He stumbled, then tripped and fell headlong to the dirt, which was foul and miasmic. The urge to vomit was close. He groped in the soil and found he'd tripped over an arm. He reached out, perhaps intending to discipline its owner, but as he pulled at it, it came away in his hand, cold and lifeless. "Amputated," he said. "Goddamn it." He tossed the useless limb aside.

About this time he heard a sound he was familiar with,

something from deep in his childhood perhaps, vague. He couldn't quite bring the memory forward. A wet, sucking noise and he was finally distracted from it by the litany again.

I'm kilt, I'm kilt, oh Gawd have mercy I'm kilt!

He struggled back to his feet, determined to find the bastard, to shut him up any way necessary. He felt the lack of opium again, and his entire body shook in disorganized, random waves. He felt himself going away, detaching. His innards boiled and he had need of a latrine ditch, but his bowels held for the moment. He began to drool like a rabid dog. He took two more steps and tripped again, this time over a leg. It, too, was alone and the extremity was moldy and black with fungus, but he recognized it for what it was. It gave off the strong, cheesy odor of rancid meat.

The place reeked of the dead. Boyd covered his lower face with his handkerchief and stood. His nose told him what had at first escaped his eyes. Lying before him, in several piles that collected into one horrific mass, were the disembodied limbs of hundreds of soldiers. As he gazed over this memorial of inhumanity, it seemed that every limb he'd ever amputated was there. Worse, he realized what the wet, sucking sounds were. Not sucking, he told himself, but smacking. And chewing. And ripping. A vision of his childhood flashed through his mind.

A vision of his family's hogs.

The hogs at feeding time.

And then, there they were. A dozen or more wild hogs feeding on the unburied, discarded limbs. The dead arms and legs were no better than fodder. The hogs snorted and rooted about, ripping the flesh bare to the bone, then crunching the bone as well.

I'm kilt, I'm kilt, oh Gawd have mercy I'm kilt!

Twisting back and forth in the cold wind, Boyd screamed. A terrible and agonizing noise, barely human.

He shook violently and his bowels let go. His breathing came in harsh, shallow gasps and he realized the devil's litany that had haunted him through the night

I'm kilt, I'm kilt, oh Gawd have mercy I'm kilt!

—was his own.

I'm kilt, I'm kilt, oh Gawd—

Josiah Boyd's eyes popped open and he stared at the roof of the ambulance. Gasping for air, he stumbled to the door and leaned out, vomiting in the muddy road. He held himself in that spot, shaking and drooling over the edge of the wagon, wishing more than anything else he would die. He didn't though, and an hour after he'd entered the ambulance, he stumbled out, feeling as if he'd come in from the woods.

As if he'd risen from the dead.

***

"You're crazy," Dr. Hardy said, looking out over the dim interior of the church. "You'll kill him. Besides, it won't make no difference. He's dead anyway you look on it. Can't you see I've accepted that?"

Boyd was tempted to point out that operating on a man who was going to die wouldn't do much harm, but he didn't. Truth was, he didn't see it that way. Ellis had been right when he'd said Boyd cared about what happened to the men passing under his knife. The level of futility in Boyd's universe was high, indeed had climbed another notch with each shattered frame laid before him. But here was one he just might be able to help, one who deserved the same consideration he'd given to all the other poor souls more shot up even than this. The symptoms of compression of the brain were obvious: stupor, stertorous breathing, slow pulse.

"I had this patient once," Boyd explained, "he got

himself thrown out a wagon, never mind how. He looked okay at first, then collapsed and died a day later. In between though, he was good, damn near normal according to his boss. Anyway, I didn't have anything better to do, so I posted him. I opened his head."

"He'd fractured his skull," Hardy said, as if a fact.

"No. See, that's the thing. There was no fracture, no broken bone at all. If there had been, I might would have operated when he first came to me. So after he was dead I used the trephine and managed to drill a hole big enough to look in. What I found was the same thing I would've found if there'd been a fracture though. A big clot of blood filling half his head. I thought then and still think now that what killed that fellow was not the blow to his head—hell, he was awake and good for a time after that. What did him in was that lump of blood pushing where it ought not 'a been."

"You ever trephined a man still this side of the grave?" Hardy said, voice between ridicule and contempt.

"No."

"Well, I have," Hardy said. "And I'm telling you it can't be done without killing him. Christ, man, he's my son. And they shot him in the head."

Boyd saw it was pointless to argue. Hardy was beleaguered, used up, clearly physically ill. He'd lost his son already in his mind. Maybe he couldn't take the idea of losing him again. Then came the thought that Hardy was too proud to admit he'd been wrong in putting his son aside in the first place. What a hard thing that must be, Boyd thought. "You go get some rest, Sol."

"What you gonna do?" Hardy asked.

"What I have to. What you'd do."

Hardy closed his eyes, said nothing aloud but his lips moved. A moment later, he leaned over and kissed his son's cheek, then took a few awkward steps backward.

"Good luck, Josiah."

The older surgeon turned and descended the altar steps. He was shaking hard and collapsed before making it out of the church. He had to piss, he said, could somebody bring him a bucket?

Not much later, a steward showed the bucket to Boyd before emptying it. An inch of blood covered the bottom.

***

They took Spencer Hardy outside and laid him face-up on a table, under a rain-swept awning. Boyd wanted to be outside where the night was finally giving way to morning. He wanted the light to see by. Spencer had a baby's fuzz on his chin and wore Union blue trousers with a thin yellow stripe along the outer seam. His dingy gray undershirt had specks of blood down the front. Boyd noted the young man's breathing had grown irregular, first a few quick and shallow gasps, then several deep breaths, then the gasps again. He laid a hand on his wrist, felt the pulse; slow and weak it was and the surgeon thought: *whatever that indicates, it ain't good.* For him this was uncharted territory. A head injury was a thing best avoided from a surgeon's perspective. Cutting offered little to gain and much to lose. Hardy's words rang in his head.

You ever trephined a man still this side of the grave?
I'm telling you it can't be done without killing him.

The skull itself was a rigid and unyielding box, with little or no way to know what was going on inside it. It didn't tense up like an abdomen gone bad, or cough up cruddy phlegm like a consumptive's lung. Any physician worth his salt could diagnose a stoned kidney from the sharp flank pains and bloody water it produced; could acknowledge a failing heart by the way the blood backed up to congest the liver and swell the legs. But the interior of the skull was a no man's land, a void as mysterious as the sky was blue. All but unreachable and therefore unknowable. Its domain had seldom been entered, and then only at its barest fringes and under the most extreme of circumstances.

But, as Boyd understood it, here was such a circumstance, tailor made for his intervention. The patient's life signs were burning down like one of the candles dotting the inside of the church, moving toward what could only be one endpoint.

Do nothing, and this boy would surely die.

Hardy again: *Christ man, he's my son. And they shot him in the head.*

Do something, and he'll probably die anyway. They had a place for such, a woods where they deposited hopeless cases like extra baggage nobody had room for. But hundreds of youngsters had crossed his table and at least some were alive because he'd intervened where he knew little enough, only slightly more than most.

That's how it was, he decided. Those who knew helped those they could.

He cursed Hardy and thought of Thomas Ellerby, the soldier he'd met at the start of this damned war. He actually had met him, not just found him. The two had actually conversed. *I's Thomas Ellerby. My folks has...a plot for me up...up on Sumter Ridge, South Carolina.* How the hell could he have done that? *I's Thomas Ellerby. I gots half my head blown to the wind...* How the hell do you talk with a plum size hole in your forehead? It had spooked Boyd then and it spooked him now.

The surgeon tensed, felt the squeeze of his stomach up under his ribs again. He could still taste the bitterness of the laudanum on his tongue—like black bile it was—and cursed himself for having taken a medical education. He hated he knew enough to help some and not others, hated his hands for the way they wielded a blade. For a thin moment, he even hated his patients, hated Spencer Hardy most of all.

"Major, you ready?" Ellis asked, leaning toward him.

He thought *no,* wanted to say no in the worst way, but somehow it came out the way it always did. He pinched a wad of tobacco and pushed it into the pouch of his cheek, bulging it pregnant. He put a hand before his face as if checking the wind, saw only a slight tremor. He'd had worse.

Boyd felt certain a clot of blood was pushing on the young soldier's brain. But where exactly?

As he stared down into Spencer's youthful face, it suddenly occurred to him he had no idea what he was doing, where to drill. And if he drilled in the wrong spot, what then? Should he try again? And again? How many holes should he put in Spencer Hardy's skull?

Standing in the dawn, the gathering light had never seemed so dark.

Boyd wanted to vomit.

SIXTEEN

The Sabbath morning broke cold and wet over the churchyard.

Liza Coffin, on the very margin of that unholy place, opened her eyes to the sound of rain pattering the trees. The rain stopped a moment later, and it was the cessation of the pattering as much as anything that had aroused her. The varied smells and noise of the encampment had taken her off guard. She had wandered on the camp in the night and for a moment she forgot where she was. The lapse lasted only a moment though, and the horror returned to her soon enough. She sat up and with that the baby in her arms took on weight and Liza pulled him to her bosom.

She'd fallen asleep against a stone wall, not comfortable but she had been exhausted. This was just outside the cemetery and the little Lutheran Church. The baby boy, his name was Samuel, she'd held close against her bosom all the long night and for two days before, while hiding in her root cellar. Now her cheek was crisscrossed with lines of twigs and sand from the wall and she and the baby both were chilled and wet. Hungry too. Liza looked at his face and saw how it was pitted with tiny black marks. *Vermin,* she thought, *fleas or ants maybe.* She scratched at her own side, saw the ants moving up and down the stonewall.

Samuel remained still and she wiped at the ants crawling

across his stomach. She unwrapped the shirt that did for a diaper and, seeing he had produced nothing, closed it up again. These things she did calmly and with little emotion. She jiggled him a little and his head lolled side to side. She said, "I ain't got none for ya," but put him to one of her teats anyway. He didn't glomp on to her immediately and so she opened his little mouth and in went the nipple.

The rebels had occupied the roads around her place in heavy numbers until the day before. They'd pulled out in the afternoon just passed, though they'd left the worst of the lot behind. She'd seen those wounded men by the dozens as she walked through the night, the ones too damaged to have any chance at all of surviving the wagon ride home. Her own home was now a ruin and her only family the baby. Maybe the baby's pa too, though she was far from certain he was still living. Ezra Coffin was a soldier and not much for letter writing. His last letter had arrived eight weeks before and in it he'd said how they were about to go into battle against 'Uncle Bobby,' which she took to mean the rebel general Robert Lee. A huge battle had been fought at Chancellorsville about that time, and a lot of men had died. She had heard nothing of him since.

She wasn't eighteen, she thought, and already she'd been a homeless orphan, then a mother. Now maybe a widow too.

She'd not known the hospital was here, had more or less stumbled upon it. Samuel was an eating machine and she had no idea how she was going to look out for him. The world was an upside down place just now, but she figured a hospital was as good a place as any to beg a few scraps. She doubted they'd turn away a homeless mama with a baby to feed.

She'd lost everything to this goddamn war. Wasn't it about time she started getting something back?

***

The wind howled around them, but the rain stopped abruptly. Boyd looked up from the soldier on the table, toward the cloudy sky. He didn't pray though, knowing beyond any doubt that God had long ago abandoned him. He was not a prayerful man.

He could have been the last physician in a land besieged by plague.

He spat tobacco gruel and tried to concentrate on the problem at hand. From the corner of his eye, he noted Tobias Ellis watching him. The assistant surgeon stood directly opposite, waiting to take his cues. To Ellis's left was a skeletally thin negro stretcher bearer named Abel. Abel's job was to hold a lantern, to fan Boyd, to hold an umbrella, whatever might be needed. Tiny, Boyd's long-time assistant, stood at the head prepared to administer the chloroform whenever the word was given.

The right side of Spencer's head was discolored the blue of days-old bruised skin. Boyd smoothed the blond hair back and saw the small hole where the bullet had pierced him. Another hole just behind and above the ear where it had exited. "Guess that's as good a place as any to cut," he said with a lack of enthusiasm. "Sleep 'im."

Tiny let go a few drops of chloroform into the mask and Spencer's heel stopped moving. The lack of movement was eerie, like he was dead. But he was only playing at dead, for every now and again he swallowed or suffered a slight cough. Boyd waited what he thought was a full minute, probably longer, as he was in no hurry to get this thing started. Once started, however, he would be most certainly in a hurry to get it ended.

"Give me a knife."

Tiny wiped the blade on his apron and slapped it hard

into the surgeon's outstretched palm.

Boyd sucked hard at the wad in his cheek, putting the cold edge of the steel against Spencer's temple. He ignored the hair and pressed the blade into the skin, cutting not quite to the bone, and dragged it upward over a distance of two inches. He made a second incision at right angles to the first, the effect of which was to fashion an 'X.' The incisions were half in, half out of the hairline so that if Spencer survived, the marks would be forever obvious to all.

The skin parted and a brisk stream of bright blood jetted out, as if proof of life. The stream pulsed twice more in quick succession, each time striking Assistant Surgeon Ellis in the belly. Ellis was quick to act, though, knew the import of blood after more than a year of watching it spill. He put a stubby finger over the artery and halted the flow. "Ligature," he said, and tied off the exposed ends of the temporal artery and vein with lengths of silk thread Tiny handed him. Done smartly, Boyd was impressed with the assistant surgeon's hands.

Boyd deepened the cut through the muscle over the side of Spencer's head, running the knife over the same path as before, this time sinking the knife all the way to the skull. The wound filled to overflowing with the dark red of venous blood. "Retractors." Ellis continuously swabbed the wound with a lint sponge, but the effort did little good until Boyd inserted a couple of curved metal tongs under the skin on each side of the X-shaped incision. "Here," Boyd said, indicating Ellis should take control of them. The assistant surgeon tugged them apart from each other, opening the wound as wide as the split skin allowed. Boyd wiped again at the blood, then leaned back to spit and wiped his hand across his forehead.

"Hold that lantern up now."

"Yassah," Abel said and came around the table to a spot

NOT ONE AMONG THEM WHOLE

behind Boyd. The long shadows of morning leaned lazily against the exterior of the church. The spot was the same a priest had given last rites a few days before, though not a man here had been present for that solemn observance. Once or twice the white skull chanced into a fleeting view, but for the most part Boyd worked blindly, by feel. "Elevator." The instrument was six inches long and resembled the gnawed clean bone of a chicken leg the way it flared at one end. The other tip was flat and blunt and he scraped this back and forth against the hard skull, detaching whatever muscle was there and confirming the need for the trephine. Dark blood and gray matter slowly percolated up through the hole in the skull. All the while a steady stream of blood oozed from the skin edges, enough to be a nuisance but not so much the man would bleed out. Ellis pulled the skin edges taut with the retractors and the bleeding slowed to a trickle.

Boyd pushed a naked finger against the skull and felt around, rolling the digit under the skin and making a small pocket. He tried not to think too much about what he was doing, hoping only that he was making a difference.

"Trephine." Three minutes had passed since the incision. Boyd was exhausted.

Tiny passed the T shaped trephine to the surgeon. It had an ebony cross bar handle and a metal shaft that ended in a hollow conical drill with a flange of teeth. The whole thing was built compactly, no more than five inches long, and was solid, so that one could put his weight behind the turning of it; a human skull is hard, not meant to be penetrated. He gripped the handle in his palm, the shaft between middle and ring fingers.

He knew the drilling would require muscle and backbone, though he was hesitant, having never done this before—at least not in a living person where the drill could potentially plunge brainward. He thought for a moment about that word. *Brainward.* Like rightward or leftward, though it didn't seem a direction one wanted to test that often. But he was committed now, and so he leaned over the open head and pressed the teeth of the drill against the bone. He tested the unyielding nature of it, gaining confidence, then simultaneously pushed down and turned the handle the way one might work a stuck door latch. The teeth bit the bone and stopped. He tried a second time using more force. The teeth moved slightly, then popped out of the skull and skittered across Spencer's forehead, leaving a pattern of tiny bleeding nicks.

Hardy's words haunted him: *You ever trephined a man still this side of the grave?*

He hadn't pressed hard enough, that's all. He replaced the thing and turned the drill, learning the art and work of it. It sank deeper into the bone and Hardy was at him again: *I'm telling you it can't be done without killing him.*

He ignored the thought and pressed forward. The work was tedious and the minutes passed like days. At one point Spencer stirred and Tiny poured a few more drops of chloroform into the mask. Ellis too strained, holding the retractors and the head both. The assistant surgeon swallowed at the sight of the drill poking out of the head but didn't falter when the thing skittered.

Boyd turned the drill in small jerks, a quarter arc at a time. Simple brute force, with no way to build momentum. Despite the cool morning, sweat dripped from the tip of his nose. After every few turns, he leaned over and spat, sometimes on the floor and sometimes on the trouser leg of the man beside him.

From the post-mortem trephination he'd done and the several skull fractures he'd seen, Boyd recollected the skull to be about a quarter-inch thick. But a quarter-inch came and went and the drill was still anchored in firm bone. Several times he took the trephine out and tapped the cut skull with a mallet and chisel. Finally, on the fourth such occasion, it gave slightly. He tapped again and the bone popped free and floated up, a clot of blood welling up with it.

Ellis grinned at Boyd, still holding the retractors in place. "Hot damn."

The blood was thick and almost black. Several large chunks pushed out and slid down the side of Spencer's head. Boyd pushed his little finger into the hole and twirled it, feeling the inside of the smooth skull and dislodging several additional pieces of clot. There didn't look to be any fresh bleeding, though, and after a few minutes he considered how to put paid to this thing. He decided not to put the bone back in place, there being no good way to secure it. In the case of a fracture the bone would simply be discarded and he saw no reason to deviate from that. Ellis removed the retractors, and Boyd proceeded to stitch the skin with a needle and silk thread. The entire operation had taken just under thirty minutes. When done, the right side of Spencer's head was dimpled where the bone was missing. They wrapped his head with a length of muslin and waited for the chloroform to wear off.

Boyd spat in the dirt again and stepped back. He picked up the trephine, stared at it a moment or two, then set it back down. Leaning against a wall, he closed his eyes and slept standing up for several minutes.

Another half hour passed before Spencer Hardy began to come out of his stupor. As he did so, he crossed his legs and reached up to grab his head. This was more movement than he'd done in a day and those present glanced at each other and perhaps even smiled.

Boyd at least was satisfied. He slumped to the bloody grass, and slept.

***

In the morning light, Ezra saw the field that held him captive as if for the first time. A rock strewn slope of festering bodies, on the extreme edge of a large grassy knoll. Overnight the wind had died down and the morning air bore the proof of death.

Everything was wet through and the cold permeated him like water through a sponge. The bodies he had piled as a break against the weather—the same ones he'd conversed with in his fever the night before—had swelled in the night and he was thankful he didn't have to look into their faces now. He stirred and every fiber of his body gave up a frenzied wailing, terrible in its implications. He felt himself an open sore, a malignant stew of sickness. A dark realization then: *I'm dying by parts.*

He pictured the grim reaper coming to get him, a slow, teasing creature that refused the whole of him. It wanted only a piece now, an arm or perhaps a leg. In an hour or a day it would return for his skin maybe, or possibly a lung. Only when he was totally parted out—rendered a thin figment of wasted flesh, a mere illusion of life—would it take the thudding muscle in his chest and end his suffering.

He felt a pang of regret he hadn't loved Liza better; he'd wrapped his legs around a common whore not long after his bout with fever. The sad image of Liza's face as she read the letter informing her of his death was more than he could bear. He pictured her in mourning and his son growing up without him. He pawed at her tintype, which was still in his breast pocket. He didn't have the strength or dexterity to remove it.

He wished he'd written her more often.

Tom Jersey lay beside Ezra, his breathing heavy and loud. Ezra welcomed it. He took hold of the major's hand, which was hot and dry. He thought back on all the fevered men he'd seen during his stay in the hospital, tried to think what made the difference in those who lived and those who died. His mind wasn't up to it, though. He couldn't get it to recall the men that way. It seemed they'd all died. He was sure that wasn't true, but he couldn't remember the face of a single one he was sure had lived.

A breeze came up and he propped his head on one of the dead. A black spot blowed across the grass. The mackintosh. Some distance beyond it another moved, then several others as well. He fought to focus and as his vision resolved to something useful, he saw them take the form of animals. The wild hogs were back. They were far enough away he couldn't hear them grunting and for this kindness he was grateful. To his eyes the scene was still, and he was curious about how little emotion it held. He flashed on the image of the reaper again, then passed it by with a nod. Overhead, a sea of gray clouds moved across the vista and he knew the rain wasn't done with him yet. He thought once again about dying, how it must be warm in the ground. Will the army or the hogs find my body first? What will Liza think if I just go missing, if I'm never found?

He thought about his son.

Jersey stirred beside him. The rebel's color didn't look good. He squeezed his hand the little he could and Jersey opened his eyes.

"Morning," the major said. His lips were dry and cracked.

"Morning," Ezra said.

"We're still on this damn field."

"Yes sir, I guess so. Could be worse though."

"How's that?"

"My son could be here."

Jersey nodded. It seemed he understood exactly.

***

Dr. Boyd crawled over the canvas floor, trying desperately to sop up the laudanum he'd spilled. He was wearing his blue government issue trousers (they were unbuttoned at the crotch and his suspenders had been removed, he had no idea why or by whom), a badly sweat-stained undershirt, and the socks he'd put on a week before. He had not a clue where he was or how he'd gotten there, only that his mind was racing faster than a runaway locomotive and his head felt as if that same train had run over it. The ambient noise reverberated a hundred times over in his ears and his skin crawled with static charge— everywhere he touched seemed to leap out and touch him back.

He took off his undershirt and sopped the spilled liquid with it. His actions were desperate and disturbed, more those of a mad man than a surgeon in the US Army. He was agitated, severely so, like a cheap drunk hoarding the last of his liquor. He looked the part too. A sheen of sweat wrapped him in a wet blanket and his jaw tremored hard enough to make his teeth chatter. A coarse, week-old stubble roughened his jaw line. He looked like an escaped asylum patient with the shaking palsy.

It dawned on him the place was familiar, even very familiar. His vantage point on the ground was strange, though, not a view he'd generally appreciated. The items around him seemed distorted, like in a house of mirrors. The cot was low to the ground, beside it an off kilter table towering as high as the cot was low. It held one of those traveling lap desks and the burr chestnut case was open, exposing the rich blue velvet of the writing tablet. He somehow knew the velvet was embossed with gold on its periphery and that a small plaque engraved with the name *Parkins and Gotto* was screwed to the outside of the box. He thought, there will be another plaque as well: *Made especially for Josiah Boyd, MD.*

He stopped his frantic sopping motions and lay against the cot. *My cot. My tent. I share it with Sol. His cot's just there.*

He hesitated. *Where's Sol?* It occurred to him a war was on, that they were smack in the middle of it.

I'm a surgeon.

Christ almighty.

He bit the cloth of his undershirt, sucking at the remnants of laudanum, the copper taste of blood rising fresh in his mouth. It came back now. All of it, whether he wanted or not.

Yes, a surgeon.

Oh God, a surgeon at war.

The wounded. Patients.

Jesus Christ, the patients.

Mother of God, the patients.

My name is Thomas Ellerby and how the hell can you talk Thomas? How in tarnation can you talk with a plum size hole upside your head?

He didn't want to remember, but there seemed no choice.

He said no chloroform. Goddammit, he said no and I cut and may God have mercy on both our souls... If it even looks like you're sawing his leg off, I'll blow your brains all over that cross... I'm kilt, I'm kilt, oh Gawd, I'm kilt. Somebody! This'll hurt like hellfire... Somebody tell me where to cut... I don't know where to cut. Jesus Christ and Mother Mary, I don't know where to cut...

Boyd began to shiver. The tent, which was not cold, had become the coldest, most remote place on the face of the earth.

***

"Lady, I'd like to help you, I really would. But I can't.

Plain and simple. There's thousands of casualties here. I can't just be giving away supplies to every person what comes this way. Baby or no."

"Nothing you can do?" Liza asked. "Ain't even got a little napkin for the baby?"

The man threw his hands up and shrugged. "I'm sure I'm not the women's commission," he said, then, looking taken aback, added, "Something wrong with that baby?"

She ignored him. *Such a good baby. And so quiet.* "Well, what exactly do you do around here?"

He pointed to the sign on the tent behind him. *Sanitary Commission.* He looked at her, at the thing in her arms, pulled at the neat bow tie crowding his neck. "We see the troops are cared for best they can be, present conditions— you sure there ain't nothing wrong with that kid?."

"I'm sure." She smiled coquettishly. "I bet you real good at your job too. Ain't I right?" She took his hand. "Whyn't we go into that there tent o' yours."

He pulled his hand away. "I'll give you some linen, for the baby of course. But that's it. And I don't want whatever else it might be you're offering."

"I don't know what you're talking 'bout."

"Yeah, sure. Keep it that way." He ducked inside, pulling the door closed so she wouldn't follow, and reappeared a moment later with a blanket. The words US Army were stenciled across each corner.

"Much obliged," she said, taking the blanket and covering Samuel. "He don't like how it's bright out here."

"Course not. He don't look too good, you know."

"He got the sunburn, that's all. On account of won't nobody give me nothing for him. What you expect?"

"That didn't look like no sunburn I ever saw, lady. That boy's sick if'n you ask me. You best get him over to the docs. I'm not saying they'll have time for you, but I was you..."

"You ain't me. Sam is fine. He's a good baby. Just a little quiet now. Resting. We've had the devil's own day, mister."

He looked at her, uttered something under his breath.

"Could you be kind enough to tell me which way I might go to find something for me and the baby to eat?"

"Lady, you know where you are?" he asked. "What kinda place this is and all?"

"That's a obvious question."

"Then you must know that for the likes of a little woman like yourself, baby or no, the pickin's gonna be mighty thin. There's lots of folks what haven't eaten, some going on three days now I expect. You'll be in line behind them. And don't think they'll be the least interested in your charms."

"You ain't gotta say all that. Samuel and I, we ain't ones for charity. I can read some, write too. I can provide for our keep."

"Uh huh." Another muttering.

"We'll just be moving on then. Thank you kindly for the blanket."

"I got some fruit," he said. "I could spare a couple of oranges and maybe an apple might do for the baby. Can't help no more than that."

"Thank you kindly."

"'Cept to say you might try the hospital proper. Times like this, they need all the help what they can get. They won't favor the baby, mind you, but you tell 'em you're looking for the boy's father. You did say he was a soldier, right? Make up how he's missing and you think he might be among the wounded. Seems like maybe you the type to make that work. And make yourself useful somehow."

***

Liza tore a part of the blanket into a smaller cloth to swaddle Samuel in and the words covered his backside. The rest she tore into strips and from these she fashioned a tolerable sling with which to carry him across her front. She even made a little bonnet sort of thing to protect him from the sun. It also managed to obscure him from the eyes of others, though that was not her intention.

She crossed the grounds, poking her head in various tents randomly, seeing whatever there was, seeing everything and nothing at the same time. She hung around one of the cook tents in the late morning and talked a loaf of bread out of one of the bakers after she winked at him. Later, she walked past the back of the Lutheran Church. A hive of activity and the sorry sight of the sick and invalided in its yard made her turn away. She'd crossed that same ground—that cemetery—a dozen times in her life, but it was a strange and tainted place now.

Sometime after midday, she came to a long row of tents, a few wagons mixed in besides. Someone had sunk a signpost into the mud. The words Undertaker's Row were scrawled in coarse, uneven letters that she took several minutes sounding out. Beyond it, a half dozen folks were busy in the alleyway, others moving in and out of the tents. The ground was a mud slop field slewed with puddles at irregular intervals. An old man with a green bowler hat on his balding head was working over a body in the lee of a tent awning a stone's throw down the road. A row of covered dead, a dozen and more, lay in the mud to one side of it all.

The close smell of the place nearly knocked her over.

Fifty yards or so up the road from Liza, in the direction opposite the row, a negro boy of ten or twelve was tending a fire. He was a nappy-headed youngster, thin-framed but muscular looking nonetheless. He was barefoot and wasn't wearing a shirt. His trousers looked a size small. He appeared busy roasting something, potatoes maybe. It made her mouth water.

"Whatcha doing?" she asked, flinging her head around, and with it her flaming red hair.

Cuuda looked up from his position opposite her, the fire between them. He didn't say anything, motioned with a slight dip of his head toward the potatoes and what looked like some sort of rodent on a spit. Two rodents actually. Still kneeling, he of a sudden put his arm out and a monkey thing came running from the bushes and up onto his shoulder. He rose.

"What the hell's that?" she asked.

Cuuda held Archimedes's tail in his hand. He stared at her but didn't speak.

"You one of them niggers what can't talk?"

"I c'n talk good as you, when I got something to say."

Archimedes screeched.

"That some kinda monkey?"

"That some kinda baby?"

"His name's Samuel. You wanna see?"

"I seen babies afore."

"Not this here one."

"Sumpin special 'bout that one?"

"Special to me," Liza said.

"All babies is special to dey ma." Cuuda bent to turn the potatoes.

"You got any more of those?"

"Why?"

The man in the green hat came up to the both of them then. He was old, thin as a twig, and wore dark trousers and a stained undershirt. As she waited, he retrieved a white, long-sleeved shirt and buttoned it fully to his neck despite the humid rain. Dark sweat stains already marred the armpits. He coughed several times in the process.

"Howdy," he said, after making himself presentable.

"Afternoon," Liza said. She startled at a bang, a coffin lid slamming somewhere, and squeezed Sam.

The man wiped his brow with a kerchief. "Never mind that, missus, you get used to it. You come claiming a body? Loved one maybe?" He bared a broad smile. "Cuuda, put a extra potato on that fire. I got me a appetite today."

"No," Liza said. "But I'd be obliged for a potato."

"Well, perhaps you want us to find somebody then? A brother on the battlefield perhaps? I'm awful sorry if'n that's the case." He took his kerchief to cover his mouth as he coughed. "Awful sorry."

She observed a tinge of blood on the kerchief. "No, no that's not it at all. You injured?"

"Come to say a few words over someone then?"

"No, can't say that either." She eyed him from across the fire.

"I see." The old man turned and spoke to the boy. "I could use me some Oil."

Cuuda put the monkey down and made a curious hand signal and the creature ran off down the road toward the wagon.

"I, uh, I'm looking for my husband," Liza said as she watched the monkey scurry away.

"Well, I am sorry for your loss," Jupiter said, and pointed to the covered bodies laying beyond the road. "Cuuda will—"

"No, no. My husband ain't dead. Lest not so far as I know. He's a private in the Union Army. Name of Ezra. Ezra Coffin."

"Coffin you say?"

"Yeah," she said.

"Good name," Jupiter said.

"I believe he's wounded."

The undertaker looked at her, not appearing to know how to take this bit of information. "Oh," he said, clenching his teeth together. "How long on them potatoes, boy?"

"Dey be done directly," Cuuda said.

"I got a son needs his pa." She began to unwrap the boy from his linens. "He's hungry."

"That baby's not gonna eat. Besides, this ain't no kinda place for a baby."

She stopped in her efforts at unwrapping him and rearranged him in the sling across her front. "He a pretty thing," she said. "Quiet too."

"I don't do babies," Jupiter said, then "Miss, you got a name?"

"Liza. Liza Coffin. My husband is Ezra. Our son's Samuel."

"My name's Jupiter Jones, Liza. You know my work?"

"You're an undertaker."

"That's right. You must know I don't get much call to search out the living. Don't believe I can help you with that." Archimedes came back just then, bringing with him a bottle. Jupiter uncorked it and turned it up to his lips. He recorked it and set it down on a log beside the fire. "As for your baby there, well, I don't do babies."

Liza watched him drink, smelled the alcohol. "You don't mind if'n I have a sip do ya?"

Jupiter wiped his mouth on his forearm. "I ain't exactly partial to drinking with a woman."

"Oh," she said, and put her head down. A moment later, when she looked up, she appeared to be crying.

"Jesus K. Reist, woman."

"It's just that...with all what's going on...we ain't hardly had nothing...I'm just trying to get on, me and the baby, is all." The tears continued the whole time.

Jupiter said, "I ain't one—"

"How long since you et?" Cuuda interrupted.

"We had us some little bit of stew night before last," she

lied. She wiped her runny nose on her sleeve.

She saw Cuuda look at the old man, saw something unsaid pass between them, saw the old man shaking his head no.

"Got a extra potato I guess," Cuuda said. "Some squirrel too, you want that. Kinda stringy I suppose, but it'll fill your belly all the same."

"We'd be much obliged."

"Your baby though, he won't be eating," Jupiter said.

"How do you mean?"

"I mean your baby ain't just sleeping."

Liza said, or some part of her that hadn't spoken up till now, "I know."

Then she fainted.

***

Ezra shivered. It had begun raining again. He sucked from a dribble coming off the blouse of one of the dead men in the walls of his tomb. Jersey lay beside him and every few seconds, the sound of another gasp was some comfort.

He watched as a cricket crawled down his sleeve. When it got to his hand, the thing turned and began to traverse his palm. With the peculiar strength that only comes of sheer exhaustion, Ezra closed his fingers over the bug. He lifted his hand to his mouth, and dropped it between his lips. He chewed dispassionately, making no judgment upon the taste or the crunch.

It began to grow dark and he figured he would be dead before the sun rose again. He could think of nothing worse than waking alone in this place. He hoped Jersey would go first, but the thought of that breathing silenced was almost too much to stand. The major's breathing, such as it was, anchored him to life. He didn't know what he'd do if Jersey stopped breathing for good.

That was rich. Of course he knew what he'd do. He'd die, that was all, just die. In truth, he supposed, he'd die either way. He wondered where the major's revolver was, then discounted the thought. Not because he couldn't shoot himself, but he couldn't shoot them both.

There'd be too much shame in his own suicide, like running in battle. He'd have to take the major with him if that were the case, and he couldn't do that. He'd sooner shoot his own brother.

That, of course, was the fever talking.

Still, where was the weapon? It had to be nearby. He closed his eyes, tried to remember. He imagined the major shooting the scavenger man, the scavenger man falling beside him, and the exhausted major himself falling back in relief. Where would the gun have gone? He would have dropped it Ezra decided. So was the major right or left handed? Ezra closed his eyes, pictured the major there beside him those several days. The man had used his right hand in preference. The revolver had to be to the major's right.

Jersey lay to Ezra's immediate right, his head against Ezra's shoulder and breast. To get to Jersey's right side, he would have to either sit him up or roll over him. Neither seemed possible.

And yet, slowly, he inched Jersey off of him. The major groaned, a pitiful noise. He propped his right shoulder and arm over Jersey's left, making him high enough to swing his arm around to the ground on Jersey's right. That he could do this was almost a miracle in itself, and his muscles screamed every inch of the way. He couldn't see what lay on Jersey's right though, and his own right hand was nearly useless. Swollen to twice normal size with the bullet hole through it, no feeling, and barely a grip. Nothing more than a piece of wood.

And then an idea.

Removing Tim Jewel's harmonica from his breast pocket was the easy part. Gripping it well in his damaged hand required a good deal of effort. Once he was sure he could hold it tightly, he leaned over and extended his arm as far as he could. He flexed his wrist stiffly, depressing the harmonica into the grass. He extended his wrist, bringing the harmonica up again. He moved his arm an inch or so, repeated the process. Slow, grueling work, and every minute made him pay, but he made himself think of the goal rather than the work. He stopped frequently to regroup, once or twice to reset the harmonica in his clubbed hand. Finally, at the very limits of his reach and endurance, he brought the harmonica down and was rewarded with the hollow clink of it hitting something other than grass.

He fell back exhausted.

The light had faded to shadows and a misty rain dampened the air. Jersey still breathed—thanks be to God—but he had no awareness. In a flash of wit he could have done without, it occurred to Ezra what he'd found could easily be a rock. He tried to think of an easier way to do things. Nothing came to mind. Well, he finally decided, if it be a rock, so be it. He had nothing but hope left, and he was short on that.

It had to be the revolver. But how could he get it?

He concentrated everything on that spot and stuck his arm out again. He tapped the object with the harmonica. Again the clink. He put the mouth organ back in his pocket and pushed himself another inch up on Jersey's chest.

Jersey's heart beat a frenzied drum inside that chest. Ezra coughed, and pain splayed through his body as if his bones were a highway for agony. He spat, gritted his teeth, and inched further over, all but willing his arm to grow an eighth of an inch, then a quarter. The butt of the weapon came into view—the revolver. Ivory handled he saw.

Teasingly close. He reached, but was a palm's width away. He sighed, cursed, gritted his teeth again, and wiggled his ass best he could over the major's torso. The cold butt of the gun teased his fingertips. A final inch of stretch and something popped in his neck. His arm came alive, burning with fire along its whole length. He slumped back again.

Ezra tried to get back up but couldn't do it. His arm stung shoulder to hand, like he'd been chopped in the collar. Every time he moved, the pain surged and made him grimace like a man with a tic. His fingers grew numb over the minutes. The clouds rolled by overhead, obscuring the stars and dropping rain. He held still and listened to the night approaching, the wind howling. He noticed how the dead around him had turned green after four days and the thought twisted his gut queasy.

He couldn't stand another moment on that field, had to have the gun.

Jersey's arm jerked and Ezra startled. He shook the major, but the only response was a gurgle. He grabbed the man's arm, found that it moved easily. With care, he stretched the arm open at the shoulder and extended the elbow. Ezra got excited when the fingers passed over the gun, and stopped breathing when he hooked the trigger on Jersey's thumb. Slowly, he bent Jersey's elbow and the gun rose out of the grass.

A moment later, it was his.

A litany of emotions. Pain was at the forefront, followed by loathing for what he'd been reduced to. He hated himself, the war, even Tom Jersey. He realized in that instant that he could kill him, could kill them both.

He gripped the revolver and rolled off the major. There, in the late dusk, he determined to get it over with, to finish what the damn war had not. He would shoot Jersey first, in the head to make it quick and painless. Then himself the same way. He held the revolver and spun the cylinder—and the air suddenly went out of him.

In the growing darkness, he could just make out the chambers, saw there were six of them. Five had been fired.

He had one shot left.

One ball between the two of them.

***

"Ah shit," Jupiter said.

When the girl, she'd said her name was Liza, fainted, the baby rolled out and his head struck the ground with a thud. Jupiter stood looking down on the pair of them, wondering what the hell he'd done to warrant this kind of torture. He wasn't partial to women or babies and here was both in one not so neat little package. *Jesus K. Reist.*

Of course, there was one bonus. The baby was dead. He'd said he didn't do babies, and he'd meant it. You couldn't talk to babies the way you could talk to normal folk. Didn't make no sense. All that babbling and cooing. Listening to that was apt to drive a person bat shit, no matter what side of the grave it came from. And if all that verbal diarrhea meant anything before death, it meant even less once the shroud dropped. How the hell could he tell he was doing what the person wanted if he couldn't talk to them—or they to him?

Thing was...the more he looked at that poor sonbitch baby laying in the mud, well, the more he thought the situation...interesting.

She didn't know her baby was dead. That was plain enough. Shock? Probably. Who knew what she'd been through these past few days. The devil's own playground? Maybe. Whatever, it had likely been enough to bend her mind—maybe even break it. War could do that. Oh yeah, that and more. He was almost a goddamn expert on that subject.

I don't do babies. He had said that of course. But maybe...

There was a dent in the kid's head where it had struck the ground. Right in the middle of his—Jesus K. Reist—forehead. Jupiter wondered what he could do with that dent, how he could fix it all lifelike so folks wouldn't even know it was there. So his mother wouldn't even know it was there. That'd be a job. And done well, it'd be more than just tolerable, it'd be an honest-to-Jesus miracle.

He could take the baby over to his tent and have him back before his ma—Liza, he told himself again—knew he was gone. In her exhaustion, she was probably gonna sleep for hours. Even if she didn't, her mind was halfway out the door anyway. He had an idea if he *didn't* take care of the kid, that door was gonna slam and smack her in the ass hard. She wouldn't need Cuuda's stringy squirrel then, no sir. Her mind would be like a piece of burnt toast then. You might butter such a piece, trying to make it look good, but as soon as you tasted it you'd spit it out and toss it in the trash.

There was decomp of course, but the Oil would take care of that. Jupiter's Oil and Jupiter's toil, he mused. Between the two, the boy *would* look like he was just sleeping. It might be a week or more before decomp set in again, and by then she'd have figured out he wasn't just such a quiet baby—if her mind had only bent and not broken that was.

How often do you get a chance like that, Jupiter, old boy? *It's the perfect Jesus K. Reist test of my skills.*

He worked fast. He took a gulp of Oil, thought *screw the stringy squirrel.* Too big a moment to waste time on anything as mundane as eating. He bade Cuuda to keep an eye on the woman. "If she wakes, feed her. If she asks about her boy, make like you don't know nothing. But keep her here. Everything depends on her being here when I get back. Come on, Archimedes."

The baby boy was a mottled, veiny blue thing. He was still, the way a bowl of apples is still and inanimate when depicted in a still life painting. It was wrong, this stillness. Jupiter felt this wrongness to the very fiber of his own rotting insides. As if to confirm this, he coughed and brought up a wad of those insides. Black, no blood, which pleased him.

His thoughts returned to the boy. On his forehead, right between and above his eyes, was a dent big enough to hold a walnut. Jupiter looked at it and felt the old juices flowing. *Interesting,* he thought, *I can work with that.*

The first thing he did was rub the body with the Oil, which took care of most of the decomp, as well as the smell. The smell had been only a small distraction. In another few hours, twelve at the most, it would have become overwhelming. Now it wouldn't be an issue for a week or more, even in the best heat Pennsylvania could muster. In the background, on the other side of the shroud this was, the baby coo'd, or at least Jupiter heard it so. He didn't coo back.

After that, he got out the pewter syringe. He argued with himself briefly, groin or neck, and chose the groin. What mark there was from this small intrusion would be less visible in the groin he reasoned. He made a small incision on the inside of the thigh, found the femoral artery, slitted it, and passed the needle point of the syringe into the artery. As he had done countless times in the past, he worked the plunger mechanism on the syringe and filled the tiny body with his concoction of embalming chemicals. It didn't take long.

By the time he'd finished these things, the body already looked a fair bit more presentable, though there was still the dent to deal with. The eyes too were wrong and needed dusting up. The combined effect of these two things—the dent and the wrong eyes—left the child looking monstrous, like one of God's mistakes.

Jupiter took a deep breath. Not great—not yet—but better. It was the dent that needed doing now and he turned his considerable skills to it. He even forgot Archimedes. The monkey jumped from the undertaker's shoulder to the table and stood beside the baby. Every once in a while he licked his lips or moved his tiny hands, but he seemed to sense this was not a time to disturb his master.

First he rolled the baby onto his face. He found himself taking pains to be gentle. From the far side of the shroud, he heard that inane cooing. He guessed if he wasn't gentle that cooing might go to crying, which would be all the more irritating. So he took pains to be gentle.

Sam's hair was short, but he thought he could hide the incision along the back of the head nonetheless. He thought it was unlikely Liza would look there anyway. She wasn't the looking type.

He took up one of his many scalpels and dragged it across the scalp over the crown of Sam's head from ear to ear. He was clever about it, cutting the skin at an angle so as to bevel it. He put a finger under the forward edge and worked it back and forth, dissecting the skin from the bone in deliberate effort.

He might have been scalping the kid.

He continued these efforts until he was able to pull the skin all the way forward and down as far as the eyeballs. There was no bleeding since the baby's heart had stopped days before. For the same reason, there would be no swelling in the aftermath of his work. He would just put things back the way he had found them, minus the dent of course.

With the skin pulled off the forehead, the dent was plain to see. He took a moment examining it, giving it a clinical once-over, the way he'd learned to do on his surgery rotation so many years before. He'd spent a month as a surgery house officer then, eating and sleeping in the hospital beside the poor wretches whose conditions were so desperate, so wrenching and wretched, that they agreed to be cut on. He had graduated from his medical studies a full ten years before the folks in Boston had discovered Ether and its curious ability to dull the senses briefly, thus making painless surgery possible. Those were mostly good times, he thought, with nearly every person he met demonstrating proof of life: the woman with the eighty pound ovarian tumor; the man whose moth-eaten skull leaked clear spinal fluid constantly; a young man with some kind of problem that caused one side of his body to retain water until that arm and leg had enlarged to monstrous proportions. They were *mostly* good times, because the proofs caused the people so much pain. He was not a sadist. Their pain brought him pain, left him uncomfortable. He'd have preferred to see them stilled, to have seen their misery at an end, to have discovered what made them who they were.

He didn't like sick people. Sick people were a nuisance. What he did like, he discovered during that month of quick and bloody surgery, was a preference for the stilled.

He preferred the dissecting room to the operating room.

Samuel's skull was not fractured. He saw this clearly now, saw how the bone was pushed inward, bowl-like. He had only to pop it back out. He used another device from his bag of tricks. A small trephine. He held the crossbar of the 'T' and laid the downbar against the side of the Sam's skull an inch from where the bone pressed inward. The trephine had a serrated edge on the tip of the downbar and as he turned it, it chewed the bone drill-like.

It took only a moment and he was intracranial, deep to the bone and inside the skull proper. The brain—Sam's brain—rested quietly. Jupiter stopped, listened. All was quiet behind the shroud. "I think this is right, Sam." He inserted a flat spatula, running it along the bone until it was under the dent. He popped the bone out and the bowl was suddenly flat again.

He patched the hole in the skull with a bit of putty and spent the next fifteen or so minutes reapproximating Sam's scalp until he had it perfect. He used the smallest thread he could find and stitched the incision together as if Sam's life depended on it.

He took a long time getting the eyes just right—mom would look at them. She wouldn't be able to help herself, she'd want to see those baby blues to see he was all right in there. He dusted them with a light coat of Oil as a final step and they brightened immediately. He wiped the rest of the face and that was that. He stepped back, only now noticing how his hands tingled from the caustic chemicals in the concoction. He couldn't help grinning. "Jesus K. Reist," he said.

Archimedes screeched and bared his shiny teeth.

Samuel Coffin was ready to face the world.

SEVENTEEN

Tom Jersey kept on breathing as if mocking life— *mocking me,* Ezra thought. He had to be close to death, but nothing ever seemed to come of it. Each breath came as if the last, followed by another, and another, and...

Enough to drive a man insane.

Ezra had tried putting their heads together, tried to arrange a position in which one shot would take both of them out. He could never devise it to his satisfaction, though, never be sure the bullet would pass cleanly through both skulls. He imagined putting the gun against the side of his head, only to leave Jersey untouched. Such a suicide was intolerable. He wouldn't leave his friend that way. But he wasn't unselfish enough to put the barrel first to Jersey's head either. He couldn't imagine being left alone. Not for a day, not an hour, not a minute in that wretched place.

All night long, he listened with ghoulish expectation to Jersey's breathing. In and out it went, in and out. Time and again. In and out.

Make it stop, he prayed over and over, screaming it out other times. "Make it stop! Make it stop!"

Once or twice, Jersey took a breath, and nothing followed. Each time it seemed the moment of salvation was at hand, but before he could get the revolver in place, the raspy sound of Jersey's chest rising again interrupted him.

A mental torture of the worst kind. So much so, that when the first gray of morning appeared in the eastern sky, he didn't realize the two of them had survived another night.

He finally found an uneasy peace and slumbered.

***

Tobias Ellis hunched over a man whose lower jaw had been blown away on the second day of fighting. The same man Archer—Ellis's late hospital steward—had described, the one who'd left him shaken. The fellow hadn't died. Had instead achieved a certain notice amongst the surgeons in the days since his wounding. His wound was remarkable both for what it revealed—the thing that wiggled with each breath (like the crop of a bird feeding was how Archer had termed it) was his epiglottis, a flap of tough flesh that normally served to prevent bits of food from going down the wrong pipe—and what had not been damaged: the paired carotid arteries carrying blood to the brain, and the jugular veins carrying blood back to the heart. A disturbance in any one of these vessels would have produced a quick and bloody death. The man was a walking miracle, if any poor devil with the lower part of his face blown to hell could be described as such.

He hadn't died, and now he was paying the price.

The most pressing problem in the first two days after his injury had been how to get food and water into him. Most of the bony lower jaw, all of its teeth, and a goodly portion of tongue had been subtracted by the shell fragment. With larynx and epiglottis thus exposed, feeding him was a problem. However, necessity breeds action and after thirty-six hours and out of desperation, Ellis had found a way. He put a hollow quill down what remained of the man's gullet. Seeing no ill effects, he poured a shot of whiskey through and observed the response, which had been quite positive. Thus emboldened, he and a corpsman were then in the process of removing the quill in favor of a rubber tube, which the quartermasters had found. He had rolled his sleeves to his elbows and had his fingers in what passed for the man's throat when word came he was needed urgently elsewhere. Ellis cursed and instructed Archer to take his place beside the patient, then followed the messenger sent to fetch him.

Only after departing did he realize he'd called the soldier assisting him 'Archer.' He couldn't recall the man's name, but it sure as hell wasn't Archer. Archer was dead.

**

Liza Coffin stood in the doorway of the tent, watching the scene unfold with growing horror. Ten patients in the tent and a moment before she'd been talking to one of them, Wooster he'd said his name was. He was the only one who had seemed at all awake. He'd been sitting up in bed and she'd been running her hand over his chest, wondering if he or any of them had any money and where they might keep it.

Samuel had been at her bosom when she entered of course, but now he was sleeping in the corner. *Such a good baby,* she thought for the hundredth time. *Always such a good baby.* There was something different about him now. Ever since her visit with that Jones fella. She had been very tired at that visit, had fainted from the lack of rest she guessed. Jones, or maybe that negro boy who hung out with Jones, had been kind enough to watch Sam while she slept. She guessed they'd bathed him too, since he smelled better. He'd needed a bath but she had been too tired to give him one. Now she wouldn't have to for another day or three. And they'd fed him too. That Jones fella had said as much.

Nice man. Queer, not the sort she wanted to know too much about, but...nice.

She had brought over a wash basin, had sat on the edge of the bed, had just offered to give Mr. Wooster a bath. To clean him up. To clean *all of him.* He had seemed to like the idea, if the size of his smile had been any indication. Now he was sitting up on the cot, groping desperately but ineffectively as blood burbled between his fingers and through the dressings on his thigh. "Oh no," he kept saying.

She didn't at first know what to do. Then she started hollering. "Someone. Hey, someone." Then louder. "Someone! There's a man here's what needs help. Nurse!"

A man rushed into the tent, a nurse, and took one look and began to yell at the top of his voice, at the same time having no luck at curtailing the flow with his fingers.

Another man rushed past Liza. Ellis—dressed in blue uniform trousers, a long-sleeved undershirt, and a soiled apron—seemed to take no time at all to understand the situation. Wooster was prostrate now, panting, his hands no longer groping. The cot beneath him had turned red and it made his features look all the whiter. He was paling before their eyes. Ellis began shouting orders. "Get me a surgeon's kit and knife. Now! No time to quibble."

He measured the pulse. "Weak and rapid," he said to the nurse. "Somebody find a surgeon, Boyd if he's available. Tell him there's no time to lose." The nurse ran out. "I need some morphine—no, that bottle there." He pointed to a small table next to the tent flap, to a tall, dark bottle stoppered with a piece of cotton. "You there, give him the whiskey. Pour it down his throat."

Liza hesitated.

"Come on miss, do it now or stand aside." His voice broke her stare. She started to pour a glass—the liquor was warm against her fingertips. "Not the glass, dammit, the bottle. Pour the whiskey bottle," Ellis said.

She dropped the glass and it shattered on the ground. She grabbed the bottle and turned it up to Wooster's lips, her hand shaking all the way. He swallowed drunkenly, like a man stupid with thirst. Looking into his eyes, she saw pleading. They stuck on her for a long moment, then rolled back and forth, bounding randomly in their sockets like billiard balls loosed on a table. He screamed and grabbed her arm, his hand sticky with blood. She dropped the bottle and it clanked across the wooden floorboards. She heard Ellis talking, 'ignore the blood,' or something like it. Wooster moaned—the kind of ugly sound a young lady should never have to hear—and mouthed something like *don't leave me*, but his voice was nothing and she couldn't be sure. She felt mounting panic, heard her own heart pumping; the swoosh of her pulse was heavy in her ears. She didn't leave, though, squeezed Wooster's hand by way of affirming her presence. She turned and saw the doctor sliding a finger into the messy raw meat that was Wooster's thigh. At quick, regular intervals, a jet of bright red blood shot out. It struck the doctor in his apron front and arm. Another nurse was suddenly at Ellis's side, wrestling the leg up and trying to twist it such that Ellis might get a better angle on the wound. It looked to Liza as if Ellis was working blindly. And hard.

"Turn him up on his side," Ellis hollered.

She helped and it was accomplished fast, like they'd done it a hundred times. Wooster's thigh had grown to twice its normal size, a mottled blue like the ankle she'd twisted bad as a girl.

"Knife!"

The word reverberated and she stared at the blade as it sank into the bruised skin. More raw meat appeared, the doctor had two fingers in the hole and looked to be feeling for something. What was he doing? She wanted to run, but Wooster's hand squeezed hers as tight as any she'd ever held and she couldn't move. He felt strong and she thought in that moment it was impossible for such a man to die. She thought of Ezra and gripped Wooster's hand tighter still, feeling the warmth. She saw the wash basin at the bedside, thought *Damn!* and spontaneously grabbed a wet towel and placed it over Wooster's forehead.

"Tenaculum!"

"What?" the nurse asked. He fumbled with the surgeon's case. It must be unfamiliar to him, Liza realized. The nurse ran his hand across the gleaming silver instruments resting against the dark velvet.

"That one there," Ellis said, "The instrument with the hook, the one with a point on the end. Christ, man, hand it over!"

The nurse passed the device, slow and tentative.

"Where's Boyd?"

Another man appeared at the door of the tent. "What is it, Ellis?" he asked. Liza thought the voice was both smaller and older than it should have been for a man his size.

"Secondary hemorrhage," Ellis said without looking up. "Dr. Hardy, I think it's the femoral artery. Boyd wanted to amputate his leg thirty-six hours ago, but the man refused."

Liza turned her head and saw the other surgeon in the doorway. He was puffing a segar, and she noted, in the curious way one sometimes does when the details don't matter, the tiny curls of smoke rising from it. She also noticed the way he held his side, the way he splinted with each breath. At that moment, Wooster vomited and the rancid smell of liquor mixed with bile filled the close air of the tent.

Liza suppressed her urge to throw up too. She looked into Wooster's eyes, saw in their receding light a glimpse of her own beau, Ezra. "Don't go," she said, then saw how he had paled, how his flesh had gone from a creamy rose to a stark eggshell white in just a few tortured moments. In that instant, she realized he *would* die and wondered who he was, who he *really* was. Did he have a family, a girl back home? Would she get along without him? "I can't get along without you," she said, and the thought was like a winding-sheet passing between her and Ezra.

"Burst femoral? Boyd knows better. Should have amputated," Hardy said.

"I can't get this," Ellis said through teeth clenched to the point of breaking.

"He's dead," Hardy said. Liza heard nothing in his voice beyond the words: no passion, no anger, no remorse or sorrow. Just fact.

"What, no, eh, no," Ellis said, continuing to probe Wooster's leg with the tenaculum.

Liza tried again to pull her hand back, and watched Wooster's limb fall away lifelessly. She looked down and saw the bloody imprint of his hand on her arm, saw the detail where his fingers had pressed her skin, the blood on her fingers. *My blood,* she thought, but knew in the same instant that wasn't right. It was his. "Oh Jesus. Oh Christ in heaven."

Ellis seemed the last in the tent to realize what the others already knew. Liza saw blood was no longer squirting from the thigh, saw Ellis was still trying to bring Wooster back—or keep him from going in the first place. He was digging in that thigh with such concentration that only after the nurse grabbed him and shook him—"He's gone, goddammit"—did Ellis see the man was gone. Ellis stood erect, the instrument in one hand, the other empty. Both hands were red to the mid-forearm.

He looks like a man in shining red armor, Liza thought. Blood slowly congealed on the tent bottom around him. He rubbed at one forearm with his free hand, wiping away the blood. Liza saw something on the back of that forearm—a scar, she decided. Ugly too. The blood wiped indifferently over the heaped skin, showed a different sheen. A burn scar, she guessed.

Ellis dropped the tenaculum, walked away without a word, slumped on a trunk by the entrance. He kept rubbing at that scarred wrist and forearm, like it suddenly pained him a great deal. She looked away, looked down at Wooster. He had relaxed as well. His chest was still, his eyes open but no longer seeing. Like painted eyes. She hadn't known a man could die like that, with his eyes open, and this simple observation almost undid her. She pictured Ezra lying dead on the battlefield, his eyes wide to the sun. "Oh Jesus," she said again, and then her mind seemed to glitch a moment and she said the words over and over again. "Oh Jesus, oh Jesus, oh Jesus..." At the same time, she reached down and pulled the dead man's lids closed. Only then did the glitch right itself.

Hardy said, "A man with a stuck femoral don't live. I suggest you remember that, doctor. Might save you some grief in the future." He puffed his segar, turned, and walked out.

Liza felt herself being led out, but at the last minute remembered Samuel in the corner. Still quiet. Such a good baby. She rushed to him and pulled the cloth back from his face. There was a tiny blemish on his forehead. Was that there earlier? He looked so beautiful sleeping like he was. A tiny version of Ezra. She kissed him. Bundled with him, where she'd secreted it, was the bottle of Jupiter's Oil she'd stolen when Jones's back had been turned. She pulled the cork and gulped a large sip before leaving the tent and going out into the day. The rain was still coming down and she noted with an odd clarity that others moved in it as if nothing had happened.

As if death had become the norm.

***

Hardy exited the tent into the same rain. Despite his comment, he'd watched Ellis work and thought him capable. He didn't *want* to think that, didn't even want to like him. But he did and Ellis would make of himself a splendid surgeon someday—if the demons didn't get him first. This battlefield doctoring was damned bloody business, not for but one in ten. He seemed to be that one, the way he'd fought Hardy about his son notwithstanding. In fact, it was because of that argument he'd made up his mind about Ellis.

He crossed the ground, the stub of his segar dying as he went. He passed men lying in the wet dirt, some looking very poorly and others less so. They'd escaped the moil of war and now had a meagerness about them, like starved dogs. Except their eyes didn't possess the fiery glint of such wretched beasts. They were mostly just wasted, used up and biding their time until their next piece of misfortune. They were, he thought, very much like fine chaff, like grist that would blow whichever way the wind took it. To look on such men was hard and it gave him no comfort to know he'd been a part of their grinding. He thought of Spencer, who lay even then on a cot in a tent (such beds were scarce and, by God and Jesus, how unfair was that but such were the fortunes of war that you got wounded and happened by chance to land in your father's hospital and got first call on any available bed) yet unconscious, maybe dying, probably dying. He'd seen his beloved Maggie die in childbirth. Seeing his son nearly dead in that churchyard had been like losing her all over again. Was there no end to suffering in this war?

The humid air was warm and close, and he was feeling it about as much as he ever had. He was still pissing blood and guessed he had a fever. Pissing burned too, like peeing boiling oil. Every drop was agony renewed and it had taken him most of an hour to empty his bladder the last time around. That, in fact, was what he'd been doing when the call for a surgeon had gone out. Standing in the pisser sweating like a pig on a spit, holding his side

(He thought he could feel a deep, boring discomfort there as well; he prayed not, but he thought he could feel it just the same and, oh Christ almighty, that could only mean his kidneys were tainted and the news went downhill from there)

with one hand and his pecker with the other, praying to the mother of all gods to "please, please, please" let him piss at a low simmer instead of a hard boil. He had actually cried at one point. Here he was, a grown man, a surgeon whose very stock and trade was suffering, and he had cried. He had cried like a baby and that's what he'd been doing when they came looking for him. Crying like a baby who ain't been broke from his mama's tit.

And now he felt the need again. He had to piss and there just wasn't any way around it. He'd felt the urge in the tent, had been able to ignore it for a few moments—almost as if he'd been whole once more—but it was back again. He felt as if he was carrying a pound of lead shot in his low belly. *Sol, you ain't gonna be able to ignore this one, no siree. And you thought you cried before? Wait till you see what's waiting for you when that miserly gate you call a pecker opens up this time. You gonna be pissing steam is all. Superheated steam.*

The idea sent him quivering.

The pisser was a few hastily dug holes in the ground. A shed had been erected around them, no roof. He entered, feeling very much like a condemned man going to the gallows. It rained on him as he stood at his business.

It took an hour—drip by tortured drip—and he wept and prayed to that great sonbitch in the sky the whole time.

***

Cuuda pulled the body of Corporal Jonathan Archer, hospital steward, from the long row of dead just after midday. It had greened to a hue that made recognition of the features near impossible, but the body had been tagged on the field of death days before and so identification wasn't an issue.

Archer had a hole in his chest big enough to set a melon in. His innards had already begun to run and his juices sloshed as they moved his body to the embalming table. Archimedes ran up into his place in the tent awning, screeching the whole time. Cuuda, who had long since plugged his nostrils with cotton and learned to breathe in deep, chest full breaths stolen at long and awkward intervals, hardly frowned at all. Jupiter coughed in the sick, wet bark he'd had for months. The exertion was taking its toll and he allowed to himself he was more dying than living these days. He coughed again and saw more blood on his kerchief than usual. He shook it off.

He plugged the usual openings and gave the naked body a once over. "Mr. Archer, afraid that's a big hole you got yourself. Going to be tough to do much with it." He made a few more such observations, then eyed the half-palm of Archer's left hand. "Well, what's this now, Mr. Archer? You got your hand all shot to hell. Three fingers gone and half the palm too." He looked at it another moment, sort of humming and sort of not. "I wonder..." he said, and placed the maimed hand over the hole in the chest, saw the shape was similar. "Ain't that a bitch," he mumbled. Proof of death, he supposed.

Jupiter shook his head and coughed again. A deep, convulsive hack that wouldn't quit. It came at him again and again until he felt his air going and the tent began to spin around him. He bumped the board and Archer's mutilated hand slid off his chest and over the edge. Jupiter fell to his knees, choking on his own phlegm. He was surprised to feel fear climbing his spine, fear of the unknown.

Fear of dying.

He fell backwards. Archer's damn two-fingered hand dangled in the air above him. He had time enough for just two words, "Jesus K." and his world telescoped to a point.

Then nothing.

***

Josiah Boyd lay on his cot in his underwear and a robe untied at the front. His eyes rolled back in his head. He'd finally found a few minutes to himself and was enjoying what he considered the improved Josiah Boyd. He'd sipped from the opium bottle (more gulped than sipped really, but that was a mere technicality). The dark circles under his eyes could have been a map of his life over the previous six days. He might have needed such a map too, since he couldn't remember much of what had transpired. It had all happened so fast, and with such vivid, terrible languor. Like a dream where you remembered everything, but can recall only in jumbled fits and starts. Twisted pieces of the living and the dead, life and death at the speed of a bullet. He saw the dream through a red filter, and over and over again the various parts of it fell out and assaulted him.

It would have killed him but for the laudanum. Ah, thank God for life's simple pleasures. He'd secured a few bottles of the stuff, not an overabundance, but enough if he didn't waste it (like yesterday, goddammit, when he'd turned a bottle over and half of it had spilled across the floor of his tent). He couldn't let that happen again. And he wouldn't gulp it anymore, he decided then and there. Sips, evenly spaced. He'd restrain himself, use it like it was meant to be used—as a medicine. That was right, as a medicine. The stuff was goddamn life-giving—goddamn life improving if you wanted the truth. It certainly improved him.

The improved Josiah Boyd could think better, without all the goddamn

I'm kilt, I'm kilt! Oh Gawd, I'm kilt!

clutter. And with all that clutter removed, the truth had become increasingly obvious.

The truth of the flesh.

We are made breakable, that's all, that goddamn simple. Nothing immutable about the human form, nothing special. A horse or a man, and, once opened up, all the same. Could you tell the difference between cow shit and horse dung? Between cow shit and his own shit? Well, maybe you could, but in the end it was all just shit, right? Shit was shit whether it came from a bird or goddamn elephant. It was just a matter of degrees, of amount.

A tiny sound, and the improved Boyd (his hearing was more acute than it had been in years and wasn't that a goddamn remarkable thing) turned his head. He spied a cockroach in the corner. *Shiteater.* The thing moved with the ease and grace of a dog crossing a road. Didn't know any better.

And what of the cockroaches, shiteaters that they be? Scavengers of rot. Are we any better? Any different? Step on one of those rot suckers and what'll you see? The same old shit, that's what. Blood, guts, and puke. A lot smaller package maybe, but crap is crap anyway you package it. Just a matter of degrees, of amount.

The improved Boyd sat up, his feet now on the tent bottom. He trapped the shiteater against first one foot and then the other as the tiny creature scurried around seeking a way out. He bared his teeth and knew in that instant the bug was his to do with as he might. "I'm your God, goddammit." As if the bug might pray to him.

"It's a kill or be killed world," he said. "You wanna die? Or live? Which is it gonna be, fella?" The roach bounced off his foot and changed directions.

Be merciful to let you live? Would that really be the kindest thing to do? To let you go on mucking around unawares, like you was actually getting somewhere or accomplishing something? But that ain't reality, is it? In reality all you're doing is going from one shit pile to another. Isn't that the truth of it? Isn't that the real truth of the flesh? We're all just shiteaters scavenging from one shit pile to the next.

He cupped the roach in his hands. Held it there, pinching it between thumb and forefinger, feeling its little legs scratching back and forth against him. "I'm your God, goddammit. Answer me!"

But there was nothing. Not a goddamn plea, nothing. If the thing was praying, he couldn't hear it.

"Ah, shit." He squeezed his fingers and the roach popped like a ripe berry. Its back split down the middle and its guts squirted out its ass end, where he pill-rolled them between his fingertips.

"The truth of the flesh," he said. *I knew it. No different than the piss and guts I see every goddamn day. Bug or people, it don't matter. It's a kill or be killed world, Mr. Bug. Either you eat, or you get eaten.*

The improved Josiah Boyd sucked the squished bug into his mouth, licked his fingers, and swallowed. Thinking about all of this had given him a headache—a small one, but it would get worse. He needed to take a squat, too. He had just about decided he would walk over to the latrine, take his squat, then come back and lie down. He'd take a sip of the laudanum before lying down, of course. But just a small one. Medicine, treat it like medicine.

He had just about decided these things when they came

for him. He stood, pulled on a pair of trousers and his boots, then tied his robe loose across his front.

A boy had been brought in. He lay in the churchyard dressed in a pair of too-big overalls, one strap broken and the other pinned over a shoulder. He had no shirt, no shoes either. His feet were callused and hard. He was blissfully unconscious, probably dying. His right leg had been blown apart below the knee and his foot hung by mere bits of sinew. A twist of hemp was tied around his shin and the bones protruded below it like dead tree stumps in the middle of a rotted land.

Someone told how the boy had picked up an unexploded grenade, how he'd shown it to his mother, how she'd taken it from him, how she'd dropped it and it had exploded and the mother had been (the teller lowered his voice to a whisper) reduced to bug food. Boyd put a hand up at hearing that. He'd heard enough. "The truth of the flesh," he said.

Standing to one side of all this—maybe listening, maybe not—was a young woman with something strapped across her front. A baby? *No,* Boyd decided, that couldn't be right. What kind of a madwoman would bring a baby into a place like this?

"He's the son of the minister," the woman said. "His name's Jerem—"

"Stop. Okay? Just stop," Boyd said. "Don't care to know his name. We'll do well enough without it and just call him boy."

"That don't seem right," the woman said.

"Wha—" *the hell you know of what's right? You ever even heared of the truth of the flesh, woman?* Boyd stopped himself. It wasn't a question he cared to have answered and he never asked a question he didn't want to have answered; he'd learned this much in the army. He had done his last operation several hours before, but now he sighed and put his hand to the wounded boy's mouth. He felt a humid breath, and ran his hand to the eyes and pulled one open. The large pupil quickly constricted in the light and the eye rolled up in its socket.

"I guess we oughta do something about that leg," the recently improved Boyd said. "First, though, I gotta squat."

***

Liza tapped her foot waiting for the surgeon to finish his assessment. His name's Jeremiah Penn, she'd wanted to say. She'd been listening intently. She was in the thick of it now. After the thing with Wooster, she couldn't resist the hospital. And nobody seemed to care anyway one way or t'other. Hot damn and all that, so much work nobody ever questioned her or where she had come from. So there she was, Samuel wrapped at her chest so that maybe nobody even knew he was there (such a quiet boy, a good baby). His presence soothed her. He was a Godsend, manna from heaven. She couldn't even begin to imagine a world without him.

She hugged her baby close and watched the one they called Tiny (he was anything but and that amused her) place a wad of cotton material over Jeremiah's face. The boy relaxed after a few moments, though he hadn't been combative to start with. His relaxing amounted to his body settling down on the operating table, and again that odd clarity struck Liza: the boy relaxed in exactly the same way Wooster had at the end.

The team went to work with practiced speed. The only one who hesitated at all, to her unpracticed eye, was Surgeon Boyd. His movements seemed to lack confidence and were stuttering, as if he had to plan his every move. Sometimes they appeared to be wasted effort and he seemed...lost.

Could that be?

He dropped an instrument. In the next moment he fumbled with tying a knot and she flinched, swallowed a tiny lump in her throat. Then, as Boyd looked up from his work, that odd clarity again. His eyes held...nothing. No look at all, as if they were—she suddenly thought of the dead Wooster—painted glass, yet to be stamped with thought and intuition.

That was when she became afraid.

EIGHTEEN

Cuuda was the first to find the undertaker. Mr. Jupiter lay in the mud, his legs under the awning and his head and torso exposed so that the rain fell gently upon his face. His eyes were open, crossing back and forth like they'd finally become unyoked. Cuuda wiped the accumulated water from his eyes. He held the old man's hand in his own, rubbing those fingers, hoping for some tell-tale sign the old man knew he was there. Those fingers were long and thin, the knuckles big and knobby. Cuuda thought how they looked well used. If he'd been burying Jupiter—planting was the term the old man liked to use and the thought made him grin—he would have looked at those hands and thought farmer, brick mason, or carpenter. He'd have thought *proof of life*.

They'd been together six years. Each was all the other had. Cuuda had stood beside this old man for hundreds of embalmings, which amounted to hundreds of lessons.

Cut down on the neck, the vessel's easier to find.

The femoral artery is here, on the inside part of the thigh, maybe two inches deep in the meat. A little deeper if he's fat.

You get more concoction to the face if you use the carotid.

Nobody much cares what his innerds look like—except me. Mr. Jupiter was always a perfectionist.

You got to look on a body—on a patient—the way you would a horse.

Where's his heart? By way of answer, Cuuda would lay his small fist over the left side of the patient's ribs—Mr. Jupiter had a tendency to refer to them all as his patients—between breastbone and nipple.

And always the last lesson: *Where would you needle him?*

They'd been over it a hundred times.

Where would you needle him? They'd never actually done it. But "Sooner or later, it'll come in useful," Mr. Jupiter would say.

"Hot damn," Cuuda said. "Mr. Jupiter, is this the moment you was always talking about? Seems like it might be. Tell me, Mr. Jupiter. Say something."

But the old man was mostly beyond saying anything. Actually, he was bluing up.

He felt for the old man's pulse at the carotid artery. He had a hard time finding it, even though he did as Mr. Jupiter had shown him a hundred different times on a hundred different stills (that was Cuuda's term; he thought a patient should be a living thing). He found the adam's apple, then slid his fingers an inch to the outside, into the groove caused by the big muscle on the side of the neck. He found the beat: weak, barely there at all. He felt for his own, found it bounding, not something he could miss.

A whippoorwill whistled in the distance and its song was mournful. Cuuda wished with all his being he hadn't heard it. A bad omen that. He put his ear to Mr. Jupiter's mouth. No movement of air. The old man was quitting him.

"No, you cain't do that. Mr. Jupiter, oh, Gawd. No."

Where would you needle him?

When Cuuda's head rose from before the old man's mouth, Archimedes was standing beside them. As if Mr. Jupiter had tapped his cane twice, the monkey held a bottle of Jupiter's Oil in its tiny, perfect hands. Cuuda looked at it, looked at the undertaker lying in the mud, at the water accumulating again. He looked back at Archimedes. The monkey screeched. Cuuda put a hand out and nodded, took it.

Things went quick after that.

He set the bottle down and rapidly gave a set of hand signals to Archimedes, who scampered over to the wagon. Cuuda laid the undertaker flat upon the ground, he had been propped over on his side at first, and pulled his shirt and undergarments off over his head. The old man was naked now from the waist up. He saw how the man's eyes had stopped crossing back and forth. For the first time ever in Cuuda's recollection, they looked straight off into the distance together, seeing—or not seeing—the same thing. Cuuda reached up and closed them, the way you'd close a dead man's eyes. He supposed what he was about to do would either work or it wouldn't, but he didn't need Mr. Jupiter looking at him the whole time either way.

That old man could be death with his criticism.

He started to place his hands, saw how that chest was more like somebody's feeble idea of what a chest should look like. Thin and frail, all the more so in the rain, which gathered unevenly in the depressions between his ribs. He placed his small fist over the left side of the old man's ribs, between the breastbone and nipple. He tried not to cry, but a few tears came nonetheless. "The heart is right about here," he said sobbing, then felt for the tip of Jupiter's breastbone, dropping into the hollow just under it.

Archimedes reappeared, carrying the large pewter syringe and its unholy attachment, the long, hollow needle that looked like a grannie might use it for knitting. Cuuda quickly filled the syringe with the Oil, then attached the needle and found again the hollow under the tip of Jupiter's breastbone. Mr. Jupiter was, he noted, decidedly blue now.

Archimedes climbed onto Cuuda's shoulder, but the boy took no notice. He concentrated, put the tip of the needle to the skin in the hollow. "Upwards, a little to the left," he remembered aloud, "about three inches." He pushed.

Jupiter did not flinch as the needle sunk in, but Cuuda did. He felt a tough resistance at the skin, then a *pop* as the needle went home. There was a spot of blood, no more. *One inch, two inches,* he counted in his mind, thought *spongy, nothing firm.* Another push forward, three inches, and now there was something firm, something that seemed to cause the whole apparatus to quiver in his hands. *The heart? Is this what you wanted me to do, Mr. Jupiter, find the heart?*

Cuuda trembled, was suddenly aware of Archimedes' weight on his shoulder. At the same instant the monkey screeched. "Oh Gawd in heaven," Cuuda intoned.

Then he drove the plunger all the way to the base of the syringe, injecting the Oil into Mr. Jupiter's heart.

***

Jupiter's skin went from the color of death to transparent in an instant. Cuuda thought he was too late, that he was seeing the birth of a ghost. But in the next moment, veiny blue lines radiated out from the old man's heart, staining his skin and branching over and over again before his eyes, until that entire scrawny body seemed bloodshot with veiny blue—an impossibly tattoo'd man.

And that body began to dance.

Cuuda backed away. Archimedes jumped into the awning above the tent flap.

Jupiter's arms flailed randomly and his legs kicked about. He sat bolt upright, then relaxed down again. His back arched and Cuuda heard what he thought were the sounds of bones popping out of place. Jupiter's eyes came open—crossed again, and Cuuda had no idea where they might be looking—and the old man sat bolt up again and puked.

He fell back into the mud and the dance stopped. His head lolled to one side, the side where Cuuda was standing, and Jupiter's mouth fell open and his tongue came out. His eyes rolled until Cuuda imagined they might be trying to focus—on him. Cuuda thought, *he looks like the tiredest man in the world.*

The boy stepped forward, knelt in the mud. The sound of Jupiter's breathing was loud up close. He heard something else too, Mr. Jupiter's heart maybe. This was impossible—a beating heart can't be heard outside the earshot of its owner—but Cuuda didn't know that and so heard the impossible.

The old man's hand came up then. Weak, still scrawny, but sweaty too. In fact, Mr. Jupiter was drenched, as if just pulled out of a lake. Even that part of him that had been under the awning was soaked. His veined, blue skin gradually faded to Jupiter's more normal yellow, waxy tone. Except for the center of his chest. There, over the breastbone and in the hollow under it, those veins still branched and crossed back and forth across each other in vivid, creepy crawls—like a barren tree writhing back and forth in an impossible winter gale.

Cuuda, breathing hard himself, reached down and felt for the syringe sticking out of the old man's chest. It thrummed mightily, as if on the cusp of some great engine within. Touching it sent a warmth through the boy— uncomfortable, but tolerable.

The old man came alive of a sudden. His arms embraced the boy and pulled him close with the strength of ten men. His eyes swung open wide, the eyes of a hungry predator— a lion on the edge of a watering hole measuring his prey. His breath was like steam and his skin near scalding to the touch. He screamed then, a foreign noise never heard before. Cuuda screamed too, an ungodly mixture of pain and fear and surprise. The boy tried to pull away, but it was no good. Another instant and the old man was not beside him, but inside him, probing his mind. *Go*, was the sense of it. *Go now, work to be done.*

Mr. Jupiter's lips parted. "Jesus K. Reist," he said, "boy, you done good. Now do gooder."

The old man let go and Cuuda fell back against the side of the tent. He pulled the needle from the old man's chest in one mighty effort and the old man seemed to deflate some in the aftermath. He shrank back, holding his chest, taking in great gouts of air.

Cuuda sat beside him, his mind a blur. For some time, he had no idea how long, he couldn't remember his own name. He thought it might be death. *I am death, I am death, I am death...* played over and over between his ears like a dirge. He struggled to organize his thoughts, like catching his breath after a hard run. A single, dreaded image kept bubbling to the surface of his pokerish mind. A little boy sitting beside two men. The men were prostrate, didn't seem right. The boy neither. He carried a creel but no pole. And he had only one shoe.

In the next tiny beat of time, like a heartbeat this was, Cuuda of a sudden knew Jupiter really could talk to the dead. He'd seen how the shroud between the two worlds sometimes came down.

The knowledge seemed to do him no particular good, for he knew only one thing at that moment. He had to walk. He had to walk or he would die.

***

Exhausted beyond what even sleep could cure, Liza Coffin sat propped against a headstone in the small cemetery outside the Lutheran church. On the ground to her right was her baby, Samuel. She was trying to feed him bits of the loafed bread she'd taken from the baker, but he wasn't cooperating. "You ain't hungry I guess." She gave up the effort and turned to her left, where lay the boy Jeremiah Penn recuperating from his time under Boyd's knife.

Jeremiah stirred periodically in the midnight darkness, but it was a stupid, unknowing kind of movement brought on by fever. A distemper. Maybe even blood poisoning. She caressed his forehead, his short, blonde bangs reminding her of a time before all of this misery. It made her think of the week before, of Samuel at home in his crib (Ezra had made it of his own two hands before his birth and she had thought that a glad omen; what could she think now?) and for a long instant she wondered what kind of mother she was.

Her mind shuttlecocked back and forth through the events of the days passed. The odd undertaker with the green hat, the nigger boy with his monkey, Wooster sitting up in bed one moment and dead the next. Ellis covered in Wooster's blood: like a man in shining red armor.

She fumbled for the bottle of Jupiter's Oil.

She looked at Jeremiah, a boy she barely knew, son of the town's minister. Something about him stirred her, and she cried for him. For Samuel too perhaps, and for herself, and most of all for Ezra. The tears wet her face like blood from her torn heart.

A young soldier beside Jeremiah roused. He had big, moon pool eyes and asked in a croaky voice if maybe she had any water. She startled, catching her breath in curt gasps the way a child will after a hard cry. "No. No water. I'm sorry."

"Durned it all then."

"I'm sorry," she said.

"Ain't no matter. I think I shall go up afore morning anyhow."

She caught the import of these words and looked closer at the soldier, who was no older than her Ezra. Both his legs were crooked above the knees and lashed with crude wooden splints. He had the noxious look of someone who had been abed for days. "Don't be saying that," she said, and forced a smile, "you must keep your courage."

"My courage don't falter," he said. "I'll be among my fellows."

"I don't think you're going anywhere."

"Sure could use that water."

She stopped stroking Jeremiah's forehead. "I've something better." She leaned over and gave the man a sip of Jupiter's Oil. It brightened his eyes and features both and evened out his breathing almost at once. It also brought a sure smile to his face. She took a swig herself—suddenly the world wasn't such a dreadful place—and before too long half the bottle was gone between the two of them.

***

He had to walk.

Cuuda neared the last of his endurance an hour after midnight. His body screamed for rest, his legs heavy and clumsy. He'd fallen four times in the last half mile. He would have stopped to sleep and maybe eat something, except there was nothing to eat. He'd stuck Mr. Jupiter (that old man's skin had gone nearly transparent and, hot damn, he still couldn't believe that) and then touched that apparatus sticking out of his chest. He remembered that, by Gawd, like touching a hot stove. And then everything misted like a fog across his memory.

He needed to walk, he knew that much. Like a disease, walk or die. His legs couldn't carry him fast or far enough.

There didn't seem any particular rhyme to it either. One foot in front of the other. A slog is what it was. Pure slog.

The ground seemed to spin away from him a moment and he stopped. He bent at the waist and his stomach twisted on itself. He retched and the last of the squirrel he'd eaten hours before came up. He stood tall, catching his breath, looked around. He had no idea where he was.

He leaned against a tree, closed his eyes. "Gawd, just a hour of sleep. Just five minutes." But now came the boy again. Only one shoe, and a creel looped over one shoulder. No older than ten. He stood opposite Cuuda, maybe a dozen steps between them. *You done good, now do gooder.* The words came into his head sounding like the old man, but the old man wasn't there. *You done good, now do gooder.* Get to walking. That's what those words alluded to. The boy beckoned. Cuuda's legs stepped off almost without his knowledge. It had been so all night.

Something about that boy was off-fettle. Cuuda had an idea what that something was. A ghost. Prosper had told him of such things in the before time, back on the plantation with massa. Before his parents had been carried off to the *sure dead.*

He stopped now to take a squat. He closed his eyes for only a moment and his mind instantly became a jumbled mess again—

Jupiter on the floor of his embalming tent, half-in, half-out of the awning, with Archer's two-fingered hand dangling above.

Two negroes swinging in the wind, while a young boy sits at the base of their hanging tree.

The girl with the baby sitting among the headstones in the Lutheran cemetery, trying earnestly to feed the baby she doesn't know or can't accept is dead.

A young white man tussles with a negro boy in a back alley. "Well I could use me a dumbshit baby nigger darkie.

Maybe I buy you, boy. Maybe you come with me then you eat." The underside of the young man's wrist is ugly, scarred and discolored by what looks like an old burn scar.

A man he doesn't recognize screaming something incomprehensible about the truth of the flesh—as he drags a knife across the back of his own arm, then licks the blood.

Prosper smiling at him in the before time.

A burned out house—four charred walls and a roof that has fallen inward—with the body of a small dog at the front door.

The sun high in a cloudless, vivid blue sky.

An artillery wagon over on its side, and the skeletal remains of the horse that had pulled it.

The stilled, piled four and five high on the roadside, awaiting casketing.

The boy again, wearing the same pair of soiled coveralls, muddy and smelling faintly of fish, with the creel looped over one shoulder. His trouser knees are worn and one of his suspenders has come undone and dangles down in front. He has short, fine fingers and blond hair. His eyes are stunningly blue. He wears only one shoe.

The vista opens out now and the boy is not alone. He is kneeling beside two men, both of whom are themselves not well. Sight opens still wider to all of this on a field of wheat and cadavers. The dead lay everywhere, as if they've picked their spots and are just waiting to be planted...

All of this had come to Cuuda when he touched the apparatus still stuck in Mr. Jupiter. All this came back on the instant whenever he closed his eyes—or maybe not. It had a decidedly unreal tenor to it. It didn't feel right—not wrong exactly, but not right either. It was like a carnival he'd once been to, the hall of mirrors. That place had distorted his appearance from every direction. One moment he was impossibly tall and thin, the next squat and fat. In one mirror he had the pinhead of an imbecile, in the next his head had grown to the size of a monster. This had that kind of feel, as if not his body but reality was being distorted. And yet, somehow, it was real, as real as the air in his lungs: he couldn't see that air, but it was there just the same. Impossible to imagine otherwise. That was the quality of the boy with only one shoe.

Cuuda couldn't imagine him not being real. And so imagining, he had to follow him.

Or die trying.

On his journey this night, he'd crossed a wooded gully and heard the mute testimony of a hundred or more dead soldiers. He'd seen a burned out house and it was just like the picture in his head, dead dog and all. And the bodies and the skeletal horse too.

Cuuda waded a stream and climbed the hill on the other side. The grass, wet from the rains, was greening up. It felt cool against his leaden legs. He was at the end of his endurance when he crossed a wide muddy lane. His feet sank in the muck, and it was the near last thing he could do to pull them out again. Across the road, he came upon a huge tree with a scattering of bones underneath. He stared hard at a skull. A dried, ancient bone that reminded him for all the world of the soothsayer he'd known back on the plantation. Prosper. He couldn't say with any authority why that skull reminded him of such, but it did.

Cuuda stood in the profound silence under the large tree, all the while feeling the press to keep walking. He couldn't do it though. The spot seemed to compel his presence. Or maybe his fatigue compelled his rest. For a moment, the tree seemed the only other thing living in that place. The trunk was the biggest he'd ever seen. He couldn't encircle half of it. He gave up and collapsed at its base. The last thing he saw as his eyes closed was the oak's wide canopy above him, and the gnarled, bulky, elbow limb that jutted out at an odd angle from its intricacies.

A crow perched there, no doubt watching how the boy's legs continued their walking movements even as he fell into sleep.

Book IV

The Cauling

NINETEEN

The dog wandered the streets of the town, looking drawn and hungry. His white on brown coat was mangy and hung loose on his frame, as if by some curse he'd thinned to a figment. His bones poked out odd and clumsy, suggesting not only an age beyond his natural life, but starvation besides.

He moved with a lazy gait, as if the next corner offered no more promise than the previous and hurrying was a thing of the past. So he moved like the people of the town—slow, not regarding much with interest, pausing occasionally to ponder a bloodstained walk or a hole in the side of a building. His stilted activity could have been the last remnants of shock or the first tentative movements toward a new and unsure life.

His old life was gone and that he'd lived to see this day was a near miracle. When the booming had started he'd run for cover, spent the early part of the confusion holed up in a forgotten corner of the livery, then escaped to the thickets on the edge of town. He'd eaten gophers and frogs and stumbled into a wasp's nest; had sprained a leg bounding a field and cut his head above one eye scooting under an overturned caisson. He'd puked blood and burned a paw. Once, seeking refuge from the heat, he'd gotten himself stuck in a log and had wiggled two days getting out. He'd rubbed himself to near exhaustion after crawling through poison sumac and nearly died from the trots after eating a passel of bright colored berries.

The dog had returned to town a figment of his former self. The town, of course, was a mere figment itself.

***

The soldier with the crooked legs lingered and never did die, at least not to Liza's knowledge. She nursed him through the wee hours, both of them a little giddy from the Oil, which perhaps was some kind of cure after all. He rallied with the coming of the sun and went on to the surgeons not long after that. They determined to take his legs, one above the knee and one below, but in the course of doing so somebody questioned even this, for he was found to be of a singularly unusual constitution. In the several days since his wounding, it seemed he had mended better than most.

Liza searched the wounded man's garments after he was carted off to the operating tables and found coin and paper worth one dollar and sixty-two cents. She thought it adequate payment for her time and comfort to him through the difficult night. She'd expected he would be dead by first light and, when he still breathed an hour after that, figured she'd witnessed, if not a miracle, then at least a wonder.

She hoped Ezra was made of such stout material.

***

Ellis breakfasted on cold grits. He didn't feel like eating, not really, but he supposed he was famished, or at least his stomach was, and so forced himself to take something. It might be a while before he had time to sit again. He sipped a little coffee as well. He hated coffee, but somehow what he liked and didn't like didn't seem to weigh much anymore. He ignored the weevils floating on the surface of the drink. Weevils were easy to ignore, unlike most everything else in that goddamn place. He sat on a wooden stool and pretended everything and everyone around him were weevils.

"I seen you yesterday," Liza said.

He looked away from the girl. Weevils.

"The bleeding soldier. You told me to give him whiskey."

"Did I?" He glanced up, not really interested to do so but looking up anyway. She didn't look like much, a baggy drab cheap-looking dress, dirty and ill-fitting. A bundle in her arms. A baby? He'd seen her, he guessed, couldn't say where. "I see a lot of bleeding soldiers," he said.

"Not like that one, I'm guessing. You were covered with his blood after it was done. I saw you rubbing your arm. Looked like you got a pretty bad scar there. Mind if I sit?" She spoke the words as if they were a single sentence.

"Free country." In another time and place he'd have told her to get lost, that his scars were none of her damn business. But he was too tired for argument this morning. "What'd you say your name was, miss?"

"It's missus. Missus Liza Coffin." She knelt down on the ground beside him, Indian-style. Samuel's hand of a sudden fell out from her bundle and Ellis startled at the sight.

"What was that?"

"Oh don't mind him. That's Samuel, my baby. He and I, we're looking for my Ezra."

"You ok, missy?"

"I said, it's Missus. Coffin, Liza Coffin. This here's my little boy Samuel." She said the words as if they were the most natural ever to come out of her mouth. She smiled too, a queer smile as Ellis saw it.

"You don't look so good, Missus Coffin."

"I'm fine. Me and Sam, we're fine." Still that queer smile. "You wanna see my boy?"

Ellis had by now stopped eating and set his plate aside. "Yeah, let me see the boy," he said, but not eagerly.

"He ain't been so hungry lately. Mostly just sleeping to tell it like it is."

"That so? Let me see."

She untied the linen strap holding the whole thing and pulled the bundle away from her front side. The hand fell out again and this time he was sure of what he saw. She put the bundle on the ground in front of her and Samuel's head lolled out like his neck was boneless. His entire head had the splotchy, blue, veiny look of the departed. And not the nearly departed or even the recently departed.

Ellis guessed Samuel had been dead two days, maybe twice that.

He looked at the poor girl. She seemed ignorant of Samuel's...condition, as he finally termed it. What in the name of all that was holy was happening here? "Your baby's . . . .dead, Missus."

"No no no. He ain't dead. I'd know if'n he was. Sleeping's what he is. Babies do that."

"Not this one. He's dead, all right. He's about the deadest baby I've seen."

"You ain't gotta say all that, mister. You don't want us around, you just gotta say."

"You ain't listening missus. That boy's—-"

A crowd was gathering around them. "Oh my god," someone said. "That girl ain't right in the head," another pointed. Still another, "It's the devil's work."

"Well, I guess we'll just be leaving then," Liza said primly.

Ellis said, "Umm, I can't let you do that."

"But he's just sleeping. Please, you don't understand."

I guess I'm about the only one of us that does. "I understand your baby's—"

"Not dead." She was crying now. "Our house was surrounded by dirty rebels. Those heathens. They would'a raped me. Plain an' simple. I seen it in they eyes when they come up the walk that first time. They asked how I might be able to give 'em some food. I told 'em no, that I didn't have nothing. They left but they took my cow.

"They come back not two hours later. They was six of 'em then. Only two come in first. I didn't answer the door. They come in and rummaged the place. Me and Sam, we hid in the root cellar. They didn't know we was there but I could hear 'em the whole time. Sam, he was trying to be real quiet, but then he started crying. I put my hand over his face. I just wanted him to be quiet. It worked too. Not another peep. He got real quiet. He's such a good baby. Such a quiet baby. You see? Lookie here how quiet he is. Sam, I like to call him Samuel mostly, he's a powerful good boy. He don't make no peeps."

"Jesus Christ," someone said. Another, "the poor girl's crazy."

"You all shut up now. Go on 'bout you business," Ellis said. "Missus, your baby...he isn't sleeping."

She lowered her head slowly. Murmured, "I knowed as much. No baby sleep that long."

"Yeah. All right. Whyn't you come with me?"

"Samuel too?"

"Samuel too."

"I seen you was nice when you tried to save that bleeding man. You couldn't save him. Nobody coulda saved him."

"Let's go now."

"Mister?"

"Yeah?"

"You can't save Samuel neither."

- 260 -

Ellis knew by the tone of her voice, as well as her look, that it was a statement, not a question. He picked up the dead infant. "Missus Coffin—"

"I'm looking for my husband. He's a soldier in the Army of the Potomac. I think he might be among the wounded. This here is, was, our son, name of Samuel. Samuel Jaspers Coffin."

"Might be your husband's among the dead too."

"No, he ain't. I'd know if he was dead. He's alive." She said it without losing a beat.

How could she be so sure?

"You're wonderin' how I can be so sure, ain't you?"

Tobias nodded.

"Cause if'n he's dead, my life's over too. I ain't got another thing in all this world what means so much to me as that man. I'm gonna make another baby with him just as soon as I find him and we're gonna have a life. Ain't nobody gonna take that from us. Specially not nobody associated with this goddamn war."

Ellis looked away from her, toward the trees. The letter from Tucker was still burning a hole in his pocket. He'd meant to forward it on to the man's widow, but he hadn't gotten around to it just yet. Bullshit. He hadn't posted it because he couldn't bring himself to part with it.

"I hope you find him," he said. Then he took her hand and went in search of someone who could help the poor girl. He knew he damn sure couldn't.

***

On the morning of July seventh, Cuuda awoke to the twittering of a dozen crows in the branches of the large oak. He was confused, not certain where he was or how he'd come to be there.

You done good. Now do gooder. This time it wasn't the

old man he heard, but a boy's voice. He had an idea it was the boy from last night, though he couldn't prove it. He didn't even know who the boy was.

That old walking urge started up again.

He took up his shoes, he'd removed them from his feet sometime in the dark night, and leaned against the oak. It was a massive tree, as big as he'd ever seen. In its shade across the ground in front of him were the bleached bones of some long dead animal. He thought of old Prosper, and of his dead parents. He glanced up into the branches of the oak, took note of the gnarled limb with its elbow bend jutting out in solitary salute. Looking closer, he saw the notches. Not fresh, but as obvious as the sun against a vivid blue sky. At least a half dozen notches marred the branch before it bent and turned upward. Their import was apparent to anyone who'd seen their like before, who'd seen what rope could do to the skin of a tree. Or the front of a neck.

A hanging tree.

Cuuda suddenly wanted—needed, needed in the worst way—to be as far from that place as he could get. He had a need to walk again, bad—like he needed to squat that very second or shit his pants. He was on his feet, bushes scraping his arms and legs and the wind rushing his face, and had run near a mile before he had any conscious idea he'd moved at all. He still had his shoes in his hands. He slowed then, feeling the ground against his bare feet.

He came finally to a stop in the lee of several house-sized boulders on a field strewn with yet more tragedy. He put his shoes on. Before him lay an impossible sight: tens, maybe hundreds, of corpses the graves registration units had yet to reach. Interspersed among them were a score of bloated horses. Broken wagons littered the landscape, their axles twisted at odd angles. The few trees were nothing more than craggy reminders of what they'd been, no leaves filling them out so that they looked skeletal against the gloomy sky. The ground itself was brown and tarnished, the wheat field barren and devoid of life for large swaths. The rain had done nothing to green this ground. Puddles of murky water and black blood dotted it. In the far distance, Cuuda saw men working. Black forms bending, stooping, digging, and generally toiling in the terrible dawn.

That sight was a slog on his eyes.

The air was breezy, wet, and weighted with the awful essence of rot. He didn't want to move. Didn't want to but he did. The need to walk had not left him, and he picked his way forward between the bodies. There came the rumble of thunder as the rain renewed itself, slow and sparse. He walked toward the black figures toiling in the far distance. It was a long and difficult walk, more so than it might should have been, as if something unseen plodded along with him, pulling at his every step like soggy mud. The field was a quiet place, not unlike a cemetery, and the rain pelting the dead was an eerie, discomforting noise. He darted his eyes to and fro, locking on nothing and seeing everything. He covered his mouth and nose with his shirt; the stench was the worst part of everything he'd ever smelled, magnified well beyond the close air of Mr. Jupiter's tent. He saw how the bodies were terribly swollen, how they were only historically soldiers. Some still held their rifles—hands gone bony, faces ugly and spoiled, meat left too long in the broiling sun. More than a few had congregated with their fellows into small groups, preferring perhaps to die in the company of others. He wondered what one might say at such a time. He wondered if they'd known they were dying, or if it had come as a surprise.

That feeling again. As if something—or someone—plodded alongside him. *You done good. Now do gooder.*

Something moved on that killing field, something in the corner of his vision. He stopped abruptly, the movement unexpected. A crash of thunder, and for just a moment, the open field became as claustrophobic as that hole his father had buried him in, the one he'd come to think of as his salvation.

He saw before him his father's tear-rutted face in that final moment of the before time. *No! No, ya can't put me in there. Please pa, don't put me in there!*

Where's that nigger boy o' yours?

His mother's sweet, golden singing: *Will the circle be unbroken—*

They slapped her and Cuuda pissed himself all over again standing in that field. His own face stung. He cried, his fear of them now more powerful even than his love of her.

(Not true, he thought, and the moment thumped him with the hard, physical pain of a blow to the head. *I loved her, loved both of them. I was a boy. Just a boy for God's sake. What was I suppose to do?*).

Don't ya cry boy. Ya cry, dey finds you.

He calmed himself and thought of his father, of the towering giant he'd been. Hard muscle throughout, skin a polished black like burnt ash. It was his pa he missed most, who still loomed as a giant in his eyes. That last week, the two of them had chopped wood together and he could still smell the musky odor of his pa's hard built sweat, could see the big man's muscles rippling with each throw of the axe. Many was the night he saw him holding that axe high over his head, arms outstretched powerfully, looking as solid as a tree and as strong as ox.

Pa, how could you die?

Movement again. This time Cuuda turned toward it and saw the outline of an arm waving back and forth. The wind, a dead arm blowing in the rain. He saw the arm moving back and forth and suddenly remembered *them* moving back and forth, under the tree branch. He remembered it all

as if it had happened yesterday, as if he was still in the in-
between time. He hadn't seen it, not most of it anyway, but
he had heard it. And that was maybe worse. Hearing was
like seeing, only magnified.

They beat you senseless Pa. As big as a horse and they
beat him senseless. His mother's singing again. *Amazing
Grace! My God,* he thought, *they waited for her.*

They must have been awed. But not awed enough to
spare her. His mother's last touch he could still feel when
the wind was right and the smell of honeysuckle crowded
the air. The wind could remind of other things too,
however. Like the whispering of the heavy ropes as his ma
and pa swung beneath their place in that hanging tree.

He had been back to that tree only once, a few months
after the start of the war. There was nothing to it except a
large oak with a few notches on a wayward pointing limb.
No sign of his parents, of their graves. He'd built a sign and
tacked it to the very tree. Erasmus and Sara Monk, 1857.
Adding the year made him feel better. They'd lived.

Cuuda looked through the rain and saw the arm move
again. Dead men didn't wave. The hand opened and closed.
He walked toward it.

The boy with the creel and only one shoe stood beside a
cluster of bodies, stacked so as to provide some small
measure of protection against the weather. Cuuda moved
closer and saw two men lay beside and within it, one
dressed in blue, the other in dirty butternut gray. Neither
was moving. The head of the man in blue was buried
beneath the shoulder of the other, who was face up.

Cuuda looked at that face and recognized it. The face of
the boy with the creel—only not.

It was the boy's father.

***

The cost of a man's life had shrunken to a miserable low in Ezra's world. The proof was all around him, and if he couldn't see it, he could smell it. It came as something less than a surprise then when he awoke in the rain and saw the dark figure hovering over Tom Jersey.

Another scavenger.

Without any more thought to it than that, Ezra raised the pistol, aimed it in the general direction of the figure, and pulled the trigger.

***

A misty rain fell as Ellis left the shelter of his tent. They'd received word of a large contingent of wounded rebels at a farm, the Benson place, six miles distant as the crow flies. He had been ordered to ride out and confirm the information, and make arrangements for their care if the story bore truth.

He broke wind and rubbed his forearms. His damn arms hadn't pained him so in years.

He looked in on Spencer Hardy first. He'd regained consciousness sometime in the night. Spencer was sitting up on his cot. While not looking perfect, the young cavalryman looked a damn sight better than he had when his father had been willing to consign him to the woods. Ellis wondered how a father, any father, could do such a thing, could be so cold. It seemed callous even in war.

Well, that was the nature of being human. A person couldn't always account for his actions. He thought about that a moment and decided it was a subject he didn't want to think on any further.

Spencer said little in response to Ellis' questions. What he did say was slow and slurred, difficult to understand. His scalp was badly swollen, with what felt and looked like a bag of water under it. He looked like he'd gone too many rounds with a prize fighter, or been kicked in the head by a horse. Undeniably ugly above the shoulders. But alive and that was what mattered. Alive and talking no less. A miracle? No. Just the new science of surgery. *Someday, Ellis thought, we'll operate on the brain and it won't be anything special. It'll be as common and straightforward as amputating a leg or an arm.*

He left Spencer behind and rode out across the hills. He'd gone a few miles, the hospital camp faded to a bad memory in the distance, when he came by some men digging in a field. It was still raining, though only slightly, and he used the brim of his hat to shield his face. He took his outer jacket off in the heat and humidity. The men were mud-covered teamsters; negro soldiers who, lacking the fighting spirit as some said, had been put to work on burial detail. He rode by at a distance.

There were four of them and they were built stocky and rigid. He thought they could probably have dug up the huge oak he'd passed a ways back if they'd been so ordered. Three had taken their shirts off in the heat. The senior was a sergeant and his shirt was dark with rain and sweat.

They paid him no mind, probably didn't even see him across the fifty yards separating them. He made no effort to announce himself, had slowed his horse to a walk. The bugs were bad here, eye-bothering gnats and blowflies big as roaches, but the scene had captured him. Despite all the dead he'd seen, he'd thought little about their burying and his mind suddenly seemed stuck on it now. He counted four lined up. Four bodies and one grave. It didn't register until the negroes lifted one and carried it to the edge of the hole they'd dug. They tumbled him in and stepped over to the next, tumbling him in as well. A mass grave.

The men they buried out here would likely be lost forever. He thought how every one of them must have friends and loved ones somewhere, and how those loved ones would search for years and never find a trace of where their father or son had been laid at their last accounting. That seemed unfortunate.

He swatted at the gnats.

He watched as they placed a third body in the open ground. Ellis wondered how deep they'd dug it. He'd seen hogs on the road and suspected—he swallowed and was suddenly glad his stomach was empty.

A shout broke his train of thought. The diggers were hollering amongst themselves.

"Lookahere, don't that just beat all," one said.

"I'm guessing we need us a foot more," another said, apparently measuring the dead man with his eyes as the body lay beside the hole. "He a tall feller, sure enough."

"Y'all can't bend 'im?"

"It ain't gonna happen. That feller's stiffer than a soldier in a two-dollar whore house."

A round of chuckles. *Niggers*, Ellis thought, *they'll do anything and be happy at it.* He had stopped now and was staring from across the field.

"We jus' gonna have to dig's all," the one still wearing his shirt said.

"Like hell we does."

"What in hell you doin', Preacher Man?"

The one they called Preacher Man picked up an axe leaning against the tree and stepped forward. Ellis had only an instant to consider what was coming, but when it came it played out before him as if slowed especially for his eyes, as shocking a thing as he'd ever seen in the army. Preacher Man hacked through the tall fellow's legs in two quick, powerful strokes just below the knees. As a rule, the dead don't bleed and this corpse proved it. The stunned assistant surgeon spurred his mount.

"Now he'll fit." Preacher Man held the axe loosely in one hand. "You'll see."

"You dumbshit niggers!" Ellis shouted as he rode up. His initial impulse was to get down, but once amongst the diggers he saw their size. To a man they were bigger than two of him. He also discovered the advantage the animal's height gave him. They had to look up at him, up into the rain. "If I could, I'd bury every one of you worthless niggers here," he said.

"Cap'n sir, he didn't mean no harm, sir. I mean, the man, he dead an' all," the shirt wearing sergeant said.

"I'm aware of how dead the man is, sergeant. You are a sorry lot," Ellis said, trying to look them all in the eye at the same time. "Haven't you respect for these soldiers? For what they did here? You hack 'em up like you're splitting cordwood. I'll have the bunch of you bucked and gagged for a week. Cowards."

Preacher Man looked at the sergeant, eyes stupid with regret.

"Now Cap'n," the sergeant said, "you don't wanna be doing all that, sir."

"How's that, Sergeant?"

"Well sir. Preacher Man here, he just a stupid and why you wanna be wasting your time, suh, wit a stupid nigger? All due respect Cap'n, you bein' an' important man an' all, your time is val'abel. Too val'abel to be messing with a bunch of no accounts like us, suh. We respect these men an' what dey done. We just tired o' waiting our chance to show it's all." The sergeant grinned cheaply.

"What's your name, boy?"

"Tibbles, suh. Sergeant Tibbles."

"Tibbles—Sergeant Tibbles—how you expect to fight if you can't even handle a few no-goods on a burial detail?" He looked around, spat with the wind. "Fact is, though, I expect you'll get your chance to fight soon enough. I hope you don't regret it. But this," he swept his arm through the air, "this isn't right. Mind it don't happen again."

"Course not, suh. Never."

Ellis wondered if Tibbles was patronizing him. He was thinking on that notion, trying to decide whether he should answer, when he heard a sound in the near distance. A loud bang. An image of Archer lying dead on the ground with a hole gaping his chest suddenly flashed in his mind and he thought: *gunshot.*

***

Cuuda felt the heat of the ball as it passed through his cheek, spinning him around and knocking the wind out of him. He fell to the ground the way a dead man might have, with purpose, meaning to catch the ground quick as possible. He hit hard enough to knock the wind out of him a second time. He lay several moments with his head buried under his hands, tasting the wet dirt, waiting for the blood to come, expecting to spit teeth.

You done good. Now do gooder. The air smelled faintly of fish and he felt the boy beside him, whispering in his ear. His breath was warm and soothing. His cheek did not hurt.

There was no blood.

Cuuda waited for whatever would come next, but when nothing did he lifted himself out of the mud. He rubbed his cheek and ran his tongue around his mouth. Nothing out of the ordinary.

He looked down and the soldier in blue was staring up at him with the waxy look of a store dummy he'd seen once. Not saying anything, just staring. Staring and breathing in a low, sick sounding sort of way. A revolver dangled at the end of one hand, but the hand didn't appear to have much strength and the gun fell the inch or two to the grass as Cuuda reached for it. He stuffed it in his belt and gave the second man the once over.

Plain to see he was a rebel, an officer based on the gold

on his uniform. He was face-up but his eyes were shut. He had the look of a tired soul, one who was done with living and just waiting to catch the train to Heaven. Cuuda heard old Prosper's voice from the before time in his head again:

Dere's the hebben-goin spirit what goes to duh sure dead, duh place where duh hebben-goin spirit can rest. Dat where His eye watch ya.

"Whose eye, Prosper?" Cuuda said now, aloud.

Gawd's eye chile. But den, dere's duh trabblin spirit too. Dat one come an see us fum time tuh time. Duh trabblin spirit is free, like a birdie.

The rebel looked very much as if his Spirit had already left out of him. Cuuda turned and looked out across the field. In the distance, a group was coming toward him—a rider on horseback and three or four negroes pulling a dray wagon. He looked back at the two on the ground. They hadn't moved. Between them something glinted in the rain. He bent and picked it up and turned it over. On one side a few letters were engraved in the bright metal. The thing looked interesting, maybe some sort of musical instrument.

He stuck it in his pocket and waited. It was just after ten am on Tuesday morning, July seventh.

TWENTY

Surgeon Josiah Boyd was bandaging his own arm when the diggers brought the two in on the late afternoon of July seventh. Sometime in the night just passed, he'd managed in his exhaustion to slice his forearm in a dozen places. These were deep cuts, the blood must have flown freely he thought but had no recollection of it, and they'd opened again. He was actually rebandaging them.

He'd just finished rounds. In fact, he was in no shape to make rounds and Tiny, who was not a doctor and never pretended to be, made them himself—and not for the first time. Boyd had found salvation in a little bottle and now that salvation was killing him one swallow at a time. He was staring the reaper in the face and half knew it.

Boyd, of course, could have argued it was the war killing him. He had begun to see things, to hear things too. Many he suspected were not real, like the little boy he saw now standing beside the wounded rebel major. The young boy wore a pair of muddy trousers and had only one shoe. A look of youthful ignorance shone from him. Looped over one shoulder was a wicker basket, a creel. A faint odor of fish hung on the air and Boyd caught himself thinking he must have a couple of fish in that creel.

But despite all of this, he didn't think the boy was real. Like the man who'd suddenly been in his tent the other night—suddenly been there and then not. It was otherwordly the way he hadn't heard him and that's how this boy seemed to him. He rubbed at his coarse beard (he hadn't shaved in more than a week and he was going to have to do something about that. His heart raced with the familiar pangs of a need now as much a curse as it was a salvation. He ignored it best he could and turned his attention back on the boy, but the boy was gone. He sniffed. The fish smell had gone too.

He left the rebel major for, well, for later, that was all. If Hardy felt up to it maybe he'd examine him, or maybe Ellis would get back from wherever he'd gone (Boyd tried to remember where he might have sent the assistant surgeon, but, what the hell, he couldn't be expected to remember every goddamn little detail, could he?). The other fellow the diggers had dragged in, whom he now saw wore Union blue (and the rebel be damned), had what was obviously a bad thigh wound. He motioned to Tiny, and Ezra Coffin was carried into the church, to the altar that had run with blood for a week now. It was dusk and the lanterns burned with a lazy intensity that gave shadows to the men as they moved around.

Beads of sweat grew on Boyd's face as he cut out a piece of flesh over Ezra's swollen thigh. As the skin parted it came alive with a teeming mass of worms. They crept over Boyd's hand, and of a sudden he had the impression his own skin had disintegrated into the writhing mass. He pulled his hand from Ezra's innards and stepped back. Stood contemplating his hands, turning them in the flickering light, watching the maggots move and writhe over his flesh. His skin was intact after all. They were just worms, just bird food. He'd begun to hyperventilate, but now he concentrated on controlling his breathing. "Sonbitch," he said, looking at Tiny. The fat corpsman (and he was fat, Boyd thought, a goddamn human eating machine—no pride, no pride at all) was staring hard at him with those fat, accusing eyes. "Sonbitch," he said again, and sneered at Tiny. "You never seen a maggot?"

He watched Tiny shake his fat head and open his fat lips. "I seen maggots before. Major, sir, you okay?"

Now that's a goddamn stupid question. "What?"

"It's just..."

Tiny's fat head swiveled on his fat neck as he tried to get his undoubtedly fat brain to work. *Must be a lot of shit in that fat pig of a body.* "What is it man? Speak up. You questioning me? You impertinent, fat sonbitch. You questioning me?"

Tiny's hands went up before him and he stepped back, as if pushing himself away from a wall. "Major, I wasn't questioning you."

"Damn right you weren't questioning me. Best remember who's doing the operating here, fat man."

"Yes sir," Tiny said. "Maybe, maybe you could get back to the patient, sir?" His voice was tentative, not that of a man who'd been two years with Boyd.

Yeah, yeah, yeah, I'll get back to the patient. But I don't need you to tell me my business. I'm not done with you, that's for sure. We gonna talk, you and me. Don't ever question my judgment, you pig. Boyd looked down, saw the maggots crawling out of Ezra's thigh. "Okay," he said, "so they're real. I can deal with that. Yeah, I can deal with that a whole lot easier than if they're not."

"How's that, sir? You say something?"

"Why don't you just shut
(your fat face—your fat, dumb ass little face)
your mouth and pass me the damn scalpel."

Tiny retrieved the blade from where Boyd had dropped it. He wiped it across his apron and handed it over without any show of his usual enthusiasm.

Boyd lengthened his incision and began to pick out

chunks of bone and other debris, working with his customary diligence and attention. He found the ball, which had squished flat against the shattered femur. He tossed it in a bowl and it made the tinny sound of metal striking metal. He made no indecisive moves, was quick and to the point. Looked almost his old self, except he mumbled the whole time.

Tiny moved in closer, but Boyd's one-sided conversation abruptly stopped and he looked over at the hospitalman. "There a problem?"

"No. No problem, sir." He shook his head.

"Then stop making so much goddamn noise."

"Beg pardon?" Tiny asked.

"What part of SHUT UP don't you understand?"

Tiny took a step back from the table, a look of confusion about him.

"A man can't hardly hear himself think for Christ's sake." Boyd redirected himself to the soldier on the table, his own pulse a water hammer slapping his skull. The sound was heavy in his ears and he found it increasingly difficult to concentrate on the task at hand. He removed the last of the maggots and palpated the fractured bone, tried to remember what *Tripler and Blackman* had said to do with a femur busted all to hell. He'd memorized every page of the 1861 textbook, but the only part of it he could recall just then was the full, weighty title: *Handbook for the Military Surgeon: Being a compendium of the duties of the medical officer in the field, the sanitary management of the camp, the preparation of food, etc; with forms for the requisitions for supplies, returns, etc; the diagnosis and treatment of camp dysentery; and all the important points in war surgery: including gunshot wounds, amputation, wounds of the chest, abdomen, arteries, and head, and the use of chloroform.* He'd studied *Tripler and Blackman* like a Baptist preacher studying the Scripture, had worn the spine thin till the pages fell out. Just then however, he couldn't recall one damn word. There he stood, the bones and muscle of a man's thigh naked to the air, a sheaf of flesh hardly thicker than his trousers the only thing between his fingers and the man's life blood pulsing hard in the exposed femoral artery, and all he could conjure on the subject of gunshot wounds was *Handbook for the Military Surgeon: Being a compendium of the duties of the medical officer, etc., etc., etc.*

He stared wide-eyed at the leg, feeling like he'd forgotten how to walk.

***

Having seen to the welfare of both the Union private and the Confederate major, Dr. Tobias Ellis had spurred to a gallop and made it out to the Benson farm by late morning. There he found a rebel surgeon and forty-eight rebel troopers suffering from any number of serious and life-threatening injuries. They were spread out between the house and the barn and though injured, not one of the forty or so conscious men acknowledged him with anything more than a contemptuous grunt.Several were downright ornery and one went so far as to suggest the noxious fumes which everywhere suffused the air had worsened with his arrival.Ellis chuckled and replied that the only thing he smelled was Johnny Reb's pungent sweat as he fled the countryside to escape the wrath of George Meade and Abe Lincoln.

"Lincoln ain't fit to lead a johnny detail," the rebel retorted.

"Maybe not," Ellis said,"but then I suppose the President of the United States doesn't have to dig too many latrines.And I'm betting that right about now, Bobby Lee's wishing he'd never heard of General George Meade."

After a thorough accounting of the casualties, he met with a Major Jonathan Sutter, who outranked him. The man had either been injured in the past or was born troubled because one side of his face drooped. Ellis had showed the necessary military courtesy nonetheless. "Sir, my condolences on your situation. You have accorded yourself with the highest standards of our profession and I only wish I could do this without taking you into custody, sir."

"Captain, all I've done here I did because it would have shamed these men to do any less." Sutter spoke out of only one side of his mouth. "If I might be allowed to continue to care for them, with perhaps the requisite necessities, it would have the best positive effect on them."

"Of course, sir. But you understand that such a decision..." He gestured; *out of my hands.*

"Of course. But I mention it all the same."

"I'll pass it along, sir." He paused. As the junior he had to give the major opportunity to speak last if he so desired. He said nothing though, and the awkward moment passed. "I must be getting back. I'll send ambulances for your charges by first light tomorrow, sir."

"We'll be ready."

Ellis had ridden up to the Benson farm and seen the destruction wrought by the rebel occupation. He'd been prepared to actively dislike the man in charge of that occupation, but found he didn't. The major's sense of duty and professionalism—all this despite his obviously palsied face—had caught him off guard and reminded him of his own place in the war. The major was making the best of a very difficult situation and doing a decent job of it in the process. Ellis found he respected the man.

Tobias arrived back at the church just past dusk. The rain had finally stopped and the air had a crystalline quality that allowed him to see for miles as he came over Snyder's Hill and passed through the remains of the Peach Orchard and across the battlefield, including the Trostle and Weikert farms. He'd long since recovered wounded from all these places and a hundred more besides. He wondered how many more were out there, wounded rebels hiding in the rocks perhaps, or being cared for in private homes. And then there were the dead. He had a sudden vision of a vast and grand cemetery, rolling green hills covered with white crosses for as far as the eye could see.

He put such thoughts out of his mind and enjoyed the last mile of his ride, crossing the Spangler farm and finally Rock Creek. He found the Baltimore Pike and turned south for a quarter mile, saw the churchyard looming in the twilight at the top of Butler Hill. He dismounted outside the stone wall and stood to the west watching the last remnants of light pass out over what had been a modest cemetery, the dark banks of Rock Creek just visible beyond. A hundred or more tents now covered that land, shadowing the tombstones in the end of day.

He thought first he would get some supper. Now that he was here though, outside the church that had become the focal point of the hospital grounds, he had a mind to check on how things were faring inside. He was a surgeon after all, and the place any surgeon worth his scalpel wants to be is in surgery. He ascended the several steps and entered.

Darker inside than out, it took his eyes a moment to adjust. He knew immediately something wasn't right. The familiar rhythm was lacking. And Tiny was saying, "Major, you all right, sir? Want me to get Dr. Hardy or maybe Captain Ellis?"

Boyd was yelling, "You can get whoever the hell you please, fat man. Cause I'm outta here. I don't need this crap. Don't need it at all."

"Sir?"

"Don't sir me, you pissant. You got what you wanted. I can't work with that tongue of yours jawing at me constantly." Boyd backed away from the table, swung a gaze that nailed Ellis like a hot spike. "Here, you fix 'im. I'm done."

Ellis listened and stood dumbfounded in the vestibule of the church. Even as Boyd brushed by him, he couldn't believe it. Not until he saw the surgeon's eyes close up. Glassy, like he wasn't using them.

***

The ball that felled Tom Jersey had crashed through his right hip, bounced off his pelvis and deflected upward, where it passed through his bladder and eventually passed close under his rib cage in the general vicinity of his liver. It exited his flank several inches to the right of his spine, where it left a large hole that bled profusely but spared him the indignity of paraplegia. He might well have bled to death but for the dirt in the wound that acted in some measure as both poultice and packing. Still, he was left prostrate, and Hardy (he was spending most of his time abed himself, his flank pain a sharp colic he recognized as the dire spasm of a stoned kidney), who examined the rebel major at leisure several hours after he was brought in, noted the rapidity of his pulse. He'd ordered a half grain of morphine and probed the flank wound, remarking in the process that only the divine hand of providence could save the major. He then added, rather pompously and to no one in particular, "A wound not to be treated, as the Romans might have said."

The probing stirred fresh bleeding, however, and he tasked a rebel private (the man had lost an eye in the fighting, but he only needed one eye to see with and he had two able hands, unlike Hardy, whose fingers still cramped at the mere thought of operating) with holding pressure over the site. When this worked only marginally well, he instructed the private in packing the large wound with lint and prescribed twice daily shots of whiskey to stimulate the officer's spirit.

When the same able-bodied private asked after the major's prognosis, Hardy replied as if the answer was obvious: "Such wounds are invariably fatal. A few days, a week at most. I expect he'll have a hard time of it until then. It would have been merciful if the ball had killed him outright."

Major Sutter and his rebel charges had all been moved from the Bensen farm to the church by the next midmorning. Forty-nine wounded plus the surgeon himself. They were set to one side of the grounds, where the land was low and the waters of Rock Creek had drowned a dozen at the height of the rains a few days before. They joined two hundred and three other confederates, most of whom had been doctored and operated on by their own surgeons. One was a major who'd yet to regain any useful consciousness. He lay among the others, a pile of straw doing for a bed.

Dr. Sutter leaned over Major Jersey, examining him as the private relayed Hardy's prognosis.

"Horseshit," Sutter said. "Now give me a hand with him."

***

Undertaker's Row had grown, over the passage of a week, to a string of tents with notices of helpful intent, such as

All persons are respectfully invited to see the operation.
And
Bodies recovered from the field of battle at no additional cost to the family.

These signs were well made but weathered. This was not

their first use. The tents were placed slightly off to one side of a muddy lane, but still managed a haphazard and slipshod appearance. What had been a field of tall grass and gopher holes a month before was now a busy mess; burying the dead had become an industry in the wake of the great battle. People came from all over in the quest to find and identify their loved ones. Those who were successful were still more than the system could handle, however, and it sagged in the effort. Unidentified bodies were stacked under canvas between the tents. Burying them—or making them ready for transport—was a race against man's perishable elements. One was better off not seeing what became of them.

In short, not a place for the living.

Fully ten different morticians of one ilk or another had taken up residency in the lane. A near-constant stream of wagons kept them in business. Jupiter's shop was sandwiched in about the middle of the row, not a prime location if the wind wasn't blowing, between *Drs. TD & Edward Cooper, Embalmers,* and *Goldspur, Whitehall, Cruddy & Co., Undertakers & Morticians.* A large sign atop Jones' tent announced he was *The Leading Embalmer to the United States Army.* Not entirely true, of course. Another, beside his workbench, notified the observer that: *By order of the US Army, no dead soldier can be sent to his parents or family without first having been embalmed.* Another lie. His workbench was outside under the awning. Working in the open was preferable under such conditions and was the norm on the row. A man was not so apt to faint when he could breathe freely.

Jupiter himself was back at his bench, having made an usually quick recovery from his collapse. He still had his cough, still wheezed intermittently, but at least for the time being he had stopped bringing up pieces of his insides every few minutes. He felt able to work unmolested for the first time in years.

Cuuda was present as well. He was mixing a new batch of the Concoction, a necessary if mundane part of his chores. He'd made it dozens of times. Arsenic and chloride of zinc mixed with alcohol and some amount of water. He could have done it blindfolded.

It allowed time for a person to think. Right now he was thinking about Captain Tobias Ellis. He had told the assistant surgeon on their meeting a few days earlier that the two had never met. Now, however, he wasn't sure that was true. Ellis had administered aid to the wounded pair Cuuda had found on the field. He'd done it quickly, and with authority. And he'd done it in short sleeves.

Cuuda thought the scars on the captain's forearms was pretty ugly. Probably burns.

And probably exactly six years old.

Thinking about that got his hands tingling. Or maybe that was just from handling The Concoction.

TWENTY-ONE

Tobias was worried. He'd taken over for Boyd when the surgeon had walked away from his table. The patient, he didn't know his name but that wasn't uncommon, had yet to regain consciousness. He was a fevered wreck, pulse weak and thready, his life almost historical. Ellis had splinted the soldier's broken wrist and cleaned out the hole in Ezra's hand as well, but it was the thigh that bothered him most. He'd followed Boyd's lead in surgery and not amputated the leg. That might have been a mistake, he thought now. Normally, from his painstaking study of *Tripler and Blackman,* such a large and open wound would warrant amputation. But that hadn't been on Boyd's mind, not judging from the way he'd cleaned the hole of dead tissue. Hell, the wound had looked practically polished. Even in his obviously disordered frame of mind, Boyd was a better surgeon than Tobias could ever hope to be.

Disordered? Tough to argue against that. But Boyd was under pressure, they all were. Different people react differently. *Give him a pass this time,* Ellis thought. *After all, it was an isolated incident.*

Was it? Boyd had been erratic of late. But he'd done a hell of a job on Hardy's boy. Boyd had saved Spencer Hardy's life. No doubt about it.

But what about this soldier? Had Boyd done good by

this man? Had he done all he could? Had he done him a favor by not amputating?

Ellis kept trying to say yes to this, but his mind kept flashing back a few days, to a tent on the other side of the compound, and to the soldier bedded there. His name was Wooster and he'd been dead every bit of seventy-two-hours now, but in Ellis's mind the man's blood still jetted freely from that damn hole in his thigh. Hardy's words then echoed uncomfortably.

A man with a stuck femoral don't live. I suggest you remember that, doctor.

Like Wooster's, this private's femoral artery had been clearly visible at the base of his wound. It hadn't looked injured, but that was just it. It wasn't supposed to have any look at all. It should have been buried several inches under muscle and sinew, palpable maybe, but protected from any harm deep in the meat of the thigh. But it had been visible and that bothered Ellis in the extreme just now. What if Wooster's artery—his femoral—hadn't been injured either? What if it too had only been in the line of fire, so to speak?

What if a busted shard of bone had slowly, inexorably, worked its way into the artery's wall? What if Wooster had sat up one too many times? Well, the blood would flow then, wouldn't it? Like a goddamn burst dam it would flow, covering everything in its path.

What was it the woman had said of him after it was over? That he had looked like a man in shining red armor. Her name was Liza Coffin, bright red hair. It had stuck with him.

Like a man in shining red armor.

Boyd had brushed past him in the vestibule, had looked him hard in the face, apparently hadn't seen him: Like a man with glass eyes.

A chilling thought and his head ached with the idea. What if Boyd hadn't intended to leave the leg? What if he'd been so disconnected he hadn't known what the hell he was doing? What then?

What if Wooster's artery hadn't been injured?

Hardy: *A man with a stuck femoral don't live. I suggest you remember that, doctor. Might save you some grief in the future.*

Then again, it might not.

Ellis had a notion that maybe this private was a stuck femoral just waiting to happen.

***

They were all there, crowded into a large tent cleared for the purpose. The general mood was dirty brown, which matched the canvas sidewalls around them. The space was close, the ceiling sloping so a man of average height had to stoop except along the very center. It smelled of frowzy men, stale burlap, and the coarse tobacco of cheap segars.

Tiny, the oversized hospital corpsman, tried to make himself small in the rear of the tent. Several others, nurses who'd been with Boyd a year plus, aimed to make themselves smaller still. An admin clerk and a records officer squeezed into the small space to one side of a desk at the front. Ellis stood before it, wearing the only semi-clean uniform he had. Hardy, still sick but still too the senior surgeon, sat behind the desk in undress uniform. A bit of the fever lingered in him and his skin held gray in the lantern light. He struck a lucifer and puffed his segar with a saturnine look.

And then, of course, there was Boyd himself. The surgeon stood before Hardy and the others, keeping his sangfroid. He'd slept the sleep of the just the night before and was tired, but the bone weariness that had gutted him in the days past was gone. All were assembled to hear his explanation of why he'd walked out of surgery thirty-six hours before, why he'd left a man on his operating table with his inwards exposed. He had not concerned himself with this thing up to that moment and saw no reason to do so now. He'd gulped half a bottle of laudanum and felt the measure of it coursing through him, instilling confidence.

An ether of anticipation charged the air. Hardy poured a small cup of water from the croft on the table. He sipped. When he finally spoke, his voice was sick with fatigue but he made it work. The murmurous tent quieted in the process and the senior officer's carried all the way to the back despite their hoarse tone. "Dr. Boyd, you understand the nature of this inquiry?"

"I understand certain individuals believe I have, how would one say, acted in haste."

"In haste? It's a goddamn disgrace if you did what I'm hearing you did. I can't credit it though. No sir. Not with the Boyd I know."

"He done it all right. I seen it with my own eyes!" a frumpy-looking sergeant hollered, pointing at Boyd as if the man was guilty and soon to go to the gallows. His voice squawked like a chicken suddenly startled from its roost, loud and obtrusive. The room filled with the sound of men speaking and hollering at cross purposes.

Hardy pulled the segar from his mouth and slapped the table several times. The croft of water lifted and moved a fraction but didn't spill. "Quiet now. Won't have any more outbursts like that." The room quieted.

Hardy cleared his throat and redirected himself. "Boyd, you and me, we go back some. We've got history, you and I, been together awhile now. Had our differences, and I can't say I've always liked you. But I've never known you to endanger the welfare of one of your charges. Quite the opposite, I'd say." He gestured toward Boyd with his segar. "What have you to say? Why'd you leave that man on your table? What in God's name happened, doctor?"

"What happened? What in hell you think happened? The truth of the flesh."

"The truth of the flesh?" Hardy said.

"That man ain't made in his image."

"His image?"

"That man's made breakable. Christ man, you seen it yourself. I know you have. Haven't you been paying attention?"

The tent became raucous again and Hardy slapped the table once more, then again. "What in blazes you talking about?"

Boyd looked around the crowd. Tiny averted his eyes, shaking his head. A nurse in the back looked at him like he'd suddenly grown a horn. The frumpy sergeant mouthed an obscenity. Hardy himself sat with mouth gaped; a fly could have nested there. In that instant, Boyd was blessed with a clarity of biblical proportions. "Sonbitch," he said. They didn't have his knowledge of war, didn't understand. Well, he would enlighten them. That's all. He'd enlighten them and then they'd know how it really was, how the world turned on the grease of macerated flesh. How shit was shit no matter the package. He was juiced now, feeling no pain. Samson himself couldn't have stopped him.

"I had one of them broken men talk to me once. He was dead, of course, like we're all gonna be someday."

(And how messed up was that? No matter how much you accomplished, no matter how far you went in this life, it was all going to turn to dirt sooner or later. What was it the squirrel said to his doctor? I done all this, accomplished all this, and for what? Nuts, that's what. This revelation had just come to him—it was all so clear now.)

"He had a plum size hole in his forehead. Told me his folks had a place for him over in South Carolina." Boyd's head lolled back and forth. He pressed his lips together, voice now a teasing whine. "Up on Sumter Ridge." Back to his own detached voice now, full of fire as he spoke. "I suppose you could argue that a dead man speaking might have something more profound to say, but that's not the point. The point is he was proof of the hell that's waiting for us all. I seen too much of that hell right here, too many goddamn men what shoulda been dead and too many dead what maybe shoulda been home sparkin' their gals." He was speaking fast now, very fast, and they had to listen hard to catch the words. "I saw a man with his jaw blown off. Blown clean off! Another with half his chest missing. You could look in and see his heart beating—only it wasn't beating. It was wiggling. I thought then how the truth was right before me, right in the flesh of that wiggling heart. We're all of us breakable, all of us. You see, we're doomed, too smart for our own damn good."

He eyed the croft of water and licked his lips. Don't stop now, no sir, not when you got 'em in the sweet spot. To hell with thirst.

"The human body's a wonderful thing, when it works. And the mind, oh, the mind. Marvelous in all its accomplishments. But a damned hateful thing too."

(And this, too, was a new revelation. Christ but clarity was a wonderful thing.)

"We, most of us, we don't do no more with it than figure out how to kill our brothers and sisters. Hell, a bug does that. We don't use no more brain power than a bug. You ever seen how a cockroach works? It just bounces back and forth, moving from one shit pile to another. We're all of us cockroaches. How's that make you feel? Makes me feel mighty low friends, mighty low. Like God's pissing on me and laughing about it."

I'm kilt, I'm kilt, oh God, I'm kilt. (Where had that come from?)

Boyd took two steps toward Hardy, halving the distance to the table. The clerk scribbled madly and the sound of his nib working the paper reminded Boyd of the cricket that had so tortured his youth and he cupped a hand to his ear.

The place was quiet, the people staring. "You folks even breathing?" Boyd said. "Cockroaches, goddammit. Cockroaches. We all gonna go to hell. I know that much. Mark my words on this. We, no. You. You goddammit," he corrected, and pushed a finger through the air, pointing at various of the assembled. His other hand scratched at his ear and skin collected under his fingernails. They stood as if at attention, mesmerized, simultaneously avoiding his stare and unable to move. His eyes grew large and were shot with red. Inside his head, the cricket scratched and now he began to pull at his ear like it needed to come off. "You'll wake up like me one day, with a God-given clarity that'll let you realize how screwed you really are. You'll feel your scrawny little asses frying in the oil pits of hell till your arms and legs ain't nothing but burnt bones, like a piece of over-roasted chicken on a spit. That spit will be a poker in your ass and you'll turn there all your days, sweating your guts out in a place so hot your blood will steam. And why this unholy salvation? Because," he saw them taking the premonition in—soaking it up like sponges in a pail of piss. "Because you stupid sonbitches...."

(And that was right, wasn't it? Just stupid sonbitches. No better, and no better off, than cockroaches. Or crickets goddammit. They were all just a bunch of crickets.)

He yanked his ear and the skin on the side of his head tore and a gout of blood appeared. "We ain't made in his image." He took another step toward Hardy and now all that separated them was the table. He gestured grandly, taking his hand away from his ear and cocking his head with a grimace as he did so. He took in great gulps of air and held his arms aloft till his hands touched the sloping sidewalls of the tent. His eyes widened and a long drip of blood rolled down in front of his ear and onto his neck.

"We're flesh and bone, you and me. And let me tell you something. Flesh and bone is breakable. I know this, I been there, seen it. It burns too, and all what's gonna be left of any of us is teeth. Teeth don't burn and that's what's gonna be left. Nothing but teeth—"

"Dr. Boyd!"

"The whole goddamn lotta you, every last cricket and cockroach, ain't gonna be nothing but a pile of teeth chittering in the pissed dirt—"

Boyd's hand brushed the croft, knocking it over. The water spread across the table, soaking the papers and smearing the clerk's writings into a useless gibberish. Boyd collapsed to a knee, his head still cocked like a man in the midst of an apoplectic fit. He swiped at his half-torn ear.

"Dr. Boyd!" Hardy shouted. His segar hit the ground. "That's enough, mister. Quite enough." Water spilled over the table's edge into Hardy's lap. He stood, wiping his front with his open palms. "Dammit, man, that's quite enough."

Boyd knelt on the tent bottom, his lips moving rapidly as he chanted: "Handbook for the Military Surgeon: Being a compendium of the duties of the medical officer in the field, the sanitary management of the camp, the preparation of food, etc; with forms for the requisitions for supplies, returns, etc; the diagnosis and treatment of camp dysentery..."

"You're finished," Hardy said.

Boyd grabbed at his dangling ear then, and before any of the assembled men could stop him he tore it off completely.

Anything to stop the crickets.

***

Jersey rallied for a day, but his wound began to fester on the ninth, when a watery discharge appeared at the hole in his back. He complained of severe flank pain and lay with a toilworn, cadaverous expression.

Dr. Sutter counted Jersey's pulse against his own, found it thin, quick, and irregular. Skin cold and clammy, respirations hurried and laboring. His pelvis was distended and the surgeon introduced a catheter into Jersey's bladder, recovering a dark, strong-smelling mixture of urine and clotted blood.

Ellis, who'd just removed himself from the tent where Boyd had collapsed in spectacular fashion, joined Sutter after the catheterization. The two stood in the yard together, Sutter toweling his hands and somehow managing to look kempt despite his half paralyzed face.

"Your man, how does he do today?" Ellis asked, recognizing the injured rebel major lying supine on the straw. "He's had quite a time of it I'd imagine."

"Not well. He's nauseous and diarrheal both. I've cleaned his wounds best I could here, but..."

"I'm sorry. There's a great deal of foul humors in the air all over the camp," Ellis said.

Sutter shot a glance at the Union assistant surgeon, handing the towel to a rebel soldier assisting him. "I don't subscribe to such black magic, doctor." He stepped over an unconscious soldier and knelt for a moment, peeking beneath a dressing on the man's abdomen. The patient made an unintelligible sound as if passing gas by mouth. Sutter rose.

"Surely you believe in the benefits of fresh air?" Ellis said. Sutter's skewed face was almost painful to look at. .

"Of course." Sutter glanced at the assistant and the towel was proffered wordlessly. He took it, wiped his hands a second time, then looked at Ellis. "What I do not believe is that foul air enfeebles." He made a show of glancing about. "I cannot fathom the atmosphere contains an essence that may be either good or evil according to the vicissitudes of some unseen nature. The air contains nitrogen, Priestley's oxygen, which by the grace of a merciful God gives all of us life, and a few other incidentals of little import. Nothing more, nothing less."

"You're anti-phlogiston." Ellis observed. A statement, not a question.

"Of course. My good sir, any physician worth his weight in this modern day and age is anti-phlogiston."

"Indeed. But perhaps foul air possesses a lack of Priestley's gas."

"Then in such case it should make us all unwell." Sutter knelt before a man with a rakish look and a sunburnt face. "How're you doing, sergeant?"

"Tolerable, sir, but I could do with a bit o' the spirits. If you catch my drift, sir."

"I do sergeant, and," Sutter's eyes shifted to Ellis, "as soon as our hosts enjoin us with such libations, you'll be the first."

"I ain't sure what you just said doc, but if it had anything to do with drink, I'm your man."

Sutter patted the sergeant's shoulder and moved on.

"Perhaps it requires an enfeebled constitution to gain a toehold, sir," Ellis said.

Sutter took the towel and held it up, as if letting the sun shine through. "Like you, sir, I have seen many such enfeebled constitutions on the battlefield. Most will live or die at the hand of the surgeon, not of the atmosphere. No, Dr. Ellis, it is not a malignant vapor that kills our soldierly colleagues. It is our own ignorance." He rubbed his hands across the coarse cotton.

"Our ignorance?"

"There are those who believe the murderous agent is carried not on the breeze, but by man himself." He turned to his assistant. "New towel, boil the old."

Ellis watched as the assistant bundled the towel in one pocket of his satchel and pulled another from the opposite side. "I'm aware of such theories, doctor. No such infective agent is proved, though."

"That hardly means it doesn't exist."

Sutter knelt and Ellis watched as he cut the dressing away from a stumped arm. "Six days on this one. Isn't that correct Mr. Dean?" Ellis observed the lack of any discharge, saw the wound was pink and only slightly puffy.

"Six, doctor. If today be the ninth," the man said, grinning at Ellis.

"Curious how there's no laudable pus—" Ellis began.

"The only thing laudable about pus is its absence," Sutter said. "I am among those who believe it to be a derangement of the natural juices, sir."

"A minority."

"An ever increasing one." Sutter took the fresh towel and wiped his hands again.

"You've wiped your hands a half dozen times in the past few minutes," Ellis said.

"It is a theory. My own."

"What's that?"

"The infective agent is borne on our hands, not the air."

"Now that sounds like black magic, doctor," Ellis said. Before Sutter had a chance to answer, he added, "Is there anything I can do for you or your men?"

"A touch of apple brandy'd be nice to do Major Jersey some good."

"Of course. I'll see to it at once. You shall have a cruet by evening," Ellis said.

"And perhaps a bottle of spirits for the men. To buoy their constitutions, you understand."

"Yes, their constitutions." Ellis was distracted now. Not by Sutter's theory, which was interesting but hardly a thing to be given over to serious consideration, but by thoughts of the work he had waiting for him. Hardy was physically incapacitated (Ellis doubted he'd ever operate again and suspected Hardy knew this as well) and Boyd was—he hesitated—mentally deranged. *Deranged.* The word was like bitter lemon on the tongue. If a man like Boyd... He shied away from going there. "I'll see what I can do," he said.

"Much obliged," Sutter said. He toweled his hands once more, stooped, and peeled back the next dressing.

***

On the banks of Rock Creek, three miles east by south along the Baltimore Pike, lay the Lutheran Church and its cemetery. Once an abode of worship, the grounds were now a great hallowed retreat of humanity.

In a clearing somewhere near the center of this pitiful concern, a fiddle player tightened his bow. Slight, elderly, he slowly tuned the fiddle's strings and began a long, lamenting melody. He played as if he'd waited all his life for this moment. The vibrato was a tremulous, eerie thing that seemed almost to hug the countryside. Solitary in its musings, it reminded one of home. Wandering in its stirrings, it rang of ma and pa, of Billy Bob and Mary Jo, of gals back home, of wives and children kneeling to pray beside quilted spreads stuffed with feathery down. It awoke those parts of a man poisoned by a war nobody wanted, a conflict everyone hated.

Liza listened to the musical piece as she sat alongside the cot of a boy who'd lost both arms a few days before. He was a wasted, distant lad with ash gray skin, scruffy whiskers, and concussed eyes. He sweated much and from time to time passed bowel gas. The flies alighted on him frequently, but he appeared to pay them no mind. Indeed, he paid no attention to anything and had said not two words to anyone until he heard the musings of the fiddle player. "My Julie," he said suddenly, unexpectedly.

Liza, who'd sat vigil for numerous men and boys in the past few days, fumbled for her pen and paper. She scribbled: *My dearest Julie.*

The ash gray soldier continued. "I was shot a week ago at Gettysburg." He turned to the red-haired woman. "Do you think that's okay to say? That it won't come too much of a shock?"

He sounded like a little boy, though she was some surprised by the strength of his voice. She'd almost convinced herself he could not speak except for simple utterances. "Yes, yes. I'm sure any words from you will do her well."

"You're kind. My Julie's kind like that too."

"I'm sure she is." She wrote: *I was wounded a week ago at Gettysburg.* "Please, go on."

He didn't look at her. His eyes rolled back and forth as a light breeze came through the open flap. An up tempo lifted the music, followed by a haunting series of lingering tones. He seemed to concentrate on this, as if in the notes he heard a distant voice. "The surgeons took my arms and so I am invalided. The hand of this letter is that of a woman who has been very kind to me in my hours of misery. – I'm sorry," he said, "I never asked your name?"

She told him.

"Her name is Liza. She reminds me of you in so many ways. I wish I could see you. I was a fool ever to have left. There is so much I would like to say."

He continued speaking in halting sentences, letting the music speak to him in between his words. Liza continued writing. Occasionally she inserted a word or chose a phrase she thought more meaningful. Mostly she just listened and wrote. These were the times she felt closest to Ezra. They kept her sane in her grief over Samuel. The camp doctors had put her to the task.

When he was done, she sealed the note and pocketed it,

promising to post it immediately. She stepped out into the evening air and took a large breath, feeling the warmth but tasting the rot as well. She stifled a gagging and moved across the yard to the clearing where the fiddler was still at work by the light of a large fire. She wondered if he knew the effect his music had. A small crowd was gathered and a petty sutler had set up a grill and offered roasted peanuts for a few pennies. She watched a negro boy, he looked vaguely familiar, give over a few indian-heads for a bag. He skipped off into the night.

She stood leaning against a tree, the exhaustion of several days falling upon her shoulders like saddlebags weighted in granite. She slipped to the ground and closed her eyes. Later, when the negro boy came back through the clearing with an eye out for her, she was still sleeping and so missed him.

TWENTY-TWO

M urder.

Funny how the world works, Ellis thought. There were perhaps ten thousand dead on the fields of southern Pennsylvania just then—all to a man dead at the hands of another in some way—yet none would be classed as murder in a legal sense. War was like that. You could kill a man, or ten men, or a hundred men, and justify it all. But cause or permit the death of just one under the right circumstances, and the hangman's noose might not be far behind.

It was enough to keep a man from wearing tight-collared shirts.

Boyd was under arrest, charged with dereliction of duty, conduct unbecoming, and a half dozen lesser charges. Ellis was still concerned with the man Boyd had operated upon—or failed to operate upon, as the case was now apparent. If he died, Boyd could be held accountable. A zealous prosecutor might even hold for murder. At the least, it wouldn't be just his military career ruined.

He deserved better.

Ellis leaned over the wounded private. He was still largely insensible, not unconscious but not in his right mind either. A clerk had gone through his pockets. A few letters addressed to "Ezra" had been found so this was the name scrawled in red letters on a tag pinned to his undergarments, which was all he wore. The letters had been shoved under the cot, as was usual. Ellis picked up the bundle.

On top of the pile, crisscrossed by twine ties, was a tintype of a woman standing in front of a willow. He fingered the image, sliding it out from the bundle. The girl looked vaguely familiar, and Ellis thought for an instant he knew her. Had the likeness been in color, had her bright red hair been able to shine out from the mixture of silver nitrate and gun cotton coating the surface of the iron, he might have known her immediately.

Ezra stirred on the cot. He mumbled unintelligibly and turned on his side, his stomach rumbling with deep borborygami. Ellis put the tintype back in the bundle and out of his mind. He returned the patient to his back and untied the mud-tinged dressing around his thigh. Underneath the flesh was pink and healthy looking, with a few spots of black-brown where the air had dried out the fat. He saw no laudable pus. Sutter's words came to him: *The infective agent is borne on our hands, not the air.* He doubted that—doubted it very much—but just the same he decided to make an experiment of this case. He'd wash his hands and change the dressings daily. Such a proposal would be a bother on a larger scale, but for a single patient it was no more than a minor nuisance and could do no possible harm.

He had a corpsman find a bucket and instructed him to wash his hands and change the private's bandages afterwards. Thinking about it another moment, he decided he might have trusted Archer with such a duty, but not just any corpsman. He had the aide bring him the fresh water and changed the dressings himself.

"Can't hurt," he said, but he felt foolish even so.

He left the private and returned to his own tent, where he removed his shirt and boots and lay down on his cot. The scars along his forearms were itching again, as they had a tendency to do when he was over tired. The scars were a gift from his pa. The old man had made him lift a pot of boiling water with his bare forearms back in the summer of '57. Ellis had wanted to kill the old man for that. He did too, the next day. The old man keeled over dead while drinking his own stinking hooch. Go figure. Even that hadn't been enough though. He'd dug a grave in the family plot out back of their Western Virginia farmhouse. Ellis himself had put the old man into the canvas sack for burying. Then he'd squatted and shat in it. "Deal with that, you old hoot," he'd said. "You can smell my shit for all time now." He'd have pissed on him too, but by then his mom had joined the affair and blubbered as he shoveled dirt over her beloved. One fool crying over another. Her goddamn weeping and carrying on had made him want to puke. He'd left the next day. She hadn't even come out to say goodbye.

He was tired and doubted he could go on without at least a few hours' sleep. The damn scars itched. They always itched when he got really tired. But he could deal with that. Always had. The memories were another matter. Because when he remembered, he desired. And when he desired, well, in the end he always got what he desired.

And these days, with who he was and how far he had come, that might be a problem.

He rose and went to his trunk, opened it. He removed a few items, trying to find exactly the right object. A girl's hairbrush. A young child's bow tie. A pendant necklace. A pair of glasses too small for him, one lens cracked and a fingerprint of blood on it. All interesting, the glasses especially, but none quite what he needed at just that moment. Then he spotted the bag. He unrolled it, turned it upside down. A boy's shoe fell out, and along with it a faint but undeniable fishy odor.

That would do, he thought. Yes, in the absence of

anything better—anything living—the shoe would suffice very well.

***

Cuuda had to walk again.

He had been listening to the fiddler play his tune, had been munching roasted peanuts he'd bought from a sutler and sitting on the edge of the clearing watching the people come and go. He'd had a pleasant moment recalling his parents in the before time, and then

You done good. Now do gooder.

He dropped the peanuts. Nearly pissed himself. It was the boy's voice, and when he looked there he was, standing beside a tree down the lane. As always, he had the creel over one shoulder and wore only one shoe. *Where's your other?* Cuuda had time enough to think, then was on his feet. He had to walk.

Coffin. Her name was Coffin. Like the boxes he built for the dead.

He had to find her. One of the men he'd found on the field was attached to her in some way. He wasn't sure how exactly, but he knew it was true.

Old Prosper, in his creolized English, would have called it the *caul*. A sense—more a certainty in this case—the private and the woman were connected. Here was the man she'd spoken of to Jupiter. Cuuda was sure of it. He guessed he'd sensed in her that the man she sought was still alive, that his hair still grew. That's what Prosper used to say when a man died: *his hair don't grow no more.*

Problem was, the caul wasn't a thing you could pass over and ignore, no matter how much you might like to. The knowledge would burn inside him like an ever growing bonfire until it either consumed him or he proved it out. Already he could feel it heating his insides, like a hot ash about to erupt.

He had to walk it out. It was the only way.

He knew she hadn't left. He could feel that too. That and no more. Now he had to find her. He began by checking random tents and moving among and between the various sutlers. He checked the church itself, where he'd seen her kneeling once in the accumulated blood, which had been nearly as bright as her hair.

Bright red hair. He could see it plainly. Her face too was coming back to him.

He waited outside the tent of the Sanitary Commission, the only place he'd seen ladies coming and going in finery. Why he supposed she should be dressed such was beyond him. After an hour he gave up the post. But as he walked away, an idea came to him.

Or rather *cauled* to him.

***

"Mister Ellis, suh." Cuuda looked at the ground as he spoke, afraid he might be interrupting something important.

Assistant Surgeon Ellis looked up from the crumpled sheet of paper. His face appeared distant at first, then he balled and pocketed the note. He looked at the boy, and Cuuda saw his hard features soften, or at least thought he did. All the same, he avoided the man's eyes.

It don't pay to look toubob in the eyes. Prosper's voice again.

"Cuuda, ain't it?"

"Yassuh." He looked at the surgeon's forearms, saw the scars and knew. *You're the one, you toubob sonofabitch.*

"How you been? How you gettin' along?"

"Thank you, suh. I guess I'm...tolerable."

"You sure we ain't, eh, haven't ever met?" Ellis said.

"I don't think so, suh. I think I'd remember something

like that." *You just a dumbshit baby nigger darkie.* "Not no more I ain't."

"How's that?" Ellis said.

"Nothin' suh. A moment?"

"You know I got that. For Jupiter's boy. What you want?"

"It's about that soldier, suh. The one what come in the other day with that rebel. When you was with the diggers." Cuuda nodded as if he expected this last bit to jog the surgeon's memory.

"I recall the man. A private. What about him? He's bad hurt if that's what you're wondering."

"No suh. I mean, yassuh. Sorry 'bout that, suh."

An awkward silence.

"I do have work," Ellis said.

Cuuda raised his head until he was looking the surgeon straight in the face. He said, "I thinks that soldier is the mister what that lady been looking for, suh."

"What're you talking about?"

"The red-haired mistress, suh. She been looking for her man."

"You mean Liza? How did you know... And you think...?"

Cuuda nodded again, averted his eyes.

"What gives you such a notion, boy?"

"Can't readily say, suh." Prosper: *The caul ain't something toubob unnerstands.*

"Don't play, boy."

"No suh. Course not. It's a feeling. Sometimes I gets them."

"Like Jupiter, eh? Not sure I can credit that."

"You seen a likeness of her." He had no idea where that came from, or even that he was going to say it. The caul talking. "A tintype I think."

Ellis looked at him and Cuuda saw in his eyes how he

was right on the edge of recognition. He turned to leave, then stopped short and looked back. Ellis was still looking at him. "Suh," he said, tossing the harmonica to the surgeon. "It's his."

"How's that?" Ellis asked.

"I found it on the field beside him. The private. Name's Ezra, I think."

"Ezra?"

"Yassuh. Ezra Coffin. Like the boxes I make."

***

It didn't take Ellis five minutes to get to Ezra's bedside. He found the bundle of letters where he'd tossed it under the cot and pulled from it the tintype he'd admired earlier that morning. The girl stared out at him and he had no trouble placing her face.

Liza, as she might look as a grayish-haired woman. Was her last name Coffin? Ellis couldn't remember. He stood in the tent trying to make sense of the information.

"Help me. Liza? Please help me."

He looked down, saw Ezra was awake. "Soldier, you've been badly wounded."

Ezra's eyes closed then opened again. "I gonna live?"

"No telling," Ellis said. Then, "Your name Coffin?"

"Ezra Coffin." It came out sounding choppy as he choked a bit on talking.

"And this Liza. She's your wife?"

Ezra nodded.

"Then you shall have her, of course."

Ellis put the word out immediately that he was looking for the red-haired girl. Not that he'd found her husband, just that he wanted to speak with her at once.

Before leaving, he handed the harmonica to Ezra.

The private wept at the sight and feel of it.

TWENTY-THREE

The night of July tenth passed with the racket of black crows cawing in the trees.

Cuuda passed the time eating another bag of roasted peanuts before he and the old man slept under Jupiter's wagon. He expected Ellis would remember him eventually, and when he did there'd be hell to pay. A man like that didn't take kindly to changing circumstances. Or to being lied to.

He supposed the caul had left him, at least for now.

Assistant Surgeon Tobias Ellis spent a miserable night in the tent with Private Coffin. The pulse in Ezra's leg weakened to a thin, reedy thing in the evening, then regained itself in the early hours after midnight. Ellis kept an eye on it but things seemed to go along well enough. His trouble sleeping was more personal. He had an idea he'd seen that Cuuda kid somewhere before, but where?

Ezra himself rested comfortably enough, passing the night humming small tunes on Tim Jewel's harmonica. He worried about Tom Jersey and wasn't the least bit sleepy. He'd slept enough.

Dr. Hardy hadn't though. He slept the night through without rousing once. The first time he'd done so in nearly two weeks. He dreamt of his son's thirteenth birthday; they ate cake. Josiah Boyd slept without dreaming and the night proved a dark one indeed for him. He passed it under guard on a railroad siding between Baltimore and Washington, DC.

Major Sutter, the Confederate surgeon, was up and down repeatedly. He lost two soldiers before morning, but saved a third when he dislodged a plug of meat from the man's windpipe. Tom Jersey, who'd rallied late in the day, failed again. He became delirious after midnight and repeatedly asked to hold Little Tom, even reaching out to the vapory air.

And on the ground just outside the low stone wall surrounding the Lutheran Church, Liza Coffin spent the night dreaming of Samuel, of what could never be, of what might have been. She dreamt too of Ezra, who was dead on the battlefield and no more than history to her now. A dog sniffed at her in the wee hours, but she didn't notice and the animal was long gone by first light.

***

First light found Tom Jersey's flank badly distended. A rancid odor of stale cheese assaulted Sutter when he lifted the dressings; the major's side had turned in the night. The skin, black and blistered and dead looking, sloughed as he touched it.

Sutter worked fast. He'd seen it before, this flesh-eating stew. He had word sent to Ellis that he needed chloroform. The assistant surgeon himself appeared with the anesthetic barely a quarter hour later. He offered Sutter his assistance, which was accepted without hesitation.

They operated out in the open air where the light was good and the air breezy. Ellis was awed by the spectacle of Sutter operating. He didn't simply pick up a blade and cut, preferring instead to clean his instruments first. "Such is not always practical," Sutter allowed, "but when it is it has the best effect on the outcome."

Once Jersey was slept, the two physicians inspected his flank and observed the full measure of the damage, which was extensive and terrible. The necrotic tissue wrapped fully from his groin around to his back, encompassing all the skin in between. That the skin itself was dead was of no debate—it came away in great swaths, as if greased on its underside. The fat beneath was hardly better, though here and there the buttery look of normal adiposity showed through.

"He's a dead man," Ellis said.

"Sir, I'd be much obliged if you'd keep such sentiments to yourself," Sutter said, adding, "he sleeps, but by some accounts he can still hear us."

"But the muscle too is involved."

"So it is. I suspect the source is just here," Sutter said, pointing with a probe. He called for a scissors and snipped a thick rind of membrane that lay beneath the muscles of Jersey's flank. A viscous effluent of pus and piss rolled forth and the man's belly deflated like a gravid woman at a caesarian. Ellis was thankful they were in the open air.

Word came that Ellis had a visitor waiting for him at the church, a lady. He sent word back he'd be there directly time allowed, but that it might be awhile yet. When the operation was over, the gaping hole in Jersey's flank was bandaged and he was taken away to convalesce. Ellis was impressed and said as much.

"Too little too late, doctor," Sutter said. "You were right. He won't survive."

"By no fault of yours, sir."

"When this war is over, I should very much like to take a long vacation," Sutter said. "I have never been, but I am told Europe is nice in the summer."

"I can't imagine any place is nice this time of the year," Ellis said. It wasn't the season he was speaking of. "Good day, sir."

Sutter tipped his head, "Doctor."

***

Ellis made his way across the compound to the steps of the Lutheran Church, where he found Liza Coffin waiting. He apologized for her wait. He saw she wore a pomander about her neck. It smelled of citrus and he marveled that sutlers could find such wares in a place like this.

"Have you found my husband?" she finally asked.

He was tongue-tied. What if the man wasn't her husband? What if he had made a mistake? "We've found a soldier."

"Captain, I would be much obliged you'd take me to him."

"Yes, of course. But there's a chance of a mistake. You must understand that."

"A mistake?" Liza said.

Ellis nodded. "I believe this is yours?" He pulled what at first appeared to be a playing card from a trouser pocket. A fold of paper, several smears of blood upon it, fell out with it. This he retrieved from the ground and returned to his pocket.

Liza took the card. A tintype. She turned it over and her likeness stared back at her. She closed her eyes for a few seconds, steadied herself, and said, "Alive or dead?"

A moment of hesitation. "He's alive."

"But? You hesitated. That means there's a but."

Ellis nodded at her. "It is so. He's badly injured. I don't know that he will survive. And he may yet lose his leg."

"I don't care about his leg," Liza said quickly. "I must see him. Please. Now."

"Very well."

***

They crossed the hospital grounds and she caught a fleeting glimpse of Cuuda on the way. He appeared to see her too. Nothing verbal went between them, just a look of recognition.

They arrived at the tent and started to enter. Ellis stopped. "You go ahead," he said.

Liza passed under the flap. A medicinal smell, something like camphor, heavied the air. It took her eyes a moment to adjust. A dozen men were cotted around her, and at first she didn't recognize her husband among them. She panned their faces, but they hadn't shaved and were woolly and shaggy. She paced the tent floor, looking into their eyes. It wasn't till the last pair she saw something familiar.

Ezra sat propped thirty degrees at the waist, an olive-drab blanket covering his lower half. He blinked several times, as if her presence was a mirage he must wipe away. Gradually, a smile brightened his bearded face. "Is it really you? Are you really here?"

She stood locked in place, her breath caught in her throat. She stared, not believing the proof of her eyes, as if he too was a mirage. He looked perfectly splendid, the way a man was supposed to look on the best day of his life. She had the sense she'd waited a lifetime for this moment, two if you counted Samuel. Her eyes misted and she began to cry. She made a memory then, and over all the time to come whenever she recalled this moment it would be as if through a window streaked with those tears.

She stepped toward him, slowly at first, and then all but fell into him. She hugged him against the cot, ignoring the awkwardness. She felt his arms come up; heavily bandaged, they were club-like. She pressed her cheek to his, loving the way his stubble abraded her. "I love you so much," she whispered, and wrapped her hands around his waist under the blanket.

"I love you too," he said. But it came out sounding throaty and forced and she drew away. She saw his eyes roll, saw his chest heave. A slick warmth embraced her hands and she knew even before she looked what she'd find.

Liza screamed as the blood began to saturate the blanket.

***

Ellis had not wanted to intrude. He'd spent most of the night at Ezra's bedside, feeling the pulse in his leg wax and wane. Several times he'd considered re-operating, but he doubted himself and his skills. Now, as Liza screamed and he ran in, he beheld Ezra's life dripping onto the dirt, but Wooster's face stared back from the bed.

A man with a stuck femoral don't live. Hardy's words came at him like a speeding bullet as he reduced the length of the tent to three long strides. He hollered for a corpsman.

He pulled Liza away and tore the blanket off. The dressing around Ezra's thigh had loosened and a jet of bright red blood geysered with each squeeze of his heart. It struck his arm and he thought: *like a man in shining red armor.*

"Horseshit," he said. He must be decisive. To nobody in particular he announced: "Get Sutter in here, the rebel surgeon. Do it now and do it quick." But he knew by the time Sutter got there it would be all but over. He stuck his hands against the man's groin. "Get me a goddamn knife!"

He groped at the inner thigh and found with a little experimentation that he could control the hemorrhaging between a torrent and a manageable trickle with firm pressure against the thigh bone. But the clock was ticking, no doubt about that. Every time he looked at the man, he was paler than the moment before.

Wooster had paled too and that knowledge did nothing to comfort Ellis.

Liza inched back to the bed and took Ezra's hand in her own. She squeezed and hung on.

Where was that knife? Ellis's gut knotted and he felt like a man being stampeded. He was soaked with sweat and consciously worked to slow his breathing. He pushed two fingers through the incision, popping the stitches, feeling for the great vessels that passed under the skin of the thigh. He tugged at the wound and the edges separated to reveal pink muscle and alabaster bone. The hole quickly filled with blood and Ellis rooted in the depths of it. His hand holding pressure on the thigh slipped; a gush of blood taunted him and he quickly reset his hold. With the other hand, he continued to search the meaty wound for the ruptured vessel.

He glanced up and there was Sutter coming through the tent flap, as impeccable as ever save for that twisted face. Ellis pulled his fingers from the wound and increased his weight against the thigh. The blood slowed, but was still too much.

"Stuck femoral." Sutter said, more a statement than a question. He didn't even sound out of breath.

"Yeah. I should have amputated three days ago when he came in but..."

"Now's not the time for regrets," Sutter said.

"He's going to bleed out."

"I'll ask you again to keep such thoughts to yourself. Let's get the bleeding stopped and do what needs doing."

"Yes, of course," Ellis said, looking at Liza, realizing she was still there for the first time. "Do what needs doing," he repeated.

And they did.

TWENTY-FOUR

Hardy crossed the compound, walking in the cool air of a new morning. It had been a week since Boyd had opened Spencer's skull and subtracted the clot that threatened his life. In the interval, Spencer had awakened and regained much, though he still had plenty far to go. He was out of the woods, however, and this day would see him moved to one of the long term hospitals in Washington, DC. Hardy meant to say goodbye.

Ellis stood outside the boy's tent. "I've checked him. He looks good, should have no difficulties with the transit."

"I'm grateful. Don't recall I said that before now," Hardy said.

"It's what we do, you and I. Boyd too. He's the one who saved Spencer. He's the one you should be thanking."

"You're right, of course. But my boy would be dead were it not for you. You believed and for that, well, I'm grateful is all."

"Thank you. That means something coming from you, sir."

Hardy looked as if he needed to say something more. "I didn't want him to die. You must know that."

"I do. War does peculiar things to a man. Creates its own agenda."

"I didn't even know he'd joined the army. After his mother died, I didn't know what to do. I left him with my sister and her husband. I saw him regular, several times a year anyhow. The last was just before Sumter fell. Two years that's been. My God, two whole years. I've missed so much. So very much."

Ellis had questions, but they'd have to go unanswered. He was too respecting of Hardy's privacy to ask them. "Well," he said, "I guess you've got a second chance. That's more than most of us get."

"And that, doctor, is why I'm grateful." Hardy shook Ellis' hand. "You're a fine surgeon, don't let anyone tell you otherwise. If you should need a letter—"

"Thank you. I'll remember that."

"You should know I've put in for a transfer. I'm sure it will be accepted; these hands won't be much good for surgery anymore. I hope to follow my boy to DC."

Ellis nodded. "Good luck, sir." He stepped aside to allow the senior man to pass, but Hardy stayed put.

"One more thing. I'm putting you in for promotion to Surgeon."

"I'm obliged."

"Don't be. I'm not one to do something without cause— good cause more often than not. You've earned it. A man with a stuck femoral. I can't recall I ever seen one live before. Helluva job, Surgeon Ellis."

"God bless you, sir."

Hardy ducked under the flap and was gone.

***

Liza Coffin wept softly as she leaned over the prostrate form of her husband. Where once had been a leg, the blanket was flat against the cot. The surgeons had controlled the bleeding, and then gone on to do what was necessary.

Her tears were not for his leg, however. Neither were

they for him, strictly speaking. She had told herself she was cried out, that she wouldn't cry again until she found him. Now that they were together, crying was all she could do. She couldn't help feeling the loss of Samuel acutely now. She'd pushed his passing out of her mind. Now that she had Ezra back, Samuel was center stage again.

Ezra stirred on the cot and opened his eyes for the first time in hours. She was leaning over his chest and he smelled her familiar scent in front of all else. Her presence was better than any pill or medicine they could give him. The pain ebbed away. They held each other for some time. She wept and he embraced her, feeling the thrum of her heart against his chest.

The best thing he'd felt in a very long time.

Ezra and Liza talked. Samuel was on both their minds and he came first. "He died in my arms. I was so scared. They was all around me and we was hiding in the cellar and I tried to keep him quiet and...and I'm sorry. You ever gonna forgive me? I'm so sorry. Please don't be mad or upset. I tried so hard, but he was so small and..."

"Shhhhh." He silenced her with a finger to her mouth. He knew something of the fragility of life. "It must have been a hard moment for you. You ain't gotta apologize."

She stopped weeping and sat up in the chair, looked at him. "They took him from me, buried him too. Wouldn't let me see. I asked they lay him under a tree. That's what they done, put him under a tree." She sobbed between words. "I got this though. Ain't much." She reached into her bag and withdrew a piece of linen. It was stamped with the words *US Army* on one side. The edges were ragged and unraveling. It was the swaddling cloth she had carried Sam in at the end of his days.

Ezra didn't recognize it. Sam's entire life had taken place outside his embrace, and now the boy was gone from him forever. And in his place was this cheap rag. He fingered the cloth, turned it over in his still-stiff fingers. Tried to imagine Sam wrapped in it. He might have said anything at that moment, but what he chose was this: "Somebody once told me that sometimes we have to suffer, because only then can we know when we ain't suffering. I think we have to get through the bad to know the good. And the good can be so very good, especially when we keep the ones we love close. But the truth is, those we love—they are never really far from us. Not in the time of suffering, and not in the better days either. That's what I think."

"That's exactly what I think too," Liza said.

And she lay down on the cot beside him, the scrap of cloth between them.

* * *

Tom Jersey died at a little after three in the afternoon. His final day was a peaceful one. He had regained consciousness shortly after his operation, but a few hours thereafter he slipped into a state of delirium and then a quiet, restful sleep. Several times he appeared to be talking with somebody, but the conversation was one-sided and seemed the random misfires of a gone mind. Sutter was present when Jersey uttered his last words: "The creel, Little Tom, don't forget the creel."

Among Jersey's effects, Sutter found an undated letter. It read simply:

Dearest Elspeth,
It is peace. Perfect peace.
TJ

Sutter folded the letter and posted it to Tom Jersey's wife. He included a note with his own condolences and, as was his habit, a copy of the Twenty-Third Psalm.

***

Tobias Ellis never mailed the letter he carried from Tucker. He found he simply couldn't bear to part with it. It reminded him of what he'd been through, not so much the hell, but the honor of battle. It became another one of his trophies, one of the many things filling his trunk.

His promotion to surgeon came through faster than expected. He'd anticipated staying on with Tiny and the others, especially since Boyd and Hardy were about as used up as used up could get. Unfortunately, that wasn't going to happen. Their hospital group was being disbanded, the personnel reassigned. He had been reassigned to a unit in the west, under Sherman. He was Major Tobias Ellis now.

He packed his trunk up, had taken out the bag with the shoe as well as the letter from Tucker and put them in his saddle bags with his personal things. He had a ten day furlough coming en route to his new hospital and one never knew when one might need a little inspiration or motivation for extracurriculars. Besides, it was high time he did something more about his problem than just scratch his forearms.

He rode out of camp at first light, three weeks to the day from the start of the battle.

***

On the morning of the day Ellis set out for his new position, in the early morning hours of 21 July this was, Jupiter and Cuuda were awakened to the sound of somebody ransacking their set-up. The man was in high feather, turning over tables, disturbing bodies, and kicking things. He was looking through various cupboards when

Jupiter crawled from under the wagon to confront him. "Jesus K. Reist, what the hell's the racket?"

The man turned round, a stream of spittle running out one corner of his mouth. It was John Magruder, the portly, soft-looking barkeep from Monroeville. Only he didn't look so soft now. In fact, he looked as if he'd made a fair amount of progress on the road to hell. Jupiter thought *uh oh* and took a step back. "There a problem here?"

"Where is it? Where you keep the stuff?" Magruder spoke in a voice all but out of breath. Either he had been drinking—or he was mad. Experience being on his side, Jupiter supposed the latter.

"I don't know what you're talking about."

"The hell you say. You sold me that goddurn tonic. Jupeeder's Oil or whatever. What the hell was in that stuff?"

"I didn't sell you nothing you didn't ask for, mister."

"You told me that stuff would last. I bought four bottles and you told me they would last."

"And so they have."

"I ran out four days ago. Ain't slept or ate since."

"I told you they would last long enough."

"Do I look like a man what been cured to you? You call this long enough?"

"Well, mister, I never promised a cure. But, yes, I do call this long enough."

"What?" Magruder said.

Jupiter nodded and Cuuda stepped forward behind Magruder. He pushed the apparatus—the grannie type knitting needle and the empty syringe—through the back of Magruder's ribcage, on the left side.

Magruder's last utterance was "ngok" or something very much like it. The trocar passed through his heart and he was dead before he hit the ground. Now Jupiter addressed him further, the way he did all his 'patients.'

"Jesus K. Reist, I'm sorry about that mister, but you didn't give us no choice. And I did tell you it would last long enough. You just never asked long enough for who? Long enough for me is what I guess I was getting at. Long enough for me. Almost too long, you wanna know the truth.

"Now, how we gonna do this? You want I should go through the carotid, or the femoral? Your choice, I can allow that much. Jesus K. Reist."

TWENTY-FIVE

Cuuda had to walk.

Late on the same day John Magruder died at the tip of Jupiter's trocar, Cuuda had another caul. He had become a small industry, was making pine boxes by the dozens. He had just assembled one and it sat before him, awaiting a lid.

"You done good. Now do gooder," the boy with only one shoe said, and this time Cuuda saw those thin lips of his move apart as he spoke from inside the box.

The words were like a summons and his feet answered. He had no idea where they were taking him, just the knowledge that he had to follow their lead. No choice really.

He had to walk. Walk or die. Because somewhere in the sandy soil of the North Carolina Outer Banks, the bones of a dead boy moldered at unrest in his grave.

And the man who had put him there was on the prowl once again.

THE END

ACKNOWLEDGMENTS

Writing a book is a long, lonely road. Not a slog, mind you. I never find writing a slog. But, for me at least, it's an intensely solitary experience. I'm not much of a people person when you come right down to it. Oh, I try to be. I'd love to have scores of friends I can call at all hours of the day and night, to golf with or invite over for a movie night. Another couple to go out to dinner with would be handy. And somebody to trade tools with or play catch with on a Saturday afternoon would be fun.

Problem is, my life doesn't run that way. I've never been able to make friends easily, and, if I'm being truthful, I'd just as soon not be bothered with making dates to play ball or shoot hoops. And what happens if you just don't feel like going out to dinner on that previously scheduled night? I like my alone time. Maybe I'm selfish, or maybe it's all on account of how much time I have to spend doing other people's bidding at my day job, being a neurosurgeon. Sixty hours plus a week, used to be eighty or more. When I'm off, I want to spend my time my way.

Usually that means either watching baseball, curling up by the fire with a good book, or writing. Sometimes a variation of all three. The writing is daily though. Over the years, I've realized I need to write the way others need to breathe. It's sustenance.

But no man is an island, and no writer is truly alone. Even if it's just coming up for source material, or to eat and drink, you just can't do it alone. Besides, that'd be boring.

Thanks to my wife, Jean, for putting up with this attitude all these years. She's there when I need her and mostly even when I don't. And god bless her for knowing there ain't much difference between those two.

Thanks to my kids too, Edison III, England, and Ehvyn. They've had to listen to more than their share of stories, which I could see in their eyes was pretty painful at times, especially when I cajoled one or two of their friends to tag along. I hope they noticed their friends kept coming though, and I hope the stories have gotten better over the years.

My mother is, perhaps, my ideal reader. She's never been able to wait for the next thing to come off my pen and for that, thanks. She's been nothing but encouraging over the years.

David Poyer deserves a round of applause for his patience and assistance over the years, as does Lenore Hart. I've learned more from their edits than I ever learned elsewhere. I appreciate their faith and persistence with me over the years. I've no doubt it was a slog for them at times. Thanks, folks.

Tim Farrington helped me when I was at my lowest. Thanks, Tim.

Over the years the nurses and techs at my hospitals have listened patiently as I read the occasional passage or bounced ideas off of them. Linda Vogel in particular deserves special mention for her time and encouragement.

There are, undoubtedly, many others I could name, but I'll stop here. I haven't left anyone out on purpose. All who have been along for the adventure know who they are. You are, each and every one, close to my heart.

Now let me go and write.

ABOUT THE AUTHOR

Edison McDaniels's writing is informed by medicine and the supernatural. His work received honorable mention in the seventeenth edition of *The Year's Best Fantasy and Horror*, and has been published in *Paradox Magazine*, *The Summerset Review*, *The Armchair Aesthete*, *On The Premises Magazine*, and others.

McDaniels, a graduate of Stanford University, is board certified in adult and pediatric neurosurgery, with over 7,000 operations to his credit.

Edison and Jean collect historical etchings and attend at least 1-2 baseball games a week between April and October (more, if the Minnesota Twins are in town).

His first novel was *The Burden*. *Not One Among Them Whole*, his second, will be followed by *The Matriarch of Ruins*, a novel of one woman's struggle to keep her family going in the midst of the fighting at Gettysburg.

Visit Edison McDaniels at www.surgeonwriter.com, where you can read his blog, Neurosurgery 101 — about life and some of its harder or more interesting moments.

Northampton House Press

Northampton House LLC publishes carefully selected fiction, lifestyle nonfiction, memoir, and poetry. Our logo represents the muse Polyhymnia. Our mission is to discover great new writers and give them a chance to springboard into fame. Our watchword is quality, not quantity. Watch the Northampton House list at www.northampton-house.com, or Like us on Facebook – "Northampton House Press" – to discover more innovative works from brilliant new writers.

CPSIA information can be obtained at www.ICGtesting.com
Printed in the USA
LVOW11s2306080415

433779LV00031B/1135/P